Clevehold

The Lost Descendent, Volume 3

Liz Bunches

Published by Liz Bunches, 2024.

This is a work of fiction. Similarities to real people, places, or events are entirely coincidental.

CLEVEHOLD

First edition. December 22, 2024.

Copyright © 2024 Liz Bunches.

ISBN: 979-8227318848

Written by Liz Bunches.

Table of Contents

Chapter 1 1
Chapter 2 6
Chapter 3 17
Chapter 4 26
Chapter 5 39
Chapter 6 48
Chapter 7 60
Chapter 8 72
Chapter 9 94
Chapter 10 113
Chapter 11 128
Chapter 12 140
Chapter 13 157
Chapter 14 171
Chapter 15 181
Chapter 16 196
Chapter 17 214
Chapter 18 234
Chapter 19 250
Chapter 20 259
Chapter 21 283
Chapter 22 299
Chapter 23 314
Chapter 24 328
Chapter 25 358
Chapter 26 371
Chapter 27 390
Chapter 28 409

Chapter 1

LENA OFTEN WONDERED what the castle had been like before glass was fitted in the windows. Had noise carried from room to room? If that were the case, how did anyone keep secrets? Perhaps that was how Avild had discovered the whore's plan to have the prince killed. Did bugs fly through freely? Birds? For whatever reason, of all the questions Lena had never gotten the chance to ask, the glass was what bothered her the most.

When the windows were being fitted for her bedroom, they had asked her what type of glass she wanted. Three windows, knee height to ceiling, faced north. Her request had been stained glass, something no one on the other side could see through. The glassmaker had reminded Lena how high off the ground she was, but that didn't dissuade her. Lena had tapped into her girlish nature and said, "I suppose it'll just make me feel safer."

Now, she stood in the bath of light, basking in the reds, oranges, and yellows from the middle window. Each one had been built using a different palette, all of them warm colors, but she liked this one best. Through it, she could see bits of the city below, blooming into a metropolis once more. The yellow made her think of hope, growth. It was the preferred lens to see Clevehold through.

Shifting her focus away from the city, she looked at herself. Her green eyes popped nicely in the yellow reflection. It made her hair look almost black.

Her mind hadn't changed about the want for privacy. Magic still felt like a silly explanation for anything, but it was her reason. There was so much magic could do, most of it unknown to her, and that made for the most unsettling assumptions. Magic, she supposed, was the second most troublesome thing she wished to have asked Avild about.

After getting dressed, Lena had the inclination to wander. It was something she had been allowed to do in Steepwharf, back when no one had monitored or much cared what she did. Since taking up residence in the castle at Clevehold, there were always people who hailed her during her walks, no matter the hour or location—save one, that is. There was one place she could wander unfretted.

As she opened the door, Socks ran in, a black-and-white cat with the whites only on his paws, underbelly, and chin. He scampered around the room, excited and aimless, and eventually jumped onto the bed to stare at her.

Lena laughed and shook her head. "Didn't anyone feed you?"

"Meow," answered Socks. His tail was straight up, and his legs were posed as if he was ready to dart away. He was a skinny thing, a resident of the castle when they had arrived, and was naturally skittish around people. It had never been formally discussed, but Socks was Lena's cat, though everyone collectively cared for and left food out for him.

"I suppose I can get you something first." Lena dramatically sighed, followed with a smile, as she walked to a long dresser and opened a small chest. At one time it may have been used to store letters, coins, or even fine jewelry. The shiny brass was adorned with gold flakes and embedded pearls. It came with the room Lena had chosen. The chest had to have been over a thousand years old, yet by the grace of magic, it sparkled like new in the reflections of the stained glass.

What Lena kept in it, however, was cat food, little dried pellets of mostly meat. Whenever she opened the chest, a pungent smell wafted out. The workmanship was quality enough to keep the odor

CLEVEHOLD

contained when closed, and the food fresh enough for Socks' liking.

He sprung up as soon as the lid opened.

Lena put the food on the floor, then quickly snuck out of her room. She kicked open the small corner flap a woodsmith made in the door so the cat wouldn't get trapped. Between that and the secret passages—something only as small as a cat could access by going under the bed—he had options. The access point had originally worried Lena. Rats or bugs could make their way into her room, she had feared, but Socks made good work of keeping them at bay.

As she made her way down the hall, Lena nodded politely at those going about their day. Many people lived on the grounds, such as advisors, servants, groundskeepers, and their families. Initially, the barracks built between the inner and outer walls of the castle had been refurbished to house those who worked in it. A time later, the barracks were split between housing the Royal Guards and the people who came to Clevehold before it was fully livable.

The barracks didn't see much use from the public anymore. There were enough rooms in the castle for those who worked to occupy the empty space—more room than they knew what to use it for.

Her feet knew the way down the long halls and grand staircases. It had taken months of wrong turns, dead ends, and laughably getting lost to earn it. The castle was magnificent, restored akin to how it must have looked in the days of the Stone King. New banners and glass had been their own added touch.

However, there were some places that magic wasn't permitted to restore. Lena pushed open a door and was revisited by the memory of the first time she had done so. Her heart had nearly wanted to quit. If she let her imagination take hold, she could feel that day again, see it, smell it. The heavy door had symbols lining the sides, slashed out. Another thing she never asked about.

Lena closed the door behind her and took the spiral stone staircase with unhurried steps. She refused to let the memory get the better of her. If she strayed down that path, it would only dredge up the sounds. The laugh. The clattering of swords. The screams.

At the bottom of the staircase, she stopped. Cells lined both sides of the hall before her. Those on the left with broken walls and floors remained as such. This couldn't be fixed. It would have been an insult to the memory to fix it.

The cells on the right were open and vacant. The only amendment had been clearing away the blood in the second to last cell. It was a point of pride and had been cleaned by hand.

Lena traced her fingertips along the wall. The iron keys hanging on the rough stone clanked as she knocked into them and kept trailing. The light that bled down the walls wasn't much, but enough that she could recognize her surroundings. She knew this place. It came to her many times in dreams.

She stopped at Selgen's cell. Hands bracing the cold bars, she took a deep breath. It didn't feel empty; the energy radiating from the place warred with her sight. This wasn't a trick of magic, but of memory.

Back turned to it, she leaned heavily against the cell. Her eyes moved to the second set of stairs, heading up. A flash of blonde hair ran up them, hellbent on revenge. They had followed. And after the fighting and screaming had stopped, only she and Avild were mobile enough to come back this way. The bloodstains on the ground had been their guide.

Lena felt no need to go up the stairs. The hall there, the ballroom, and the balconies had been left in a state of disrepair. She had asked to not have those fixed. The castle didn't need the space.

CLEVEHOLD

Eyes clenched shut, she focused on the void of darkness. The memories didn't live there. Nothing lived there. It was static, quiet, and undisturbed.

The stark emptiness reinforced her desire to amble. She felt she couldn't accomplish that inside the castle, didn't want to do it in the locked off section. Her feet needed to move.

Lena opened her eyes and followed where the trail of blood would have been, had pride not scrubbed it from the stone.

Chapter 2

TWO ROYAL GUARDS ACCOMPANIED her as she crossed the bustling drawbridge into Clevehold. Lena knew she couldn't go far without their watchful eyes. At first, the sensation of being followed by the guards, coupled with the inherent shame of not knowing their names, had bothered her.

But the streets here were energetic. People were everywhere. It was impossible to avoid. What were two more guards along her route? As it had been in Steepwharf, she knew some names, was always polite during her social encounters, and had accepted it was impossible to know everyone. She'd had in-depth conversations with Socks in the beginning, and he had agreed that of the many duties she was taking on, knowing all the denizens by name wasn't the best use of her expertise.

For instance, she knew there was an ebb and flow of how densely packed the streets were. As districts were cleaned up and refurbished, people moved there. The density lessened. Then a wave of newcomers would arrive in Clevehold, people would live in closer quarters until more space opened, and thus the process repeated. The city breathed in, and it breathed out. Lena helped oversee which districts required work, and she coordinated the funds to get it done.

The market she now walked through was the main thoroughfare of the city, the focal point of their rebuilding efforts, nestled along the main canal. All else expanded from there. Which stalls went where was an undertaking coordinated by someone else, and whoever it was, they kept the market running smoothly.

The illusion of this place being akin to Steepwharf—the stone, the crowds, the newly cleaned canals—broke at the first sight of magic. There was one shop Lena favored idling outside. A shoe mender, though his services extended to other cloth and leather goods. Similar to how Harth had mended the book in the library, the shopkeeper used green threads of magic to pull an item together. The glowing green strands would soon disappear, and the shoes would look as good as new. She imagined it saved many a worker from having to buy new shoes.

Memories of the library felt warm, like the fire they had built, not cold and off-putting like the cells. Drawn to its warmth, Lena left the market and headed that way. To reach the library, she crossed a canal, an arching bridge with a railing on both sides. Like most bridges, it was wide enough to pass a horse-drawn carriage. The bridges along the side canals, like this one, were all affixed. If she wanted to cross the main canal to the other side of the city, she would have to use a wooden bridge, which were removed when ships exited the Royal Dock to go downriver.

People smiled and inclined their heads at Lena as she passed by. Some probably knew who she was, some were only being courteous, and others who didn't look twice at her clearly had no idea. She liked it that way. They didn't need to pay attention to the guards following her, either.

Lena took the walk over the stone bridges slowly. The elevation wasn't enough to see far and wide, the buildings too tall for that, but it provided a prize view. A living city. A center for trade between the land of Istedinium to the west and the coastal cities to the east. Buildings were put to good use. Hard workers cared to make an honest living. A future lived here.

All around, there was evidence of magic. People summoned light from their hands in darker alleyways or shops. Workers mended boats, canals, sidewalks. Those carrying items over their heads used a small shield emanating from their hand to better balance and spread the weight. There wasn't an obscene amount of power amongst the common people—they weren't *too* well-grounded—but the simplicities made everyday life a touch easier.

Lena smiled at the city guard posted outside the library as she approached. He returned it and nodded. The door was propped open.

Only two of the library's wings had been restored. The other parts of the building were closed off. There were plans for renovations, but it was too low a priority to justify doing yet.

What had been built of the library was magnificent. The clean earthy smell greeted her as she approached the lines of bookshelves. There was nothing she particularly wanted to see. Something about being around the books simply gave her comfort. New books were placed on the shelves all the time: ones travelers brought with them, or those newly restored. The employed librarians doubled as menders and transcribers.

A lower priority on Lena's personal list was to learn another language. Books spoke of much technology and advancements long forgotten by Steepwharf, and they were written in symbols she didn't understand. Iste was her probable choice, the language of Istedinium, their plains neighbors. Perhaps Rufino, a native Iste, could help her.

It was odd to think about the path of language in their past. The Stone King had insisted they all speak the same language, or rather his great-grandfather, however many times removed, had. Pockets of native languages had survived, though, and resurfaced when the Stone King died. Lena didn't want all people to revert to all one language, but for multiple tongues to coexist.

One of the guards behind her clattered clumsily along the marble floor. She pressed her lips together and tried to ignore it. The illusion of peacefully ambling was so easily broken.

"Brick boots, sit down," she heard in her head. She shook away the memory and walked on. *Not now.*

Lena headed for the central staircase. More books sat on higher floors. Lanterns kept the way lighted, but the majority of the illumination was from the glass dome roof. Clean clear glass let sunlight in. Feeling its warmth as she climbed, Lena decided to travel all the way up.

The library had three floors, making it among the tallest buildings in Clevehold—save the castle—but there were many tied for that height. The advantage of the library, however, was an observation tower that reached another story and a half above the roof. That was where she wanted to go.

On the third floor, she headed toward the door to the roof. A guard on post perked up at her footsteps but stopped himself before he stood completely. He smiled and nodded at her as she passed by. It was his job to stop anyone from going onto the roof, but she wasn't just anyone.

Lena loved that first feeling of the warm breeze on her face when the door opened. She stopped a moment to breathe it in. It felt like peace, even with the backdrop of commotion. Below, people continued about their days, pushing carts, herding children, or whatever their occupation entailed. She took a few steps forward and, before going up the observation platform, looked over the side.

"Miss," one of the guards beckoned.

"It's alright," she assured them with a passive hand gesture behind her. There was a slight clench in her stomach, as heights still made her nervous, but she had decided to not let those types of fears rule her. She wanted to look down over the side, and therefore she did. Things could be simple.

Satisfied with her effort, Lena took the steps up to the observation platform. It was a new addition, made of wood. The librarian guards took the structure apart and brought it inside when the weather threatened to damage it. The steps and platform were mostly sturdy.

"I'll be fine up here alone," she called back to the guards. The wobble and give was easiest to navigate when she was the only one on it. That, and with them out of her line of sight, it was easier to pretend she was alone.

She made it up to the top, the deck no larger than a small bedroom, and rested her hands on the railing. She looked east. The sun shone down on the large river at the mouth of Clevehold and made it sparkle. The broken archways bracketing its mouth had been removed, two large pillars left in their place. There had been talk of expanding the pillars into a wall to encase the city, but the proposal was scrapped. If the inhabitants of Clevehold needed protection, the castle would serve well and could hold everyone.

Dark hair escaped her braid and tickled her face. The short cut of her two-toned grey dress fluttered in the wind, though the green trousers she wore beneath protected her modesty. Her clothes were now professionally and personally tailored. The multiple colors were purposeful, and the types of fabric matched. The trouser legs tapered down to her ankles, tucked into closed-toed leather shoes.

She looked south. Another branch of the river that came off the mountains stretched and wound out of sight, eventually curving west into Istedinium. *How did their women dress and behave?* she wondered. There were a variety of women in Clevehold. Some were Iste. The only woman she personally knew from that region, however, was Marisol, a kind woman born of dainty nobility. Likely not the best comparison, she reasoned.

The heat from the sun was becoming uncomfortable. Before getting down, Lena looked to the castle. Her home now, restored and alive again. She took a deep breath and climbed down. At the last few steps, a guard offered a gloved hand, and she took it.

CLEVEHOLD

Lena led them back inside, down the stairs, and exited the library. She had wandered as her heart needed, but there were things to be done. The balance was constantly tested as to what to do for herself and for others. For now, it was time to return.

The journey through Clevehold and over the drawbridge was uneventful. People moved to let her by, and she smiled politely. The guards departed her company once they passed their post within the outer wall.

The Commander of the Royal Guard greeted her by asking, "Why do you ignore my advice?"

Lena smirked and clasped her hands behind her back. She supposed innocently, "I took guards."

"You took guards?" Harth evaluated the two who had followed her as they walked toward the barracks. "Or they followed *you?*"

"You tell them to follow me. I don't need to ask."

"You wouldn't take them otherwise," he reminded, crossing his arms. Harth wore typical non-combat guard clothing, including a loose-fitting tan shirt under a heavy cloth vest. He was without his bow but kept a dagger on his belt. The only visual difference between the Commander and the men he oversaw was the rank insignia etched into the vest. In the vicinity of forty, he wasn't older than all of his men, but certainly among the most seasoned.

Lena tucked hair behind her ears as they walked toward the inner wall's main door. "I won't be stuck in here."

"The city is being revived at an alarming rate. The future queen needs to be kept safe."

She felt no threat. Not from Clevehold, and not in his comment. He was playing serious, and he mostly was, but he wasn't scolding her—he understood both her point and her naivety. It was protective, caring in the only way he knew how to display.

The part that weighed on her was the title. Part of her brain couldn't properly wrap itself around it, and for that reason, she didn't feel ready or even deserving. Yet, it was something she had to do. It had been decided. That prospect had first borne her decision to weigh things that she wanted versus the things that were wanted of her. The trouble was, she was able to use that exercise to process every other obligation except her impending title.

But there was no use in debating it, was there? She had to take it up. Clevehold wouldn't move forward otherwise. It forced on her a maturity she didn't feel worthy of at twenty-seven.

"Lena," said Harth patiently.

She shook her head, then changed to a nod. They were already at the inner wall entrance. He was holding the door open for her, but she had stalled outside.

"I'm hearing you. You wish to be informed before I leave," she said, walking through.

"*If* you must leave."

"If I'm to have the city rebuilt, I need to know where the weak points are," she reasoned.

"When you leave on Council business, let the Council know," he countered.

"I can only compromise so much." She hadn't intended to sound so harsh. Harth was a good man, appointed because he was skilled and trusted. He didn't deserve grief for his proven efforts to keep her safe. "I'm sorry."

"There are only so many compromises you should make, but unless the reasoning is profound, your safety shouldn't be one of them."

Lena nodded. "I can't promise to never leave the castle without giving the entire Council warning, but I can promise to provide *you* better warning, and only go individually when I truly need to wander."

"I appreciate it. It'll give me time to give you better guards than those two."

"They were fine." She hadn't taken more notice of them than necessary. Her baseline was that they hadn't harassed her.

"One of those men cracked his head open last week getting a shoe on," grumbled Harth in that voice she had learned meant he was amused but needed to retain serious composure.

"Neither fell over today."

"Where are you off to?" he asked as he stuck his chin out toward the stairs within the castle doors.

"The vault, where I will be dutifully chaperoned," she answered.

He raised his eyebrows. "I ask because it was requested I tell you the Council will be meeting late this afternoon, before dinner."

"Did something happen?" Lena stepped closer to speak more quietly. They stood on a main path; people crossed behind her with low density, and there wasn't somewhere a person could hide to eavesdrop.

"Ships were spotted crossing the sea. They'll make landfall on the coast soon. Not a normal concern, but they don't fly the banners of our known neighbors in the East," he explained. "I'm sure your advisors will tell you more."

"I'll be quick at the vault," she said as she thought on it. This was an unknown. She had hoped they had already gotten past all the large unknowns.

"They didn't ring the bells for it, Miss Lena."

Lena pressed her lips together in a tight line and made a small nod. "Thank you for the information. I'll be quick about my business and will see you in about an hour's time."

"I'll pass along the word you returned early."

The route she took to the vault was practiced. There were likely multiple ways she could have made her way there, but she had a particular route—at least, that's how people described her insistence to only go the one way. In truth, she used the one practiced route because it was the only way she knew with certainty to reach the vault. It started by a golden statue of an old man in an alcove, which she followed down a line of windows, made several turns that she counted, and eventually found her way into a part of the castle only ever lit by fire's light.

The vault was built into the mountain the castle was perched on. From what they had all managed to determine, there were no tunnels or caves leading into the mountain, save the vault. The vault's secondary air hole was on the ceiling and led to another part of the castle. There was no means of reaching the vault from the outside. The air hole above was too small to fit a person, not to mention well guarded—she assumed by both people and magic. The door to the vault was itself a conundrum.

She nodded at the guard on post as she approached. Just one, and it was for show.

Lena put her hand on the smooth wall just where Avild had shown her. There wasn't a clear vault door until the magic was applied. After her hand rested on the stone for a moment, the familiar pins and needles began. Then, an outline of a door depressed into the stone. The lines grew thicker. She stood back to watch.

The impression of the door moved inward, the wall becoming thinner as the four sides converged on the center. It took a few seconds, but once it overlapped where her hand had been, the stone thinned more until it faded into a haze.

"You and those you allow may walk through it," Avild had told her.

Lena stepped through the haze and thought about the question she had responded with: "How does it know who I allow?"

"Physical contact is the easiest way, unless your thoughts betray that."

She hadn't asked what Avild had meant. There were too many questions Lena had never asked. To remedy the unknown, Lena had been given sole charge of the vault. Only those who had the right knew it was due to the inherited Stone King's magic.

Everyone else, including the majority of those who lived inside the castle and knew of the vault, assumed it was done by intricate magic. It was merely respect or lack of grounding that stopped others from trying to open it. As she passed by the mounds of gold and chests filled with jewels, Lena wondered how her access to the vault had changed people's perception of her. Did they think she was all-powerful? Or that she had a unique skill?

Lena took a deep breath, counted out ten gold coins, and considered a change in perception implied they had thought of her before. As the majority knew little of the vault, they also knew little of her. Assumptions must have been made after the reveal of her existence, but those conceptions had been heavily influenced by insight to the result. Due to respect and station, no one asked of her past.

The glow from above flickered. It wasn't from the access hole a hundred feet above her head; the light within the vault was a green-tinted glow, a haze that hung off the walls and ceiling. She assumed the magic light activated once the wall opened for passage. She had made the determination early on, when first here with Avild, that the magic light was tied to the person.

When Lena was somber, it dimmed and solidified into a thicker green. When she was in a giddier mood, the light brightened and danced. Times of turmoil in her thoughts made the lights flicker.

She pocketed the gold and made for the exit. There was no use in pondering things already decided, told, or too unknown to have been asked. A different unknown was upstairs—the unidentified ships.

Lena stepped through the hazy wall of the vault. Once through, she turned back and hovered her hand where solid stone had been. A thin sheet of stone reached toward the walls, floor, and ceiling. With the thin layer in place beneath the haze, the rest of the stone rose and filled in. Lena stepped back and watched it rise.

"What happens if you get caught in it?" Lena had asked Avild.

The last of the stone reformed and closed. The wall looked solid and undisturbed, as she had found it. The guard was unfazed.

Lena smirked as she remembered Avild's response.

"Don't."

Chapter 3

LENA WAS THE THIRD member of the Council to arrive at the designated meeting room, situated on a middle floor and overlooking an elevated garden. Three guards were stationed within the garden and two more on the door.

The man who was always early, which Lena suspected had to do with him not wanting to be around his family, was Norman. He was a taller man, skinny, with thinning hair peppered grey. He was the representative of the cities of the northern coast, where the main commerce and trade were furs, whaling, and liquor. With his beard shaved off, soft hands, and in his lighter clothes to accommodate what he considered a warm climate, there was little evidence to suggest he had once lived anywhere rugged.

Across the table from Norman, on the other side of the head chair, was Rufino. There was a natural kind snark to him that Lena found amusing and Norman tolerated. Rufino was in his mid-thirties, married to a woman he unabashedly loved, and had semi-unruly curly hair and a disposition that would have made him a good teacher. His main physical change since coming to Clevehold from Istedinium was his faded skin tone. Though his naturally dark skin had lightened a shade or two, the calluses on his hands hadn't. Rufino was as skilled at horse rearing as he was in politics and kept up both in Clevehold.

"Miss Lena," they both took turns greeting her.

"Mister Rufino. Mister Norman," she returned, taking her seat next to Rufino. It was her preferred place for two reasons. Firstly, she normally sided with Rufino, and thus it gave the visual of the younger Council members being on the same side, both physically and diplomatically. One would have thought a woman of the southern coast would find more to agree on with the other coastal attendee, she had been told, yet she found herself most often aligning with an unexpected ally. Secondly, when seated here, she had a kinder face when Norman made an asinine remark. The farthest to his left that Norman ever looked was forward left, where Lena sat, never to his direct left. His attention mostly stayed right, at the king's chair.

"I was told briefly of a ship crossing the sea from the East," she opened conversationally. A pause followed. Driving the question more directly, she asked, "Have either of you heard more of it?"

"It is what we are here to discuss. With the king," said Norman.

"Yes, we should wait to discuss anything about the four antique-style ships from the East, flying no banner, until the king arrives," said Rufino in a tone of agreeance.

Lena's lip pulled up in a tight smile she tried her best to hide.

Norman lightly rolled his eyes and straightened out his shirt. He looked toward the door.

Footsteps approached from the hall. Two sets, both quiet, one with the rhythm of an extra beat built in. The door opened, whining despite how many times it had been oiled recently, and Harth appeared. He held the door open for the man that followed.

Rufino, Norman, and Lena stood out of courtesy.

Led by his cane, Tulir entered. By now, the cane was an extension of him and moved as such. Despite the best efforts of multiple doctors, his right leg had never fully healed. For short distances, he could walk without a cane, but all those bold enough to speak candidly with him advised against it.

The lasting leg injury wasn't all he carried of that day—Tulir's right arm had also been used as a shield against a sword swing. It hadn't been swung with enough gumption to cut through, but it had sliced down to the bone, fractured it, and taken a chunk of flesh. Months, he had spent with it wrapped, the fear of needing it amputated lingering. Worse still, his right had once been his dominant hand, but it was no longer useful as such. Yet he had been able to keep his arm, thankfully, and the dent of a scar was always kept covered.

"Your Majesty," greeted Norman.

"Sit, all of you," Tulir beckoned. Despite his direction, he was the first to be seated at the head, the other three only sitting once he was.

Harth let the door close and then took his place at the table to the left of Norman, across from Lena.

"Is anyone not aware of what we know thus far?" Tulir hung the cane off the high back of his chair. The woodwork of both were delicately intricate.

"Four ships with no apparent banners—old-style ships, mind you—were seen crossing the sea from the East," said Rufino.

"Not just old-style ships, *antiques*. Not something manufactured in our world, or even in other parts of the known world," added Norman.

"You're calling them otherworldly?" proposed Tulir.

"Reports on the ships tell us they're too big to fit through the strait that closes the sea in the south. There's too much ice in the north," said Rufino.

Norman jumped in on the other man's breath. "But there are wide expanses of land on both coasts that bracket the sea. Thousands of miles on each."

"But you've insinuated the ships couldn't come from there," reminded Harth.

"Is it possible that, in desperation, these older ships were taken out of retirement? Possibly by a people who needed to flee in a hurry?" asked Lena. She looked to Harth and Rufino, though she knew Norman would have been better suited for the question.

"Their trajectory suggests they are coming directly across the sea," said Norman.

"What do we know of those neighbors and what ships they may have kept?" Rufino leaned forward on his elbows.

Tulir gestured at the map carved into the table. A beautiful fixture, created by a craftsman's hand and maintained by magic. Across the sea directly from Clevehold was a giant bay. "That region was upset and diluted long ago. It's fishing villages and farms, nothing large. The closest city to the bay rivals Mudfalls in size, the largest on that coast, and we know their banner."

"Your ancestor upset that region for a reason." Norman gestured at the same area. "Perhaps these boats were stolen by the heathens that live there."

Tulir breathed out slowly through his nose. "How? How do you suppose farmers and fishermen, untrained and generally uneducated, stole boats such as these, yet we've heard nothing of it?" His tone was serious, his jaw tight.

Norman likely took it personally—anger for an insinuation that the king was uneducated. Such was not the case, but their new advisors wouldn't have known that. *Ancestor*—a loaded word. The reminder the Stone King's blood lived in a man born into indentured servitude, who had been captured and tortured until he agreed to give in and wake the stone. But Tulir had bested the villains with his new power and aimed to restore what was lost uncountable generations ago.

That was how the story was told. Tulir had no living male elders, and he was the eldest son of his family. Some accepted his story just as he had accepted his new station: as a necessity.

"I don't think we should firstly assume thieves," said Rufino.

"Are the ships larger than what our coastal cities build?" asked Harth as he tapped on the map. "Because that's where they're headed."

CLEVEHOLD

"We don't have reason to assume they're warships," said Lena.

"Our ships are only built big enough to fit through the southern canal, the size of most rivers. We built them. They're purpose-built, see? There's no need for large ships like these," defended Norman. He was getting red.

They would fit up the King's River to Clevehold, thought Lena. The river was wide enough for three of Steepwharf's large fishing vessels along most of the way. Those antique ships would have no issue sailing in from the coast.

"I don't wish to speculate and drum up fear if its unneeded," said Tulir.

"Yes, sir," agreed Rufino.

"Send word to have our ships meet them out at sea if they don't port soon. Have them directed upriver to Clevehold," requested Tulir.

"I don't doubt they're ignorant as to the capital's whereabouts," said Norman.

"Call it a kind gesture," Tulir said with a flick of impatience.

"Armed men?" proposed Harth.

Tulir rubbed a finger over his upper lip and considered before answering, "Not so armed we make it look as though we're picking a fight, but enough so they could handle one, should the occasion arise."

Lena nodded. It was a good plan. "We should learn more of them in the next few days."

"Should we move on to other matters, then?" Tulir looked around the room and was met with nods. "Alright. Our latest expansion project."

Lena retrieved the vault coins from her coin purse and set them on the table. They were stacked neatly, the raven and *V* emblem facing up. She took a deep breath and began her briefing.

LIZ BUNCHES

IT FELT BETTER TO NO longer have the weight of the gold on her person. Lena never needed to ferry it far, but the trip from the vault to the meeting room made her anxious. She never fully acknowledged the restlessness until the coins were off her person and she could experience the fleeting anxiety with the feeling of reprieve to follow. She was sure if she spoke with Harth, he could arrange a trusted guard to walk with her. Perhaps he would even volunteer for it himself.

That wouldn't remedy it. Ten gold coins was a great deal of money, and she continuously plucked it from the vault as if it were nothing. Only time would dim that anxiety.

Socks met up with her on the trip to the lower floor. She was sure to walk slower to let the cat keep up. He was a young lad, spry when he wanted to be, but without much of a brain or anything to hunt, he was needy. His steps were slow as he tried to rub against her legs. Lena knew if she walked too far ahead, he would meow until she stopped. Then he would scamper ahead, rub his face on her trousers, and continue his moderate pace.

Lena didn't mind taking her time. She didn't want to falsely create any sense of hope by rushing. If she were completely fair to herself, she knew any word from her family would have been personally and expeditiously delivered to her. Going to the mail station at all was merely entertaining the illusion.

Socks wound between her legs as she ruminated. He was a nimble creature. Mostly, he avoided other people and scattered at any loud noise, but once he was familiar with someone, he made it their job to get out of his way.

Lena scooped him up and kept walking. He didn't like being held, and she knew to let him climb up onto her shoulders. Perched with just a hint of claw in her shoulder, he remained there as she went down the stairs and took the last turn. The people she passed didn't try to pet the cat, whose black fur blended in with Lena's hair.

"Morning, Missus Marisol," greeted Lena.

Socks leapt off her shoulder and onto the shelves of the mail station. To the amusement of the postmaster, the cat made a game of climbing shelves, darting from one high place to another, wary of disturbing any mail that sat in his way. He had never knocked anything over purposefully.

"Afternoon," corrected Marisol with a smile. "Almost dinner, really."

"The days all blur," excused Lena. She hugged her friend. When they parted, she asked, "Any luck? Any news?"

Marisol blushed. She was a pretty woman with dirty-blonde hair, a rarity for an Iste. Rufino always commented on how he had found the rarest beauty. Marisol was as tall as Lena, slim figured, modestly dressed, and had rough hands from horse reins. She answered, "No, but I'm still hopeful for this year."

"It'll happen soon enough, I'm sure." Lena lowered her voice for only Marisol to hear. "Especially since you and your husband have such constant perseverance."

"Why, my lady!" Marisol shoved her playfully.

"I look forward to meeting that child to tell it how much it was loved and wanted before it came into this world."

Socks meowed at the postmaster, who replied, "No, no mail for you."

"Meow," said Socks as he sat on a high shelf and batted at the postmaster's grey hat.

"I've always wanted a child, ever since I was one," said Marisol thoughtfully.

Lena smiled and thought of her own future children. She pictured at least two, one with light hair and green eyes, the other with dark hair and dark brown eyes to match—a good blend of their qualities. The thoughts were warm. She would become Tulir's queen to ensure the power of the Stone King was passed down to future generations. Their children would be much loved, princesses and princes, and legitimate. Perhaps one day, those children would even be told the truth.

"You can't have my hat," the postmaster said, pulling Socks' claws from the fabric.

"Meow," protested Socks as he tried for it again.

The women laughed. Lena offered, "Sorry about him."

"He's alright." The postmaster smiled. He scratched behind Socks' ears. "Nothing for you, Lady Miss."

Lena let out a breath and forced herself to maintain the smile.

"Letters are slow to the coast. Your family may yet reply," encouraged Marisol.

"They've yet to come. Last year, I was confident enough in this place, in what we'd built and discovered, to send the invitation. Their reason was the approaching winter. Winter came, winter went," explained Lena. There was a heaviness coating her throat. She missed Nela fiercely. Though she had comradery with some of the women of court, nothing could compare to her bond with her sister.

"It's only early summer. They have time yet," soothed Marisol.

She nodded. Looking to Socks, Lena called, "Are you staying?"

"Meooow," he responded, a long-held note while he batted at the postmaster's hat again.

"He says he's staying," replied the postmaster.

With a giggle, Lena pointed a stern finger at Socks and directed, "Don't you be out too late."

Marisol put an arm around Lena's shoulders and walked them out. "I'm sure he'll cause all sorts of ruckus before his bedtime."

"Kids," said Lena with a huff. "They're exhausting."

CLEVEHOLD

"Do you have any nieces or nephews?"

"No." Lena shielded her eyes as Marisol walked them out onto a terrace. "My sister is a widow, and they had no children."

"I'm sorry."

"No need." Lena directed them to sit on a stone bench. There were birds soaring about, waiting and hovering for scraps of dinner.

"I should be. I know we've talked about your sister before," apologized Marisol.

"It's alright all the same." Lena patted her arm.

Nela. How had her life changed? The first letter Lena had sent from Clevehold, naturally, was to her sister in Steepwharf. Months had gone by since the incident when Selgen was arrested. Things weren't altogether calm or set, and she had begged in the letter to share the news with no one, but Lena had been so terribly homesick.

The answer came weeks later. By then, Lena had surmised it didn't matter what she had asked of her sister if the letter was intercepted. Luckily, Nela's response was kind and cautious. Lena shouldn't return to Steepwharf, not yet. Let the heir's legitimacy take hold first, she said. All corners of the continent were buzzing with various degrees of conviction. She had underlined a particular line of Nela's letter as a reminder: *"Steepwharf is slow-moving. Give it time."*

Sun on her face, Lena thought about now. What would she tell her sister? What *could* she? The secret was hers, foremost, but it wasn't only hers to tell. Telling anyone could put them all in jeopardy. And yet the longer the ruse was kept, the harsher the potential fallout.

Perhaps it was better that Nela didn't come. In a few years, Lena could visit Steepwharf. By then, perhaps her propensity to fib to her sister may have regained strength.

Chapter 4

HEAVY KNOCKS POUNDED on her door. Socks scampered away, dashing about the room chaotically before hiding under the bed. Lena sat up quickly. Another round of knocks.

Out of bed and with a robe thrown over top her nightgown, Lena crossed the room. It was dark, not yet dawn. She opened the door. "What is it?"

"Sorry to wake you, Miss," he began.

Lena rubbed sleep from her eyes. *Vilars . . . ? It cannot be.*

"The king needs to convene the Council at once," said the guard.

She shook her head. It was no one, a dark-haired guard hidden by shadows. Too short, too young. It wasn't him. The voice was wrong.

"I've been asked to bring you there immediately."

Lena tightened the fastener of her robe. She was decent enough. The shoes next to the door were easily toed on. "Of course."

IN THE MEETING ROOM already were Norman, Rufino, and Marisol, all in their nightclothes and robes. The guard guiding Lena kept the door open behind her. Harth and Tulir followed in soon after.

"It's fortunate the king knew the exact whereabouts of the Commander at this time of night," commented Norman.

Marisol wrapped her arms tighter around herself. "Should I go?"

"You were roused in the middle of the night. I believe you have the right to know why," said Lena. Her heart was in her throat. Harth's face was his typical seriousness, and there wasn't much she could glean from him, but she knew in an instant Tulir was fuming beneath his composed exterior.

The guards closed the doors, leaving just the six of them in the dim light. Norman went to a lantern and turned the dial to increase the burn. "Well?"

"The newcomers in ancient ships have raided Steepwharf," said Tulir, grit in his tone. He clenched a white-knuckle grip on his cane.

Marisol gasped, and Rufino took her hand.

"How do we know this?" asked Lena. A million questions clattered around her mind, but at the forefront were those looking for holes in the legitimacy.

"News came by bird not a half hour ago," answered Tulir.

"Raided Steepwharf? Why?" questioned Rufino.

Harth held up a folded piece of paper. "All we have is here. The newcomers came in, made a ruckus, fatalities unknown, and then they went back onto their ships to camp offshore. We know that, and some of what they look like, talk like."

"May I see that?" Norman held his hand out and took the paper when it was extended to him.

Marisol was pale, her tone shrill and scared. "Why would they do this?"

"To know that, we first need to know who they are. *Who* would do this? Who are these people from across the sea?" asked Tulir. He rubbed a hand over his brow. His clothes hung loosely and partially untucked, hair tussled as if he had been having a fitful sleep.

Norman handed the paper off to Rufino. Norman said matter-of-factly, "It's not a friendly people."

"As though I fucking needed you to tell me that," snapped Tulir.

"What I mean is, the way they're described—their language, their clothes, their ships—I don't know that they are our neighbors from across the sea at all."

"I have to agree," said Rufino, almost remorsefully. He held the note in one hand and kept the other secure to Marisol's.

"We haven't gotten any news of raids in the East, but we aren't in constant communication with them. It's possible these people sailed from the East but didn't originate there," said Lena. She ran a hand through her hair and thought about it more. "But we're still confident these ships wouldn't fit through the strait in the south?"

Before Harth could produce words from his opened mouth, Norman cut him off. "Were the king's ships able to reach Steepwharf before the raid?"

Tulir sighed.

"We're confident these large ships couldn't be from outside our sea. And no, those ships were targeted to arrive early afternoon today," answered Harth.

"Whoever they are, these ships of theirs are fast," commented Rufino.

"Where did they come from? Ships this large, this advanced, had to have been noticed by someone," said Tulir.

"We can send out messages of inquiry at first light," suggested Harth.

"What do these people want?" demanded Norman.

"We don't have any more answers than what's on that paper." Tulir shook his head and tapped his cane once on the floor. Lena expected a near-silent swear to accompany it.

"May I have the note for the descriptions? I want to consult with the librarian, see if we can make headway," offered Lena.

"Of course." Rufino handed off the note to her.

"No demands have been made. We can't expect this news to stay quiet, but we, as the Council, don't want to incite panic. Be cautious as to your public reactions and who you speak to of the details," advised Harth.

"That means no more rousing anyone in the middle of the night," added Tulir. "We can draft the inquiries tonight, but nothing to the librarian or messenger until morning."

Lena clenched the note. Though she hated the idea of waiting, she understood his reasoning.

"We are to lag for the people that died?" questioned Norman.

"The exact number is unknown, but they put the estimate low. We're not pardoning murder, but it looks like it was a quest for supplies," justified Tulir. "We can't help them, but we can protect our people from panic."

"By now, Steepwharf has people behind strong walls. She's a defendable city," said Harth.

"I'll begin drafting inquiries," said Norman.

"I'll see Marisol back to our room, then return to help," added Rufino.

Tulir waved to dismiss them. "I'll leave you to it. Find out what you can."

Lena looked at the note in her hand. She hadn't read it. Her mind felt blurry with the news, equal parts exhausted and concerned. What had been done to her home? Was her family alright? Surely with ships, these people attacked from the water. Her sister's and parents' homes were far enough inland, they shouldn't have been threatened.

The door swung closed. Lena picked her head up. Only she and Tulir remained. He went to the lamp Norman had adjusted and dimmed the light.

"What happens now?" asked Lena.

"You should get some sleep, if you can." He walked to her and extended his hand, a patient kindness in his eyes. "I'll walk you back, if you like."

"I don't know I would be able to sleep." She took his hand.

"The next few days are going to be long ones," he said wearily, the biting undercurrent of anger having lessened. In its place was a coating of confusion at the unknown.

Lena pulled the door open for them, his hands occupied by the cane and holding hers. She didn't want to lose the sense of security it provided her. They walked the halls silently back to her room. Though empty, there was no gambling who could have been listening. Most people in the Council and trafficking the castle were trusted, but it only took one bought man hidden in a cove to break that.

At her door, they stopped. She didn't move to open it. The words to ask him to stay constricted her heart and danced on her tongue. There was no personal reservation in her wanting to make the request—her intentions were pure, and she cared little for how others might interpret them. But in this time of turmoil, what would this add to the king?

Tulir squeezed her hand, then released it. He turned the knob and let it swing inward. The new view revealed Socks on her bed, crouching down as if ready to run. His tail was up and his eyes wide. It made them laugh.

She could stand to hear more of that. The king was mature enough to make the determination for himself. She asked, "Will you stay?"

His free hand gestured for her to walk in before him. She did, he followed, and he shut the door behind her. In a conservative tone, he admitted, "I don't care for being alone right now, either."

"It's different," she agreed. The clarification of "for us" was left implied. Steepwharf was their home. Before Clevehold, it was the only home they had known. The city had defied them, given them cause to break the law, but there were still people there they cared deeply about.

"I'm sure your family is fine," Tulir assured. He went to her couch by the windows and sat, cane braced next to him on the wall.

"The casualty estimate is low, and my family has no reason to be at the docks or waterfront during the day. Father works in the Central District, and Nela would only be there at night . . ." Lena stopped as she felt her voice cracking. She put a hand over her mouth and clenched her eyes shut. Tears squeezed out of them as she trembled.

She heard Tulir crossing the room, then felt as his arms wrapped around her. "It's going to be alright."

Lena wanted to wholeheartedly believe him. Arms secure around him and face buried in his shoulder, she did manage to believe him enough to stop herself from breaking down. "Why would this happen?"

"I don't know." He smoothed a hand down her hair. "We can't reach any answers tonight."

No answers. They had to wait. Even if she went to the library now, or helped Rufino and Norman draft their inquiries, it wouldn't give her the answers she sought. Lena pulled back and rubbed her hands up and down his biceps. "Thank you."

"Please don't. I feel as if I've done less than nothing," he refuted. He was leaning slightly left, favoring his weight there.

"For staying." Leading them to the couch, she clarified, "You know what would become of your reputation, should Charlot hear of you staying in my quarters."

Tulir smirked and shook his head. He was first to the couch and sat heavily. After a huff, he said, "It's been years since Norman and his wife shared a room, and I've heard tell she sleeps heavily and snores like a goat. She wouldn't wake up for this debacle. Your reputation won't be tarnished."

"I don't care what they think of me. Their rumors are all hush work." Lena sat with her leg bent on the cushion to lean an elbow on and face him.

Socks jumped onto Tulir's lap. Looking him in the eye, the cat let out a long meow. The end trailed up as if it was a question.

"Is that right?" Tulir asked with a smile. He pet the cat and earned a steady purr. In a serious tone, he said to Lena, "How could you not feed this poor animal?"

Lena shoved his arm lightly. "He's only skin and bones because he runs amuck so much. You know it well."

"Are you calling the prince a liar?"

"Oh, he has a *title* now?" Lena pet Socks and pulled lightly on his tail.

"Meow," said Socks.

"Don't talk to your mother like that," Tulir faux scolded.

"Meow." Socks jumped into Lena's lap and rammed his head into hers.

"Where did he learn that language? I know you don't talk like that," said Tulir.

Lena laughed. "*You* do. He gets it from you."

"Ah." Tulir made a clicking sound with his mouth. "That'll do it."

Socks went to the far side of Lena's lap and pawed at the cushion beside her. There wasn't more than a few inches open, but he had snuggled himself into much smaller spaces. "Meow," he protested when she didn't move.

"What do you want?" she asked.

"Clear as anything, isn't it? He's telling you to move over for him to have a space of his own," answered Tulir.

How he got the cat to do his bidding, she had yet to determine. Perhaps it was a man-to-man thing—man-to-male cat, that is. Despite the cheap invitation, Lena took no issue in scooting down closer to Tulir. There was a warm sense of familiarity under his arm.

She kept the slight angle to look at him, and it brought their faces closer. With only a few inches between them, she could whisper. Before she had looked into those deep brown eyes, wasn't there something she wanted to say?

Tulir brought up a hand and brushed hair off her shoulder. "I'm used to seeing it in a braid."

"I didn't quite have time when my door was being rattled," she jokingly apologized.

"No, it looks nice. Comfortable." He looked at her softly.

Something you could grow accustomed to? She thought about their future and smiled. "You look comfortable yourself."

He blushed.

"You handled yourself well today," she complimented.

Tulir smiled and looked away. "Are you trying to get me into bed, Miss Lena?"

She took his chin in her hand and turned his head. With his face close to hers, she hesitated, but only so long as it took to look for refusal in his eyes. He closed the distance for her.

When their lips met, her heart thrummed faster. It wasn't their first kiss—not that they were seasoned, either—but it always felt like the first time. Her hands traveled from his chin to his neck, down his arm. It was familiar, comfortable, but at the same time burning. *Does he feel it, too?*

Lena adjusted her sitting position to face him more and increase the pressure on their lips. His small moan confirmed he felt something akin to the fire under her skin. The pressure his hands applied as he gripped her neck and waist alternated between light touches and longing grasps.

He broke the kiss. Lips red, eyes hazy, and voice low, he reminded, "We have to be reasonable."

"What *you* decided was reasonable," she combatted but allowed him the space.

Hand still on her neck, he conveyed in earnest, "Let me do this right with you."

Lena nodded. In the daylight, with company—in those times it was easy to agree. Their emotions were running too rampant right now for it to have been right. He was a king. She would be queen. All there was to do was wait. There was no set date but the planning had begun, at least in a general timeline: after the newcomers were dealt with and the Steepwharf business was settled.

Soon, she told herself. She could have him soon.

She tucked herself under his arm again and rested her head on his shoulder. As she settled in, she looked at Socks. Prince. Their first son. She smiled.

Moments like this, it should have been hard to question his true intentions, but there was a small gnawing feeling that crept in. Did he *want* to marry her? His hold was secure around her. She always felt the passion reciprocated in his kiss. He was present when his skin was pressed to hers, yet when they parted, she couldn't help but feel some small reserve.

Lena yawned. He wanted her. Reserve was late-night paranoia. In the daylight, she was sure she would agree to reasonableness.

THE SUN HADN'T BEEN up long when Lena made her way to the library. Other people were up, and the halls were buzzing. The atmosphere was strained. There was no questioning why with the note clutched in her hand.

A recognizable face she couldn't recall the name of was at the table nearest the door when she entered the library. After exchanging pleasantries, she asked, "Do you know if my cousin is here?"

"He was putting away books along the back wall, last I saw him," they answered.

Lena inclined her head and went that way. Rows and rows of books filled the Royal Library. The shelves had survived the test of time, but numerous original books had not. While many had been mended, some had proved too eaten through to revive. Gradually, the shelves had been refilled with items from all over. Gifts presented to the king, usually. They regularly rotated select stock with the library in Clevehold to share the wonder of words with the people.

The Royal Library wasn't as grand as the library in Steepwharf. Lena couldn't help but make the comparison, especially when she quickly reached the back row and saw her cousin standing there.

Selgen was thin, more than his natural figure. Pale skin, dark circles under his eyes, a lackluster posture—he looked ill. If it hadn't been for their time in Avild and Klaus' cabin, Lena would have had no issue recognizing him as the introverted librarian she grew up knowing.

However, she had witnessed him grow. For what felt like an instant, in retrospect, she had seen him come alive. There had been gumption in his step. He was finding purpose. There had been want to thrive enough for him to run for his life when trouble found him.

All of that was now gone. At first Lena had pitied him, but over time that pity morphed into disappointment. She wasn't sure if, were the library shelves to tip, he would have enough will to live to even move out of the way.

"Selgen," she greeted.

"What can I do for you, Miss Lena?" he asked flatly.

She resented the tone, though it was earned. The only times she came to see him as of late were for requests. She knew he probably thought her compassion for him had dissolved with her impending ascension to the throne, but it was quite the opposite. He was important to her, and she couldn't stand to see him like this.

Lena cleared her throat. "It's about the ships that arrived in Steepwharf."

"I heard of it." He slotted a book on the shelf.

"It was only yesterday," she said as she moved closer.

"I heard of it over breakfast. Your men sent inquiries this morning." There were no more books in his hands, but he stared at the shelf as if there was something more he needed to do.

"The people, they aren't anything like what Rufino, Norman, or I recognize," she said and then took a breath. Her hands felt clammy.

Selgen hummed. He nodded, then turned to her. Instead of responding, he gave her a wide berth as he walked around.

"Can you read it?" Lena followed, holding the note out to his back. "Tell me if you recognize anything about the descriptors?"

He kept walking, headed toward the nook in a corner where his desk lived. Stopping at it, hands flat on the desk and staring at the wall, he finally responded, "No."

"No?" she questioned. Lena moved around the desk to face him. Insistently, she held out the note.

"I won't." He shook his head.

Her hand lowered slowly. "Why?"

"What use would it be?" he returned. There was no fight in his eyes. The tone was tired, disinterested.

"What use?" she repeated incredulously. He said he had heard of what happened, but had he really? Was this the extent of his want to help his home city?

CLEVEHOLD

The home city that nearly hanged him, she reminded herself. Breathing out through her nose, tone patient, she offered, "This is the account of what they saw. Can you just have a look?"

"They were people who went to Steepwharf to raid. I don't care what they look like, and I don't care for the damages." Selgen waved a hand. "Let the king deal with it. It's your district."

"And I'm curious," she insisted.

"Curious to know if they came to usurp a false king?" Selgen bit in a whisper.

Her tone lowered. "You know nothing."

"Then leave"—he stood to the side to let her pass—"before I pretend to the wrong people I do."

"You wouldn't," she said confidently. "You wouldn't do that to me or to Tulir."

"I wouldn't?"

"We saved your life. Tulir and Vilars were your best men," she reminded. They were family. She was the first among the family he had come to, or had he forgotten?

"And now you're in a position to put me to death," he said passively.

Lena hesitated. "Do you want that?"

"Leave me alone." Hand toward the exit, he pleaded, "Just go."

"If I could take those memories from you, I would." If such magic existed was one of the questions she had thought to ask Avild. There was no cure for it.

"Perhaps one day I'll have the nerve enough to bore them from my own skull," he said while looking at the floor. His arm flapped down.

Lena cleared her throat. "Do you have an objection to me doing my own research?"

"It's your library," he answered.

She wanted to yell. She wanted to shake him. Didn't he have the constitution to move past it? Only once had he spoken to her of those revived memories. They were as gruesome as she had imagined. She didn't expect him to simply forget again how he had killed, violated, and removed the hands from those bodies—at times not in that order—but she had hoped time would let the reasoning lessen the burden.

Selgen had never wanted to kill people. He wanted this: a library full of knowledge to fawn over. She thought if she could give him that back, he could become who he had been before magic ruined him.

Too much flooded into Lena's mind to say, and though she paused to summon the courage to do so, a little voice reminded her of something. They had done this before. She had tried. Every time she left the same argument, she cycled ceaselessly through wondering what more or what else she could have done.

There wasn't time for a rehash performance now.

She nodded and walked away. "I'll see to the books."

Chapter 5

THE HALL WAS ALIVE with noise at dinner. Three long tables spanned down the room with a shorter head table at the front, decorated with a dark-purple runner. It was at the front that Lena sat next to Tulir, Harth on his other side. Across from them were Norman with his wife, Charlot, and Rufino with Marisol. There were ample empty seats, and they remained as such unless there were guests in attendance.

The head table could seat up to fourteen. Lena expected the space beside Harth would be taken by his wife, if he ever chose to marry. The ones next to Lena would seat the future prince and princesses. As for the rest, perhaps more Council members would be added as the reign endured. More voices for the people.

Lena had scanned the three long tables a few times over. Selgen wasn't there. It was hard to tell by how packed the room was, but after the most recent sweep, she was sure of it. She had examined the crowd thoroughly while explaining to the table what she had found in her day of books.

"If the strait closed only a few hundred years ago, that means it was open when the Stone King reigned," concluded Harth based on her information.

"Why does that matter?" asked Charlot. She had a high-pitched voice, all her statements sounded like questions, and her hair always looked as if it were wound too tightly to her head. She wore a lot of powder makeup and only light-blue clothes.

"Do we think the ships are from that age?" proposed Rufino.

A group of servants took away their bowls from dinner. Their discussion resumed thereafter when Tulir spoke, "The ships wouldn't be the only thing to survive that long."

"That would require a lot of magic to remain hidden for all this time," said Marisol.

"Not to mention the magic upkeep for them to still be in sailing condition," added Rufino.

Lena nodded along, keeping silent. She was glad they were coming to the same conclusions she had.

"Magic like that would be hard to keep hidden, as well. The outlawing of magic was enforced on both sides of the seas," said Harth.

"Is it possible these ships are replicas?" asked Norman.

A band had set up along the side near the open windows. It was a nice night. Patrons were clapping along as the instruments began to play.

"It's possible." Tulir scratched the side of his head. "Neither options are settling, because neither should have gone unnoticed. How big a shipyard would be needed? It takes much magic or many years to build ships like that."

"Are there pockets to the East where magic wasn't outlawed? How much was controlled on that side of the sea?" inquired Marisol. She dabbed a napkin at the sides of her lips.

"From what we determined, it wasn't really encouraged or outlawed outside the large city. The communities there were downtrodden, and they lost it. They didn't have it or the grounding for it," explained Tulir.

"The kind of magic we're talking about would have given them trade, made them more than dirt-poor," said Norman. "Every few years we send a ship, and nothing has ever changed."

"When was the last time the northern cities sent a ship east?" asked Lena.

Charlot acknowledged the question by turning up her nose.

After a pause, Tulir seemed to realize the question was to go unanswered. "Norman."

"Last year, in the spring, I believe. There's that nasty storm—that weather imbalance cove—but once you get past that, nothing. Nothing of note," he explained, then continued pointedly at Lena, "and nothing I haven't disclosed previously."

"Excuse us if we weren't enthralled by your stories of keeping your buyers poor," said Harth.

Tulir smirked and hid it with a drink.

The music ramped up, and people got up the dance to the beat. The first people to the open floor were a woman and a man recently married. Lena recognized the man, as he had come to ask for the king's blessing at the last open forum.

As a servant passed by, Lena hailed them. The girl asked, "Are you in need of something, ma'am?"

"My cousin, Selgen, he hasn't come. Will you take a plate of food and eat with him?" requested Lena.

"You want me to serve him?" the girl clarified.

"Take something for him but also for yourself. Company is what he needs." Lena took a breath, then warned, "He may not eat. You can bring another with you to be more comfortable, for he may not talk, either. I just hate the idea of him being alone."

The girl smiled. "Yes, ma'am."

Lena nodded and the servant walked away. There were many things to balance, and one attribute of being nearly queen and on the Council was her capacity to delegate. That, and perhaps a new friendly face or two could make Selgen forget his demons for a little while.

When she looked back to rejoin the conversation, she saw Marisol whispering something in Rufino's ear. The man then addressed the table, "Thank you for the company, as always."

"You have a takeaway to think on," said Tulir almost teasingly.

Rufino rose and clumsily pushed in his chair. "Of course, sir."

Marisol was on Rufino's other hand, pulling lightly. "Good night, all."

Lena smiled.

After the couple left the table, Charlot followed them with her eyes, watching them openly. She then turned back, confused. "They're not going to dance?"

A laugh turned into a cough when Lena kept her mouth closed.

"Rufino's shy. He prefers to dance privately," answered Tulir.

"The drums do carry. We'll be lucky to sleep tonight," complained Norman.

A group of girls approached the head table. They were a few years older than Lena, likely Tulir's age or older. Giggles and smiles were exchanged between them. One in a pale-yellow dress was pushed toward the table.

"Mister Harth, sir"—she glanced back at her pack of girls briefly—"would you care to dance with us?"

He put his drink down. Politely, he refused, "Thank you, but I—"

Tulir interrupted, "Go on." When Harth didn't immediately respond, Tulir elbowed him lightly.

"I don't think—"

Another girl interjected, "Please?"

Tulir whispered something to Harth, who then let out a long breath and stood. "Good man," commented Tulir, giving him a pat on the back.

Lena smiled.

Harth left the table and was soon enveloped by the group of girls leading him toward the dance floor. Music from violins, horns, and drums floated around them.

"I'm surprised you let your personal guard go," said Norman with raised eyebrows.

"The ones I may need protecting from tonight, I can handle myself," replied Tulir. He leaned back in his chair.

Norman smiled forcibly.

"We should pivot to watch the band," suggested Charlot.

"Yes, dear." Norman did the work of resituating their chairs until the backs were facing the table.

"It's comforting to see people having fun, despite the tribulations of what's going on," said Tulir.

Lena nodded. "I'm glad you like it, because the performance funds were taken from the vault this afternoon. You can't stop people from hearing of the troubles, but you can . . . distract them, as bad as that sounds. Keeps them from sitting around and overthinking it."

"Give them an alternative," he proposed.

"Give them comfort," she agreed.

Tulir had his cup raised partially to his mouth, but he stopped. He was smiling at her. There was an evident fondness in his eyes.

"Yes?" she questioned kindly.

He put the cup down. "You're well suited for this."

"I'm playing my part."

"No, you're not. I am. Harth"—he gestured to the awkward Commander attempting to dance—"is. But this doesn't look disingenuous on you."

Lena smiled and leaned in closer. "Perhaps I carry it well."

"I hope you don't mean 'carry it' as in deceit. I have no room for it," he spoke softly as his eyes flicked from hers to her lips. The tone was far from the warning, the words implied.

Blushing, she looked down.

"I didn't mean . . ." he trailed off.

"I was raised to know degrees of expectation." She looked to him and continued, "I also enjoy it."

Tulir rested a hand over hers. His gaze moved to focus behind her, and his expression became serious. He sat straighter and asked, "What is it?"

"News best received privately, my king," a man behind Lena answered.

"Norman," Tulir said to get the man's attention. Once he had it, he beckoned, "We're to receive news. Make sure the room behind us is clear."

"The garden would be more secure," said Norman as he stood and looked between the messenger and Tulir.

"Then ensure it is such," responded Tulir impatiently. He then returned to the messenger, "Will you inform Harth and meet us back there with him?"

"Yes, sir," the messenger said and went toward the festivities.

Lena reached back to where Tulir's cane rested against the wall.

Tulir stood slowly, hands braced on the table as he got his legs straightened out beneath him. He winced slightly before pushing the look away. Letting go of the table, he stood straight and took the cane when offered.

"You alright?" she asked quietly.

"Sitting too long." He took a cautious first step. "I'm not old yet, but this will get me there."

"Should we try to get Rufino back?" Lena kept in step with him as he moved toward the door behind them.

"Once we get the degree of it, we can find him or fill him in come morning."

Harth got ahead of them and opened the door. He held it for them and followed. The messenger was with him.

"Always a gentleman," commented Tulir. There was an attempt for lightheartedness, but his tone was distracted. He regained normal walking speed as they crossed the room and made their way to the garden behind it. The greenery was raised high off the ground and open on three sides with a view of the mountains and Clevehold. The lighting was a combination of the glow from a few floors above and bright moonlight. Harth added to it by emitting light from his hand.

"Is this everyone?" asked the messenger.

"Proceed," said Tulir. They stood in a circle, Tulir flanked by Lena and Harth, Norman and the messenger across the way.

"The ones who attacked Steepwharf, they are coming upriver. They are headed for Clevehold," delivered the messenger.

Lena's heart clenched.

"What of the communities along the river?" asked Harth.

"No one else has been attacked. They aren't getting off the ships."

"What of our ships on the river?" asked Lena.

"Those leaving Clevehold have been allowed to pass, but no one can come up behind them. It's scared most traffic off the river," he explained.

"Still four ships?" Tulir asked, and the messenger nodded. "Anything else?"

"No other news yet, sir."

"Go down to the Royal Docks, tell them not to send anyone else out on my orders. Then have men sent out into Clevehold to say the same to the ships in the canals," instructed Tulir.

"We mean to tell everyone?" questioned Norman.

The messenger went inside and closed the door behind him.

"It's not a question of trying to hide it. People are going to know before long." Tulir looked out toward Clevehold. He then looked to Harth. "As warden of the city's safety, what would you have me do?"

"We don't have a wall around the city, nor the manpower to defend such a wall if we did. The city's too large, and there are too many dead areas people could hide in. Clevehold isn't defendable," summarized Harth.

"But the castle is," said Lena. Their walls were strong, and they had room enough to house the city in the lower levels.

"It's our best bet. We should make the move into the castle somewhat gradually. Unless we think they'll be upon us in a day, we don't want a rampage," agreed Harth.

"We will start passively by bringing in supplies in the morning, should it come to housing everyone here. We can't stop people from knowing, but we don't want to incite a panic," said Tulir.

"We also don't want to bring people into the castle before it's necessary. Aside from panic, an enclosed area opens us up for disease, disputes, fights," said Norman.

"Say it does come to that. Everyone inside; they're knocking at our door. Then what?" asked Lena.

"Assuming we can get everyone and everything inside," amended Tulir.

"They brought four large ships worth of men. Unless skeleton crews are sailing them, we have guards enough to keep peace, but not enough to fight them outright. Our options would be to bargain, threaten, bribe, or outlast," said Harth grimly.

Tulir rubbed a hand down his face. "Bargaining or bribing can show them we have one hand of gold or goods, and the other empty of a weapon. Threatening them only works if we can make them believe it."

"Does that mean we do nothing, then wait them out?" asked Lena.

"We should send an emissary to meet them, see if we can come to terms. They have to want something," suggested Norman.

"Was anything else sent from Steepwharf? Were they specific on their casualties?" asked Tulir.

"Not many were reported," said Harth.

Tulir opened his mouth and looked down. "It wasn't bad."

"I thought you cared more for your home," scolded Norman.

"From what we were told, the deaths were all in defense. The ships ported but they came for supplies, not blood," expanded Harth.

Lena narrowed her eyes. There was relief in knowing the intention of the newcomers wasn't just destruction and murder, but what sense did that make?

"If they wanted to lay waste to our cities, they had plenty of opportunities. There are towns dotted up and down the coast. There are more along the river," pointed out Tulir.

"It's possible they aren't intent on a fight, but it's more so possible they're saving energy and resources for a fight. Or a siege," said Harth.

"They're headed here. Ships are allowed to leave but none to come through," Lena repeated the messenger's words, hoping to gain some insight that would help the situation make sense.

"What do these newcomers want from us?" questioned Norman.

"Was the librarian able to provide any insight?" asked Tulir.

Lena shook her head. "Only what I've relayed about the strait. Nothing more."

Chapter 6

THE PRESSURE OF AN external force could be felt subtly squeezing the spine of Clevehold. It reminded Lena of Steepwharf when the murderer had been at large, unknown. Once Selgen had been arrested, the city exhaled. No one living in Clevehold knew an accused murderer lived in the library of the castle; these people had only known the exhale. Clevehold was the heart of where magic had been revived, and here they could start over. Everyone started fresh.

Lena had made sure to tell Harth she planned to leave the castle and gave twenty-four hours' notice before doing so. When she left, there were three guards waiting to accompany her. One was older than Harth, in his mid- or late forties with a scar over his eye, armed with a long sword. He had darker skin, a short beard, and looked like he was from Istedinium. The other two were younger and not visibly armed.

She knew well enough the other two men had concealed weapons. Typically, she would only have two guards to accompany her, but the third was there to push the cart of supplies Lena had gathered to be brought out.

Harth's men were working to bring grain stock and other food stores within the castle walls. What Lena did was not in detriment or defiance of these efforts. What she carried and planned to distribute were small tokens of comfort: sweets for children, oil for lamps, blankets. Things that could be parted with.

As Lena and her men walked along the main canal, she saw many weary faces. Though she knew few who lived in Clevehold personally, she prided herself on at least recognizing faces. There were many new ones here.

CLEVEHOLD

"People are coming here from farms and settlements along the river, aren't they?" Lena asked the seasoned guard.

"Yes, Miss Lena," he answered.

A group of children ran up to the cart, plucked some sweets, and darted away. The guard pushing the cart was about to protest, but she put up a cautionary hand.

"That's what this is for." She then pointed to an open market stall. "We can station ourselves there and give out until we have no more to give."

The guards did as she instructed. While she waited for them to push aside a crate to make room, a frail-looking old man approached her. He eyed the cart.

"Do you need a blanket?" she offered.

The man continued to stare. His one hand was concealed beneath his thinly worn brown traveling cloak. He looked hungry and dehydrated.

Lena took a blanket from the cart and held it out for him.

The man reached out quickly with the visible hand, and the concealed one then sprung out. A metal gleam accompanied it.

Lena's hand came up. A green-hued shield protected her, one made of magic. It tingled as it rested atop her hand, and she didn't feel the knife as it bounced off the shield.

The man recoiled and took a step back. His mouth twisted in a snarl.

One of the younger guards came around her and punched the man in the jaw. It dazed him enough for the guard to wrench the knife from his hand and toss it into the canal. The guard punched the man in the gut before taking hold of both arms and fastening them behind the man.

"Quick thinking, Miss," commended the seasoned guard.

Though she wanted to think the best of people, she knew to be cautious. Turning to him, she dismissed the shield and asked, "Is the stall set?"

"Yes, Miss Lena," he answered.

"I'll get this one worked and send someone back in my place," offered the guard who had hold of the man.

"No need. We won't be bringing the cart back." Lena let herself feel the racing of her heart. She looked down at her hands. For that being the only thing she knew of magic, it never failed her. It could cover her from head to toe, two feet in each direction, if she needed it to.

"Yes, ma'am," he responded.

"Thank you." She looked up and cleared her throat. "Thank you for stepping in so quickly."

Lena went to the stall. She stood behind the cart and by the time she looked up, the man and the guard restraining him were gone. The two remaining guards were at her side, preventing anyone from getting behind her.

"Brave, Miss," said the seasoned guard. He rested a hand on his sword. "Do you feel up to staying?"

"I still want to give out what we came with." She nodded and smiled at the people in the street. They had missed the debacle, it seemed.

A woman came up with two small children. For her, Lena handed off two blankets and some sweets. When the woman tried to pay and was refused, she thanked Lena profusely.

When there was no one at the stall, Lena said, "The man was tired, hungry, and desperate, and I look like an easy target."

"You handled it well," the other guard commented.

Lena smiled and went about handing out items as people approached. She made small talk, gave reassurance, and listened to people's woes. None but herself knew it took more than a half hour for her heartbeat to return to normal. That she still felt the phantom tingling in her hand where the shield had blocked the knife. Those sensations, she kept quiet.

During the course of the day, she heard and was told many things. The magic menders had a line out the door. The estimation of newcomers from the last three days alone was almost a hundred. School sessions had been cancelled. Families were already rationing their money and supplies.

Endearing news reached her as well. Men had taken it upon themselves to block the canal entrance with sunken wood. There was enough room for the water to flow, though it had caused slight flooding in the district closest to the mouth. People had also pooled weaponry. They were prepared to fight. More than one man boldly declared to Lena he had no intention of giving up his new home.

Near the end of the day, however, they were met with harsh news. The newcomers had arrived. Camped just around the bend beyond the pillars of Clevehold, they had stopped. They now blocked the river with their ships.

The grip of unsettled nerves tightened. Lena took a few breaths to steady herself. *They're here.*

"Miss Lena, the few items left can distribute themselves. We should return," the seasoned guard recommended. Lena nodded.

She didn't know what she felt. Part of her was numb. She recognized the threat but felt no dominion over the situation. Her position was no different than anyone else in the street. In that moment, they were all the same.

In the distance, she heard a loud creaking noise. Others reacted as well. A father hung onto his child. Murmurs flared up. "The castle" and "the docks" were heard amongst the whispered words.

Lena stepped out from the stall, recognizing what they were hearing was the sound of the Royal Dock gates closing. The news had reached that far. "Only as a precaution," she assured them.

"We need to be inside," said a woman.

"It isn't safe," said the father with the child fastened tightly to him.

"These newcomers are not in Clevehold. They stopped outside. They have not attacked us. We will be cautious, but we will not panic," said Lena. "It will do us no good to panic."

<hr />

WHEN LENA RETURNED to the castle, she felt the need to change and wash. Normally, being out in Clevehold didn't give her that sensation. It was a combination of the old man's attack and the news of their new neighbors, she reasoned. Lena didn't wonder after that man, if he would get charged or not—she didn't care. She wanted to be rid of it. All of it.

Due to her time in the bath, she missed dinner. She imagined there wasn't as much fanfare as there had been two nights ago. The atmosphere was too tense. She did assume, though, there had been equal drink included.

When she returned to her room, there was food waiting for her beneath upturned bowls to keep Socks from eating it. The cat was pawing at the bowls unsuccessfully when she arrived. She closed the door and snapped once at him, then kicked up the door's corner exit for him.

Unafraid, he looked up. He greeted, "Meow."

"Oh, alright." She went to his food box and took out bits. They were no sooner dropped on the floor before he began munching.

"I don't know that I can eat," she murmured to him.

Socks made a grumbled meow in response as he ate.

CLEVEHOLD

Lena went back to the dishes. Beneath the first cover was a piece of chicken dressed with carrots and peas. Beneath the other was a bread roll. The latter, she picked up and began munching on.

Socks jumped onto the bed.

The piece of chicken didn't look seasoned. She separated it from the vegetables, putting them into a bowl, before pushing the chicken toward Socks. "Enjoy it."

He didn't hesitate to eat it. One paw on the meat, he ripped pieces away with his teeth. His tail stayed in the air, enthused.

"You stay in the castle, alright?" Lena finished her bread and wiped her hands. "Things are touchy outside. I want you safe."

Socks continued eating.

Lena left him to finish it and set the bowl of vegetables on her dresser. He would do little more than sniff at them. If she came back to hair in the bowl, she would know not to eat them.

The halls saw low traffic as she walked through. This wasn't a casual or aimless amble; she knew where to head, and it wasn't far.

She knocked on Tulir's door.

"What is it?" he called from the other side.

"May I speak with you?" she asked at the door. She clasped her hands and waited. Sounds of movement approached the door.

Tulir opened it. The cane wasn't in his hands. "Everything alright?" He looked pale.

"Yes. I didn't mean to worry you," she pushed out quickly.

He let out a big breath and combed a hand through his hair. After a nod and a moment's hesitation, he moved to the side and said, "Come in, please."

"I'm sorry I missed dinner," she apologized as she walked in. His room was familiar to her. The deep-blue sheets, purple tapestries, and polished wooden dressers. Of his three windows, two were clear with the slightest hue of pink, the middle one blue. The size of his accommodation was similar to Lena's, but his had the addition of a formal sitting room. Most guests would knock and have been received through that door, but she wasn't most guests.

"You worried me when you didn't show and then weren't in your room." He closed the door.

"I lost track of time in the bath."

He leaned back against the wall and looked at her fondly. "I missed you at dinner. It was a somber affair. Charlot took it upon herself to do most of the talking."

"Did Rufino and Marisol sneak away the first chance they got?" she asked.

Tulir pulled a half smile and nodded. "Harth didn't stay much longer than them and left me with Norman and Charlot. Something about coordinating something or other," he joked.

Lena looked around the room and twined her hands together. She noticed the cane resting next to the desk at the foot of the bed. Tulir's belongings were orderly and put away. She supposed he hadn't been raised accustomed to having much and hadn't taken up the habit.

The more she looked around, the more she wanted to look. A feeling within her spoke of something she didn't see. An absence. She stopped herself from gawking and ran a finger along the carvings of the cane.

"How was your afternoon in the city?" He pushed off the wall and limped to the bed to lean on the frame instead.

She looked to him, then at the bed. "You still make it as if you're in the barracks."

"I wasn't in the barracks that long. Private employ meant private quarters." He patted on the top blanket pulled taut over the mattress. "I did always pride myself on the better made bed."

"Start the day with a sense of accomplishment," she agreed.

CLEVEHOLD

"When I can make myself get out of it," he joked, and she laughed. "The sun always comes up too early. Night shifts were my favorite."

Surveying the room again, she picked up what she had felt whispers of before. They weren't alone. Under scrutiny, the thought developed. There couldn't have been someone else in the room—she would see them.

She took two steps toward the windows to view the private sitting room. It was empty. Just an unlit fireplace, high-back chairs, a fantasy novel on an end table. There wasn't another living thing present. She didn't feel like she was being watched, necessarily, and the sensation wasn't wholly uncomfortable. Being in Tulir's presence never was.

She felt it but she saw no proof—someone else's imprint on the room. Was it that Tulir was so accustomed to living his life as one of a pair that it always felt like there was company?

"Lena," he said to get her attention, continuing once he had it. "The city—did something happen?"

"A small incident. Quickly resolved, no harm done, and nothing compared to the other news we received," she answered. She dropped her fidgeting hands and said confidently, "I think I should go speak with them."

"What?" Tulir stood upright, balanced on his left leg. He took a limping step to the desk and grabbed his cane.

"They have to want something. They stopped in Steepwharf, raided supplies"—she put her arms out and began pacing—"but they didn't stay there. They didn't attack or kill everyone once the fighting started. And then they took their time coming upriver, not attacking our towns or farms, just to settle outside our front door. They haven't come into the city. I'm curious, and I think I should speak with them."

"Or they could be readying an attack. Or setting up for a siege."

Lena pressed her lips together. *Perhaps so.* But their first action couldn't be violence, particularly if unprovoked. Steepwharf hadn't been left bloodless, but the city had certainly had brawls with higher body counts. "What if they're out there waiting to see what we do about it? What if they want to talk? Shouldn't we give them that?"

On her next lap toward him as she paced, Tulir took her by the wrist. His grip was light, and the touch trailed up her arm once he had her. "You plan to negotiate?"

"I plan to find out why they caused damage to my home." She looked him in the eye and put a hand to his shoulder. "And hopefully settle whatever it is to prevent them from doing more damage."

"It's a good idea." He looked down at his cane and dropped his grip on her.

"Thank you."

He began to walk away and didn't look her in the eye when he said, "But I don't want you to be the one to go."

"They can't hurt me."

"They could try. It's not a risk I want to take," he rebutted. He stopped at his windows and looked out.

"I can defend myself." The issue was, Tulir had never seen it firsthand. The stories of her using the shield were just that to him—stories. Telling him what had happened in the market would have been of no benefit. All he would see was her safety threatened and her stubbornness stopping her from returning when he thought she should have.

"Why must it be you? I can speak with them," he asked as he turned to face her again.

"Sending you is too high a risk," she combatted.

Sternly, he complained, "Can't send a cripple king."

CLEVEHOLD

"You know that's not what I meant." Her heartbeat quickened as she crossed the room to stand close to him. She took his free hand and locked eyes with him. Words weren't needed to convey the sincerity or justify how she meant it. The sentiment danced on the tip of her tongue: *Because I love you too much.*

Could he see the unspoken words in her eyes?

Tulir squeezed her hand and closed his eyes. Menace gone from his voice, he whispered, "I hate the idea of you going out there. I hate it selfishly."

"I promise, I'll be fine." Her other hand came up to caress his face.

He opened his eyes and nodded. "How do you plan to convince the Council?"

Lena leaned up and kissed him lightly. A small spark. She sighed into the kiss and broke it. "I planned to get the king's permission and not go to the Council."

He groaned and leaned his forehead against hers.

Backing away from him, she brought to life a small shield. "If we go to the Council, you will need to justify why I'm the one who must go."

"But you don't," he combated.

"I do," she matched his tone.

Tulir opened his mouth, returned his jaw to a stern closed position, then groaned again. With stressed patience, he asked, "How do you expect me to afterward justify sending the future queen to meet with murderers?"

"That's how you justify it," she encouraged, letting the shield dissipate. "Diplomacy, not a rash reaction of war. We speak with them first to find out what it is they want and if there's a rational, peaceful resolution to all this."

"And if they try to hurt you?" he asked pointedly.

She thought back to their plot to break Selgen out of prison. The stakes had changed; she was more attuned to the plan this time, but the throughline was there. "I'm a woman. Even if I am accompanied by guards, they'll underestimate me. They will have less want to kill me."

"Less want does not equal none," he pleaded.

"I may not be a fighter, but I can defend myself."

"With that magic you hardly know."

"It's kept me alive. It's saved all our lives." She tried to keep her voice low without losing the impact of her words. It was an old habit that reared when emotions ran high, to keep talk of magic hushed.

"But it couldn't—" Tulir clenched his fist and finished with a loud exhale from his nose.

It couldn't save Vilars. Lena licked her lips and looked to the floor. They didn't talk about him, and she knew better than to mention his name.

Tulir rubbed a hand down his face. "How confident are you they can't kill you?"

"Under the circumstances I'm going to create for the meeting, very," she answered with conviction.

"You're set on this?"

"I am."

He beckoned her closer. When she stood before him, close enough to feel his breath on her face, he said, "Alright. Take a boat downriver. Go with a white flag and have one of them brought aboard to negotiate with you."

They were of the same thinking. "Our boats are smaller, less imposing. This will work."

He sighed and wrapped an arm around her waist.

"I'll go in the morning," she said.

"Any sign of trouble . . ."

She lightly put a hand over his mouth before he could finish. "I will be careful and mindful."

Using his face, he nudged her hand to the side. Her hand cupped his cheek, and he leaned down to kiss her. It was brief, chaste. When they parted, his forehead rested against hers.

He whispered in a loving tone, "Please, be careful."

Chapter 7

LENA HAD KNOWN TO EXPECT larger ships, but seeing them in person was daunting. Her people had no trouble finding them along the river. They only had to go around the bend for the magnificent works of craftsmanship to come into view. The ship she had taken was mid-sized from the Royal Dock, a few feet narrower and shorter than the largest. Now, she realized there had been no need to choose a conservative-sized vessel to lessen their threat.

The guard beside her was the seasoned guard from Istedinium. She had learned his name was Salvatore, and he spoke both her tongue and Iste fluently. Just as he was at the market, which she could scarcely believe was only a day prior, he was armed with a long sword and a concrete expression.

The sun was rising in the east and cast a long shadow over Lena's boat, almost fully enveloping them. The white flag at the top of the mast reached the banister of the newcomer's ship. Theirs was a dark wood. Creaks and moans from the ship echoed in her ears.

Voices carried over the natural noises. No doubt they were talking about her arrival. She listened intently, but she couldn't hear much and understood none of it. There was a fear their languages were different. The guards she had brought with her were from different regions and spoke other languages. They had planned for as many contingencies as they could.

A hatch along the side of the giant ship opened. The scrape made the motion feel longer than it was. Darkness was all they could see inside the opening.

Salvatore's grip on his sword tightened.

"Hold," she commanded.

CLEVEHOLD

A man poked his head out. He had unkempt ginger hair down to his chin, tucked behind his ears. He wore leather armor and an open-mouthed smile. Cold blue eyes stared at Lena, and he swayed more than the ship necessitated. He stomped twice.

There was a twitch of a flinch in her posture she couldn't help, though her chin remained high.

He closed his mouth partly and his nose scrunched. He looked her up and down, and his tongue came to rest under his front teeth. The ginger man disappeared into the darkness.

Lena glanced to Salvatore, whose eyes were trained on the opening.

Wooden boards ran out and were slotted onto the railing of Lena's ship. The hatches were lower, and it required an upward angle. The ginger man reappeared. His fingers wrapped around the sides of the hatch as he slowly emerged. A full body view showed he was tall, armed with a sword. There was a pause. He stared at her for a few seconds before he let go and crossed onto her boat. He dropped off the plank onto the deck with a loud thump.

Two others followed him, their expressions more serious. One was a blonde woman, muscular and dressed like a man in partial plate armor—breastplate, shoulder, arm, and shin pieces. She wore a dagger on each hip. The third person was another man in leather armor, not as tall as the first, with a bow instead of a sword. He had shaggy brown hair. Both looked to have been about Tulir's age.

The lead man was still looking at Lena curiously as his companions crossed the board. She did her best to evaluate what she was seeing. He was about her age, perhaps younger, but not by much. The leather looked strangely styled. Beneath it, his clothes looked like brown rags held together by blue threads. He was strong looking and as tall as her largest guard.

Words were spoken by the ginger man, who then gestured back to his companions. When he looked at Lena, he waited. There was an intensity in his eyes, amplified when his head tilted to the side. If not for the barren soul reflected in his bright eyes, the expression looked pleased. His smile widened when he didn't get a response.

She looked to the few guards with her. They knew to come forward if they had insight on the language. No one moved.

The man spoke again, repeating the same arrangement of sounds in a mockingly slow speed. Lena squinted and looked at his lips. She thought she understood a few words. The phrase started with "my," included "stay," and the last word may have been him asking, "yes?"

"My name is Miss Lena," she replied. She made no move to get closer.

The woman and archer surveyed the ship but stayed close to the plank.

The ginger man spoke again.

She took a moment to process. It was no coincidence that she could pick out some words—they did speak the same language. The consonants were close, but the vowels were stressed differently. The Stone King's invisible hand over the situation prevailed: make the whole world speak your language.

Finally, she understood he had said, "You want to talk, yes?"

"We are here to talk. Forgive me if I ask you to speak slowly." Taking a step forward, she asked, "What's your name?"

He turned to the woman with him. "My name?" it sounded like he asked.

"I think that's what she said," answered the woman.

Lena felt a headache coming on from what felt like reading a book written with a faulty bleeding pen, but it sparked hope. This was promising—they could understand each other. It wasn't bad to have to take it slow.

"I am Kazio," the ginger man answered her. "You are Misleena?"

"Lena," she corrected, dropping the title.

He nodded.

She spoke slow enough to aid understanding without sounding as if she was talking to a child. "Who are your people?"

Kazio responded with two syllables.

Of-nigh? Lena couldn't piece the word or words together. "Sorry?"

"Ovnite," he repeated. "We come from across the sea."

Lena nodded. "You'll have to pardon me, I don't know where, or what, that is."

He looked back to the woman again and asked, mimicking Lena's pronunciation, "Tapurdunmeh?"

"Forgive her," the woman responded.

Kazio turned back to Lena and scratched the side of his head, a broad smile under his dead eyes. "*Pardon me,*" he mocked in her accent. The smile dropped as his hand did. "Are you their leader?"

Their. Did he not know where he was? Caught off guard, she responded, "Not yet."

He asked a question. When Lena gestured for him to repeat himself, he spoke slower, "You are in line for it, yes?"

"I will marry the king," she answered.

Salvatore kept an eye on the archer as he moved around the side of the ship, looking around curiously. The archer kept his hands visible. The guards gave him space.

"Maybe you should look more into who you are marrying," advised Kazio.

Either understanding him was becoming less taxing or the decoding less active the more they spoke. "Why do you advise as such?"

Kazio rested his hand on his sword and paced to the side a few steps. "Did the king tell you of the city across the sea, encased in magic and left to rot?"

Flashes of the cabin came to mind. The wooden arrow toy. The dog. The basement cell. Had it been Klaus who once mentioned the trapped city? "That's where you are from?"

He rocked back and narrowed his eyes at her. "So, you do know what it is?"

"It was a story I was told," Lena answered. She forced her mind to focus on the present. There would be time to validate the revelations later. She wished she had brought Harth—surely Klaus would have told him about that city.

"For nearly a thousand years, we were trapped behind a green wall of the king's doing. But we are free, as you can see, and we've come to talk to the king about . . ." He paused and considered. "The *impact* it's had on our lives." It wasn't just the strange accent that put an unnerving stress on his words. Threats could be deciphered in any language.

"I can assure you, the king knows nothing about it," she responded.

He tsked.

"You know my station. What are you to the Ovnites?" A sense of dread crept up on her when it dawned on her: He wasn't in a hurry. He wasn't worried. The threat was backed by confidence in his eyes.

"I lead the Vitki," he answered as if there was implied importance.

She didn't understand the last word, but she assumed it was a title, which meant he wasn't their leader. Looking up at the large looming ship they stood in the shadow of, she asked, "You answer to someone. Did you bring your king? Is he on your ship?"

"We have a leader, but she has no need for hollow titles."

Lena paused, running back over the words. She had heard him correctly, she was sure. Their leader was a woman. Awareness regained, she asked, "Do you know what she wants from us?"

Kazio laughed and rubbed his hands together.

The circumstances had changed. How could she hope to negotiate with those who had been trapped by the Stone King's curse? She had put off reevaluating their situation, but that was a mistake. Breaking the curse had changed everything. Her tactics had to change, too.

"The king would like to meet with your leader to discuss terms." *Terms?* She hadn't meant to make it sound like a surrender or compromise.

Vocabulary aside, they needed time. They were lucky to have gotten this far. People trapped by centuries of magic had a right to their ire. Receiving her party was an act of patience Lena was surprised they had been offered. If not for Kazio's brash confidence, perhaps they wouldn't have been.

"As if you have anything to offer us," he scoffed.

"We know what you did to a coastal city, but we also know you haven't attacked any others along the way. You haven't come into Clevehold, and you agreed to meet with me here today," Lena said assuredly. She provided a pause for him to speak, then continued, "Any fighting is rash, and I hope it doesn't come to that."

"That sounds like advice from a city not equipped to fight, yes?"

She summoned some of Tulir's snark to ask, "Does your leader not recognize diplomacy?"

Kazio smirked. He stuck his chin out. "You can't be hiding an army in those walls."

"She's built into the mountain. Tell your scouts to go look again, if you like." The bluff felt natural.

"Is that right?" he questioned.

"We have fighters to the west in the plains and to the east all up and down the coast." Her tone wasn't boastful, but factual. She fastened her hands behind her.

"Now *you* are threatening me, yes?"

The archer returned to Kazio's side. The woman in plate armor hadn't moved. Kazio looked to each of them, tilting his head to the side and scrunching his nose.

Lena proposed, "Two days. During which time we shall not attack, so long as your people agree to do the same. In that time, I expect you to talk to your leader, your counselors, whoever. On the third day, we will reconvene. Our leaders will meet to discuss terms."

Kazio took a lengthy, heavy step forward and looked down at her with an openmouthed smile. She held her stance. Her hands tightened behind her back, and she let that be the only faucet for her nervousness. The stench of his breath reached her. She let him hover and kept her stare steady.

He turned away and went to the plank.

"Are we understood?" Lena called after him and took a step forward, arms coming down to her sides.

The woman put hands on her daggers.

Kazio put his hand up and turned back to Lena slowly, one foot on the plank.

"My pride allowed me to ask you to repeat yourself when I did not understand. You've done none of the sort. We speak the same language but differently. I need to know I am understood," she said pointedly.

He smirked. "No attacks."

"No violence of any kind," she clarified.

"Hollow words."

"You will always have the option to leave."

Kazio laughed and scratched the side of his head. "I will take this back to my leader, Lena."

She waited. "And? The terms?"

CLEVEHOLD

"If we don't attack in that time"—he shrugged—"you will have your answer, yes?"

"Is there anything else you wish to discuss?" She didn't bother with any pleasantness in her tone. Her attempts clearly went unappreciated.

"Tell your king to bring food with his offer. Bring plates—fancy, shiny ones. With the pointy eating sticks, too," he requested, tone coated in amusement.

Lena licked her lips and shook her head. "How many plates should I tell him to set?"

"Five. Our leader, Vitki"—he gestured to himself, then to the woman—"two Drengr, and our elder."

"In three days, we will return," she promised.

Kazio sucked his teeth, then turned to cross into his ship.

RECOUNTING HER CONVERSATION with Kazio necessitated a diluted version of how infuriating the encounter truly was. When her audience already assumed the worst of the newcomers, her personal feelings on the matter didn't need to play into things. Her task was to explain all she had learned and assumed, paired with her best effort to pronounce their specific words correctly.

Ovnite.

Vitki.

Drenr?

"They had others in the woods, but they did nothing but watch," added Salvatore.

Lena looked to him and nodded. Of course there had been others watching. The woods, the ship, from the hatch. Why hadn't she paid more attention?

"Could you estimate their numbers?" asked Tulir. He sat at his normal chair in the Council's meeting room. Lena and Salvatore stood at the other end.

"No better than we did before," answered Salvatore.

"They were lucky to keep out of view," commented Norman. He was the only other one seated at the table.

Rufino leaned his forearms onto the back of his chair. His curls were a mess with how much he had been running his hands through them.

Harth stood off to the side near a window. He was turned away, but Lena knew he was listening. His posture was tense. Nothing had been heard from him since her and Salvatore's arrival.

"Luck played no part in it. What I can reckon is, they're learned. When that fire-haired boy boarded to meet us, there was no concern in his eyes. They were prepared, cautious, but they don't fear us," explained Salvatore.

"Rufino and Norman will speak with each of your men later, find out if they picked up anything else," said Tulir.

"I'll make them available," replied Salvatore.

"Anything more?" Tulir looked to Salvatore first, who shook his head. Then to Harth, off to the side.

Lena imagined what was running through his head. Salvatore was trusted and seasoned, enough so that Harth had sent him with her into the city. When the diplomatic mission had been put together, Lena had an inkling of what Harth's reaction would be—refusal, which was the reason she hadn't asked him to come. How much goodwill and trust had Salvatore lost from his superior by going on this mission?

Harth's answer was a question. "Was this mission the only one of its kind?"

About to jump in to defend, Lena was beaten by Tulir's justification, "I sanctified the mission this morning. It was singular. We had to move quickly."

Face unreadable, Harth told Salvatore, "Dismissed."

Salvatore gave a short nod, then turned to exit the room.

The door closed, and the Council was alone. Lena pulled out her chair but decided against sitting. She cleared her throat and said, "We can discuss what a risk it was to me later."

"She's right," agreed Tulir. "We need to discuss what tactics we will take with the Ovnites." He hesitated, under-stressing the vowels of the word.

"I don't know what there is to discuss. They attacked the coastal cities," asserted Norman.

"One city," amended Rufino. He pushed off the chair and stood straight.

"Casualties were low. If our number estimates and Salvatore's assertions are correct, they could have done far worse," said Tulir.

Norman jabbed a finger onto the table. "May I remind you, Steepwharf was your home. *Any* casualties should be too many."

Lena was about to make a remark but thought better of it. Norman would only continue to do what he always had done—ignore her. She clasped her hands firmly behind her back.

"The coastal cities are also where the largest part of our army is," said Rufino.

Harth moved closer to the table. His footsteps were purposefully heavy, and they all looked to him. "Steepwharf will be looking for retribution, regardless of what we do."

"It's all a misunderstanding." Tulir put an elbow on the table, grasped at air, then put a hand to his face. "That's what it comes down to, isn't it?"

"What would you think if you were trapped in stone for centuries?" asked Norman.

"A magic binding, in this case," corrected Lena.

"It is a misunderstanding but a long-enduring one, born of your grandfather many times removed. It's not a rationality they may care to hear," said Rufino.

"I think we should try to make them understand why they were bound as long as they were. They weren't the only ones held captive by the acts of a power-hungry king," said Tulir.

"It won't matter. They want a fight. Both sides will, for that matter," reminded Norman.

Harth looked at him. "Are we willing to lose lives over not first trying for peace?"

"Negotiation puts the king at risk," said Rufino.

"The king is willing to risk it," refuted Tulir passively.

"I asked them for two days. It should give us enough time to put a plan in place," said Lena. She should have asked for more time. It had been her decision to make on the spot, and she had undersold them.

"We can try for peace, but we should be ready for war." Rufino put a hand to his neck and took a deep breath. "I'll go east, see if I can calm our neighbors on the coast. Prepare them for the possibility to either bite their tongues or raise their men."

Before Norman could argue, Harth interjected, "It will take very little effort to rally them for a fight, if it comes to it."

Norman clenched his jaw and squared his shoulders. "If someone is to go to the coastal cities, shouldn't that be me? It's my area."

"You're too close to it," answered Lena. "The trip should be diplomatic, not personal."

"Do you want—" began Norman to Tulir.

"I think she's right. Rufino will go. Harth." Tulir looked to him. "Arrange guards to take him by land. Rufino's the best on a horse."

"I'll send him with the best riders," agreed Harth.

CLEVEHOLD

Norman drummed his fingers atop the table.
"No arguments," said Tulir.

Chapter 8

SOMEONE KNOCKED ON her door. Lena stood straight, confused. She had been in the middle of feeding Socks his dinner. A glance at the sunlight told her she wasn't late for anything. After the day on the boat and talks over dinner, she had purposefully set the next day up to be on her own. The expansion project was on hold. The vault didn't need opening.

News from Steepwharf? The Ovnites?

She crossed the room quickly and opened the door. It was a servant about to knock a second time. The way Lena threw the door open made the servant girl flinch.

"Sorry," Lena apologized. "I'm accustomed to getting bad news at odd hours."

"Not this time, ma'am," the girl recovered gracefully with a smile. "The king wanted to extend an invitation to a private dinner on the western-facing terrace."

Lena knew the one. She had remarked it was one of her favorite spots to watch the sun go down. She asked, "Any required dress?"

"Come as you are, he said, ma'am," the girl answered. There was a twinkle in her eye. "He did look fancy."

"I'll be there shortly," Lena agreed. With a nod and a smile, she closed the door. There was an innate disdain she felt at being called "ma'am." "Miss," she was accustomed to; "missus" was something she wanted to earn. Your Grace, Your Majesty—the monarchy had been encased in stone for too long for those living to agree on which the correct form was. Another question Avild could have answered.

Lena ran a hand through her hair. She was stalling. Should she put her hair back up in braids? Did he mean "come as you are" in a literal sense? The girl had said he looked fancy—did that create an expectation he was too shy to enforce? Tulir wasn't one to make Lena jump through mental hoops. He was direct. Some shyness, he could stand to learn.

Socks jumped onto the bed. He pawed at the covers. "Meow."

The top blanket was pulled back and bunched up for him in the way she knew he liked. "The stress is making me overthink everything," she complained.

He flopped down on the pile of blankets and purred.

"I don't want to set my expectations too high. There's too much going on." She picked up a brush from her armoire and combed it through her hair.

Socks rolled over onto his back, paws limp in the air.

"Nothing bothers you. Nothing besides people," she said as she combed out the last of the knots. Looking down at the short dress and trousers, salmon and dark brown, she sighed.

No, she wouldn't change. That was just an act of procrastination. Instead she put on a necklace, a shiny chain with small jewels embedded in the links. It had never been assessed or appraised. She liked it, and Tulir had agreed on its prettiness once.

"I'll be back late, possibly," she warned Socks, giving him a quick belly rub.

"Meow," he replied.

"Of course, I'd say yes," she answered casually. Her heart caught in her throat. She was overthinking the invitation. The action had already been decided; he didn't have to ask. Her agreement was a focal point in their telling of the story. There was a time she had remarked she would like something romantic and personal, but he didn't need to.

She leaned down to kiss Socks on the head and turned to leave the room before she could procrastinate further.

Lena locked the door behind her and kicked up the cat corner flap. She stepped quickly and lightly through the halls. Wondering briefly if her known route was longer than the most direct one, she decided not to dwell on it. She would get there soon enough.

In the final hall, the guard at the door stood at attention. She smiled kindly and slowed her approach. It would do her no good to show up out of breath. Hair tucked behind her ears, she made a point not to fiddle with her hands.

A few feet before she reached the door, the guard opened it for her.

"Thank you," she said. He might have been one of the guards she often took to the library. On a less stressful day, she would have been more certain.

Lena walked in, and her smile for pleasantries developed into a genuine one. She was far enough inside to allow the door to close behind her when she stopped. The sun was setting in the west over the mountains. The view was nothing short of stunning.

The room echoed the beauty outside. The walls were painted to mimic the vines and tendrils of a garden. The room was half enclosed, transitioning into a balcony with the real thing wrapped around the stone railings. Lanterns hung from the ceiling and provided a warm light in yellows and oranges. The green carpet, a novelty even in the castle, was soft beneath her shoes as she slowly made her way to the table.

Tulir stood. He was dressed in relaxed well-fitting clothes that thankfully did not make her feel underdressed. He was the only other person in the room. He had been sitting at a table prepared for two, set up on the cusp of the transition to the balcony. The food was steaming, and the wine had been poured.

"I hope your day was calmer than yesterday," he greeted.

She approached him and allowed him to take her hand and kiss it. "It was, thank you. I will return to being fully present tomorrow."

"I'm not worried you will neglect your duties," he assured. He was holding on to her hand a beat too long and rushed to add, "I hope that doesn't mean you object to dinner."

Lena wasn't accustomed to not seeing him put together, either by truth or ruse. She smiled and answered kindly, "No."

He let go of her hand. His mouth was open.

"No, I have no objections," she clarified.

"Right." He nodded and then pulled out the second chair. "Then please, sit."

Lena did so, taking in the view again with the fragrant food under her nose.

"You look beautiful," he complimented.

Her hand came up to the necklace when she saw him notice it. "This is all stunning."

"I wanted to speak with you and saw no reason why we couldn't speak in one of your favorite places." He also sat and hooked his cane onto the chair.

"Will anyone else be joining us?" she asked out of courtesy.

"No, and we shouldn't be disturbed." He picked up his glass of wine, waited for her to do the same, and then clinked them together.

"What are we toasting to?" she questioned warmly.

"You." He looked her in the eye. "And the brave thing you've done."

Lena smiled and nodded. She sipped at the wine. It was fresh, but very sweet.

Tulir swallowed a mouthful and set the glass down. It caught the lip of the plate and nearly fell over, but he was quick enough to catch it and set it upright. The sudden movement made his sleeve pull up above the indented scar. He sighed at the wine glass as if it had wronged him.

Taking him gently by the wrist, Lena brought his arm in close. As she carefully righted the fabric, she said, "I wanted to understand why they did what they did."

"Do you?" asked Tulir. He watched her fingers work. When she was done, he clasped his hand over hers.

The touch of his skin was warm. She shrugged. "Not completely, but we're on our way to answers. We at least know their origins, and I'm hopeful we've avoided the fight."

Tulir hummed and nodded. He looked pale.

Lena took a deep breath, looked at the spread of food—the grapes, pork, and bread—and then down at their joined hands. "Is it my going that bothers you this much?"

"No. It was brave, very brave." He withdrew his hand and cleared his throat.

She didn't like his tone. This wasn't joyful nervousness anymore. "If something's happened—"

"Lena," he said to stop her. He closed his eyes briefly, then looked to her. "I want to be honest with you. Completely honest. There's merit in honesty."

"Alright." She tried to keep her tone relaxed, the opposite of what she felt.

"There's another."

Her brain felt as if it were frozen. Then a wave of thoughts rushed in. There was no misinterpreting what he was saying. One meaning, one intention.

She retracted her hands into her lap. Mind cluttered, her mouth luckily operated separately. "Kings are allowed multiple wives or mistresses, if they so choose."

What did that do to her standing? Which did he expect her to be?

"Multiple wives? You haven't accepted my proposal," he reminded.

"There wasn't one," she immediately combated. She pushed back from the table.

"What did you assume—?"

She interrupted, "But you may as well have. It was done."

"I wanted it to be your choice," he said firmly.

Her eyes widened, and her breath caught. "You mean to undo it?"

Damn her for getting so comfortable to overlook her instincts. There *was* someone. The unseen presence in his chambers. What woman had he been sneaking in the shadows with? Was she to emerge from the balcony during this apology dinner?

She began to protest, "For the line of legitimacy—"

"Harth."

Lena stopped. For an instant she didn't breathe, blink, or feel her heart. For a second time that evening, she searched in her mind to see if there was another interpretation to consider. *One intention.*

The cane clattered noisily as Tulir unhooked it from the chair and leaned on it to stand. His face was red, eyes averted. Uneven breaths pushed out his nose.

She also stood, slowly, with a hand on his arm. The question was on her face, in her eyes, not her lips. *Stay. Talk to me.*

Tulir rocked as if he debated sitting or leaving. He licked his lips and nodded toward the balcony. He took the first step, and she followed.

"Maybe I shouldn't give you the opportunity to pitch me off." His joke came out nervous and flat. She was still on his arm.

"Just because I don't have an immediate reaction doesn't mean it's turned me to hate you," she said patiently. Her other hand gripped a vine on the banister. Eyes up to the mountains and plains, her thoughts were calmer. Concise.

He needed her to be queen. Her title wasn't threatened, only her position with him. Lena's mouth opened, and a desperate breath escaped.

"I don't expect your reaction to be immediate. Or easy," he apologized.

What was she supposed to say? What was the male version of a mistress? It had all been padding to get her to love him. "I didn't think . . . after what we've . . ."

"I know what you are thinking. There are men"—he cleared his throat—"men who screw around as they please and have a wife for appearances. This isn't remotely that."

"No?" she questioned. A tear pricked her eye.

"What I feel for you isn't a ruse." He turned her to face him. "Lena, I love you."

She swallowed down a lump in her throat. It was true, so far as her eyes could see. She wanted it to be true, but there was a new wall between what she wanted and what she expected. How much had she not seen or thought to see?

"If you find any lie in my eyes, I will have you pitch me off the side. My feelings for you have not been faked. You've not been lied to there."

"But you didn't tell me," she stopped at hearing her voice crack.

"It's not . . . for men to—w-we aren't . . ." he trailed off and rubbed a hand down his face. "It's not spoken of. And spoken of lesser for a person to look at both. To *want* both."

"You're asking." She filled in her voice with faux confidence. "You don't want to have to choose."

"I'm in love with you both, and I see no reason to choose. I also can't bear any longer to not have you know, even if it does lead you to hate me. These savages are knocking at our door, and . . . I don't know. I needed you to know. I needed to ask."

"Ask?" she proposed. This was all a question? Of what she wanted, or what she would tolerate?

"You're right when you say it is set. You are to be queen. If the proposal wasn't clear, I take fault for it. I could lie to everyone else here about what there is between me and Harth, but I won't lie to you."

"Is this some ploy to ask me to allow as many people as you want into your bed in the future?" Her hands withdrew from him and the vine.

"No." He shook his head and looked down at his empty arm. "I would be faithful."

"To both of us," she said incredulously.

"Yes."

Lena didn't want the idea flowing through her mind to spew out of her mouth. She felt a fool—in love, burning with anger, and confused. If there was something to save, the words had to be kept in her mind. She was sure if she stayed, the gate on her resolve would break.

Eyes damp and jaw clenched shut, she left.

LENA MADE IT DOWN TO the cells without anyone stopping her. She had a combination of dinnertime and her stoic expression to thank for that. Not knowing if she needed to laugh, cry, or shout about Tulir's news, she headed for the one place she knew no one could bother her.

She only got so far as the first step down. The heavy wooden door closed behind her as she sat, elbows on her knees, head in her hands. This wasn't how the night was supposed to go. There was supposed to have been a blip of joy before they faced negotiations with the Ovnites.

Tomorrow. They were headed back out tomorrow.

Why was it now, of all times, that Tulir decided to toss a lit match into the life she had tried to build? Didn't he have bigger things to worry about? Did he think her chief concern should be their romantic future?

"It was stupid . . ." Lena mumbled to herself. She picked up her head.

Stupid, but brave. He had been so nervous. Twice he had offered for her to send him over the balcony.

But it was only a joke. Always a joke. But this one was at her expense. Harth knew about her involvement with Tulir—everyone did—yet her liberties weren't afforded in reverse. How long had it been happening behind her back?

What Tulir had told her days before revisited her mind. What were his exact words? *I want to do it right with you.* No—*this time.* He wanted to do it right *this time*, implying that he hadn't previously. Harth had been allowed to see that side of Tulir without waiting to cross that figurative line of matrimony.

And why shouldn't they just move her around the board? She was a pawn. She carried the Stone King's magic, the heir's closest legitimacy, and no one outside the circle of those she trusted knew.

Lena jammed her elbow back into the door. It rattled. The pain stung as it ran up her arm, but there was satisfaction in it.

He hadn't wanted to hurt her. She exhaled as the thought occurred to her, but it didn't leave. She couldn't deny it.

Following where the thought led, she came back to the timing—the night before they were to meet with the Ovnites. He wanted to speak with her before then. *Just in case?* She didn't want to think that way. *No harm should come to him.*

Tulir had made the time and put in the effort when the more practical thing to do was wait. Perhaps he was as daft as she. The dinner, the location . . . he was trying to do right by Lena.

I love you.

CLEVEHOLD

It was the first time he had directly said it. She had felt it in his words and seen it in his eyes. He wasn't a liar, not to her. They shared the same secrets. Tulir's relationship with Harth wasn't a lie; it was an omission.

Relationship—was that what they had?

How could a man want to have a relationship with both a man *and* a woman? Tulir had said he didn't want to choose. Not only did he not have a preference of sex, but he also wanted both to exist in his life.

Loyal to them both. She shook her head and buried her hands in her hair. There wasn't a lie in his eyes when he had answered what she intended as a rhetorical question. He meant it. Could she trust that?

Nothing made sense. Yet she couldn't make it make sense sitting there.

Lena braced a hand on the wall and stood, pushing away the wetness under her eyes. Tulir had been a constant in her life. Now he was a question.

She didn't dare think about the Ovnites knocking at their door. They would be dealt with soon enough. Kazio and his leader from their strange world with their strange words. The unraveling of their mystery would take time.

The steps she took down the stairs were slow. In pushing away her thoughts and walking away from her problems, her mind wandered. Anything else to keep it occupied. She thought of Selgen.

He was at the root of it all, the catalyst. If not for him, they never would have left Steepwharf and come to the Stone King's castle. Lena would still have been living with Nela in the little home she scarcely remembered. The layout and the feelings were all there, but the details were missing. The only color she remembered of Steepwharf was stone grey.

LIZ BUNCHES

Back when Avild was a teacher. Klaus, a miner. Selgen, a librarian. Vilars and Tulir were dutiful guards, the former an object of an adolescent crush, the latter a flirt. There were so many things she had seen but not properly understood then.

Thinking back on her memories did little to lessen the feeling of not being able to trust what she thought she saw. She never paid enough attention. Was she that inwardly focused, that vain, that she couldn't see things as they were?

Selgen was always troubled, always an anomaly. He had pored over books as if they were his children. Was it really all so innocent? Or had she missed his inner workings? It must have been the case of her miscalculation. Otherwise, why was he so miserable now? Perhaps he was simply built with melancholy in his soul. He had favored Lena in Steepwharf why? Because she hadn't yet seen it?

Lena took heavy steps slowly down the staircase, one step at a time. She had made the walk enough times to know the nooks and grooves. Hadn't she known Selgen in detail? At the cabin, when he was arguably at his lowest, Klaus had given him a task: chop wood. It was mundane and unneeded, but the life within Selgen had revived. She hadn't been surprised to see him that way. It was pleasant and rewarding, but she hadn't viewed his reaction as that of someone other than himself.

Rether had soiled him with memories of murder. Selgen wasn't the sort of person who had the capacity to kill, but revealed to him were memories of him doing just that. Forcible perspective change.

Lena reached the last step and rubbed her eyes. Rether's laugh crept up into her eardrums. Did Selgen have that same memory? Was he haunted by that monster, too?

How could she expect him to outlive his memories if she couldn't either?

"Are you alright?"

CLEVEHOLD

Lena jumped back, tripped on the stone step, and braced a hand on the wall to catch herself. Eyes wide, she stared ahead. Her quick-beating heart was given no reason to slow.

Avild?

"You should advise the king to keep a better watch on who is allowed to cross the livestock bridge. I wasn't asked for papers, nor my name," she said, her back to the wall between cells.

"You're here?" Lena questioned. There was equal likelihood of that versus her memories materializing as a culmination of stress and unchecked magic.

"The tunnels are underwater still. I wouldn't recommend clearing those out until the army camped outside is gone." Avild pushed off the wall. She was dressed similar to how she had been in Steepwharf—a modestly fitting shirt, trousers, and boots. All parts of a life leftover. As if she had never left.

"Why?" asked Lena.

Avild raised her eyebrows.

"Why did you leave?" Lena stood straight and brushed herself off. "What's it been, nearly two years?"

"Your cousin sulked around in self-pity, and Tulir would have done anything in those first few months to bring his twin back." Avild put her arms out and shrugged. "I couldn't be here any more than you could have risked having me here."

"But..." Lena shook her head. Her hands pulled her loose hair to one side.

"Is it now any different?" asked Avild.

Lena shot daggers with her eyes. Which answer would give Avild more satisfaction? Neither, Lena decided, as she closed her eyes and breathed out of her nose. They had fared as well as expected without her. There was no denying the satisfaction.

"Harth survived," said Lena, hoping to hit a pain point.

"I waited to leave until I knew he would. He's strong."

"You left before he was well enough to track you down, you mean."

Avild's lip upturned in one corner and her eyes flicked down.

"You made Tulir king and left!" shouted Lena. She put a hand to her forehead.

"I gave him a reason to live, a purpose, and I knew it would keep you all comfortable," said Avild casually.

"Comfortable?" bit Lena. "We could have told the truth."

"We're far past the validity of that threat," countered Avild, a tinge of sternness in her tone.

Who was this woman? The Avild she knew, her friend, wouldn't speak to her like this. Perhaps it was better Avild remained away. She couldn't answer their questions when not present, but neither could she antagonize Selgen's state of mind.

"Do they take kindly to you?" asked Avild.

"I'm well respected," answered Lena.

Avild put a patient hand up. It morphed into a dramatic gesture when she asked, "Do they take kindly to having a woman on the man's Council?"

"I'll be queen," reminded Lena. The comfort she was set up with. A pawn.

"Queen consort, as far as they know." Avild tsked and turned to look into the empty cells. "They didn't take so well to me, and I was born into it."

"It was a different time," rebutted Lena.

"Not so different."

Lena hated how casually her old friend posed her arguments, as if her points were irrefutable, simply the way it was. Lena just didn't see it. Her fists clenched.

Through clamped teeth, Lena asked, "Why did you come back? No word for two years, and you return now? It's not to take your throne."

"It would make me happy to put the stain back on that whore's name," considered Avild. She ran her hand across the cell bars. In a low voice, she said, "I want to meet the people my father locked away."

Lena raised her eyebrows. "You think it's true?"

"I know it is." Avild looked to Lena with a blank expression. "I know you remember when it was said. If we're going to be fair here, let's not play."

Curt, but true. Lena should have known better than to dance with her. Instead, with open palms, she asked, "What more do you know?"

"The Binding around them was a wall. If they had put an earnest effort into escaping, it would have killed them. The Binding survived because my father was encased. Had I, or you, sustained it, the Binding would have remained in place."

Lena didn't have the bandwidth to absorb her words, storing them away for later. "Do you plan on making your true self known, at all?"

"No," she replied simply.

"You just . . ." Lena fanned her fingers out. "You just happened to be down here tonight?"

"I saw you down here about a week ago looking pensive. I assumed it was a place you would return to," answered Avild.

Quick breaths passed Lena's lips. Mouth agape, she finally swallowed before she questioned, "You've been lurking here that long?"

"Is that what you want to talk about?"

Lena could scream. She could cry. It was comforting that Avild had returned, and yet she hated the other woman for returning. Too much—it was all too much.

"Are there plans to meet them by boat again?" asked Avild.

"Yes." Lena took a deep breath. Of course she knew about the first meeting. Had she been ready to intervene? "Tulir plans to negotiate. Our Council is meeting with theirs."

"All of you?" questioned Avild. When Lena nodded, she continued, "When?"

"Tomorrow," Lena said simply. She had no want or energy to lie; Avild would find out with or without her.

"I'll be at the Royal Docks in the morning," said Avild.

Lena furrowed her brow. "What happened to not making yourself known?"

"Avild is a schoolteacher from Steepwharf. My old name, my old lives, they are all forgotten. I come as a consultant, a friend." Avild whistled. "Or the king can decide to send me away. In fairness, I wouldn't blame him."

A friend. A schoolteacher. The memories of visiting Avild's classroom to listen to legends of the Stone King felt like a different lifetime. Was that how Avild felt about all the lives she had built and left behind?

Avild walked past her and began up the steps.

"Wait!" Lena called. There was more to say and ask. So much more. If only her mind could work fast enough to sort the priority. How many times had she bookmarked a thought she would have asked Avild if given the chance? The only thing she could think of was the glass on the windows. Seeing the intent look in her friend's eyes, she began with, "Stay."

"No." Avild took another step. Pausing, she added, "You should say something to the king about my being there tomorrow. It will make it easier."

"Was I the first one you came to?" asked Lena. In the same way she assumed it was true, she hoped it wasn't. Didn't Harth deserve to know she was here? Couldn't she tell Tulir herself?

"Good night, Your Grace."

"I could sneak you about—there are secret passages. You must know them better than myself," Lena bargained. Avild couldn't leave. Frustrating or not, she had only just returned. There were conversations to be had, things to plan for.

"Rest. It will do you good," said Avild.

Lena followed a few steps behind her. When Avild paused at the door, Lena did as well. She waited.

"Can he walk?" asked Avild, her eyes downcast as she opened the old wooden door.

It took Lena a moment to determine who she was talking about. Her mind was too jumbled. "He can. He is the Commander of the Royal Guard. It's as if it never happened."

Avild nodded, her expression one of modest relief. Quickly, she stepped through the door and closed it behind her.

Lena reached for the handle only to yank her hand back at the burning sensation the metal caused. Looking down at her hand, she determined she was unhurt. There were no marks on her palm and the sensation quickly faded, as did the footsteps on the other side. In a few seconds' time, there were none at all.

Lena poked cautiously at the handle. It was still too hot to grip. *Damn it.*

The shield!

Lena closed her eyes and focused. A tingling extended out from her fingertips. When she opened her eyes, the green sheen coated her hand, allowing her to grip the handle and pull the door open.

As expected, Avild was gone. The hall was empty.

There was no making her stay, Lena reminded herself as she let the door close behind her. It creaked slowly as she glanced back at it. Could they carve the symbol to deny magic into the boat for tomorrow? Would that put them in more or less danger? And was there enough time to do it even if they wanted to?

Perhaps Harth would know.

Lena's breath caught. She had to tell them.

She turned back to ensure the door had locked behind her, then dashed away. As she worked through the halls, she was held up by the after-dinner crowd. Some were slow. Some smelled of alcohol. Any and all delays made her heartbeat faster.

Should she go to Harth's quarters first? She decided against it, as she couldn't confidently remember where they were and was already headed up. *Tulir.* She had to tell him first.

She came to the correct hall. There was a guard on patrol she nearly ran into. She quickly apologized, "I'm so sorry."

"My apologies, Miss Lena," replied the guard.

"Is the king available?" she asked, something she hadn't considered until now. This wasn't where she had left him.

"He is, Miss," he answered and gestured at the door.

Where else would he go? "Thank you."

The guard parted with a polite nod and continued on his route.

Which door? Lena had always knocked on the bedroom door. She wasn't just anyone.

She knocked on the door to the king's sitting room instead. Footsteps approached, an uneven step unaided by the cane. Tulir opened the door. He looked surprised to see her.

"Lena—" he tried to greet her, but it sounded like the rest was caught in his throat. He was still dressed as he had been for the dinner they hadn't eaten.

"May I come in?" she asked as a formality as she squeezed past him and into the room. Immediately, she knew they weren't alone.

Harth was there, sitting in one of the high-back chairs next to a lantern, reading. He looked up from his hardcover volume, surprised. The clothes he wore indicated he had stopped here after his shift before changing. He asked as he closed the book and stood, "Is something wrong?"

"Close the door," instructed Lena.

CLEVEHOLD

Tulir did.

"I need to speak with you."

"We can speak privately," offered Tulir. He was pale.

"Is anyone else here?" Lena asked Harth.

"Only us," he confirmed.

"Lena," Tulir began, his tone a hesitant warning, perhaps a plea.

"This concerns all of us," she began. The pause she took to dampen her nerves also provided time for her to examine Tulir's expression. He was worried. A touch fearful. Was he that concerned with what she would say, how she would respond to his proposal? She followed Tulir's line of sight over to Harth. Or was it for whom she would say it in front of?

Harth seemed to share none of Tulir's concerns.

Their fiasco could wait. Lena cleared her throat. "Avild is here."

"In the castle?" Harth set the book down.

"She's probably back in the city by now. I tried to keep her here, but she didn't want to stay."

"Why is she here?" asked Tulir. He limped to where his cane rested next to the unlit fireplace and used it to lean on. "It has to be for the Ovnites."

Lena nodded. "She wants to come tomorrow when we meet with them."

Harth rubbed a hand down his face and looked out the window.

"How did she know they were here?" questioned Tulir.

"That's the thing I'm worried least about," said Harth. He paced to the other side of the room. "What does she intend to do once there? Did she say?"

"She didn't," said Lena.

"She doesn't have a plan?" asked Tulir.

"I'm sure she has an idea. But if she didn't share it outright, I'm sure none of us will be privy to it until it happens," said Harth.

Lena looked at Tulir. "Avild's father trapped those people within the Binding that held them captive"—she stumbled over the wording, flustered, and slowed her speech—"and she corroborated what we know. They were trapped. Any attempted escapes before the Stone King was released would have killed them."

"Then the Binding faded when the Stone King was put to rest?" proposed Tulir.

"Or they found a way to break it when they knew it was safe enough," supposed Lena.

"The magic was bound in the Stone King's soul, so long as it survived. The Ovnites could think you let them go," Harth said to Tulir.

"Avild did say she or I could have done upkeep or something to the Binding," confirmed Lena. The Ovnites would assume that ability had been bequeathed to the new king.

"We want them to think they were released on purpose?" asked Tulir.

"No. But it reinforces the truth in not knowing the Binding existed to free them from," said Lena. "The story we told was that you didn't know of your heritage and ability until you were brought here."

"But we shouldn't pretend we didn't know of them whatsoever." Harth shook his head. "I thought it was just a story."

"Avild knows more than any of us about these people and what happened back then," asserted Tulir.

"If you give away her position, she will turn on you," warned Harth.

"As would everyone else," agreed Tulir. He pushed off the fireplace and used his cane to walk forward. "What I meant was, it'll be good to have her there."

"I'm not so sure," said Lena softly. Her eyes shifted to Harth, who looked to agree. They wanted to be happy about Avild's return. Under better circumstances, it wouldn't have been a question of benefit. There were simply too many unknowns.

"Why not?" inquired Tulir.

"Avild will quietly rage and plot. I don't know all of what she knows of these people. I can't advise what she might want to do or have from them," said Harth.

"Her intention was expressed as curiosity. If she means them harm, she isn't compelling us to do it," explained Lena.

"Can we speak with her before we set out? Tonight?" asked Tulir.

"She said she would meet us at the docks in the morning," answered Lena.

Tulir looked to Harth. "Any chance you can track her down?"

"Not her. Not in this city, and not in one night."

"She provided the allowance you may deny her coming," said Lena, though she expected nothing to come of it.

"If she offered it, that only means she has another means to get the same result or answers," said Harth.

"Then we risk it," surmised Tulir.

"Be cautious tomorrow," advised Harth. "Both of you. We can't feasibly warn the others, and I won't defy her in front of them, unless there's a threat to either of you."

Lena nodded.

"You think she's a true threat?" questioned Tulir.

Harth put his hands up. He shook his head and, on an exhale, said thoughtfully, "I don't know. I've only known her with Klaus there to balance her. There's no telling what these last two years have done to her."

"She gets my benefit of the doubt. She saved our lives," reminded Tulir, looking to Lena for support. "Not one of us would be here otherwise."

Lena nodded in agreement as a yawn tried to creep up the back of her throat. She wanted to suppress it and coughed to cover it. Her body wanted to sleep, but her mind felt too cluttered. Avild's return continued to be both a relief and weight.

Lena didn't feel tension. There was an obvious sense of dishevelment in the situation, but the sitting room itself didn't feel tense. It took a second for her to remind herself why she expected it to.

The book that Harth had put down on the end table caught her eye. A fantasy tale. Tulir never indulged in such types of books, having previously remarked to her there was enough extended belief in his real life. That book had been there the last time Lena had seen the sitting room. The secondary presence she had felt, but not seen.

"Are the ship and our escort ready for tomorrow?" Tulir asked.

"As ready as they can be," answered Harth.

"I'm going to try and get some sleep. Tomorrow will be taxing, I imagine," said Lena.

"Before you go." Tulir leaned down to pick something up off the couch she couldn't see. When he straightened up, Socks was in his hand.

The cat was gradually waking up. As he did, he rolled in Tulir's hand to fasten to his chest. A meow escaped as he yawned.

"How did he get in here?" asked Lena.

"The interior corridors. He snuck in." Tulir stepped closer to Lena.

She removed Socks' claws from Tulir's shirt and took the cat into her arms.

"After things settle more tomorrow, he can visit, and we can talk," offered Tulir.

The anxiety of his confession slithered back into her heart. She nodded, put on a smile, and dismissed herself. "Good night to you both."

Chapter 9

THE ROYAL DOCKS WERE busy in the morning, but Lena didn't have a benchmark for its usual traffic. She was one of the first members of the court to arrive, but it didn't surprise her to see Harth had beaten her, already giving out orders to the Royal Guards. She stayed out of his way and off to the side.

Norman was the next to arrive. He was overdressed in pressed clothes and flowing coattails. Once again, it amazed her to think he came from a city of industry.

The next person to arrive was the reason Lena was early. Avild walked out of a side door of the castle. The woman looked around curiously. Observant, but not lost.

"Avild," Harth called when he saw her.

A smile spread on Avild's face. She walked faster toward him as he did the same, and he swept her up in a hug. When they parted, they began talking. Lena was too far to overhear, but they were friendly, familiar. There was pride in Avild's eyes.

"The king," a guard announced.

Tulir hadn't stopped at the entryway where he was announced. As he passed by Lena, he joked, "If I knew they would all yell when they saw me, I would have invested in hats."

Lena took up on Tulir's left. She informed him, "From what I can tell, everything is ready."

"You were just waiting for the old man to get down the stairs," he replied.

"Looks like we're going to have nice weather for our picnic on the boat," said Harth as they approached him.

"Your Grace," Avild greeted.

"Missus Avild," he returned.

Harth thumbed back at the ship. "We'll have three guards on top deck, three more below."

"Do we think that will be enough?" asked Lena.

Avild raised her eyebrows and clasped her hands behind her back.

Is that where I learned that? Lena questioned.

Norman was headed toward them.

"If they mean to just overwhelm and kill us, we'll be surrounded. A few more men won't solve that," said Tulir.

"The guards we're taking are the best of our sailors, not our fighters," added Harth.

"It's good we're taking the larger ship," said Lena, directing them away from the conversation of the worst case.

"It won't come across as too ostentatious?" pondered Norman. He made a visor with his hand and squinted at the ship.

"Regal, not ostentatious," replied Lena. She didn't want to say their largest ship would still be dwarfed in comparison. Not as much as before, but this time the Ovnites wouldn't be able to board from their side hatches.

"The guards had a mishap." Norman looked to Harth. "Rufino is absent. It should be set for four on our side."

"We have a fifth. Missus Avild will join us," Tulir explained, gesturing at the short blonde.

Norman looked down his nose at her. "With all due respect, sir, who is she to come?"

"The historian I sent for," answered Tulir.

Someone called for Harth and he parted from them. A few feet away, he glanced back at Avild.

Is he also afraid she might disappear?

"I only mean it wasn't discussed," said Norman matter-of-factly.

"We are discussing it now," countered Tulir.

Avild put out her hand to Norman. A bold gesture, even in a city welcoming magic. She said pleasantly, "I arrived late last night. With the river blocked, it was a question of if I would arrive in time."

Norman hummed and shook her hand with a limp grip. "I thought no one knew anything of these people."

"Missus Avild is our best resource, and our fifth person to balance." Knowing Norman wouldn't acknowledge her, Lena gestured Avild toward the ship without waiting for a response. "Come, I'll show you what we have and answer any questions."

Avild nodded and followed. They approached the ramp of the ship together. Closer to the sloshing water and creaking ship, she asked quietly, "Are we pretending not to know one another?"

"Are we—?" Lena stopped and took a deep breath. It was going to be a snap remark made in anger. She was better than that. "You were a teacher in Steepwharf, where I'm from. We know each other. I'm not asking you to lie about that."

Seemingly satisfied with the answer, Avild gestured for Lena to climb up first. When they were both on deck, Avild asked, "Are you uneasy at the situation, or do I contribute?"

Lena went to the bow of the ship and heard the other woman following a few steps behind. At the railing, Lena gripped the wood tightly. It was smooth. The ships were new, within the year. She turned and took in the sight. Dark-purple sails. No emblem. Wood of various colors made up the deck and masts. Along the deck was a table covered with a cloth of the same color. Boxes were lined aft, some of which housed their cutlery and food.

"What do you want with them?" asked Lena. The remainder of their party was boarding starboard, too far to hear.

"You suspect me of what?" Avild returned.

"You were my friend, yet I don't know you. Your life was here; it was in Steepwharf. You got me this far, then you left," Lena listed out. It felt cathartic to vocalize her frustrations. She studied Avild, waiting for a reaction. What she saw instead were the first signs of aging. Lena had never taken note in Steepwharf, but she knew to look for it now.

Harth approached them. "You ladies ready for us to be underway?"

"That depends." Avild started the question looking at him and ended at Lena, proposing to them both, "If you want me off the ship, now's the time."

"Why? Are we going to have a problem?" asked Harth. He rested his hands on his belt.

"If I wanted to cause them harm, you could safely assume I could access their camp to do just that. I'm here to ask questions and see what's become of them," answered Avild.

Lena and Harth made eye contact. She nodded.

He turned to the crew and shouted, "Let's get underway!"

Behind Lena, a loud creaking started. The doors to the Royal Dock were opening. The walls sat a few feet below the water level, grated at the bottom, and turned into a solid wood reinforced by metal, stretching three stories into the air. It took ten men to move one door, and both were now opening. Clevehold came into view.

The ship began to creep forward. Lena held firm to the rail, not because the movement felt unsteady, but to ground herself. That was what it all came down to, right? Grounding. Could she use her magic well enough to protect them if something happened? Magic was volatile, subject to emotional states. Was she too worried to be effective?

Protecting Tulir was her top priority. There was no mistaking that. Personal feelings, how close she would be physically positioned to him, and his station all piled up to make him the priority. She could put her turmoil aside enough to protect him.

She reasoned it would work well with whom Avild would choose to protect. Her priority was Harth—they were practically family. He could defend himself well enough with a sword and would also treat Tulir as his charge to protect. With their combined efforts, and how close they would be clustered, Lena thought it should prove effective.

Or it makes us a well-assembled target. She quickly shook away the idea.

Norman would be left out, but she could live with that. She wished the man no harm, but they were far from being on good terms. The man lingered by the food currently, talking down to the guards, walking about in his fancy clothes. The reverberation of him again asking if the ship was too ostentatious made her smirk.

"The last time we were on a boat together, you had questions." Avild put her back to the city as they began to pass through. "I assume you have more."

Lena focused on the people in the street. Some smiled, others waved. People were walking fast, intent on their destination. She was not so far removed from them. Any key differences were only determined by chance and the ability to ask questions.

Where had Avild been? Had she hunted down any stragglers of Rether's men? She didn't seem concerned anyone would recognize her here. Had she tried to find someone to revive Klaus? Had she gone back to their home in Steepwharf?

Voices carried as people spoke on the other end of the vessel. Lena wondered for a moment how Avild had justified leaving Harth behind, but then she remembered the cabin. The phrases exchanged between Avild and Klaus when Lena hadn't known who they were discussing. *A murder. And a child. He should be with us, or safer with us. Remember him like that.* Paraphrased memories but with an easily recalled intention. Avild had planned to leave Harth behind in Steepwharf.

Then Klaus had died.

Harth himself nearly had as well. Lena shuddered to remember how touch and go it had been for weeks. That should have changed Avild's mind. Sure, she had waited until his health trended upward, but she hadn't been there when Harth struggled to get his feet back under him. She hadn't been there to see his pain and deny his pessimism.

Harth hadn't wanted people to see his struggles. Sometimes, Lena would wonder if Harth was going to disappear. Unable to do for himself and unwilling to let others do for him, she feared he would crawl off to die like an animal in the woods, alone, too proud to accept help.

Tulir hadn't let him. He had been the only one able to get through to Harth for the first few months.

Not the type for a wife. Was it Avild who had said it or Harth himself? The latter, she was almost sure. In the library. At the time, Lena's assumption was that it was due to him being a working man, dedicated to his station.

How much did Avild know? Had she seen what Lena had missed? Had Harth confided in her?

Norman was speaking with Tulir and Harth, pointing downriver. Lena averted her eyes. That little man knew. He had figured it out, or at least assumed. Lena saw it much more clearly in retrospect. The snide remarks. The looks. Did that mean Rufino knew as well?

The sun warmed them. Lena closed her eyes, turning her face to it. She tried to exhale the clutter in her mind. Useful questions, but not the ones she should have been asking. Not quite thoughts of procrastination, but distraction.

Lena cleared her throat to get Avild's attention after the long pause. "Do you know what Ovnite means, or Viti? Viki?" She wasn't certain of the second one. There was another word still starting with a *D* that completely escaped her.

"Vitki is the old word for wizard," answered Avild, though she pronounced it differently. "Ovnite, I don't know."

"A city, or a region? It's what they call themselves," said Lena.

"It's not one I know of."

The ship steered close to the right side of the canal to avoid a boat. The guards relayed information back and forth, and they passed without skimming either the wall or the boat.

"Are the Vitki who they say they're bringing?" asked Avild.

Heavy booted footfalls came upon them. The guard relayed, "We'll be out of the city soon. You should not be at the bow when we meet them."

"Thank you," said Lena. She began walking toward the table where the others were. Hearing Avild walking with her, she answered, "They're bringing five. Their leader, two of a term I can't recall, the Vitki man I met, and their elder."

They reached the table where Tulir and Norman were waiting. Avild asked them all, "What are we doing about weapons?"

"No one is being asked to disarm," said Tulir. He wore a dagger on his belt.

"Their leader is a woman, by the way," said Lena, making a point to look at Norman. He was already aware from her briefing, but it was worth mentioning again to see his recoil.

"What do we know of their magic?" asked Avild.

Lena shrugged. "We don't."

AS LENA HAD ANTICIPATED, their ship was noticeably smaller than that of the Ovnites. The ships were run up alongside one another with a few feet of space between. After dropping anchor and fastening the sails, planks were run between the vessels, forming a downward incline from the Ovnite ship to theirs.

People stared down at them from the Ovnite ship. Hatches along the side opened. Lena wondered if they would try to use those hatches again to board. The incline would have been steeper for this ship.

Orders were being given up top. Given the scarce words Lena could overhear and understand, they were readying. One of the voices she recognized belonged to Kazio. She looked to Tulir. She had warned them all about him.

The woman in partial plate came down first. A man at the top held the plank in place for her. She was dressed similarly to before, tan clothes beneath her armor and a sword fastened to her hip. After crossing the plank, she dropped down onto the deck.

"Welcome," said Tulir.

"This was one of the people I met with last time," Lena told Tulir, then looked to the woman. "I didn't get your name."

"Tisa," the woman introduced. She looked around, hand resting casually on her sword hilt. "You will make no objections to our weapons, yes?"

"No. Not to your personal weapons. But if you are to have them, I would like those arrows slack until they have reason to be otherwise." Tulir used his cane to point at the hatches.

The man who had been holding the plank climbed up. Another took his place. The man coming down wore chainmail, a sword, and a dark-green tabard with brown clothes beneath, and he looked to be trying to balance his step and repress a smile. He was as tall as Tulir, muscular, and handsome with dirty-blonde hair. His eyes were kind.

"This is Cicero," introduced Tisa as the man dropped down next to her. When he did, she leaned in to speak with him in hushed tones. He replied in kind. She looked back to the hatches and made a lowering motion.

"It is appreciated," said Tulir.

Lena watched intently as the next man climbed down the ramp. One arm bent, the other extended out, he looked off-balance, yet there was no fear on his face or any indication he felt unsure in his step. The man was bald, had a yellow tint to his skin, and wore tattered clothes held together with blue string. He had no armor or weapons. When he dropped onto the deck, his sway and odd posture persisted.

Norman shuffled back half a step. It wasn't hard for Lena to imagine why; the bald Ovnite was the tallest person they had encountered. The man's posture took some measure of height from him, but it was still no contest.

The tall man squinted at each of them, the whites of his eyes yellowed, then looked around the ship. As he scrutinized what he saw, it looked as if there was a layer of amusement beneath his seriousness. He straightened out his back to look to the Ovnite ship and whistled.

Encountering a man taller than her father for the first time made the next person to come down the plank a surprise. A blonde woman, short, wearing leather armor and green clothes. She walked slowly with her head up, staring back at them. She was also unarmed.

Kazio was the one holding the plank for her. He waited until she was at the bottom to let go, then took hold of a rope and backed out of view. After a few quick steps he stepped off the railing, swung over the side, and repelled down to the ship. He released the rope and landed next to Cicero.

The table acted as a natural barrier between them. Kazio walked between the Ovnites and the table to reach the short woman. He pointed across the table and said, "She's the one I met with. *Lena.*"

She hated how he stressed her name.

"Thank you for agreeing to meet with me. I am Tulir. This is my Council." Tulir remained still. The cane he was leaning on was strategically hidden by the chair he stood behind.

"Does a king always dress so well, or is it meant to impress?" questioned Kazio.

"We know better than to wear rags," mumbled Norman.

Kazio took a step forward. The man in chainmail interrupted his angry approach. Kazio protested, "I believe he insulted me, yes?"

The short woman whistled, and her party settled back. She stepped forward. "I am Briet. I am the leader of the Ovnite."

"Briet, you have my word you and your people are safe on this ship so long as no harm is initiated to mine," offered Tulir. He gestured at the table. "As bid, we have brought food to consult over."

The tall Ovnite mumbled a remark too low to understand.

The blond Ovnite man repeated to him some of what Tulir had said.

"We are very lucky our languages aren't so different, yes?" said Briet. Lena estimated she was the same height as Avild.

"Any questions on interpretations or intentions will be answered readily. I expect your people will extend the same courtesy," said Tulir.

"You will have it." Briet moved her chair back but made no move to sit yet. Head tilted to the right, she said, "These men are Kazio, who leads my Vitki, and Cicero, who jointly leads the Drengr."

Kazio and Cicero walked up behind two chairs to Briet's right. Kazio was in the middle. To balance, Lena took the chair to Tulir's left, Avild on the end.

"This is Miss Lena, the representative of the southern coast, and Missus Avild, a historian in my employ." Tulir switched to his right. "These men are Mister Norman, the representative of the northern coast, and Harth, Commander of the Royal Army."

Lena shifted slightly but didn't let her expression change. Would the Commander of the Royal Guard have the same title? Did Harth know he was getting promoted on the spot?

Norman stepped beside Tulir, and Harth stood on the far right end. Norman was unarmed in his dapper garb. Harth had his quiver and bow on his back and a short sword on his belt.

They had no lack of weapons, but they felt outmatched. Was it the ruggedness of the Ovnites that made it so? The guards present ensured their guests were outnumbered, but Lena didn't feel secure in a hypothetical hand-to-hand victory.

"Tisa is the other Drengr leader. Amundr is our Elder," said Briet.

The tall Ovnite stood on the left end, Tisa to Briet's side.

"Drengr—seasoned warriors?" asked Avild. Across from her, Cicero said something Lena couldn't understand. There was nothing familiar about it; it had to have been another language.

Avild replied in kind. Cicero spoke again.

"The Drengr are their fighting force. The term doesn't simply mean 'warrior'—there's a connotation of nobleness," explained Avild.

"Titles are useful," commented Lena. She flicked her eyes up at Kazio.

"That sounds like stalling," said Kazio. He dragged his chair back and sat heavily. "You are here to beg us not to attack you, yes?" He glared at Tulir.

"You are here because the explanation as to why you were trapped behind the Binding is not as simple as you think. I do not wish us to be enemies, and perhaps by the end, we won't be," explained Tulir. Subtly, he hooked his cane onto the back of his chair and sat. He gestured down the table. "Please."

Amundr spoke, but it was too accented and muffled for Lena to understand.

Tisa relayed, "It did not take much convincing for you to believe our story."

"The historian has pored over books to supplement her knowledge. I am convinced what you say about how you were trapped is true. Our records corroborate it," answered Tulir.

As everyone took their seats, Lena had the opportunity to observe how each Ovnite moved. Amundr was strange. He squinted at everything. She remembered Briet had regarded him as their Elder. Though Amundr looked weathered, Lena would have been hard-pressed to believe the man was older than Harth, putting him right around the cusp of forty. *How hard a life have these people lived?*

Tisa was poised in a way the others weren't, and that made Lena curious as to the woman's background. The second most well-mannered was Cicero, but for him it seemed to be a conscious effort. He looked like a man who wasn't accustomed to always having been strong. Both of them had tattoo lines peeking out beyond the fabric at their wrists and neck. They were the only ones who looked marked.

Something else that stuck out, amplified by Amundr being referred to as their Elder, was their collective age. They were all so young—mid- to late twenties, by Lena's guess. What circumstances had befallen the Ovnites to make their leadership all so young? She hoped the closeness of their ages to her, Tulir, and Avild's perceived age would work to their benefit.

A guard came around to deposit glasses. Another followed with wine. The Ovnites' cups were filled from the king's side of the table.

"I'll begin by telling of our history and how I became king, if that is agreeable to you," offered Tulir once everyone was sat and the wine poured.

"Shouldn't we wait for your feeble attempt to kill us, first?" Kazio raised his glass of wine and let it slosh over the side, dripping onto his hands and then the table.

Norman scoffed.

Amundr sneered something across the table at Norman.

Harth reached toward the center of the table, swapped his glass with Amundr's, then drank deeply. When he was done, he flipped the glass upside down. Small drops of wine hit the table before the rim. He looked to Amundr with raised eyebrows.

Tisa raised her own glass and smiled. "I would like to hear their story."

Kazio glared across the table at Lena. The glass was clutched so firmly in his hand, she was afraid he would break it.

"My promises are not hollow. Though I will admit, I don't have a palate for wine, so I cannot speak for how good it is," said Tulir good-naturedly.

Eyes on Kazio, Lena took her cup, sipped from it, then placed it down where Kazio's had been. The wine was bitter. It tasted expensive. Hand still extended out, she tapped the pad of her finger on Kazio's glass. He handed it to her and she drank from it, then settled in with her forearms on the table.

"If your men are satisfied," continued Tulir, a hint of impatience in his voice.

Cicero elbowed Kazio and then shrugged when the other man looked at him.

"Begin," Briet said to Tulir.

Harth waved the guard off when they approached to fill his glass.

Tulir took a deep breath and tapped a finger on the table. "I was born to a poor family in Steepwharf, the largest city on the coast. My father died on a fishing voyage. My mother sold my brother and I to a family to work. I trained as a guard, a fighter, and returned to that family to work privately for them. All the life I can remember up until two years ago, I lived in shared barracks of some sort." Tulir paused to drink. "Then, my employer came under suspicion for some sort of crime. I wasn't clear what for at the time. He was a Noble, and he was arrested on my watch. It turned out, he was being manipulated because someone wanted to get to me.

"My employer and I left Steepwharf. But then men who had gotten him arrested found us and forced us to come here. Because of my upbringing, I never knew much about the legends or origins of the Stone King." Tulir gestured down the table at Avild.

"The Stone King was the last king before Tulir. There is a wealth of information and many rumors about why the Stone King's family was in turmoil, but the most important fact is that it was. The king's son was killed. The king lashed out with magic. The magic revolted. The reason they call him 'the Stone King' wasn't just because his name was lost with time, but because the magic encased him, his family, and his court in stone. That happened almost a thousand years ago, and this land hadn't known a king since," explained Avild. She surveyed the Ovnite's faces before continuing. "The legend he's talking about, how the line survived to birth him, was that of the Princess Consort."

Lena snickered at a memory. *"The whore." I hope you don't say it that way in front of the children.*

Avild continued, "She was the prince's wife and was carrying his child. The Princess Consort was lucky enough to escape instead of being turned to stone. She was so scared by what she witnessed, she fled. The baby was had in secret. The bloodline was lost. The lost descendent was the only way to break the curse and release all those trapped in stone."

"That is why I was brought to the castle. The men who took me explained why they needed me and tried to persuade me to break the stone willingly. I knew they only wanted the power for themselves, and truthfully, I didn't believe them. I was born a guard, raised in servitude—I wasn't destined for anything more. Had I been a false heir and tried to break the stone, it would have killed me." Tulir continued to drum his fingers on the table.

Lena didn't doubt Tulir was remembering his time of capture with Rether's men. It hadn't happened quite as he told it. She doubted he would have expanded on the details, though, had he been telling the truth.

"My friends, two of which are here"—Tulir gestured along the table to Lena and Harth—"came to free me. They fought my captors. The men who had me severed a chunk from my arm and used that to wake the stone." Tulir rolled up his right sleeve to reveal the scar. "But my friends won the fight. The Stone King's power came to me. If not for that proof, I still would not believe my own ancestry."

Briet crossed her arms and leaned back. Her eyes were affixed on Tulir.

"You do not believe all that, yes?" proposed Kazio.

"It matches up with what we knew and what we were hearing in the coastal city," said Cicero.

Tisa shushed them.

"The story matches, but it does sound like such—a story. One well told, and told many times," said Briet.

"You wouldn't be the first to question the legitimacy. The king has had to tell it many times to those who believed it to be nothing but legends and falsehoods," said Lena.

"I had trouble believing it myself. The proof was in the broken stone," added Norman.

"And did the Stone King just walk away when he was freed?" asked Amundr. It took some effort to understand him, the words inferred by how he marched his fingers along the table.

"Dust and bones were all that was left," answered Tulir. He sat up straight and reaffixed his sleeve to cover the scar. "It's worth mentioning that the coastal city you attacked—that was Steepwharf. That was my home. I'm here speaking with you not because of that, but despite it."

"Attacked?" Kazio leaned forward, hands flat on the table.

Briet put up a hand, and he stopped. She looked to Tisa and nodded.

"We did not attack your home. We had crossed the sea and were in need of supplies. We wanted to barter, but your people did not take kindly to those they didn't recognize," said Tisa.

"People died," reminded Lena pointedly.

"We are expected not to defend ourselves?" Kazio opened his arms.

"We never had any intention of attacking them," said Briet.

"But you did have intentions to siege and attack this city?" asked Tulir.

Briet took a breath, eyes still locked on him.

"You mentioned a brother. Younger, I'm assuming, since you are king. I don't see a young man here who looks like you," observed Cicero.

"And if he's weak enough to leave behind in the castle, why wouldn't those who took you have taken him instead?" proposed Amundr.

Tulir clenched his jaw. "A twin brother, but yes, younger. There were circumstances that made me easier to capture, but beyond that, you can't ask dead men why they chose me over him."

"You are more portable, yes?" Kazio pointed at the hook of the cane. "Did you think we didn't see it? You pointed with it."

"Where is your brother?" asked Briet.

"I keep some of his ashes in a silver vial," snapped Tulir. He leaned back and scrunched his nose. With practiced calm, he said, "My getting here was not an easy and painless transition. You all have been wronged, but it was not by me or anyone else in this city."

In a pause, Lena spoke, "The city you are camped outside of is called Clevehold. Who knows what it was called in the era before the Stone King, because it was abandoned for hundreds of years. The people you came to attack have none to do with what happened generations ago."

"I expect if I asked you to validate his story, you would. He said you were there," Briet said to Harth.

"Yes, ma'am," answered Harth.

"You—you were a nonbeliever." Kazio snapped his fingers and pointed at Norman. "What was it that convinced you?"

Norman scoffed and opened his mouth, but Tulir raised his hand.

It was better that way. Norman was prepared to be brusque. He wouldn't answer kindly to being talked down to or having to explain himself to a woman, and this situation prompted both. Lena suspected they wouldn't take him at his word, anyway.

"Kazio is rude, but he's right," said Cicero. He sipped his wine and cleared his throat. "The Ovnite were imprisoned under the wrath of a merciless king. We arrive to face the lineage of said king who upheld our captivity, only to be told there is no fault to be found."

"What more do we need to know aside from the confirmation they're hiding something?" proposed Kazio.

The breeze picked up and the smell of food wafted around them. Lena had forgotten all about it.

CLEVEHOLD

"Part of my proof is in my city and with my people. The city, the castle, it's all in a state of being rebuilt. There's no hiding in some places where time attempted to reclaim the land. Nearly everyone in Clevehold grew up hearing the same stories about the Stone King in books, scrolls, art. Let me show it to you," Tulir proposed.

"You want to take our leader behind your walls?" Amundr shook his head and let out an amused, "No."

"A trade," said Briet. She picked up her glass by the rim but did not drink. "I go with you, but some of your people stay here."

She is quick to compromise, thought Lena. Had she anticipated this? Had Tulir's story made her that curious? Was it part of some grander scheme? It felt too optimistic to assume that Briet, despite what her people wanted, aimed to avoid any fighting.

"I wasn't prepared to ask that of my Council," admitted Tulir.

Briet furrowed her brow and leaned forward. "What were you prepared for?"

"I'll stay," offered Lena. Tulir needed a volunteer, and she was curious about the Ovnites. She could protect herself.

"I don't think that is wise," cautioned Tulir.

"I took your word for our safety on this vessel. You will take mine for hers in my camp," said Briet.

"Camp?" questioned Norman.

"Our people have set up to be comfortable," said Amundr. There was a twinge of attitude in his tone that made it sound like a threat.

"We will treat her better than you do. The future queen and a historian—positions of pity, comparatively. You didn't even arm them," assessed Tisa.

"Can she not fight?" Kazio asked incredulously, looking at Lena.

Lena tightly gripped a fist in her other hand under the table. His tone was unnerving.

"I'll stay with her," offered Harth. "Unless you think fighters, too, are pitiable."

Tulir looked uneasy. It was hidden well beneath layers of composure, but Lena knew how to see it—the twitching of his leg, how hard he blinked. He pointed at Kazio. "This one, the brash one."

"You want him to stay, yes?" asked Briet.

"He comes with us to Clevehold. I'm not leaving my people around him."

Kazio shook his head, smirked, and drank down his wine. When he was done, he crudely wiped his mouth with his sleeve. He set the glass down hard.

"I will also bring one of my choice. Cicero, my stronger Drengr," said Briet.

"I will stay as well," volunteered Avild. "The future queen should be sent with two sets of eyes to watch her back."

"You're going to send both of your poor women?" mocked Kazio.

"Makes for an even trade," answered Tulir. "And the historian can fight."

Briet looked to Tisa, who confirmed, "We can handle three."

"I will assist the king," said Norman.

"I find this arrangement agreeable. I'll go with you, but it will be now. Less time to plot and prepare. My people are also itchy for a resolution. You understand, yes?" said Briet.

Tulir nodded. He looked first to Tisa, then to Amundr. "If any harm befalls my people, chiefly Miss Lena, the safety of your leader is forfeit. You understand, yes?"

Briet smiled. "Of all the statements you've made, that is the one I believe the most."

Chapter 10

THE OVNITE CAMP WAS situated on a bend in the river, allowing three of their ships to provide cover. The river became thinner where it turned, and the large ship took up most of its width. Lena had thought there would have been enough room for two ships to pass, but she saw how narrow it was with the water low. Possible, but daunting.

Lena, Avild, and Harth stayed together on the Ovnite ship. She could see Harth was nervous when the ship came close to the bank. The depth of the ship should have been too imposing—they should have run aground. Instead, the ship pulled up alongside the bank and anchored without issue.

"One of them knows how to manipulate land," said Avild. She leaned over the side.

"More than one," said Tisa. She gestured to the ladder leading below. "We can disembark out the side hatches. The ground was raised to accommodate it."

Lena nodded. She noticed the woman had put effort into changing the way she spoke to be better understood. It was appreciated and far more accommodating than what Lena expected Tulir would experience, from Kazio especially.

He had headed back to Clevehold with Briet, Cicero, Kazio, and Norman. Should she have stayed with him? *Choosing to be with the Ovnites was rash . . . but someone had to stay.*

It had made sense for all the reasons she listed to Tulir previously: her magic, her being a woman. No, her unease wasn't that she was in danger or that she had done something wrong. She simply hated the idea that what Tulir now faced was unknown, and she wasn't there to help him.

"Keep your mind here. Eyes and ears on them," murmured Avild. She brushed by Lena to lead the way to the ladder.

Eyes and ears. Lena looked around. Dozens of Ovnites were in the camp of tents. Where was Amundr?

"After you." Harth gestured for Lena to go ahead of him.

She did and caught up with Avild at the bottom of the ladder. "Did you bring any weapons?"

"None they'll find unless they search me," she answered.

Good. Lena saw the light from the open hatches before they came into view. The ground was visible as they approached. People were staring at them, and it made Lena glad she had no weapons of her own. It reinforced how they only saw her as a pawn to be protected.

They walked to exit the ship so quickly that it didn't give her time to see much. There were doors leading to closed-off rooms, and through one open doorway she saw bunks hanging. There were people staring at them from that room, too.

The outside air greeted them with a warm breeze. Lena made sure to move to the side enough to let Harth and any others exit, but she had to stop to take it in. The setup looked like a cross between a small town and a traveling circus, tents all around the main thoroughfare. There was an obvious difference where their lodgings were versus their supplies. They were organized.

These were not the people who were meant to attack them. They were just . . . people.

"This is a different man from last time, yes?" asked one man as he approached.

Lena recognized him from the first meeting. He was about Harth's height and unarmed. There was a wrap around his fingers. His forearms were exposed, and there were no tattoos. *Do only the Drengr have tattoos?*

Tisa glanced back to Harth. "This is Harth. He is the Commander of the Royal Army."

"Are you hiding the king under your vest?" asked the man. He leaned to investigate the ship hatch.

Tisa joined them outside and pushed the man away from the ship. "The king took Briet, Kazio, and Cicero to the castle. We get the future queen, the fighter, and the librarian."

Historian. Lena didn't make the correction out loud. She couldn't imagine her cousin in a situation like this, given his state of mind.

"We agreed to that?" asked the man.

Tisa huffed a laugh. "Briet agreed to it. We sit tight."

The man nodded. He was dressed in clothes similar to what Cicero wore beneath his chainmail, a simple stitch shirt in light green. The articles were held together with blue stitching. Heavy boots. No weapons. He pointed at the bow on Harth's back. "Is that standard here?"

"It's shorter than what your people in the shadows have, but at short range, you want something quicker to notch. We have long bows, too," answered Harth. He jutted his chin to a tent. "And crossbows."

"What's the pull weight?" the man asked conversationally, crossing his arms.

"Kasper," Tisa caught his attention.

"We're here to fight the king, maybe," the man, Kasper, defended. "What else are we supposed to do with them until Briet decides which it is?"

"I'm going to put them up in a tent and have everyone else keep their distance," answered Tisa matter-of-factly.

"Do you know how long they're going to be here?" asked Kasper.

Lena kept her mouth closed, head angled down. They were here to watch and listen. She also hadn't considered what they would do in the Ovnite camp or how long they would be staying. At least a day, probably more. She supposed it depended on Briet's reception to what Tulir told her.

"Forty pounds," answered Harth.

Kasper squinted at him. "That low?"

"That low will cut through skin, even if it has to thread chainmail to do it." Harth unhooked his bow from his shoulder.

"You're giving up on power. Unless the higher weight doesn't work for you." Kasper took the bow and pulled on it tentatively. Lena recognized the wraps on his fingers as a primitive tab.

"The eighty-five-pound draw is for power. Forty pounds increases speed on the draw," said Harth.

"You alternate an eighty-five with a forty?" questioned Kasper. It wasn't accusatory, just curious. "That can't do well for accuracy."

Tisa made a clicking sound with her mouth.

"If all goes well, I won't have to prove you wrong," said Harth.

"Target practice passes the time," commented Kasper as he handed the bow back. Pointing at the strap of Harth's quiver, he said, "I've seen that symbol before. The birds."

"From Cicero's books," volunteered Tisa.

"It's the Emblem of the Kings," said Avild.

Harth passed his palm over the symbol. "It was my father's. A recovered antique."

Kasper nodded and thumbed behind him. "Want to see how well the antique and low draw weight hold up?"

Harth was good at hiding his unease at the immediate request to split them up, but Lena recognized it. Opening the conversation to the women, he said, "Avild can shoot."

"I'll stay with Tisa and Lena," she responded. Her head inclined as if she was giving him permission to go.

CLEVEHOLD

Tisa scowled at Kasper.

"It's less risky for us if they aren't all together," defended Kasper.

"No harm comes to any of them," reminded Tisa pointedly. "That includes hurting oneself."

Was it wise to let themselves be split up? Then again, was it really their choice? It covered more area, at least. They would learn more about the Ovnites this way. Friendly bonds built bridges. Loose lips of enemies gave them advantages. Kasper appeared to be an easy mark for either scenario.

If Lena asked, she was sure Harth would stay. Avild could have made the same ask of him if she was so inclined or worried for his safety. Her willingness to let him go meant to Lena they all felt the same thing—there was no innate threat. The Ovnites were just people after all.

"The camp isn't large. He can yell if there's trouble, yes?" said Kasper.

Lena and Avild separated from the men as Tisa led them to one tent in a long row of others. She pulled back the flap to expose an empty area lined with a few bedrolls. "This will have to do."

"You don't sleep on the ships?" asked Avild.

"We have shifts on them. This will be better for you," answered Tisa.

Lena looked around. Purposefully, she fiddled with her hands. What she saw surprised her, and her hands stopped.

Blue magic, not green. Avild had remarked how it was different in other parts of the world.

"You wouldn't want to make anyone uncomfortable," said Tisa.

Ceasing her gawking, Lena folded her hands together and looked down.

"These people, the Ovnites—they allow you to lead?" questioned Avild.

Lena rushed to amend, "She doesn't mean it like that."

"I wholly do," Avild corrected. There was an upturn to one side of her lip. "You're a woman leading a fighting force. How did that come to be?"

Tisa straightened up. "I proved myself."

"There's more to it than that," pried Avild.

Lena knew her friend was being intrusive—borderline rude—but she, too, was curious.

"I stepped up when my people needed me to. It's simple in concept, but not in action. I didn't strive for it, but I earned it," answered Tisa.

Silence carried for a few seconds. People still stared at them. To break the growing unease, Lena proposed, "Your family, your parents—they must be proud."

"My father was the former leader of the Ovnite. That was before Briet. He and my mother have passed. But yes, I think they would be." Tisa explained herself as if she knew Lena was fishing for information.

Lena bowed her head. Earnestly, she offered, "I'm sorry."

"You and Briet don't look like sisters," remarked Avild.

The women were also too close in age. Granted, twins didn't always have to look alike, but the height difference was the biggest physical disparity.

"Leadership here isn't passed down through blood. It's done through action." Tisa crossed her arms and kept her weight distributed over both feet.

"Does that bother you?" Avild stood across from Tisa at the mouth of the tent.

Tisa looked to Lena. "Do you need anything? Food, perhaps?"

From the supplies stolen from Steepwharf? Lena answered kindly, "No."

"Your magic"—Avild put her back to Tisa and looked around—"how effective is it?"

Lena could tell the Ovnite woman was growing impatient.

"Powerful enough," Tisa said simply.

"Do you all have it?" asked Lena.

"To some degree, yes." Tisa rested her hand on her sword hilt. "Everyone knows how to fight. Those who are well-grounded are versed in magic."

"I wonder how your magic has evolved in captivity," said Avild as she continued to observe the camp. Her hands were clasped behind her back.

People nearby kept their distance. The tent nearest theirs was open and empty. *Did they think this was possibility enough to have planned for it?*

"Tell me, can magic change over time?" questioned Tisa.

Avild smirked. She held out one hand, palm up. Her fingers fluttered to create a wave, and after a few seconds, green specks began to appear. The hazy glow traveled over Avild's hand and up her wrist, a deep forest green.

Looking intently at her hand with curiosity, Tisa opened her mouth to speak.

A teal rope fastened around Avild's arm and yanked her forward. She fell to her knees and reached out to break her fall while Tisa turned quickly to see the origin, as did Lena.

Amundr flicked his wrist and the teal rope dissipated. The whip in his hand was pointing straight out at Avild, held up against gravity, until the magic receded from it.

A weapon made of magic? No—the user's magic extended from the weapon. *Is it similar to what made Rether's sword break?* Regardless, the color was off. It was green but a lighter hue, closer to blue.

"She meant no harm," reasoned Tisa.

Amundr leaned back on his heels, hunching his shoulders in more as he reeled in the whip. "I wasn't taking that chance."

Lena looked back to Avild when she felt a small gust of wind pull her back. She had turned just in time to see Avild get to her feet and push a wave of wind at Amundr. Lena ducked and was pushed two steps to the side, balanced enough to stay upright.

The wind knocked Amundr off his feet, sending him back a short distance before he dropped to the ground on his back. The whip, still gripped in his hand, had unraveled. With the other hand, he propped himself up off the ground.

"Avild!" Lena scolded.

The other woman shrugged. There was a red mark where the whip had marked her wrist. "I wasn't taking a chance."

A nervous-looking brunette took a few steps away from the fight, then turned to jog away.

Amundr got to his knees. Now that he wasn't holding the whip, threads of magic wove around his fingers instead. They looked like strings anchored to unseen insects. His upper lip pulled back in a snarl.

"We need to stop this. Our—" Tisa wasn't looking the right way, too focused on Avild.

Lena interrupted, "Step back!"

A string came loose from Amundr's hand as he fired at Avild.

She put her forearm up to take the hit and jerked and grimaced as it landed. She lowered her arm and looked where she had been hit. Avild scoffed, amused, then shook her arm out. There was no mark.

Amundr fired a second string as he got to his feet.

This one, Avild caught. The string was absorbed into her palm and a green glow lit up her hand. She quickly closed and then uncurled her fingers to send it back.

Lena looked helplessly from side to side. Her heart was beating in her ears. People were watching—she had to stop them from trying to interfere. This had to stop before Avild hurt someone.

Amundr took the brunt of the sting, wincing when it hit him. Shoulders squared, he stood tall and flicked out the whip.

"Stop!" Lena called, looking to them both. They weren't listening.

Magic shot out from Avild's hand before her fist clenched slowly. The haze of magic directed at Amundr formed into the claws of various creatures. Bear. Mountain lion. Vulture.

Amundr thrust out the whip in front of him. The material straightened out parallel with the ground, and a shield emitted from the rope to block the claws. The green talons of a vulture ripped through the shield and dug into his shoulder.

With a yell, Amundr pulled back the whip before pushing it out with force. The haze of the shield dissipated, and the claws were forced back toward Avild as he grabbed the talon on his shoulder and wrenched it out. The magic crumbled in his hand.

Avild split into two. As she did, the claws aimed at her dissolved.

Amundr used the whip, glowing and extended with magic, to hit the Avild closer to Tisa. It struck the illusion in the neck, cutting through it, and the rest of the image was swept away in the breeze. Not losing momentum, Amundr pulled his arm back and went to strike again.

Avild caught the whip. The darker green of her magic traveled down the teal hue and as it reached Amundr's hand, she yanked, and it was pulled from him.

Lena looked to Tisa across the firing range to see she, too, was at a loss. If their Vitki were their magic users, as the translation had inferred, they had sent their best away.

Avild positioned for another attack. Across from her, Amundr did the same.

If they hurt each other, or worse, negotiations would conclude before they ever started. Whatever was to be done had to be quickly. Lena felt the pins and needles of magic in her hands. She wasn't a fighter—she knew that—but she didn't have to be.

Lena stepped between the two, magic coming at her from both sides. She bent both arms where her palms faced away from her ears. "Enough!"

The shields absorbed both shades of magic, and Lena felt as though she were being squeezed. Her heart didn't beat for that instant. She couldn't breathe. The pressure had to be relieved. She forced her arms down.

The magic rocketed back the way it had come.

Amundr fell back with a grunt, landing on grass. A small bloodstain on his shoulder was his only injury.

Avild skidded and rolled back, caught up in a tent.

"We're done!" said Lena, first looking at Avild, then to Amundr. "We aren't here to fight."

Angrily, Avild swatted at the fabric to get it off of her. She got up and stood behind it, her right arm cradled to her chest. It looked broken.

The power Lena felt instantly deflated. She pleaded to Avild, "I didn't mean it."

Tisa stepped next to Lena and stuck her chin out at Avild. "Go."

"I . . . we . . ." Lena stammered.

"They got it out of their system," said Tisa.

Lena nodded and went to Avild. Careful to walk around the mess that was left of the tent, she approached with her hands up. "How bad is it?"

"Not the first time it broke," she grumbled. Avild glared across at Amundr.

Lena could hear talking and the arrival of people behind her, but she couldn't risk taking her eyes off Avild. "I'm sorry, but I'm here to prevent a war."

"I didn't start this," reminded Avild.

"Are you going to lie to me and say you weren't looking for a fight?" whispered Lena, surprised at her boldness. She could send Avild back. If having her here was a risk, it was in her capacity as a Council member and future queen to excuse someone. Getting Avild to listen to her, *enforcing* the order—that was the issue.

Lena overheard Tisa say, "They were showing off. Your queen ended it."

Hand to her face and shaking her head, Lena tried to anticipate what would happen next. Tisa sounded forgiving enough. Amundr had stopped attempting to attack. It could be salvaged.

"What's happening?" Harth asked as he approached.

Lena stood to the side to keep Avild at her right and everyone else within her field of vision to the left. Tisa stood with Amundr, the brunette who had run away, and Kasper. Hopefully, their competitiveness hadn't ended with as much fanfare. He looked alright.

"Their magic is decent," answered Avild.

Kasper had a hand on Amundr's shoulder. Their group was talking too low for Lena to overhear, but the brunette was pointing and gesturing while Tisa nodded along.

Avild winced as Harth poked her arm. He shook his head and said, "We could do this evaluation without breaking bones. I can set it, but this will take you a week or so to heal."

"My turnaround time isn't what it used to be," she griped.

"Can we agree on peace?" Tisa called to them. She began to walk over, Amundr a few steps behind. Kasper and the brunette remained in place.

"Can we?" Harth asked quietly as he prodded at Avild's arm.

She looked him in the eye.

Lena felt her heartbeat pounding. Her face remained composed, but her thoughts raced. She had wanted Harth along as the calm hand, the voice of reason. His loyalties were to Tulir and, by extension at least, Lena. But there was history. Harth had been raised by Klaus and Avild. That loyalty wasn't to be overlooked.

Did that mean if Avild had planned something stupid, Harth would be party to it? Which would win out? He was waiting for Avild's verdict.

"As you said"—Lena responded to Tisa but was looking at Avild—"they have gotten it out of their system." Her party wasn't the only one at risk if they couldn't be civil. The Ovnites must have wanted peace as much as they did, Lena reasoned.

Or was this how they intended to start it?

"In that case, her wound can be healed," offered Tisa.

Harth and Avild looked to Tisa curiously.

"Heal?" asked Lena. Had she understood correctly? *Magic can do that?* She looked at Amundr's shoulder. There was blood on the fabric, but she saw no wound inside the tear. Was that what Kasper had done?

"Your magic can be used to heal?" Harth stood beside Avild, a physical barrier between her and Amundr.

"Show them your shoulder," Tisa instructed Amundr.

He mumbled something but moved to comply. There were two amulets hanging from his neck that he carefully pushed out of the way before pulling the collar over. Brittle nails shifted the fabric back to expose more yellowish skin down to the shoulder. The talon wound was gone.

"Amundr will heal your historian as a testament that no further harm will come to any of you while you are here," Tisa stressed the point to Avild and Amundr, but ended the statement looking at Lena.

Did they think she was going to cause trouble?

No. They were waiting for her. Avild, too, was waiting on her to accept. Lena nodded.

"You may draw your weapon, if that will help your mindset," Amundr offered to Harth as he took steps around the other man. "But I promise, it won't hurt her."

Harth took a step closer to Lena to give them more room. His hand rested near his sword. The bow was missing, but the quiver was still strapped to his back.

"She isn't the one I'm worried about," commented Harth.

"Enough," said Lena sternly. She looked to Amundr. "Fix her arm, please."

Amundr nodded. Tendrils of teal magic sprouted forth from his hands. He reached for Avild's arm, and she extended it slowly. She alternated between watching his face and his hands. He kept his eyes on her arm.

"You put a stop to it?" Harth asked quietly.

"Yes," answered Lena. She was also enamored watching Amundr's work, though she wasn't sure that was the feeling Avild would admit to.

"Are you alright?" Harth asked.

Lena hummed.

He bumped her shoulder with his. When she looked up at him, he pulled down the lid under one of his eyes.

She rubbed at her own eyes, though she knew it was useless. There was an old fear surfaced in the physical evidence of magic, the black webs in her eyes. It was nothing to be ashamed of; the same presence had been in Avild's eyes and was in Amundr's now as he healed her. The marks of magic they shared.

"It might take a day, but it will fade," said Harth.

That bad? It was just a shield. How much force had it taken to push them both back?

Kasper walked over to Tisa and they spoke in hushed tones. The brunette had left.

A snap made Lena look at Avild. She released the breath she had been holding when she saw her friend was alright. Amundr was taking his hands off Avild's arm, which no longer looked bruised or broken.

"Can't do that where you're from?" Amundr asked her as he looked down. He towered over Avild by a foot or more.

She didn't appear bothered. Chin up, she responded, "I'm sure it's not the only difference."

Tisa recounted to Kasper, "It was. That shield would have given Haldor a competitor."

With a scoff, Amundr turned and walked away.

"I only meant—" Tisa began but stopped herself.

Kasper shook his head and advised, "Let it be."

"Did it work?" Harth probed at Avild's arm when she extended it to him. From the way she didn't wince or flinch, he had an answer.

"The women of this place like to pick fights," said Kasper casually.

"It began as a misunderstanding. It escalated because tensions are high. No lasting damage, no hard feelings," said Lena.

"For our protection, we would prefer for the three of you not to stay together. This prevents any outnumbered misunderstandings, yes?" said Tisa.

"One of us will always be with her," warned Avild, gesturing at Lena.

"And my people will approach her and her chaperone in pairs," replied Tisa.

"If they're all settled, we can get back to shooting," said Kasper as he tapped Harth's arm.

He looked to Lena. "Do you feel safe enough staying here?"

They were afraid of her. That's what Tisa and Kasper had been discussing—she was sure of it. Before, they had been coy about wanting to keep the three separated, but after seeing what Lena could do and how hotheaded Avild was, they didn't mind formalizing the rule.

A pit grew in her stomach. Shouldn't she have been glad for their fear?

Lena swallowed and nodded. "We'll be fine."

Chapter 11

THE NEXT TENT THEY were led to was received with considerably less dramatics. As it grew darker, they were brought two lit candles that were set down in the center of the tent between Avild and Lena. The tent flap was down.

Avild turned over her right arm and examined it again. She was dangerously close to the fire, undeterred by the possibility of being burnt. There were no marks to indicate her arm had been broken just a few hours ago.

Laid back on the rollaway mattress, which smelled of salt water, Lena kept Avild in her periphery and her feet on the tent flap. As she scanned the tan material overhead, she could see the patches. The mending was almost seamless to the original. It had to have been done with magic. The theory loaned believability to how these people could have been isolated for so long but still had tools, clothes, and other supplies.

Where did it all come from? Lena squinted and thought hard back to Steepwharf. Growing up in a big city, there had always been goods. People harvested, thread was woven—she knew the basics, but by the time she handled the material, it was already in yards to cut down to clothes. What about books? She had seen blank pages, but where did the pages come from? Ink came from ground-up pigments. For a lack of better utensils, feathers could be used to write with. Did the Ovnites have books?

"Did birds get in?" Lena asked.

"Birds?" questioned Avild.

"In the windows, when there weren't glass panes. Did birds get in?"

CLEVEHOLD

There was a pause. Avild let out a slow breath. "They did. There were people designated to catch them. I think they ate them, sometimes."

Lena's face contorted. Had the king not fed his people enough?

"Miss Lena?" a voice called from outside, saying her name and title as if it were one word.

Lena sat upright, adjusted her position, and pulled back the flap. The smell of cooked meat greeted her.

The brunette from earlier knelt at height with her. In her hand was a large platter with two pieces of meat and two potatoes. "For dinner, if you're hungry."

"Thank you." Lena accepted the platter. She set it down next to her and asked, "What's your name?"

The woman with brown curly hair, a simple tan dress, and an amulet hanging around her neck answered, "I'm Gunna."

"Thank you, Gunna. For this and for what you did earlier." Lena caught the movement of another person standing near the tent. They must have been waiting for Gunna, or perhaps they were there to protect her.

"Do you have what you need for the night?" Gunna's tone was short, not necessarily impatient, but not open for conversation either.

She's uncomfortable, thought Lena. Wishing she could resolve that fear but uncertain if there was time or receptiveness available, Lena answered, "Yes, thank you."

Gunna nodded, stood, and walked away.

With the tent flap secured shut, Lena looked at the platter. No utensils. She thought back to what Kazio had said—"the pointy eating sticks." At the time, she had thought he was being wise or making a mockery of her station.

She hoped Tulir was faring better than they were. *Three Ovnites in the castle of Clevehold* . . . They were likely dangerous—all three of them—but despite their magic, they were heavily outnumbered. Surely, Lena reasoned, with Briet's appearance of levelheadedness, she knew better than to pick a fight under those circumstances.

The meat was sliced thin and cooked well. Lena decided to pick it up with her fingers and concentrate on eating to distract from her thoughts. It was juicy, and the taste was familiar enough. *At least it isn't fish.* She looked up when she felt Avild staring at her.

"Very trusting," commented Avild.

"They have three of ours. If I don't come back, Briet dies. If Harth doesn't come back, I'm confident Tulir would make a similar threat, or take it out on the ginger one," justified Lena. She picked up a warm potato and tossed it at Avild.

"No retribution for me?"

Lena wiped her fingers off on the cloth of her calf. "I think the smart one is going to grow on them. There's something endearing and innocent there."

"Cicero," Avild provided the name. She bit into the potato, made a face, and set it down. After swallowing, she said, "I don't expect Tulir to bargain for me."

It isn't going to come to that. By how sternly the thought crossed her mind, she was glad not to have said it aloud. Instead, she told Avild, "Knowing all that you've survived, none of us are afraid of something happening to you."

Avild raised her eyebrows and shook her head.

Lena gestured at the other woman's arm, changing the subject. "I didn't know magic could do that." The *Did you?* was implicit.

"It's going to put the need for as many doctors in question." Avild pressed two fingers where the bruise had been as if searching for where it had hurt.

Something unknown or forgotten. Lena believed her friend was unaware. "What would it take to learn magic like that?" she wondered.

"Yours has come a long way. Perhaps they can show you," responded Avild.

Lena shook her head. "I don't know this power."

"I wouldn't relay that to them," said Avild. She picked up the meat and tore a piece off with her fingers.

"I didn't plan on making them aware whatsoever."

"My mistake," admitted Avild. After a moment of silence, she added, "The shield was impressive."

"It's the only thing I know how to do. It scares me as much as it scared them." She remembered the pressure she felt holding their power back and the relief when she let go. In the span of an instant, she had gone from feeling crushed to untouchable—only then she found she had injured her friend. She shook her head, muttering, "I was a scared girl when we left Steepwharf, but I thought I had grown up. Today, I'm reminded I'm no more than I used to be."

"No," Avild said simply. She set down the uneaten meat. "You were ignorant then. I would even go so far as to say sheltered."

Easy to manipulate?

Avild continued, "Now, you're aware of what you don't know. Fear exists in growth."

"I have a lot to grow into." Lena looked down at her hands. *And so many questions.* She began with, "Where did you go?"

"I returned to the cabin. I spent the better part of a month cleaning it, fixing it, and replacing boards," she answered slowly.

Lena thought back to the small house. Two bedrooms. Garden on the side. A cell in the cellar. A reading nook. The blood.

"Do you live there now?" asked Lena.

"I burned it," replied Avild flatly. A small breathy laugh pushed out of her mouth. "I tried. I did, just like he would have wanted me to. But I couldn't stand to look at it. It didn't bring him back. It didn't get him out."

"I understand."

"No, you don't," whispered Avild. She wiped her hand over her mouth. "Klaus and I spent centuries together. I felt him in the cabin, but I could not find him."

Lena buttoned up her mouth. Avild was right. She couldn't possibly understand.

"And I could have it all back if I asked that sulking cousin of yours for his life. Why I left, why I've been spying for these last few weeks with no word—does that answer both for you?"

No, because you can't do it yourself, thought Lena, though she could understand the temptation to try. The irony was, by the time Avild was levelheaded enough to regulate her emotions and revive Klaus, she would realize it was better not to. Dead was dead, magic or not. Klaus wouldn't have wanted someone to pay for his life.

It had dawned on Lena she herself had the capacity for it. Her power was akin to that of the Stone King and his court. Learning how to revive the dead was something Avild would happily teach her if only she asked.

Lena would never kill Selgen; Avild didn't have to ask. Teaching would be for naught if the performer wouldn't actually do it. Lena wouldn't kill anyone simply because someone asked. Enemies, yes, but not good people. Not family.

Harth. A week ago, Lena would have confidently said he wouldn't trade Selgen's life for Klaus'. But Avild's arrival had her questioning it. What Lena could fall back on was Harth not being adequately grounded and being self-aware enough to not try. Lena shook her head and looked away from Avild. Her sway was great, but not enough to sway Harth's morals.

More people were showing up in Clevehold every day with bits of magic, but no one near grounded enough to try to raise the dead. That kind of power wouldn't go unnoticed.

Lena's eyes widened.

CLEVEHOLD

Avild had repositioned herself to lie on her back, arm over her eyes. She wasn't asleep yet. Her food was untouched.

You don't care about the fight, the people, the Binding, none of it. Lena controlled her breathing as to not draw attention. *Breaking the Binding took power. You're here to see who was grounded enough to do it.*

Lena grabbed the second potato with no intention of eating it. She asked, as casually as possible, "Will you stay in the castle while you're here, once we go back?"

"I don't plan on staying."

"But you will stay until the conflict is resolved?" Lena clarified.

"Depends on what this turns into," said Avild. "I'm happy to stand by and play mediator for a short time, but if talking is all it is, you don't need me here."

"You think it will evolve?"

Avild propped herself up on an elbow to look across the tent at Lena. "Are you expecting it not to? After today?"

"I expect today was an anomaly. I expect peace to be the result of the misunderstandings. Tulir will talk to Briet. If she's wise enough to lead these people, she will be wise enough to see reason." To an extent, she knew her desire was rooted in optimism. There was no reason to give up on that until proven otherwise.

Flat on the bed, loudly saying nothing, Avild let out a long breath.

THE NIGHT'S REST WASN'T the worst Lena had ever had. The mattress was comfortable enough. A breeze would have been kind in the heat, but she hadn't wanted to open the tent.

Tulir and Briet hadn't returned.

It hadn't yet been a full day. There was still time—their absence didn't mean anything was wrong. Lena hoped if she repeated this to herself enough, she would start believing it.

Gunna had stopped by with more food. Lena, with her best smile, had thanked her and asked as to where the other member of their party was. Gunna provided directions toward one of the large communal fires.

Found where she had described, Harth was sitting on a cut-out log. He was fastening his boots when Lena sat down and greeted, "Morning."

"Morning," he returned, then looked her over clinically. "You were safe? No issues?"

"We were fine in the tent. They left us alone." She handed him the second boot. "Where did you sleep?"

"Let's say I have another reason to want this done quickly. It's been a long time since I had to sleep in the open"—he grunted to get the boot on—"and on the ground."

"I'm sure we could get them to find you a tent or a bedroll." She observed the Ovnites going about their morning. Some carried baskets. There were people on the boats and in the river. She expected she would see only what they wanted to present. One aspect that surprised her, however, beyond the magic dissonance, was the women. There were no apparent divides as to which duties were carried out by whom. Men and women each carried firewood. Men and women each washed clothes.

Harth shrugged and sat up straight, extending out his leg. "How's Avild?"

"Provided our roles of pairs, she assured me she would behave while I was here," answered Lena. She looked back in the direction of the tent. It was too far away to know which was hers.

"You can admit to her wearing you out."

Lena nodded. "I'm glad she's back, but it does pose its challenges."

"Tisa's smart. She'll have Amundr keep his distance after what happened."

It occurred to her to ask, "Did they give you food?"

"Meat and potatoes," he answered. "So you know, they only eat twice a day. What you eat for breakfast must carry you to dinner."

She appreciated the warning, but his words sparked worry. How long did he anticipate they would be staying? Choosing not to dwell on it, Lena remarked, "They have no utensils among them."

"Wasn't that one of the things Kazio specified to bring?" asked Harth.

"For that meal we didn't eat, yes, he did," she confirmed. She flattened her hands on her thighs. "I found it very strange then."

"I'm not sure that's the strangest thing about them." He looked around. His hair was messed up, as if it had been pressed flat from sleeping and he had tried to fix it with his hands. It wasn't overt with how short he kept it. There was a layer of new stubble on his face.

"Is that why you wanted to stay? To evaluate their . . ." Lena considered her word choice. "Tendencies?"

"In a way."

"What have you found?"

"They've faced conflict. They aren't novices to fighting and have decent weapons. They're hiding their full numbers from us, but unless there's a secondary camp, not by much. My gut tells me this is it. It's strange . . ." He stopped, looking around again.

Lena followed his line of sight. She didn't notice anything new.

"Their leather armor is dated. The bows are old form. The swords aren't as tough, the chainmail looks handmade, and the plate is more magic than welded mends by now, but in a lot of ways, they're not much behind Steepwharf."

Careful with her words, Lena said, "They seem to have lost the prejudices of the West. From what our historian says, the role of men and women alike is fairly consistent now to what it was in the days of the Stone King. These women, though, they fight. They lead. How they're allowed to dress doesn't seem to be based on any system."

"Prejudices on jobs, duties, magic—it's what stopped the West from evolving. These people, back where they're from, they have books. *Printed* books." He mimed pulling down a press plate.

Lena opened her mouth to say something but, through a breath and shrug, admitted she didn't know the significance.

"If you go to Steepwharf's library, or any other library along the coast, the oldest plate-pressed books are four hundred years old, give or take. Before the plates, letters were affixed to a table and scrolls rolled over it. Before that, it was all done by hand. Traditional transcriptions are still manual, like Selgen's library's private collections," he explained.

"But the plate press has to be over four hundred years old if they have it," assumed Lena.

"If you go inland, plate presses predate the Stone King by centuries. By our historian's account, it was invented over thirteen hundred years ago. This tells us something about the Ovnite. They're literate, and they have a respect for knowledge. It also tells us something about the coast."

"When the Stone King died, how much did Steepwharf throw away?" proposed Lena.

In a tone of agreement, Harth added, "If the right person didn't understand it, it was too risky to have."

"Strange, indeed." She observed he had his quiver and bow, but not the sword. "Where's your other weapon?"

He laughed lightly, air pushing out his nose and hand wiping down his face to hide the grin. "I don't know if Kasper was fully aware he was trading information for a sword, but that's how I have it on my conscience."

"Is it information Tulir asked you to get?" There was no one close, and they kept their voices low.

"It's what he'll need to know. We didn't plan for this, but I'm sure he's doing alright." He said this as an assurance to Lena, she assumed, but she detected a layer of personal worry.

Lena smiled and looked down at the fire. The morning breeze kicked up the smell of flowers. Content, she said, "You care for him."

"He's a good man, makes for a responsible king." Harth strapped the quiver to his back and put the bow down beside him.

"But it's not just that." Lena took a deep breath, overcome by the irregular beat of her heart that came with recalling her and Tulir's conversation about their future. Her comment was met with silence, and she looked up. The secondary memory occurred: her, Tulir, and Harth in the king's suite. The confusion and talking around it. "He didn't tell you he spoke to me about it, did he?"

Harth put a hand to the bow. He let go and put the hand on his knee, the fingers scratching at the trouser fabric. "He told me he was considering talking to you."

"To be fair, he and I didn't finish the conversation. It might not have been much of a conversation at all. I didn't know what to think," she admitted. She observed him as he looked elsewhere. How different she and Harth were physically. He was rugged, a skilled fighter with calloused hands and a serious face. Lena had only ever fought to save her own life. Her calluses from her days of mending nets were nearly gone. Their differences only amplified her confusion.

"You are who the king is expected to marry. The one he's able to be with without legal repercussions. I am one of the few who know you need to be queen. And you can provide him heirs," Harth listed out.

Lena clasped her hands together. "I love when it's laid out so technically like that."

Harth's eyes met hers. "He cares for you."

A smile crossed her face. If that was something she had put in doubt, she shouldn't have. Tulir likely fretted for her safety as she did for his. Doubly so, if they accounted for Harth staying with her.

"I should check on Avild." Harth picked up his bow and stood. "Someone has to make sure she doesn't pick any more fights."

Lena nodded. She felt more whole then, as if she had some answers. She didn't know exactly to which questions, but she was content leaving the conversation more settled than when it began.

About to walk away, Harth turned back. "I offered to get out of the way."

"What?" Lena presumed she knew what he meant but took the opportunity to stand. They could speak quietly if they were close. In a glimpse of thought, she asked herself if she found him attractive. Her honest answer was no. She could appreciate how someone might consider him handsome; he wasn't unpleasant, but he wasn't the type she found personally appealing. *Too rugged, perhaps.*

"It would make it easier, if I went back to Steepwharf and you stayed in Clevehold. He should be with someone young and gentle. I'm over ten years his senior, and what we have puts him at risk if the wrong person were to find out. He refused the offer, but I still consider it," explained Harth. The last sentence was rushed, as if he had debated including it and hurried to say it before he lost the nerve.

"Don't," she responded automatically. The quickness of the response surprised them both, but she didn't regret it. She didn't want him to leave, especially if Tulir didn't want him to.

Did that mean she was willing to accept the compromise?

"It's about what's fair to both of you," said Harth.

"We all get a say in deciding what's fair. You can't leave Clevehold at least until the conversation's been had." Lena shrugged and added an amused, "Tulir's stubborn, you know that. He's a good talker. No wonder he's a good king."

Harth nodded. There was a softness to his face. He opened his mouth, closed it, then looked down. Slow to start, he said, "You should know I'm not like Tulir."

"In what way?" she asked before her mind could jump to conclusions.

"In my prejudices." He shook his head. "No, that's the wrong word. In . . . I don't have an affinity for women, as well, like he does." He met her eyes to assure she understood, moving a finger back and forth between them. "*Us* together isn't part of the compromise he's asking for—in case you didn't reach that part of the conversation."

Lena nodded. There was some relief in hearing that. Things still needed to be discussed and considered, but having the facts was key. A smile grew on her face. "We're an odd set, to have fallen in love with the same man."

Kasper waved at them from across the fire and moved quickly toward them, a welcoming look on his face.

"Yes, Miss Lena," agreed Harth.

Sincerely, she said, "You're a good man, too."

Chapter 12

SCREAMS WOKE HER. LENA searched first for Avild, who looked to have just woken in a similarly shocked state. The light outside the tent was brighter than it should have been for the dead of night. It was warmer. It crackled.

"Get outside!" urged Avild. She swept her hair to one shoulder and grabbed her knife, not bothering to strap it to her thigh where it was kept concealed during the day.

Lena opened the flap and crawled out. She got so far as standing upright before she was stunned, frozen in place. The Ovnite camp was burning. There were lines of fire painted through the camp as if drawn. She smelled oil.

"Stay with me," Avild instructed. She grabbed Lena by the wrist and pulled her along.

They passed by a burning tent. A woman was grabbing at a tent post to get to her feet. Was she about to go back in?

"Wait," said Lena. She tried to stop but continued to be dragged along.

There were cries for help along the river, closer to where the communal fire pit was. Avild tried to bring Lena forward but was met with resistance.

"You go—I have to help her," Lena urged. The brunette, Gunna, was about to go inside a flaming tent.

"Don't do anything stupid," Avild instructed as she let go and jogged away.

Lena ran to Gunna, who had been reaching into the fire. Her arm had caught. Lena yanked Gunna back and frantically patted out the embers.

CLEVEHOLD

The words Gunna yelled were shrill, desperate, as she fought against Lena's hold. On the third iteration, Lena understood she was yelling, "My husband's in there!"

Coughs worked their way up Lena's throat. They were too close to the fire—it was all around them. Surprised at her own strength, Lena held Gunna back. The tent was engulfed and about to collapse. "It's too late."

"He's hurt! He pushed me out," Gunna screamed. Tears flowed down her face, mixing with soot.

Something struck Lena, and she fell over as the wind was knocked out of her. She tried for a breath, but the smoke only made her cough.

A hand reached for her. *Tisa*. Lena accepted the grip to help her stand.

Gunna was getting up a few feet away. Once she was upright, Tisa left Lena and went to the other woman. Gunna pointed at the tent and lunged for it as it caved in.

"We have to get out of here," commanded Tisa. Her arms held back a thrashing Gunna around the waist. She picked the other woman up and turned them around to stand between Gunna and the fire.

"He's in there!" yelled Gunna, her shouts joining the many cries of the night.

"Then he's dead." Tisa released Gunna and pushed her back. "Don't die with him."

Ability to speak regained in her dry throat, Lena asked, "What happened?"

"Our horses are gone, and our ships are aflame. Those that could sail had to go upriver. The river is on fire to the south," yelled Tisa. She corralled the women to move closer to the river.

An oil fire. It had to be—it was the only way to get water to burn. This had been done with purpose.

"What have your people done?" Gunna demanded. She moved around Tisa and struck Lena on the face.

Lena staggered back, bumping into someone running by. The boats. The tents. The people. Everything was on fire. They couldn't stay here. To Tisa, Lena said with as much volume as she could muster, "Take them to the castle!"

"You want us all—" Gunna began.

"Wait!" Tisa commanded.

Lena cleared her throat and swallowed hard. "Through Clevehold. North. To the castle." She looked around and her heart pounded in her ears. People were dying. "I have to find my friends."

Tisa pulled Gunna away. She shouted orders and whistled before their forms disappeared around a patch of fire.

"The whip!" a familiar voice yelled. *Avild.*

In the river, people were climbing onto the shore. One of the ships remained on the water, burning brightly. The mast was tilted at an odd angle. Not the mast, she realized—the entire ship.

A teal light glowed in the water.

A coughing Ovnite near Lena threw a bucket onto a tent. They were about to head for the river. Lena caught them and said, "Water won't work. We have to leave. Go north, upriver." She let go of the person and continued toward Avild.

The teal whip emerged from the water and uncurled on shore. The other end fastened around Avild's wrist. She grabbed the teal magic with both hands, leaned back, and pulled.

Amundr was on the other end, fighting to stay afloat. His other arm was flailing, and his head dipped underwater. He was close to where the ship was going down.

Lena ran to Avild and grabbed her by the waist. Combining their weight, Lena leaned back and pulled. Steps in tandem with grunts, they kept pulling until Amundr's torso was ashore.

"My knife. Cut the net!" yelled Avild. She jutted her chin out to the gleam of metal in the grass near them. "I've got him."

Lena let go and grabbed the knife. She ran to Amundr, who was slipping back under the water. Using the light of the burning ship, she found the net dragging him down. It was too heavy for her to pull above the water. Wading in, she glanced back to the ship.

There were still people on it. The warmth felt hotter than the summer sun. Creaks and moans were muffled as it became further submerged in the river.

Amundr groaned. The whip was slipping from his hand.

Lena felt along his legs and found the net. With the knife under the water, she cut the nets away with a mix of haste and caution as not to cut Amundr's leg. Before long, he was freed enough to kick the rest of the net away.

The magic imbuing his whip stopped, and the plain rope fell to the ground. Amundr, on his hands and knees, coughed up water. He struggled to stand.

Lena put a hand out to steady him, though she didn't know how much help she could provide with his size, and guided him toward the shore.

"Briet," he called and coughed again.

"Did you see where they came from?" yelled Avild as she ran toward them.

Amundr wiped a hand over his eyes. "From the south."

"Tisa said the river is on fire that way," said Lena.

"Have you seen Harth?" asked Avild.

Lena shook her head. "I haven't."

The ship made a snapping noise. Yells picked up in intensity. As the mast broke and slapped the water, the wave sprayed them.

"We have to retreat back to Clevehold!" yelled Lena. She tried to push them in that direction.

"The Ovnite will be safe there?" questioned Amundr, his voice rough from coughing.

"You have my word," promised Lena.

"Get to the castle, both of you," commanded Avild.

"You have to come," urged Lena.

"Go. They're going to need you at the front when they're knocking on the castle doors," insisted Avild. "Go!"

WITHIN THE CITY OF Clevehold, the screams lessened, but the memories of them still rang in Lena's ears. By contrast, the city was quiet. No screams. No noise. The city was deserted.

Groups of Ovnites were ahead of her. As she reached the intersection leading to the castle, the crowd in front of her came to a stop. There were yells ahead. Lena recognized some of the accents as those of her people.

"You sent us this way," Amundr hissed. More than angry, he appeared concerned. He looked back over the crowd of people following them.

Lena pushed through the crowd. It didn't take long to get to the front. There, she was met with a line of guards, alternating with bows and swords.

"On my orders, you're to let the Ovnites through," said Lena.

Salvatore, on one end of the line, was the first to lower his weapon. He commanded, "Stand down."

"But sir," a guard protested.

Lena didn't let him finish. "See these people safely within the castle walls."

"You heard her!" Salvatore yelled, waving them forward.

Lena looked along the front row of Ovnites. Tisa and Gunna were there. They looked dirty, but unharmed. As they began walking, Lena promised, "Not much farther."

CLEVEHOLD

Salvatore led them to the drawbridge. There was a crowd waiting for them there, the Ovnite ambassadors and Tulir among them. The two crowds converged under the arch of the entry gate.

Tulir wrapped Lena in his arms tightly. "Thank goodness you're alright," he whispered into her hair.

Tears pricked in her eyes. Breaths came quickly as she turned her face in his neck. This was needed. It couldn't be afforded for more than a few seconds, so she soaked it up quickly. When they parted, she assured, "I'm alright."

"My people will be safe here?" asked Briet. She was ushering Ovnites past her, looking them over as they entered the castle walls.

"They will be," Lena answered.

At the same time, Tulir said, "You have my word."

"Sir, there are ships outside the doors to the Royal Docks," said a guard.

"The Ovnites' ships," said Lena.

Tulir looked around. He made eye contact with Briet. "I'll take Cicero to the docks. You and Lena cover this entrance."

Briet nodded.

"You'll be safe inside the castle," Tulir assured Lena. He kissed her on the forehead. His hand lingered on her face for a moment, and he leaned in to kiss her on the lips.

"Go," she instructed as they parted. He had to be at the docks. Whoever their enemies were, they couldn't get in with the crowd as cover.

What was happening to them?

Cicero left with Tulir. Lena, Salvatore, and the other guards kept an eye on the Ovnites as they flooded in. What was Lena looking for? How could she discern a foe?

The Ovnites. Briet and Kazio were receiving them. They had to trust the Ovnite ambassadors to pick out any pretenders in the crowd.

The last of the crowd funneled across the bridge. In the rear was a familiar face. Lena sighed a breath of relief.

"Sir," Salvatore acknowledged Harth as he came up.

"Is there anyone out in the city?" asked Harth.

"We began the city's evacuation when the fires started," answered Salvatore.

"This is everyone we could find." Harth gestured along the back of the crowd. "There will be others. Close up the bridge and gates. Send men over the livestock bridge to bring in any stragglers, and make sure the Ovnite validate them as their own."

Salvatore nodded and went to relay orders.

"Avild isn't with me. She left—said she was looking for you," Lena told him as they moved inside.

"She'll be alright." He wiped his hand down his face, clearing soot off. He looked dirty but uninjured. "If she wants to be found, they'll find her."

"Tisa, are you hurt?" called Briet.

"No," answered Tisa.

"Good. Go with the guards and take some Drengr. Make sure the city is clear and our people are inside," instructed Briet.

Tisa worked her way through the crowd to follow Salvatore. As she did, she was passed by someone pushing the opposite way. The mass of crowded panicked bodies were slow to move.

When Norman managed to get through, out of breath, he asked Lena, "Are you alright? They didn't hurt you?"

"I'm fine," she dismissed and looked to Briet. Kazio loomed with her. Lena asked, "Do you have any idea who attacked us?"

Briet's jaw was clenched. She looked around at her people.

"We don't know. They don't, either," answered Norman. "After the king sees the ships cleared in, we have to convene the Council, speak of what to do next."

"You mean what to do with us, yes?" questioned Kazio.

CLEVEHOLD

He looked surprisingly clean, given the rags he wore, Lena observed. They hadn't seen any troubles. Lena shook her head. "If your people weren't safe here, we wouldn't have harbored you through the front doors."

"If there's a discussion of our future to be had with the king, I will be privy to that discussion," said Briet.

"There will be time." Harth looked around and whistled to get the attention of guards. He ordered, "Clear out the eastern barracks, now!"

"Yes, sir," two guards said in tandem.

"It might not be the most comfortable, but it should fit all the Ovnite and be a roof over your heads," explained Harth.

"Put us all in one place," remarked Kazio.

Lena was distracted by a figure in the crowd. A tall woman with brown hair. *Nela?*

"Get all your people accounted for and calm. That's what they need," said Harth.

"Don't presume to tell us what—" Kazio was cut off when Briet put a hand to his chest.

"We appreciate an audience with the king shortly. Once affairs allow for it."

"You will have it," said Harth.

Disconnected, Lena said, "Amundr. Avild saved his life. Talk to him if you're worried for trust."

They might have said something else. Norman did, at least; she wasn't listening. Lena moved through the crowd to get closer to Nela. She couldn't believe it.

The instant Nela saw her, relief washed over her face. The sisters closed the distance and wrapped each other in a hug. Nela didn't smell like smoke or death. She hadn't been out there.

"When did you get here?" asked Lena.

Nela pulled back from the hug but held her sister at arm's length. Looking her over, she asked, "What's happened to you?"

Lena looked down. Her boots were muddy, one side of her was covered in soot and dirt, she must have smelled like smoke, and the side of her face felt puffy from where she had been slapped.

"I thought the city was supposed to be safe?"

Lena looked to the side. She let go of Nela and hugged her crying mother. But the last member of their family wasn't there. Worried, Lena asked, "Where's Father?"

"He didn't come," answered Nela.

"We arrived late yesterday. You weren't here," complained Mother. Her grip on Lena was tight, and tears were rolling furiously down her face.

Across the crowd, Lena saw Harth and Norman moving toward the inner wall. She struggled to push her mother off and said, "I have to go."

"What happened here, Lena?" asked Nela.

"I don't know, and that's part of why I have to go."

Nela nodded. Though she was scared, she understood.

"You have to stay with us," pleaded Mother. She pulled at Lena.

"Find Selgen. He can show you where to stay," said Lena. Was it still night? How close were they to dawn?

"At the front gate!" yelled a guard.

"Mister Rufino!" someone else yelled.

Harth turned around and went back to the gate.

"I have to go," Lena repeated as she began to walk away. What was Rufino doing back so soon? It couldn't be a coincidence of timing.

"We'll come with you," whined Mother.

"Nela, tend to her," Lena said as she pried her mother's fingers off her arm.

"Tend to me?" scoffed Mother.

Lena ignored it. Rufino was back. Three-fifths of the Council were headed inside. She had to convene with them.

LENA RAN UP THE MAIN staircase.

Harth must have heard her, as he stopped and turned back. He tapped Rufino to do the same. Norman wasn't with them. When she reached them, Harth instructed, "Tell her what you told me."

Rufino looked pale. He gulped and rubbed his hand over his mouth. Eyes unfocused to the east, he said, "That's Steepwharf's army out there." The focus zeroed in for him to look at the ring on his left hand. "I have to find Marisol."

"Once we talk to everyone," said Harth. He pressed on Rufino to get him to walk again. He also got Lena ahead of him to climb the stairs.

They weren't headed for the typical meeting room. Lena knew it once they rounded a corner. The door to the grand dining hall was open. A few voices were conversing within.

It was strange to see the hall empty. The fires were lit, but the tables had been pushed off to the side. In the center talking were Tulir, Norman, and Avild. She clutched a soot-covered sword in a damaged sheath.

Avild looked to the new arrivals as the door creaked shut. She exhaled heavily and dropped the sword. Her shoulders rounded in relief.

The release extended to Tulir, but not as heavily. Tulir must have only thought Harth was missing.

The Council plus Avild formed a circle, Tulir flanked by Norman and Harth, Rufino and Avild the next layer out, and Lena across from him. Harth put a hand to Avild's shoulder and nodded.

"I'm relieved everyone's alright," Tulir began.

"That relief is going to be short-lived. That's our coastal army who set the Ovnite on fire," said Harth.

"What?" exclaimed Norman.

Rufino, pale and shaky, wiped a hand down his face.

"They told you this?" questioned Tulir at Rufino. "Then they let you go?"

"No, no, this is a ploy to get in the gates, I'm telling you—" Norman was cut off when Tulir knocked his cane on the ground.

With strained patience, Tulir said, "Mister Rufino, please."

"I found out. I got ahead of them. I got here as quickly as I could," said Rufino. He breathed heavily. "The cities who put the death penalty on magic, they've banded together. They're coming."

"To fight the Ovnites?" questioned Lena. Did they need revenge heavier than their slight? From what they knew, there had been only a few deaths on the coast. Did they expect the king couldn't handle justice?

"They'll have their fight, regardless," said Harth.

"Did everyone from Clevehold and the Ovnites' camp make it inside?" asked Tulir.

"The gates were closed up. I sent out men to pick up the stragglers. Briet sent one of her people, too," answered Harth.

"Not all of the Ovnites made it," said Lena. The weight of the words made her close her eyes as she recounted, "The fire was set with purpose. I don't know how many Briet lost."

Norman stepped forward and pointed harshly at the ground. "Right now, we are aiding the enemy. Is that going to be the case when the armies of the coast arrive?"

"Enemies? The Ovnites didn't set their own camp ablaze," Lena argued.

"If I may make an assumption, the coastal armies attacked the Ovnites to see what we would do," said Rufino. Color was slowly returning to his face.

"They're testing your hand," said Avild.

"We failed their test," proposed Tulir.

"The river was set on fire beyond the camp. The Ovnite were being funneled toward us. There's a small chance Steepwharf knew we sent ambassadors, but the more likely scenarios are that they wanted to start a fight or force your hand," inferred Harth.

"These animals attacked Steepwharf. Of course they don't want us to harbor the aggressors," reasoned Norman.

"What right does that give them—" began Lena.

Norman cut in as if he hadn't heard her, "We need to set the proper precedent on what we think of these Ovnites."

"Steepwharf is the largest city on the coast. Whether the Ovnites came upon it by chance or aimed for it doesn't matter now. Steepwharf maintains magic should be outlawed, and they have all the neighboring cities and towns under that same assumption." Rufino stopped for a breath and to comb a hand through his hair. "They want the relinquishing of magic. In the worst case, to unseat the king for what's happened."

"They want control, and the attack opened the floodgates," summarized Harth.

"They will want to not only relieve us of magic, but of any technology they don't understand. How many centuries of innovation have they paved over?" worried Lena.

"We should have put a true representative of the southern coast on the Council. Perhaps then we would have had a pulse on this. Instead, we have a stand-in," Norman complained to Tulir while loosely gesturing at Lena.

"I'd have you replaced quicker," snapped Tulir.

Norman slapped his hand into an open palm. "That is your problem! Heart does not make a leader wise."

"Then you can be the one to go down there and attempt to evict the Ovnites, as that was an act of heart," argued Tulir. He slammed his cane once on the ground.

"I'm confident heart was the reason, but not for them. Something was missing, wasn't it? You invited the enemy in, sir. Understand that," rebutted Norman.

Lena looked to Harth. For *their* sake? Did Norman think Tulir had only opened the gates to the Ovnites for the return of his people?

Had he?

"We made a deal with the Ovnite to not attack. If we did not harbor them inside or forced them back out now, they would receive it as an act of war," explained Harth.

"We would be fighting them *and* the coastal cities," said Rufino. He gulped.

"The gates of the castle could not be breached by the Ovnites!" shouted Norman.

"The Ovnites are well versed in magic. I've not seen much, but if they had tried, it may have been possible," said Lena.

Traces of sunlight bled into the room. The night was ending. Birdsong would soon begin. Could the day be as peaceful as a melody, or would said melody provide the contrast?

"They wouldn't have had to try. If they camped outside the walls, we would be trapped here with the people of Clevehold. We did those estimates when they blocked the river. We have roughly a month within the walls for food," said Harth.

Rufino urged to Norman, "And in case you hadn't understood, it's the entire coast. The north. Your people, too, Norman."

"Our best army just became our enemy." Tulir shook his head, and his upper lip twitched. His grip on the cane clenched until it was white-knuckled.

"We could still negotiate," said Norman.

"To those who want magic to be a death sentence?" questioned Lena.

Harth looked back at the closed door. "The Ovnite are a proud and powerful people, heavily rooted in magic. Any negotiation terms from the coastal army includes slaughtering the Ovnite."

"That's not something we're willing to do, before anyone considers it," said Tulir pointedly.

Lena took a breath and felt her throat close on the exhale. In a quiet voice, she said, "They could leave."

Avild, who had been silent and expressionless, looked to Lena curiously.

"That would be ideal," said Norman.

Rufino scoffed.

Hands out into the circle, Lena tried to think quickly to get the words out. "No. They could leave. The Ovnites could go back down the river in what's left of their large boats, use their magic as shields, take little damage, and go back across the sea. We would then have to face the coastal armies. Without them."

"You're suggesting we partner with the Ovnites to fight our own people?" Tulir made eye contact with her as he asked.

"The Ovnites aren't the only ones with magic. They won't be the only ones targeted." Rufino wiped a hand on his forehead. He mumbled, "I need to sit down."

"May I, Your Grace?" asked Avild.

"Please," said Tulir before Norman could interject.

"If you feel you can't negotiate with the coastal army, the allies you have left are from inland." Avild's voice was level and concise.

As if our lives aren't dependent on it, Lena's thoughts worried.

"The Iste," said Tulir.

"They speak a different language. If you want to call on them to fight or just intimidate the coastal army, you will first need to find people like me to translate the message. Then it would be ferried there. A plea like this, when harboring an untrustworthy force yourself, is best made in person. Negotiations would happen, bargains and favors. I don't presume your knowledge, but that's time you don't have," explained Avild.

"The Iste also fight on horseback. Istedinium is plains. The advantages they have in retaining technology Steepwharf purposefully forgot is balanced by their lower numbers and their lesser ability to fight on our terrain. In the mountains, in the water—that's where Steepwharf will fight," said Harth. He, too, was calm.

Steepwharf. Not *the coastal armies.* There was no losing sight of who was at the helm coming for them. Lena swallowed. Her mind didn't want to accept the result. Steepwharf's army wasn't just coming for the Ovnites; that was simply their excuse.

"The coastal armies were smart enough to burn the Ovnites' boats. Of the three that made it into the harbor, only one is in good condition. They aren't going anywhere fast. It also gives us a good indication where Steepwharf will want to have this fight," said Tulir. He pressed his lips together in a tight line and shook his head.

"They'll have those ships mended in record time. Magic is how they did upkeep," said Avild.

"We're taking counsel from a historian," spat Norman.

Tulir leaned to the side and spoke lowly to Harth, too quiet for others to hear. Harth nodded and left the circle. He went to a tall window a few feet behind Norman and opened it. Crisp morning air wafted in, amplified by the waving curtains. Harth returned to the circle.

"Be careful not to step back," Tulir warned Norman. He then looked to Avild. "You were with the Ovnites. You know of the coast, and of Istedinium. Do you have any advice as to what we do next?"

CLEVEHOLD

Avild nodded. "Meet with the Ovnites' leadership. Not all of them, not the elder. You want their thinkers: Briet, Tisa, and one of the men she brought here. You want to be genuine in your concern for their safety and be vague about their possibility of leaving."

"Keep the focus on Steepwharf's army coming for them. Highlight a common enemy," surmised Tulir. "Briet, Tisa, and Cicero. He's heartful and intelligent."

Norman was about to open his mouth, but Avild cut in first. "And get rid of him, lest you desire more turmoil."

Lena detected a hint of an accent on her friend, and not one she had heard before. Had there always been nuances, or was the environment bringing it out? Was the Ovnite accent the way her speech truly was, and the exposure had revived it?

"To best show equal footing, when we meet, we shouldn't outnumber them," said Harth.

Rufino put a hand over his mouth and looked down. He muffled a cough.

"We'll do as we ask of them, but we want the firmness of the situation to appear friendly. Lena and"—he paused, looking at Rufino—"you, if you're up for it."

Rufino nodded. "I just need some water." He exited the group as he began to cough.

"Norman, if you would look in on our correspondence, perhaps someone from Istedinium responded," instructed Tulir.

"Yes, sir," he responded bitterly, then began turning to leave.

To Harth, Tulir said, "Double up the guards on the vault and assure the rotations on the wall are without gaps. And if it isn't spreading the men too thin, have plainclothes in the population. I want rashness down to a minimum."

"It will be done." Harth took quick steps to follow Norman.

"Shouldn't it be Avild to meet with the Ovnites?" asked Lena. She wasn't the one learned in negotiations or customs.

"I can be eyes in the barracks," offered Avild.

Tulir nodded. "Thank you, for that and the input."

Avild turned to leave.

The question Lena had asked hung unanswered. She reminded such with her eyes.

Tulir put a hand to the side of Lena's face. "You're on the Council, not her. Are you alright?"

Puzzled for a moment, she overlapped her hand on his and felt the raised mark where Gunna had hit her. "It happened when we were escaping. I'm alright."

"I never want to put you in that kind of danger again," whispered Tulir.

Lena gave him a small smile and squeezed his hand. "I was worried about you, too."

Chapter 13

THEIR TYPICAL MEETING room had been arranged to accommodate the two leaders. Tulir would sit on the end, as normal. Rufino, who had recovered his composure after his coughing fit, would sit on the right and Lena to the left. Across from Tulir was a similar high-back chair for Briet. The two seats to her left and right were open for her representatives.

Lena felt itchy. She didn't know if it was the dirt and soot on her skin or the anxiety. There wasn't time to change, and she didn't want to. The foremost reasons she wanted to return to her room were to wash her hands and find Socks. He must have been scared, not to mention hungry. She hoped he was hidden under her bed, safe from all this turmoil.

Footsteps approached the meeting room. Lena dropped her hands to stop her fiddling. Rufino straightened up and cleared his throat. Tulir remained where he was standing at the window, looking out over Clevehold.

The door opened. Salvatore, the guard on the door, said, "The Ovnites, sir."

"Send them in," responded Tulir without turning around.

Lena stood over her chair, as did Rufino, as they watched the Ovnites enter. Tisa led them, followed by Briet, then Kazio. Not the man they had asked for. Lena's hands clenched where they held onto the chair.

"Thank you for agreeing to meet with us so quickly," said Tisa. She moved slowly around the room and looked back when the heavy door creaked closed.

Briet eyed each of their belts. Tisa was the only one among them armed. She was also still covered in soot.

"You asked for my friend instead, but my presence was more practical," said Kazio. His mouth was open with a smile, save his eyes. He watched them as if he were a predator stalking lowly prey.

Lena couldn't help but let the corner of her mouth pull up. It was all an act with him. Always a show. That didn't necessarily mean there wasn't something innately wrong with him, but he had no reservations about playing it up. *How childish.*

"I trust everyone has been accommodated properly," began Tulir. He approached the table slowly. His face was shadowed by a lack of sleep.

"You effectively put us all in one place," answered Kazio.

"Giving the Ovnites the barracks was done in good faith," said Lena.

"*Ovnite.*" Kazio clamped his teeth down on the end of the word, then shook his head as he hissed an *S*.

"They opened their doors to us, yes?" Tisa stood beside Lena and gestured at the seat.

Lena nodded.

"I'll check with the stockers to make sure you have all the food and water you need," said Rufino.

Kazio traced a finger along the wall, grazing over a tapestry and skimming by a torch hilt. He then pulled back his finger and wiped it on his shirt. With raised eyebrows, he looked around the rest of the room.

"We can also have our doctors see to the injured," offered Tulir. He reached his chair and motioned at Briet to hers. He sat.

"Thank you," Briet said to Rufino, then looked to Tulir. "And that won't be necessary."

Everyone at the table sat. Kazio was the last to his chair and scraped it forward noisily. He sat with his elbows resting on the table, hands clasped.

CLEVEHOLD

Tulir spoke to Briet across the table. "I don't know how much you've relayed of our conversations to your people, and I don't know all of what mine have said to yours in the exchange. If at any point you need information or questions answered, please make it known." He leaned back and set his cane against the table. "For everyone, that is."

Lena nodded. She was impressed by his professionalism and the control in his voice. The others wouldn't know the last group meeting had involved snide remarks and a shouting match, though she assumed anger thresholds and perceptions had been amplified by the time of night. Now, they had to be gentlemen and ladies again in the daylight.

"The news I have is compiled by scouts, observers, and, in large part, my Council member from the western plains you haven't met yet, Rufino." Tulir gestured at him, then around the table. "This is Briet and two of her people, Tisa and Kazio."

"It would be more of a pleasure under better circumstances," said Rufino quietly.

Lena crossed her legs under the table. It was a good thing Tulir was the one talking. Rufino sounded too shaky.

"The coastal cities have raised an army, and not under my orders. They are the ones who attacked you. The bulk of their fighters are not yet here. They sent a small team ahead, specifically for sabotage. I have good reason to believe their intention is not simply to attack you, but to come for my city as well," explained Tulir.

"To attack their king?" asked Kazio incredulously.

Briet raised her hand and tilted her head to the side. After a pause, she brought the hand down and clicked her short nails on the table. "It is an odd story, yes?"

"But not the strangest we've heard," said Tisa. She sat straight, head high.

Tulir opened his palm at Rufino.

He cleared his throat. "I came back only a few hours ago. I was in Mudfalls. I never made it to Steepwharf, but I found out enough. Their discontent is rooted in the transgressions of the Stone King." Rufino stopped and looked to Tulir and Lena.

"They're aware," said Lena.

Rufino nodded and continued, "The continent outlawed magic. Some places, such as Istedinium, are defrosting on the idea of magic returning, but the coastal cities haven't the least bit abandoned the idea magic should be banned."

"Ban magic?" asked Tisa. She shook her head. "You've told us the legend, but what does this mean? How does a city, a continent, ban magic?"

"By use of ignorance and fear," said Lena. She took a deep breath. "I've done a lot of research and tracing since coming here. There are old books that are testament to the volatility of magic. The concept wasn't new in the time of the Stone King. When he encased himself and his family, the more conservative cities on the coast, chief among them Steepwharf, spread the idea magic was inherently evil. They set up punishments for using it. The king was dead, and the regions went on to work independently, but in order to maintain good relations and trade with other regions, certain values had to be shared. Thus, refusal of magic was adopted."

"It was the king killing his family that did this? Not the king trapping a region behind an impenetrable wall?" proposed Briet.

Rufino looked to Tulir, confused. Tulir put up a hand in caution and nodded at the other man.

With sympathy, Lena replied, "On our side of the sea, the tellings of what happened were recorded as a tale of complete slaughter. Saying the region was 'silenced' and 'lost' was translated as 'murdered.' And frankly, if the people of Steepwharf had known the truth, it only would have strengthened their case against magic, not helped you escape."

"When you say 'outlawed' and 'banned' . . ." Kazio continued speaking, his words toned as a question, but he mumbled too much in his accent to be understood.

"What do you mean by that?" Tisa translated.

"Death." Tulir held Kazio's eyes with his own. "Our librarian here in the castle—a few years ago, he was set to be put to death for his association to magic. Steepwharf's account is more complex than that, but in summation, the penalty of magic was—*is*—death."

"You employ a man who was set for death. How keen to turn away from transgressions of the past, yes?" said Kazio.

"That man was my former employer, and I still attest to his innocence," said Tulir sternly.

Don't lose sight of the argument and goals, Lena mentally pleaded.

"The coastal armies haven't taken well to magic returning, as you've showed me it has in Clevehold, and they plan to usurp you, yes?" summarized Briet.

"We happened on this continent as things got interesting," remarked Tisa.

Rufino did his best to stifle a cough.

"Why?" Tulir narrowed his eyes and leaned forward, focused on Briet. "Why did you come now?"

Kazio smirked.

"That wasn't rhetorical. Why did you come this far, for us, now?" He poked harshly at the table.

Tisa shrugged. "I don't see why that's of any concern."

"I've answered all questions you have of my city, my ancestors. Why now? The Binding was broken—you've said as much. *We* know why it could be broken, but without contact with the outside, it doesn't answer how *you* knew. Why now?" demanded Tulir.

"Is the temporary king looking to make more enemies?" Kazio coyly questioned.

"I've yet to be persuaded you're otherwise," returned Tulir.

Kazio snarled. He separated his hands and orange threads of magic hovered between them. He glared at Tulir.

Lena slapped her hand onto the table. The green glow from her palm created an aura spanning her hand. Orange magic was new. Perhaps she was outmatched, but there was an equal likelihood he had to consider the same. She concentrated on the magic seeping from her hand to make the glow appear more opaque. The more solid it became, the less she worried.

A low laugh worked its way out of Kazio's throat.

Tisa reached to place a hand on her sword hilt.

Scraping of wood reverberated through the room as Rufino nervously pushed his chair away from the table.

Briet stood fast enough for her chair to get knocked over backward. "Fae. Fae came over the Binding to tell us the king was finally dead. Both of you, enough."

Lena picked up her hand but let the aura fade slowly, purposefully.

Kazio snarled and looked to Briet. Her glare was insistent. He sighed and closed his hands, the threads dissipating.

"Fae told us the king was dead. It took us a year for the Binding to weaken enough for us to risk breaking it. The following year, half year, we used to build our ships," explained Briet.

Lena furrowed her brow. "Then you have to believe us."

"If you were waiting for the king of old to die, you knew about the Stone King," inferred Rufino.

The small green lights that had been revealed when the prince died—that was where they had gone. Lena would have considered why and what their intentions were, but she didn't know much of Fae. They were picky, vengeful, territorial. Though her interpretation originated from a child's story and Klaus' beliefs, the motives matched.

Briet leaned down to pick up her chair. "We knew his magic persisted. We didn't know why."

"Briet has come to the conclusion it wasn't the fault of anyone here or living why her people were trapped. Our sides of the world were both adversely affected," asserted Tulir.

The apprehensive look on Kazio's face told Lena he hadn't been privy to all of Tulir and Briet's discussions. Kazio wasn't just discontented with the verdict—he was surprised by it. Lena grinned.

Sitting gracefully, Briet nodded politely at Tulir. She said, "I agree your people pose no more of a threat to mine than mine do to yours."

"Not currently," added Kazio. He sniffed dramatically.

"Within the walls, we will keep peace," reminded Tulir.

"Mine and Cicero's Drengr will meet with your Royal Guards to determine any parameters our people may have to accommodate for one another," offered Tisa.

"The Ovnite will do what they can in exchange for the good faith gesture of letting us within your walls," agreed Briet.

Kazio looked at Briet. "His people are the reason, yes? They—"

"Those people are also going—" argued Lena.

"Enough!" yelled Tulir, stopping them both.

"While the Ovnite are here, we will return any earned respect," said Briet pointedly. Resuming a normal tone, she continued, "Until I decide what my people will do."

LIZ BUNCHES

A BATH. A CHANGE OF clothes. Brushing out her hair a few more strokes than necessary. Lena felt as clean as she reasonably could. She looked in the mirror and saw the swollen mark on her face. It wasn't much; it would fade in a day or two. She thought back to Avild's serum.

Medicine, not magic. She wasn't sure if she believed that anymore. Where she could get more or how Avild and Klaus had made it were beyond her. Her options were to find Avild and ask or go to the Ovnite for healing. Truthfully, she didn't want to do either.

Healing. She cursed. Tulir needed to know about their ability to heal. Had Briet told him about it? It couldn't be left to chance. Next time they spoke, she needed to tell him. For him alone, Lena could include details on how Avild broke her arm.

Harth knew. Was he telling Tulir? The thought came through with a snide connotation. She shook her head. That was the exhaustion allowing jealousy to poke through. The concept was still too new. She needed to get used to it.

She needed sleep.

But she couldn't find Socks. He wasn't in the room when she got there. There was evidence of his presence in bunched-up blankets. When she first came back, she had put her hand to the fabric to feel if it was still warm. It wasn't.

Lena had hoped in the time it took her to regain feeling like herself, Socks would return. An hour and a half had passed, at the least. No such luck.

She opened the food box and left it ajar. The meaty smell quickly permeated the air. If the cat was anywhere close, he would smell it. In a few minutes she would know if he was hiding close by.

Instead of waiting next to the smell, Lena went to the window. One hand on the wall, she leaned to look at Clevehold. She needed the cold stone under her hand to ground her. Otherwise, it wouldn't feel real. She was looking down on an empty city. Deserted. Vacant. Threatened.

It didn't feel like it had been only two years since she had first seen it this way. There had been so much life bustling about not a day ago. Despite the size of the castle, it was hard to believe everyone who had been out there was now within these walls. She had always considered the castle a huge building capable of it, but when the time came to test her assertion, it still felt hypothetical.

The situation was harder to believe still because the threat was unseen. No ships had come upriver. The group who attacked the Ovnite hadn't also tried to set Clevehold ablaze. Would they try?

Lena had given it enough time. Socks wasn't coming. She closed the lid and looked around. Not expecting to find him there but checking for peace of mind, she looked under the bed. It was vacant. Small tumbleweeds of dust and cat hair kicked up when she huffed.

Nela and Mother were downstairs. On her knees, Lena straightened her back and rubbed a hand down her face. She should go to them. They were scared. They wanted someone to comfort them.

I'm scared, Lena admitted to herself. She stood and wrapped her arms around her torso. What comfort could she provide them without answers? It hadn't been explicitly discussed, but Lena presumed everything talked about within the Council meetings was information restricted to those present. Not to say the people crowded below wouldn't find much of it out from whispers and assumptions, but it shouldn't come from her.

Her sister, she could trust. There was a yearning in her heart to talk to Nela about all of it. The issue was, Nela would not part from Mother. Not in this strange new place. Not when Mother knew there was information to be had.

Did she distrust her mother? Lena pondered the idea. No, trust wasn't the issue. The energy it would take was the obstacle. Mother was nervous and scared, and she would have no hesitation displacing her emotions onto others. Lena already carried her own fear; she didn't need more.

She realized she should check on Selgen. He was likely in need of company through all this as well. In the back of her mind, she wondered why he hadn't sought her out yet. It wasn't a secret she had gone to the Ovnite twice. The second time had been extended and ended in an attack. Didn't he want to know if she was alright?

No. She was wound too tightly to see Selgen right now. It would end in tears or a disagreement. Lena didn't have the capacity for that.

What she wanted to do was be with Tulir. They didn't have to talk; his presence would have been enough. Or they could talk about something else, anything else, to procrastinate worrying over the current affair.

She had to refuse that as well. There was a secondary issue there, one they needed to discuss once priorities allowed. It wasn't right to go to him and expect the major and secondary predicaments to *both* be ignored. He was bound to be busy.

What she needed to do was find Socks. One thing at a time. *Where would he have run off to?* He had free reign of the castle, but his options were narrowed by the commotion. Socks only liked people he knew.

Tulir's room? It was a possibility, but Lena didn't want to start there.

The mail room was out of the question. It was bound to have been busy. Even if it wasn't, the way to get there was too heavily trafficked.

The cells? Lena couldn't think of a good reason why not. The entire area was sealed off, but there were nooks and passages Socks could work his way through. He had seen her go down there before, followed her. It was as good a place as any to begin.

Lena checked her face in the mirror once more. The bruise was still there. Straightening out her dress, she took a breath. There was nothing she could do about it now.

On her way down to the cells, she used a look of concentration and intent. Her usual friendly, approachable behavior was reserved for when she meant it or when she needed to present it. People would understand her want for haste at a time like this.

The door to the stairs creaked loudly. Had it always emitted such a volume, or was she more aware now? Perhaps it had to do with others potentially being down here. Door closed behind her, Lena called out, "Avild?"

Despite her verbal protest at being in the castle, Lena doubted where else the woman would go otherwise. She had to be here. Would she risk going into Clevehold? The archers wouldn't know not to shoot her. Were they actively at war? Lena shook her head and yawned. Too jumbled. Everything felt too jumbled. She just needed to find the damn cat, then sleep.

Lena stepped heavily coming down the stairs, no regard for grace or posture. No one was there. Most of the time, she did it for herself. But why bother? She had almost died last night, and soon they may be invaded.

Fists clenched, she amended the thought. She wasn't under threat. They hadn't come for her. She could defend herself. Admittance of anything else just yet would shift her into a mindset she didn't feel equipped to handle.

It was a few degrees colder at the bottom of the steps. She wrapped her arms around herself. The weather would start changing soon. Her first winter in Clevehold had surprised her; the canals didn't freeze as much as Steepwharf's, despite being farther north. Someone had told her it had to do with the hot springs in the mountain. The water wasn't as cold as expected when it reached the bottom.

Lena took a breath, about to call out for Socks. Before she could, he poked his head out from a cell. She smiled.

He was apprehensive at first, but she could tell the instant he recognized her. The cat perked up, slinked out from between the bars, and bounced over. Purring, he rammed his head into her legs as he wove between them.

"I missed you, too," said Lena. She sat on the bottom step and scratched his head.

His eyes narrowed into slits and he tilted his head from side to side, changing the angle.

"Did you hide out when all the ruckus happened?" she asked. She switched to petting down the length of him and he squirmed. He jumped into her lap, rubbed his face against her, jumped down, and pawed at her boot strings.

"Stay away from the courtyard, alright? And stay away from the barracks," advised Lena. Her hand followed him to scratch at his ears and back.

"Meow," said Socks loudly. He pushed his head into her hand.

"No, I don't think they'll eat you."

He purred, chirped, and jumped into her lap again.

"Because I don't know if I trust them," she said. Her thoughts tried to pull her away, but she couldn't be distracted from Socks. He was moving around too much, demanding her attention. She smiled and focused on him.

"Meow," he said, quieter.

"Him, I do trust."

Socks chirped.

"Rufino, too. At least enough not to do something hasty," she considered.

CLEVEHOLD

The cat jumped down, trotted away to the wall, rubbed his face on it, and then turned back to look at her. "Meow."

"We lost track of Norman," she admitted.

Socks pawed at his ear. When satisfied, he shook his head.

"You're right. Harth would know where he is."

"Meow." He returned to her. With his face rubbing against her boot, he purred.

"I'm sure Avild could threaten him if we needed someone to." Lena raised her eyebrows and busied her hands petting him. "Someone not on the Council."

Socks looked her in the eye and let out a long "Meeeow."

Amused, Lena replied, "Avild is an old friend." She reached out to pet him.

Impatiently, he stood on his hind legs to meet her hand in the air.

"She had to leave. She lost part of herself. You'd like her, though. She was good with children. I'm sure that means she's good with cats."

A bootlace was in Socks' mouth, and as he pulled back it slipped from between his teeth. He tried again but was unable to get a better grip.

Lena looked down the row of cells. It was always so dark down here. She saw the keys sticking out of the far cell. *Selgen's cell.*

How long had they waited to give him those memories back? Was it when they arrived? Earlier than that? Or had they only been a few minutes too late? How different would his life have been if he had never seen all that his hands had done?

She sighed and rubbed her eyes. Where was her pity for him? The understanding?

Tired. After years of stagnation, she was tired.

Socks batted again at her bootlaces. He meowed and pounced.

Lena lifted her foot slightly and it startled him back a few steps. He pounced again. She smiled.

"Maybe the Ovnite can fix him."

"Meow," said Socks just before he jumped into her lap. He pressed his forehead to her nose. His entire body vibrated with purrs.

"I would like to learn it. Healing," she confirmed.

Socks stood on his hind legs and pressed his paws into her left shoulder. Lena wrapped her arms around him, and he purred powerfully.

"Even if I can't help him, it could make my magic good for something."

Chapter 14

THE COUNCIL CONVENED in their usual room. Coffee and food had been brought in. The bread and fruit had gone untouched, but the coffee was readily accepted by all six of them. No one looked as if they had slept well.

Lena pulled up the corner of her lip. It was strange how quickly her mind had seemed to accept Avild on the Council. She blended in as a natural addition. Rufino had taken well to her and asked little of the woman after being told she was a historian. Norman didn't like her, but Lena was sure it was all based on his opinion of women in general.

Rufino took a long drink from his coffee. Metal cup propped in his hand, he pointed at the map carved into the table with the other. "The coastal armies continue to move inland. The small force they sent ahead to attack the Ovnite retreated, but only so far as to join up with the rest. They're all headed this way now."

"Are they any threat to the towns and villages they're passing?" asked Harth. He had filled his cup but had yet to drink from it.

"Our scouts say no," answered Norman.

"They're taking on people as they go. Their army won't grow exponentially as they stop, but it is growing," said Rufino.

Harth rotated his metal cup slowly, mindlessly. "Accepting people and donations, no doubt."

"It's good. There's a benefit in them stopping. Their army grows nominally, but it means they're slower coming upriver," said Tulir.

Lena blew on the steam of her cup. The brown liquid was still too hot for her liking. "What have they done, armed the fishing vessels?"

"It still isn't going to give us much time," Norman replied to Tulir.

"That's exactly what they did," said Rufino pointedly. He glared at Norman across the table. Tone more professional, he continued, "They've armed both their large and small vessels. They reinforced the hulls and affixed spears. The boats aren't as large as the Ovnite's, but they have the numbers."

"How are we getting all this information?" asked Harth.

"Scouts," grumbled Norman impatiently.

"The people we send out mingle in the villages. Since they don't see a threat in the towns, our people go undetected," said Tulir.

"They truly aren't concerned." Rufino gulped down the rest of his coffee.

Harth stopped rotating his cup. "This was all planned before the Ovnite crossed the sea."

"I'm thinking the same," agreed Tulir.

Lena's heart clenched, as did her hands around the cup. The display on the map made it look so compact. There wasn't much room at all before Steepwharf's army would be at their door, stops or not.

"This all means our Ovnite *friends* won't be able to retreat downriver. The coastal armies may disagree with our stations, but the Ovnites are the reason they're coming now. The river is blocked, and they can't cross the sea on foot," declared Norman.

"I wouldn't count on them being stuck." Harth leaned back and traced his finger along the grooves of the map's edge. "With their magic, the Ovnite can manipulate the ground. It's how they carved their passage through the shallower bends of the river. Using it the other way, they can run boats aground."

"They also have shields, and they can heal," added Lena. She brought the cups to her lips. "They're fight savvy and prepared for defense."

"Apparently, not well enough," snarked Norman.

"Heal?" asked Rufino.

"We don't know the full extent of it. From what happened, we know there must be limits. It can't fix the dead." Lena looked to Tulir. "But it can mend a broken arm."

"You've seen this?" Rufino set his cup down, his eyes wide.

"They mended Avild's arm," answered Lena. She gestured to the woman at the opposite end of the table.

Rufino turned to ask her. "How did you break your arm?"

Avild stared at the map before her. Lena knew from the look and posture she wasn't going to answer.

"She took a bad step," said Harth.

Tulir moved his half-empty cup off to the side. Gesturing at the map, he said, "With or without the Ovnite, we would be outnumbered. Lesser so, if they stayed."

"The Ovnite may fight the coastal armies on river in a want for revenge. If they're smart, they won't," said Harth.

Lena nodded. "They only need enough effort to slip past and get to open water."

Norman pointed across the table at Rufino, then poked his finger into the rolling plains of the map. "The armies in the west are no closer to coming to our aid?"

Rufino hesitated.

"The armies in the west aren't going to lay down their lives for a new king. Not when those they're fighting are their trade partners, and not if there isn't conviction in victory." Tulir took a long breath and combed a hand through his hair.

"Would we have a fighting chance against the coast if Briet's people stay?" Rufino asked Harth.

Harth scanned the map. "It's possible."

Lena set her cup down. "So, the question becomes: how do we convince Briet to stay with her Ovnite and fight with us?"

"For us," corrected Norman.

"We want the same things now." Rufino swept his arm over the map. "Surely, we can use the commonalities to reach a compromise."

"She made no demands, not before or after her people were forced within our walls." Tulir looked to Harth, then Lena, to ask, "Did her people give you any indication while you were there?"

"No," answered Harth.

Lena shook her head.

"Everyone wants something," said Norman.

"They have land across the sea suitable for farming. They must have forests enough to build, given their ships, and ore enough for their swords. Their waters are good for fishing. It won't be the land that keeps them here," explained Harth.

Rufino proposed, "Gold? We have more than we could spend in a lifetime in the vault."

Norman was about to interject but Lena interrupted, "I would gladly open the vault, but the Ovnite have no currency. They wouldn't recognize the value."

"A purchased ally also isn't the most secure one," said Harth.

"Would it be worth the attempt? We don't need to build a lasting relationship, only a temporary one," argued Rufino.

"Could we use the gold on Steepwharf's army?" asked Lena.

Harth shook his head.

"I don't think any amount of money would do it," said Tulir regrettably. "Once we offer up that level of compromise to them, we've lost."

"No currency. A mark of a primitive society," grumbled Norman.

"They aren't going to evolve quickly enough for gold to mean anything to them," snapped Tulir. His elbow came dangerously close to knocking into his cup when he pulled back.

CLEVEHOLD

Lena didn't want to pile on pessimism, but she felt a duty to verbalize all their options as she saw them. Even the ones said for the sake of shutting away the option. "The Ovnite are further along than we are with magic for not having shunned it for nearly a thousand years. We can't offer them magic or techniques."

A flash of Gunna trying to fight her way into Kasper's tent rushed to mind. Lena's eyes flicked to Avild. There were no magic techniques Lena was comfortable with offering.

"There isn't enough time to round up and train our own people to fight, I'm assuming," said Rufino.

Harth shrugged. "Depends on how long Steepwharf wants to keep us hiding behind these walls. Chances are, the longer we wait, the less effective we're going to be."

"What about offering the Ovnites livestock? A lesser people may find an appeal in tangible and edible goods," suggested Norman.

Tulir covered his mouth, and his shoulders shook. He looked to Norman and proposed, amused, "What? Enough cows for them to risk their lives fighting alongside those they crossed the sea to fight?"

"We can't lose sight of why they crossed the sea in the first place. We harbored them and we are aligned enough not to fight within these walls, but we are not allies," reminded Lena.

There was a pause. They looked to the map, then to each other. The only sounds were those carried in from outside. None of them shuffled or adjusted.

Harth laid his hand flat on the table. Not looking at her, he asked, "What does the historian think of this impasse?"

The eyes of everyone else shifted to Avild. Lena noted the woman had been quiet in the debates. Avild's face wasn't blank, but the thoughts she computed weren't displayed well enough to read.

Slowly, Avild drummed her fingers on the table. Her eyes connected with Tulir's. When he gave a small nod, she said, "Steepwharf may approach under the guise of negotiation at first, but they will not accept less than what they came for. Clevehold starves, surrenders, or fights. All of those involve bloodshed. Starvation is dangerous, because it will lead to chaos. Let's avoid that. Surrendering comes with the same cost as losing. You don't want that. Fighting, or at the very least puffing out your chest, means you need numbers enough to make Steepwharf worry. You need the Ovnite to stay, but you can't threaten them, and you can't strongarm them. But unlike Steepwharf, they will bargain for the right reason. Lands, riches, magic—we're covering basic negotiation tactics. Title. Title is what's left."

Tulir sat back in his chair, not averting his gaze. He was thinking.

Harth sighed.

"It's a far jump," said Tulir.

Avild stopped her drumming fingers and laid them flat. "You can be overtly political and talk yourselves in circles and let Steepwharf get another week closer, or we can have the conversation now."

Confused, Lena offered, "They have no want for titles. They think them hollow. Besides, titles are superfluous to what they already own."

"I'm sure the king believes the one who acquires the title of queen is a matter of heart," said Norman. There was a small satisfied grin buried a few layers deep in his words.

Lena looked at him, then back to Avild. *Queen? Who, Briet?*

"Historically, a wed queen is limited in her power," said Harth. His phrasing wasn't a deterrent, but a launchpad for dissents.

Avild used it. "That is for the king to decide."

"Is it?" asked Tulir in a quiet low voice. He rubbed a hand over his mouth.

Lena felt her heart rate increasing. They couldn't—not for the sake of stripping Lena's future title, though she couldn't help but take it personally. Aside from Avild, Lena was the Stone King's closest heir. She held his magic.

"And that is something he would have to decide before making the proposal," said Avild.

Thoughtfully, Tulir said, "If I make this offer to Briet, she will recognize how desperate I am, we are. What's stopping her from killing all of us and taking it for herself?"

"The wrath of the king's magic," proposed Rufino.

Controlling her breathing, Lena tried to logic their way out of it. *This cannot be the answer. For the true line to continue, the truest it can be, it cannot be Briet.*

But Lena couldn't tell them that.

"Aside from the complications of the result acting as a deterrent, we aren't that desperate. Not as far as they need to know. Briet represents the power of the East, because goodness knows there isn't much else over there. You're both hearty magic users. With you and she, you control both sides of the sea," explained Avild.

"There's the plains people coming from the west. They will fight against the coastal armies *if* they believe they'll win," said Harth. His expression was too serious to read.

"A chance you have with the Ovnite. A chance the Iste will take because they want to reap the reward of the king's favor," added Avild. "They'll want their piece of the power and glory that comes with sacking the coastal cities."

"Sacking the coast?" questioned Norman.

Lena felt as if she couldn't think straight. This was all wrong. Yet, she didn't have a nonpersonal sharable reason to provide her insights.

"If Briet becomes queen, and I'm saying within the week, you send word to the Iste." Avild traced her finger on the map as she spoke. "The stronghold in the East has aligned with you. Magic is prioritized. Insolence against that will not be tolerated. If they want to retain influence and good favor, they have to abide these terms. In return, when the fighting is done or the deals brokered, there will be a complete overhaul of powers on the continent. More seats on the Council. Access to priority to ports here and on Briet's side in the East. Whatever it is, they're going to want."

"If Steepwharf bargains, it'll only be a placeholder. They can't be given the chance to regroup to strike again," said Harth.

"But you said making the plea to the Iste would take too long," reminded Lena.

"Sending someone in person to make a plea, yes," agreed Avild. "However, by bird, providing them an offer like this, they may be receptive. The fight only happens if the coastal armies want to take on the Ovnite, us, *and* the plains armies, and the Iste will know that. Power is your biggest influencer."

"As long as the coastal armies keep taking their time, we make the attempt," said Rufino.

"If Briet knows we're doing this and has a perceived reason why, it should build confidence with the Ovnite," said Harth. The end of the statement sounded sour, as if the words fought him on the exit.

He doesn't like this idea any more than I do, thought Lena. He knew the logistics of why they shouldn't just as well. The same reasons kept his deterrent unsaid.

"You intend to unseat those in local power in Steepwharf, Mudfalls, and all the other large cities along the coast?" clarified Rufino.

"The coastal army would have the option to submit to the king and queen, relinquish their warships, and return. Otherwise, we fight them with the Ovnite and the plains army, and we force them to do just that. Only if they fight, they'll have less people remaining and the internal political overhaul becomes easier," answered Avild.

"Is it better if they fight us or not?" questioned Tulir.

Lena's mouth opened slowly. "Harth's right. If Steepwharf bargains for peace, it will be temporary. If they don't fight, you would still have to kill some of them to make a point. Their insurrection can't stand unpunished. They would only try again."

Deep breaths puffed up Tulir's chest. He gestured at the map. "That doesn't fully solve why Briet would want to help us and risk her own people. A war that isn't hers to fight."

"Her people came across the sea looking for a fight. Redirecting their rage is safer for her than telling them to turn around and go home emptyhanded," reasoned Harth.

"If she takes her people back down the river, she's going to encounter an army. She doesn't know how formidable they are," said Avild.

"It's a risk to her either way. We have to make the risk she takes for us more appealing," said Rufino.

Tulir smirked and shook his head. It wasn't a refusal to their points; he simply looked tired.

"Don't doubt Briet knows she could start killing people down there. If she did, then she would have to fight a two-front war. Without you to fight, if you're dead or roll over, Steepwharf would actively pursue her Ovnite," advised Avild.

"Steepwharf doesn't have the ships to follow the Ovnite out into open water, if they get that far," said Rufino.

Avild turned up her palm. "Briet doesn't know that."

"The Ovnite have been locked away for centuries. They aren't ignorant, but they likely overestimate how much the world has evolved over that time," agreed Harth.

Lena let out a sound that married a scoff to a laugh. "We're going to use their ignorance against them?"

"We will use them." Tulir downcast his eyes. "And they will use us."

Chapter 15

"ARE YOU ALRIGHT?"

The question broke Lena out of her head. She was on a balcony, looking out over Clevehold and thinking how afraid of heights she used to be. It had been her greatest fear to fall through the empty space. Now, she felt numb. Indifferent. She didn't have room for such things.

Lena turned to face Marisol and answered, "It's been a trying few days."

"I can't imagine. Rufino hasn't told me much about anything, but I can see it's weighing on him." Marisol walked to the balcony and set her hands down lightly onto the stone. "We don't have to talk, if you don't want."

Lena smiled. The mannerisms Marisol displayed reminded Lena of who she used to be. How she had acted. Marisol was a conventional woman, especially in the eyes of the Council. It made Lena admire her for her composure and consistency, but also hate her slightly. Didn't Marisol know that lifestyle was a cage?

A deep breath cleared some of Lena's mind. She didn't hate Marisol. Neither did she envy the woman. They were different—their paths were different. Somehow, Lena's path had brought her to the Royal Council to discuss war. It felt too large for her life.

"How receptive were you when Rufino proposed you move out here?" asked Lena.

Surprised, Marisol pulled her head back and looked around thoughtfully. "Well, he and I weren't married when the idea first presented. He wanted to chase it. He wanted to know what I thought about him chasing it. I could tell it was what he wanted."

"Is that why you agreed?" asked Lena.

"Yes and no. I love him, always have. He's a strong-willed man. Not to say I made him what he is, but I don't know he would have done it if I hadn't come with him." Marisol laughed and rubbed her hands together. "He's so smart, but he needs a nudge sometimes. Someone to keep him upright."

Lena smiled. "I think that's fair to say of a lot of men."

The sun was encroaching on the shadows of Clevehold. From how high up the side of the castle they were, the noises of the city weren't heard. Lena imagined it was only creaking doors left open and curtains flapping in the wind. No one had gone back into the city. No one had come.

"We missed you at dinner last night," offered Marisol.

Lena hummed. She hadn't had the stomach to face them. Didn't want to give them the opportunity to speak about the future around her. Couldn't stand the idea that she had no say in it. There she was again, getting moved around the board like a pawn.

"Harth didn't join us either. Well, he was there for a few minutes, but he left so soon after," continued Marisol. "I'm sure he has duties. He's a busy man, guarding our defenses."

Lena held her chin up. Of course Harth had advocated for Tulir to do what was best to keep them all safe. Of course Harth had put the logical solution out there, or at least inferred it, and agreed when Avild verbalized it. The arrangement would make sense, and because it was the best road to keeping Tulir safe, Harth had agreed.

How big of an argument had Tulir had with him after the meeting? Had accusations been thrown around? Had they yelled? Had Tulir impressed upon him the point that he loved Harth and loved Lena and didn't want to get married off to a new foreigner for the sake of safety? Lena liked to think it had been a fight. Perhaps Tulir had able to make his point well enough for reconsideration.

CLEVEHOLD

No. It wasn't about them. The reasoning wasn't personal, or wasn't *only* personal, she amended. Marrying Tulir off, passing him off as the Stone King's heir, posed a risk in itself. What if Briet found out? The Ovnite would kill him for deceit.

Harth wouldn't betray Tulir. Lena wouldn't. Avild was the one who had suggested making the alliance. As much as she may have wanted to see her father's legacy...

Lena laughed, moving to cover her mouth. The Stone King's legacy. Avild didn't want it. She wanted it burned, wanted it gone. It had purposefully been abandoned at every opportunity to take it up. Avild wouldn't reveal Tulir to be a false heir because she didn't care of the legacy.

"Everything alright?" asked Marisol.

"Yes, sorry," apologized Lena. She cleared her throat to eliminate the last of the laughter. "Our predicament is a strange one, and it's brought out an equally strange reaction in me."

"You should join us for dinner tonight. A bit of laughter wouldn't go unnoticed," said Marisol. She pulled her loose hair over her shoulder.

There was no hiding from it. She may not have the final say, but she was allowed input. Briet posed a threat to Tulir, she supposed. The proposal of such a tangent could spark the right conversation. Regardless of the outcome, she couldn't hide from this.

Lena nodded. "I plan to be there."

IN THE AFTERNOON, LENA went to the lower level of the castle, near the post room. She had casually been around the upper premises after her talk with Marisol, but she hadn't been able to find whom she was seeking out. *I should check on Selgen. I should find Nela or Mother.*

"Sir?" Lena said to get a guard's attention. When she had it, she asked, "Do you know the whereabouts of Missus Avild?"

"A private courtyard, in the rear, ma'am," he answered.

"Thank you," she responded. Walking in that direction, Lena considered what she was doing back there. At least she was away from the Ovnite. Away from the city people.

Lena walked into the sunlight. The rear courtyard was small and didn't see much daylight. It was triangle shaped and wedged between the mountain and the castle, only getting direct sunlight in the midday hours. The courtyard was situated overtop food stores and supply stocks.

"Miss Lena," greeted Avild. The sleeves of her dark-green shirt were pushed up past her elbows and she wore trousers and boots. Her hair was pulled back in a simple fashion, kept off her neck.

Lena hadn't noticed before, but her clothes weren't Steepwharf fashion. The material was closer to that of the clothes kept at the cabin. The knees were worn thin. The boots were broken in. There were greys in her hair. Not many, but she had known Avild two years ago, and there had been none.

What had she told Harth? "Didn't operate like she used to"?

Avild was aging.

"The guards told me I could find you here," said Lena. She kept her hands clasped behind her back and casually looked around. No one else was out there.

"Did you want to talk to me about something?" Avild remained in place as Lena approached.

"I did," Lena confirmed, voice kept low. She stopped with a foot of space between them.

The corner of Avild's lip pulled up in a smirk. "It's your castle, ma'am. You're allowed to ask me what I'm doing here."

Lena took a deep breath and decided to play along. "Alright, Missus Avild, what are you doing here?"

"It's old-fashioned." Avild turned and tilted her head to the side to look up at the mountain.

"What is?" asked Lena impatiently. She walked to stand beside Avild, their backs to the castle.

"Widows getting called Missus. Most people reverted to calling Nela 'Miss' after her husband died, or didn't you notice?" said Avild. She looked to Lena. "You've not been to see your sister since she came."

Feeling the first of anger bubbling up, Lena defended, "There's been much to do."

Avild inclined her head. "It was a question, not an accusation."

"We don't have room for those," Lena returned. She thought quickly. The courtyard was chosen for privacy and space. "You were out here practicing magic?"

"I thought you didn't have to say it like it was a bad word around here?" proposed Avild. She nodded. "Yes, Tulir asked me to teach him. I obliged."

"It's a good idea," Lena agreed. The more he knew of magic, the less inconsistent their story would be. Lack of basic knowledge could have been attributed to previous ignorance. The only issue was if Tulir wasn't grounded. "No issues with his acclimation?"

"He's had the patience to learn to sword fighting left-handed. So long as he continues to approach magic with that same level of patience, he'll do fine. It was a promising start."

Tone respectful and even, Lena asked, "Do you know if he's going to speak with Briet about the proposal?"

"He already has."

Lena's heart dropped. Her breath caught. Attempting to retain composure, she clasped her hands together and pressed her shoulders back. The mere idea of a proposal had only been borne yesterday. Twenty-four hours, at the most. *When? Why?* "Has she answered?"

Avild's posture softened. Tone apologetic, she said, "All but the date is set."

"Don't say it like you're sorry," hissed Lena. It was a decided plan. Decided and done, without her. She truly had become insignificant.

"I didn't realize until just now how much you had grown to care for him."

Lena swallowed down a lump in her throat. It was all business. What was best for Clevehold. Surely, Tulir hadn't been nervous when he proposed the idea of marriage to Briet. Their relationship was transactional. Shaking her head, Lena forced a steady breath. "Would it have changed your mind?"

"No," admitted Avild simply.

Of course not. In the grand scheme, it wouldn't have made sense to object. Had Harth learned that line of thinking from Avild, or were morals more deeply sown than that? And where would he fit into all this, with Tulir marrying a foreigner?

Out of the way—like he had offered. Perhaps if Lena had seen through to an accepting conclusion when Tulir broached the subject of two simultaneous loves, they wouldn't have been at these crossroads. Or perhaps things would have moved too quickly to matter regardless. With their current trajectory, Lena didn't see a way for any version of Tulir's compromise to come to fruition. It had taken years for Tulir to confide his preferences to Lena. If he and Harth kept at whatever was intended, it would pose a risk.

Part of Lena wished there was some satisfaction in it. If she couldn't have Tulir to herself, he couldn't get his compromise, either. But that part of her was small and shrinking. Ultimately, it just hurt. She and Harth had both lost.

"He also spoke with Briet about formal titles to ensure other people's stations. You're now a duchess," said Avild.

CLEVEHOLD

Lena blinked hard against tears and pocketed her sadness. The titles didn't matter. They never had. It wasn't about being queen and the influence such a position held. It was about the legacy, as much as it had been personal.

"The line of the Stone King's magic will be broken if she marries him," whispered Lena. It should have been the last point she had to make to Avild. The other woman *had* to have known. What was her rationale?

Avild stood sideways to look around. No one was nearby. "You can marry whom you choose. Sleep with Tulir. The line continues."

Lena's mouth hung open. She exploded, "A bastard line!"

"Shh," Avild urged and stepped closer. "Your children will inherit your title. Have daughters. One of those girls will marry Briet's firstborn son. Bastards no longer."

"Marry their half-sibling?" whispered Lena incredulously.

"Then have the other man's child. It won't be legitimized until your grandchildren's generation, regardless," said Avild.

"You make it sound so simple," bit Lena.

"You're a woman of court, a duchess. It *is* that simple. You may be asked to do your part in bridging the gap by marrying an Ovnite. If you're especially lucky, they'll let you choose."

Lena pulled her head back. "Lucky?"

"There's the soldier. Strong and kind, from what I can tell. Patient enough to sit through all those new tattoos. If you want to keep a hearty magic line, there's the ginger one, the Vitki leader. Or their Elder. He doesn't look to be much over forty but may be physically unwell. Seems to vary day to day how human he looks," listed Avild.

"I . . . why would . . ." Lena couldn't force out more than a few stammered words.

Avild ran her tongue across her front teeth. "Did you think my life as a princess was delicate and kind? That I was presented with an abundance of choices?"

"I didn't ask for this station. I didn't ask for this magic," reminded Lena.

Avild scoffed and pinched the bridge of her nose. "I gave you the option to leave outright and to let this place stay dead. A different lie, one that let things be. You chose to revive it."

LENA MADE A POINT TO arrive early to dinner. She took her normal seat beside Tulir. She noticed the table was made up for twelve, with five settings on one side and seven on the other. The two settings in the middle of each row included an ornate goblet beside the plate.

The servants were pouring wine into their glasses as Cicero arrived. He looked a touch pale but brightened up to a smile when he saw Lena. The shirt he wore had sleeves rolled up to his biceps and showed off the circles and waves of tattoos winding up his arm in greyscale.

She stood and met him on the side of the table. A thought crossed her mind—*Does he know?* Had Briet told her people? Was it a secret?

Cicero alternated between an attempt to hug her and shake her hand. Fumbling with a smile, he ultimately took a loose grip of her hand. He hesitated before bringing it close to his lips to kiss overtop it.

"Was that right?" he asked as he let go.

"It was fine," laughed Lena. She gestured at the table. "Please, sit."

Cicero looked at the array. He looked over his shoulder and asked quietly, "Where?"

Lena laughed again. Kindly, she pointed to the seat across from hers. Having a warm soul on her direct eyeline may make the night more bearable.

"Thank you, Miss," he said and inclined his head. Quickly, he corrected, "Duchess."

"You'll get accustomed to it all quite quickly," she assured.

They took their places at the table. Lena saw him eyeing the wine glass and looking around. To give covert permission, she took hers, held it out for a toast, and drank from it. Cicero did the same.

A group of Ovnite walked into the dining hall. There wasn't enough room for them all, but Lena assumed the one empty table was reserved for them. Briet was with her people and pointed along the row of benches. She patted one of them on the back, then moved toward the head table.

Her clothes were formal. She wore trousers instead of a skirt. One small knife was strapped to the outside of her boot, gleaming in plain sight.

"I hope your people don't object to our"—Lena held up a spoon—"practices."

Cicero smiled. "Some of us are used to it. We'll show the others how."

"Oh?"

"People from where Kazio and I are from, we grew up with it. The country people, not so much," answered Cicero. He was looking around at the tall windows and tapestries.

Lena nodded and made a tight-lipped smile. *All for show*, she thought. She looked at the table of Ovnite. Some did have more of an olive-toned skin, like Kazio and Cicero, the utensils group. They were outnumbered by the paler Ovnite.

"Have things been going well, or as well as can be expected?" asked Lena.

"Yes. The barracks are lesser cramped than the ships, which is a relief. Don't have to sleep in swinging beds." He mimed rocking back and forth.

Coughs echoed in the hall. Lena observed her people staring at the Ovnite making the noise. They shook their heads and turned away.

Was that what it came down to? *Their* people. *Our* people.

Briet approached the table and sat beside Cicero, offering a polite nod at him and Lena. Her eyes glanced down at the silverware flanking the plate.

"It's easy," said Cicero. It sounded like he was reminding her. He picked up the fork and twirled it between his fingers.

Lena smiled. While Cicero and Briet were watching people funnel into the hall, Lena took the opportunity to study the latter. Briet had pretty blonde hair, a symmetrical face with a hint of freckles, and blue-green eyes, the color of Ovnite magic. She was beautiful. As long as her and Tulir's children were taller than her, they would be perfect.

A door at the other end of the hall opened. It wasn't loud; people at the long tables likely didn't hear it over the commotion. Lena knew what it was without looking. The private door. Only members of the Council used it.

Was it now Briet's entrance as well? Avild had said titles were provided to people to ensure station. Did that mean members of Briet's Council had them, too?

The footsteps that approached the table had an irregular clunk. Tulir with his cane. He was alone.

Cicero pushed his chair back in a rush to stand.

"No need," Tulir insisted, a hand up. He sat heavily on his chair and winced. He pulled his leg under the table slowly. The area around his knee was enlarged under his trousers, as if there was a bandage wrapped beneath. He caught Lena looking and explained,

"Sparring earlier. I took a calculated fall, but it's not something I see myself repeating."

"Is there a penalty for hurting the king?" asked Briet.

"Not when he asks for it," replied Tulir. He looked to the left and right. "I was expecting to be among the last here."

"Marisol said Rufino was going to follow up on inquiries before dinner. I don't know of Harth and Norman," offered Lena. She sipped her wine. She was surprised to find the cup was already empty.

"Harth assigned himself shifts on the wall." Tulir picked up his glass and said lightheartedly, "And I'm sure we'll all hear Charlot coming."

"She is an odd woman. Only met her once," commented Cicero. He looked back at the sounds of more coughs from the Ovnite table.

Lena wondered if Harth's absence was planned to provide space. It clearly wasn't at Tulir's orders, based on the dissatisfaction of the tone. Distance was supposed to make it easier. Her eyes flicked to Briet, and Lena thought, *She has no idea.* In her heart, Lena knew Briet never would. It wouldn't have been the first falsehood Tulir had been forced to build from.

"Is there a sickness amongst your people?" asked Tulir.

The servant came around and poured Lena another glass of wine.

Briet nodded. "There are some who are sick. Unfortunately, in the attack we lost Kasper, our best healer."

"But you still have healers?" asked Tulir.

Briet nodded. "From our Vitki, yes. They are newer to the practice, but promising."

"Why not use them to heal those with minor sickness?" Tulir reached for his water glass, avoiding the obscene goblet.

"Once we heal a wound using magic, if it isn't fully healed, the second attempt won't work. We try to avoid healing minor afflictions at the risk of missing an aspect of the sickness that causes relapse," explained Briet.

"You have to save it for when you need it," surmised Lena. She took another sip of her wine.

"Yes." Briet nodded.

Lena felt her face growing warm. She set the glass down and smiled across the table at Cicero.

"I'm sorry about your healer," said Tulir.

"I appreciate it. He was a good friend to me when I was part of the Vitki. A loyal and generous man," said Briet.

"How is Gunna doing?" asked Lena. The sounds of crackling fire encroached in the background noise of the room. The screaming. Lena clenched her hands together under the table.

Cicero cleared his throat and sipped his wine. Voice rough, he answered, "Not in good spirits, as you can imagine, but she's holding up. Unfortunately, she got sick not too long after we got here. She's strong."

"I'll speak with the doctors I have on staff and those who came in from Clevehold. I'll have them go to the barracks to do what they can," promised Tulir.

The tall man, the Ovnite Elder, approached the table. He had an odd hunched sway to his walk and looked around as if he was waiting for an ambush. The clothes were the same brown with blue threads. His head was freshly shaven. Lena couldn't recall his name.

"I can retrieve any funds that are needed to cover the cost from the vault," said Lena.

"We appreciate it," said Briet.

Amundr. She made a mental note as it occurred to her. More of his arms were exposed and she looked for tattoos, but the yellow-tinted skin was bare. She looked at him and compared his features to the other pale Ovnite. The features were the same, save the height. It wasn't lineage that altered his skin tone—Avild must have been right. There was something wrong with him.

"Just be sure not to run your men too ragged mending those ships," said Tulir.

Briet smirked. "When they're done with mine, we should be building more, yes?"

"I believe it would be advantageous. It keeps the workers occupied, strengthens our forces—I see no detriment, since you said we have all we need," answered Tulir.

Cicero looked back when Amundr was close. He asked, "Kazio?"

"Stayed to keep an eye on the river." Amundr stood behind the open chair next to Briet and squinted down at the place settings. He tsked.

"Before you sit," Briet said to Amundr, then looked to Tulir. "You trust me, yes?"

Tulir sat back slightly. "In so much that we've discussed."

"Let Amundr heal your leg," she proposed.

Tulir waved it off. "I don't need to be coddled for a novice injury. It was a fall."

"Please," she insisted, nodding at Amundr. "As a token. We cannot pay your doctors, but we can offer assistance to the injured."

Lena realized Tulir had looked at her. Behind the layers of composure was a hint of apprehension. They wouldn't see it. "You should let him."

Tulir nodded. He pushed his chair back to stand. The cane was hooked onto the back of the chair and clattered to the ground when he reached for it. He cursed.

Amundr was around their side of the table. Picking up the cane, he placed it on the back of a different chair. His fingers drummed in the air, and threads of teal magic wove around them. He bent down and put a hand to Tulir's knee.

Tulir winced but hid the grimace well. One hand propped on the table, he kept balance. He lost some color in his face.

As Amundr's hands extended a few inches above and below Tulir's knee, a residual glow grew. The power hummed. The general commotion of the room died down. They were all watching.

The glow died away. Tulir visibly relaxed.

Amundr stood and backed away a step. He seemed steadier. It was either the light, or magic, but the yellowish tint of his skin had faded.

"Thank you," said Tulir. Lena could tell he was still keeping the weight off of it.

Amundr grabbed the cane and took it with him as he took another step back.

Confusion was Tulir's first reaction to the backdrop of silence. His leg straightened fully to take his weight. His hand came off the table. A relieved, almost mischievous look crossed his eyes.

Just like that, the gimp Rether's men had caused Tulir was gone. Lena's heartbeat quickened. Her mind scrambled to find fault in Briet's motive to do it here and now. It came up justified. Performing such an act in front of the people of Clevehold, who knew little of advanced magic, could have been interpreted as the framework of a threat, or simply a display of power. Magic was their currency.

Tulir walked away from the table toward the shelf where the wines were kept. A servant moved out of his path. The steps Tulir took loosened from hesitance to his old strong, graceful gait. He took down a wine pitcher and a clean glass. He filled one, set it on the shelf, filled another, then replaced the pitcher to grab both glasses. Afterward, he walked back to Amundr. The room kept still.

Wine extended to Amundr, Tulir eyed the cane and joked, "You look like you need it more than I do now."

Amundr laughed and dropped the cane. He took the wine glass to cheers. The room erupted into hoots and claps as the men drank.

Lena joined in their amazed happiness, hands clapping and lips pulling back into a nice smile. She caught a glimpse of Kazio in the crowd. He hadn't been there before, she was sure. There was no hiding; she was looking at him, and she made a point of it.

There were two things she suddenly became quite sure of: Briet and Amundr were confident Tulir's lame leg would completely heal, and that Kazio didn't like it.

Chapter 16

"WOULD YOU LIKE ANY assistance, Duchess?"

Lena blinked a few times. *Her.* They were talking to her.

She picked up her chin and looked ahead at the vault. "No, thank you. I'll be fine."

Three men were in the hall that led to the vault. Lena supposed there were two reasons for this. Firstly, to give the idea of an increased security presence. Only two people in the world could open the vault. It wasn't a well-guarded secret that there were certain prerequisites a person needed, but it wasn't discussed what exactly those prerequisites were. She expected those details had been excluded or falsified when telling Tulir's bride-to-be.

Secondly, it gave the men something to do. Tensions were high within the castle, more so since the coastal armies had appeared on the horizon the night before last, the night after Tulir was healed. There was enough physical space, thankfully. The servants and their families had been moved to higher quarters. The barracks, the ground level, and some of the first floor were the replacement living space for the refugees of Clevehold. The Ovnite also moved about the space but mostly kept to their barracks and adjoining courtyard and stable. *So many people in so tight a space.* No wonder people were getting sick.

Lena gathered from the vault enough to pay the doctors handsomely. Some may have an issue treating the foreigners, and Lena didn't want a lack of incentive to become the point of refusal. The Ovnite needed treatment.

She attached the coin purse to her belt. It was heavy, but she knew it wouldn't be on her person for long. Rufino was facilitating payment to the doctors. She had only to deliver it to him.

CLEVEHOLD

Eight more gold. Lena took a deep breath and looked at a mound of coins. These were stamped clearly with the Stone King's insignia as it was before his death—a bird and a *V*. Not all coins bore it. The ones farther back in the vault had no insignias, nor that of a previous king. She took eight of the Stone King's gold. He owed her at least that.

The coins were deposited in the purse, and she left the vault and went straight to Rufino. He and Marisol were on the meeting floor, poring over scrolls and paperwork. The room smelled of fresh ink.

"You made quick work," said Rufino. He stretched and yawned.

"I think you just lost track of time," said Marisol.

Rufino laughed and rubbed a hand down his tired face. "That may very well be the case."

"I have the amount requested." Lena opened the coin purse. There wasn't an empty space on the desk to stack it.

"For the doctors, right?" asked Marisol.

"Yes."

"Bring it here." Marisol waved her over. "He's been looking at those logs for so long, I'm afraid he can't count anymore."

"I told you, you can take . . ." Rufino stopped to yawn.

"I'm not taking a break. I'll worry too much," refused Marisol.

Lena went to Marisol's desk and set the coins out in a space she cleared.

"You can admit you like being around me," said Rufino. He looked back to Marisol with a tired but genuine smile.

She returned it.

"Let me know if we need anything more from the vault," said Lena.

"This will do for now, but I know where to find you," said Rufino.

Lena left them to it. She had eight coins left inside her purse. A debt to repay.

She had to ask a few guards to find the whereabouts of her mother and sister. They had been settled into a room no larger than Nela and Lena's apartment had been in Steepwharf. Lena knew the rooms of this size in this section were typically occupied by single persons. It made sense given their predicament that a family of two would be expected to share the space.

The door had faded markings on it that had once been vines. Lena smiled and wondered who had done it. The person who lived here before? The fading wasn't deep enough to have been centuries old.

Had Rether's men lived here?

Lena knocked. A few seconds later, the door opened and Nela stood on the threshold. They were both still for a moment. In the next instant, they were wrapped together in a tight hug.

"I'm so glad you're here," said Lena, muffled due to how tightly she was pressed to her sister.

"I missed you," said Nela. She pulled back to hold Lena at arm's length. Looking her over, bleary-eyed and with wonder, she repeated, "I missed you."

"Is Mother here?" asked Lena. She didn't hear or see anyone in the space behind Nela.

"No. She went out for supplies and a walk." Nela moved to the side. "Please, come in."

Lena walked in. The room reminded her of Steepwharf with its stone walls, but these windows were higher and smaller. There was a small table pushed against a wall with two tucked in chairs. No stove. No different rooms. The beds were against the other two walls. Books were stacked at the foot of the made one. There was an oak cabinet next to the door.

Not like home, Lena amended. She was only looking for it.

CLEVEHOLD

"What brings you down here?" asked Nela. She was dressed in her Steepwharf attire. There was a canvas bag peeking out from under the made bed.

"I don't have too much time, but I needed to see you," said Lena.

Nela nodded. She leaned back against the table. "Things have not calmed down since we got here. I'm sure that means you're busy."

"I have something for you." Lena opened her coin purse and set the eight pieces on the table. "It's the debt. It's what I stole from you."

"Lena," she began.

"I'm sorry for the way things happened. I didn't mean for them to. I didn't want to betray your trust and steal, but the sapphire was the only thing I could think to do," explained Lena. She had to get the words out in a rush, lest she lose her nerve.

"Can we talk?" asked Nela.

"Yes." Wasn't that what they were doing? Why wasn't Nela angry?

"No. *Really* talk. Sit and . . . Lena, you look like you might dash out that door any minute."

"I'm sorry," Lena floundered. "With everything going on . . ." Her throat tightened. This was why she hadn't come to Nela sooner. She couldn't revert to the apologetic young girl in her sister's shadow. Not now.

"Honey, look at me," said Nela. When she did, Nela continued, "You left Steepwharf a girl. You were gone two years. Now you're in court. Tulir's a king? How did it all happen?"

Lena gulped and toyed with her hands. "It's a long story."

"Alright," Nela agreed. She wiped her hand over her mouth and looked down at the pile of gold. "Why don't you start with what happened to Selgen?"

"Tulir and I broke him out. I knew he was innocent. I couldn't let them hang him for it. That's why I stole the sapphire. I needed money to buy supplies and pay off guards."

Nela nodded, waiting.

Lena pressed her lips together and breathed through her nose. She looked to the floor and paced as she said, "There were men who wanted to break the Stone King from his magic to take his power. These men figured they could use Selgen to get to Tulir. Tulir was kidnapped, and the bad men brought him here to break the Stone King. It didn't work the way they planned, and Tulir inherited the power."

Nela sighed. "You're lying to me."

"I . . ." Lena stopped pacing. She combed her fingers through her hair. *How quickly can you cry?* he had asked her. *If the situation calls for it*, she had answered. Now, the situation called for it, and her tears weren't inherently false.

Feeling them prick her eyes, Lena let her voice waver. "Vilars died. Klaus died. No, Nela, it wasn't all that simple. I don't want to relive it all right now." Tears flowed freely, and she wiped her cheek with her sleeve. She sputtered, "I-I could have died, too."

"Honey, I'm so sorry." Nela moved in to wrap her arms around Lena.

Lena stepped back and sniffled. "I don't need you to treat me like a child. I need you to trust I know what I'm doing."

"I want to." Nela's hands were held out awkwardly in the aborted hug. Instead, she folded them.

"If you want to help me . . ." Lena paused to clear her voice of tremors. "If you want to help, be family to Selgen. He works in the library. He mostly keeps to himself. He isn't doing well."

Nela nodded. "Alright."

"Thank you." Lena moved toward the door. "If you'll excuse me, I do have to go."

CLEVEHOLD

"Won't you wait for Mother?" asked Nela.

Lena shook her head. She promised, "I'll come back another time."

※

LENA DETERMINED OVER dinner that the Vitki were the Ovnite without tattoos. The Drengr were littered with them. The rest of the people, non-fighters, had smaller clusters of ink.

It was a quieter dinner tonight. Everyone was present at the head table, save Tisa, who had elected a watch. Cicero still looked pale but was in good spirits. For the first time since the brokering of Briet's title, Harth returned to the table. Charlot put her foot in her mouth with obtuse statements twice.

Lena spoke a polite amount about respectable topics. The conversation concerning their occupying neighbors was reserved for Council meetings. When dinner was done, she made a point to speak with servants to assure they were doing well. The castle was their home, too. Lena was sure there was a degree of telling her what she wanted to hear, but she pursued the topics enough to have been satisfied they were mostly comfortable.

An hour. Anyone who waited until after dinner to speak with the king was provided time to stop him, which at least gave Lena enough time to feed Socks. She determined when it had been long enough based on the angle of the falling sun.

Lena let her hair down. When brushed straight, it came down to her waist. She needed to cut it. Instead of putting it back up, she swept her tresses over her shoulder and tied them together with a purple ribbon. Her clothes were the same from dinner, a green dress to her thigh and dark-green trousers. She was giving her image too much scrutiny.

With one more deep breath, Lena exited her room. She walked with her head high, and no one stopped her on the way to Tulir's room. There was a guard at the door who gave her an acknowledging nod. She returned it, went to the bedroom door, and knocked.

The footsteps to the door were quick and faint. It opened. Tulir looked surprised to see her.

"I understand," she began. Wasn't there a speech she had prepared? She couldn't recall. The image of his disheveled hair and him changed into a nightshirt caught her off guard.

Tulir stepped forward and wrapped her in a hug. Lena returned the embrace, pressing her face into his neck. He felt safe and warm. His hand cradled the back of her head.

They parted. Tulir stepped to the side. "Come in, please."

"Not too improper for a duchess?" she jested.

He smiled and held the door open as she passed through. It was closed behind her. "There's no one here to know. I suppose I could traffic you through the passages."

"Socks always comes out of there so dusty," she replied. Being in his room didn't feel like the imposition she had assumed it would. It was still his space.

"I didn't mean to interrupt you," he said sheepishly as he thumbed back to the door.

Lena nodded and tried to piece together bits of what she had concocted in her head during dinner. "I was angry. I realized the main reason I was angry over you marrying Briet is because I love you. You've surprised me so much these past few years, in the best way. I trusted you to take up this mantle, this title, because I trust you to do good with it. I hold to that. Giving the Ovnite a reason to align their interests with ours is smart."

"I appreciate that. I truly do." He leaned against the foot of his bed.

"I don't want to apologize for my statements. Maybe for my behavior. It feels wrong to say I'm sorry... I'm not sorry for feeling like this, but I've come around to understand. I wanted you to know." She stood at the window and took a breath. It felt as if a weight had lifted.

"Don't apologize. If for nothing else, it would only make me feel worse." Tulir grumbled a few words and raked his hand through his hair. He then stood straight, recomposed, and said, "There are material reasons the plan may concern you. I recognize that."

Lena couldn't help but giggle. "Such propriety."

"I wasn't lying when I said I wasn't born for this."

"The material reasons stand where I started." She mocked his regal tact of speaking, "The honor bequeathed was done in trust. Though we may face certain obstacles because of it, I do not regret the part you played in this."

Tulir shook his head. He whispered, "I don't know if I could have stood by and watched if you were the one sold to market."

"I wouldn't have been able to give her children." Lena chose his style of quip to avoid her possible impending arrangement. Another time.

"I love you. I only want what's best for you. Had I seen an avenue around this, I would have taken it." He gestured at the window.

"Our enemies have become our allies," she said. She traced her fingers along the lines of the window.

"They've greatly supplemented our defense and will hopefully secure us enough of an offensive force to not have to fight." He rubbed a hand on the back of his neck. "Though my marrying Briet poses a risk to you, I'll do all I can to mitigate it."

"Risk?" She didn't like the term he used. They were all at risk. She wasn't to be singled out.

"Should they . . ." Tulir pushed off the bed and approached her to speak quietly. "Should the Ovnite find me a fraud. *If* that were to happen, then I plan to lie, say you had nothing to do with it."

"I don't—"

"And you will agree," he insisted. He put a finger under her chin and raised it. "Promise me you would lie. Please."

"It won't come to that."

Tulir lowered the hand under her chin and clasped their fingers together.

She promised, "I would never betray you with it. Neither would Harth. Selgen was given the same story as Clevehold. Avild stands to lose if she reveals the truth. Her unnaturally long life can't be easily answered for."

"The Ovnite are magic-based people. My immaturity with magic may be what gives me away."

Lena shook her head. "You weren't raised with it. You have to learn it from the ground up, as everyone else does. So long as you keep training with Avild, you'll be able to bring the story conviction."

"She told you?"

"That wasn't where you broke your knee?"

He laughed and squeezed her hand. "Having a Vitki does come with its advantages."

"Yes," Lena agreed. Her brow furrowed. "Amundr is their Elder, but he answers to Kazio, the Vitki leader?"

"From what Briet told me, Amundr used to lead the Vitki. He stepped down. He doesn't answer to Kazio. In fact, I think it's still the other way around."

Lena hummed. She thought back to how Amundr had taken the brunt of Avild's magic. Contended with it. *Are there others as powerful as him?*

"You look worried all of a sudden," observed Tulir.

"I am," she admitted. "I'm worried about Avild."

"Not about her sharing her knowledge?"

Exactly that, she thought, just not how he meant it. "She doesn't want the crown, I know that. Do you remember what Rether said, that day in the Stone King's Hall?"

He dropped her hands and took a half step back as he breathed deeply. Looking down at his hands, he said, "I remember."

"Before that." She put a hand on his bicep to take him out of the memory.

His eyes found hers, and he swallowed hard. He looked lost. A few blinks later, the look receded. "The deal he wanted to make with Avild?"

"To bring Klaus back from the dead. A life for a life. She would need someone powerful to do it for her."

"And a boat of savvy magic users just showed up." He groaned.

"It couldn't be just any of them. I don't know exactly what it would entail, or if I would recognize it if I saw it," she explained.

"I don't think Avild is present enough to be on that good of terms with any of the Ovnite, but I will pass to Briet to have her people be cautious of Avild."

"You can't tell Briet what Avild can do," urged Lena.

"No, I wouldn't. There are ways to plant an uneasiness. I'll . . ." Tulir rubbed a hand up Lena's arm. "I'll figure something out."

"Thank you." She stared up into his beautiful brown eyes. A person could get lost there, especially the way he was looking at her.

"Was anything else bothering you?" he whispered.

She rose on her toes to kiss him. Quickly, she was embraced, his arm wrapped around her middle to bring her closer. She kissed as if she were starved for it, and he responded in kind. Breathless moments later, he parted their lips and moaned low in his throat.

"I worry of the feelings I have for you," she whispered, mouth a hair's breadth from his.

"Ones you know I reciprocate."

Body pressed close to his, she made them sway. "Big word for a king."

"I need to keep up the front," he replied. He smiled at her. There was a different level of lost in his eyes now, one it looked like his soul was daring her to pursue.

Why shouldn't she? He was not yet a married man. His relationship with Lena up to this point hadn't been a secret. Was there an expectation of faithfulness leading up to an arranged marriage? Neither Tulir nor Briet came from a regal background. The expectations were what they created.

Lena lessened the weight of her body against his but couldn't part completely. She also couldn't feign ignorance or stand to think any part of this was coercion. The reason she wanted Tulir was the same reason she didn't want him to marry Briet—selfishness.

"I can't help but think what would have happened had I gathered the courage sooner," said Tulir. He traced a finger along the outline of Lena's face.

"You wouldn't have the bargaining chips you needed," she answered.

Just once. Not again after he was married—that would become unquestionably impure. If they didn't now, she would never know, and ache for it. That possibility opened too much risk.

"Therein lies me wanting to be responsible," he whispered.

She leaned up to kiss him. A quick, chaste kiss. Her body then moved away, but she kept her hands in his. They should still be responsible. They should have the conversation, the complete one. The sun was only just dipping below the horizon. There was plenty of night left to make decisions.

Firstly, she needed to revisit with him a conversation cut short. Beyond all this, he was her friend, and there was nothing he needed to hide.

Lena led them to the recliner sofa. They sat close, their hands clasped together on her knee. "I am going to apologize for not hearing you out that night."

"You don't." He tensed under her grip. "It was, it is..."

"You caught me off guard." She eased into interrupting him. "I'm sorry if my shock translated into words or actions that hurt you. I'm not fond of what transpired without my knowledge, but in retrospect, in some ways, I understand."

"If you want to talk about it, I'll answer anything you want to know." He used his free hand to comb through his hair. "Anything I can."

"Do you have a preference for men or women, and either myself or Harth is the exception to it?" she asked as politely as her cluttered mind could assemble.

"Both. Neither." Tulir shook his head. "Not helpful. Uh, no."

"All your kingly composure was expended," she joked.

He squeezed her hand. "I don't have a physical preference. Just as certain people prefer wine or others beer, I would just as soon have them both. The appeals are different, and I have different standards and expectations within each type. They treat me differently. There's still... I don't know. Metaphors abandoned—a person's attributes are what makes me attracted to them. Dress or trousers. Doesn't matter."

"It's a good thing you like me for things other than my face." She saw the cogs turning in his head and followed up, "I was only trying to get you to ease up." She looked down at their joined hands where he was squeezing.

"Sorry." He pulled his hand away. "I would ask what you see in me, but I'm afraid I couldn't suffer the disappointment."

"Do I need to kiss you again?"

"The topic can be revisited." He tilted his head from side to side. After it earned him a giggle, he said in earnest, "You are beautiful."

She smiled. "When did it happen?"

"You grew into it about ten years ago, once you grew that last foot."

"No." She shoved him. "You and Harth, I mean."

"Ah." He passed a thumb over his upper lip. "The intrigue was there in Steepwharf. He was a hard man to figure out—I don't know. It started as a feeling, then a challenge. He was ignoring me. Then I thought I was crazy. There are laws, punishments, so it's not as if I could outright ask."

She understood what Tulir meant in thinking he was crazy—Harth certainly didn't look how Lena would expect for a man who preferred men. Harth was rugged, the kind that needed a dainty woman to balance him out. Tulir was kindhearted, but far from a gentle pretty woman. He also didn't look as she expected, she supposed. It began to feel more like a fault in her expectations than in either man.

Then was his remark about not being able to ask. Somehow, she had mostly overlooked that aspect. Had Tulir tried to pursue Harth outright in Steepwharf and found Harth *did* have a dainty woman waiting for him, it could have cost Tulir his position. If word got out, if there was proof of Tulir's deviance, beyond a civil release from the guard ranks there would have been physical punishment.

She thought back to what he had said: men who used a wife as a shield for society's sake. Tulir was too outwardly smitten for her to consider it a possibility. When she stopped to think of it rationally—not as a preference for both, but as a lack of barrier against preferring a person for their attributes—it connected in her mind.

"Then, this opportunity came upon us," she led him to continue.

"I suppose I was a touch forward in the cells," he admitted jokingly.

"You two fight well together."

"I wish I could have seen your part in it." He bumped her shoulder. "I was out of commission for the latter half. I demonstrated my affection by pitching him over the side. Strange, how fate brings people together."

"You didn't do it on purpose," she reminded.

"But I remember it." He sighed and rubbed his eyes. "I felt horrible. I couldn't outrun the helplessness I felt when fighting him against my will. Then I . . . when I hauled him over the side, he could have taken me with him. He didn't." Tulir said the next three words slowly. "He let go."

Lena could picture it all too well: Tulir's coughs. Harth's fall. Him lying there motionless, twitching. Lena had feared for both their lives. After Avild had checked on Harth, she hadn't wanted to leave his side. Perhaps she wouldn't have, if Lena hadn't bargained to not go for help unless Avild knocked down the door to get to Tulir on the balcony.

"I was desperate for retribution. Harth and I were both laid up for a time after the fight. He was my recovery, I was his. It wasn't about more than that, back then. It was about having someone to lean on, both physically and not."

"It goes without saying, but I'm glad you both survived. For a time there, we didn't know," said Lena. It was her turn to squeeze his hand.

"After what happened to Vilars, part of me didn't want to. We were always together. Those first few days, I got by because I pretended there was another bed, and he was—" Tulir stopped short. His knee bounced.

"I can't imagine. I know it still can't be easy."

Tulir looked up. A corner of his lip upturned. "I wonder sometimes what Vilars would think of all this. My choices. My station. My preferences. He would think this whole king business hilarious."

"He would," she agreed. She tried not to imagine Vilars struggling to take his last breaths. The cloth on his leg couldn't bind tightly enough. He had lost too much blood. For all the injuries sustained that day, it was a cut a few inches wide that had done a man in. It seemed so absurd. To distract herself, Lena asked, "Did you talk to him about any of it?"

"I actually—it feels strange to say it now." Tulir paused to take a deep breath and wipe his eyes clear. "I talked to Vilars about Harth once. Not much was said. I hadn't really brought up the attributes talk to my brother. He knew, but we didn't . . ." Tulir waved a hand and refocused. "Vilars had a vague idea, and I think that's why he had a chip on his shoulder for Harth."

"I don't recall you and Harth being friendly in Steepwharf," she said. There wasn't accusation, only curiosity. She wanted to understand.

"He was a handsome man with a mysterious past. I couldn't be too forward. It was part of the mystery," Tulir justified lightheartedly. "Vilars also recommended distance after the not-so-in-depth talk we had. He didn't want to see me get caught and be hurt."

"Your brother loved you."

Tulir smiled. "I don't doubt it. If it came to it, if he were here, he'd understand. I know it." He looked to Lena, and she saw a glint of mischief. "You had eyes for him."

She smiled back and admitted, "I had a childish crush."

"He did, too," said Tulir. He let go of Lena and circled an arm around the back of the couch.

"Didn't stop you from flirting." She leaned back with him. "With me, and with my sister, if I recall correctly."

"Flirting with Nela was about as dangerous as flirting with Harth. She added a touch of danger to the boring days," he jested.

"I'm sorry I'm not that exciting," she mock apologized.

"You make my heart pound as if I've run for my life. Don't pretend you don't know it." He kissed the side of her head. "I wouldn't have, though, if things had stayed as they were."

"Wouldn't have what?" questioned Lena.

"Gotten between the two of you." He toyed with her hair.

Lena smiled and looked at her hands. "Vilars was a strong but quiet man. A good one. What made me sure it was a childish crush was being attracted to the things I didn't know, more than what I did. He was a good man, and would have made a great husband—just not mine."

"I think, if you can muster wrapping your head around my blabbering, I can wrap mine around your simple concept."

"It's not blabbering. When this is all done and settled, I will still be what I had been before—your friend."

"Can we not talk about the hereafter tonight?"

"After I ask one more question on it," she bargained. "So that we all have the same stories, do you plan on bringing up your preferences, Harth, or anything that happened with the Stone King to Briet? Now or in the future?"

"No," he said simply.

"Alright."

"Not that I feel I need to say it, but please don't—"

She shook her head. "I wouldn't betray your trust like that. It puts me at risk, too."

"I wouldn't put you in that position."

"I would have risked what you proposed, had things not changed the way they did." Did Lena need to elaborate further?

Did she want to? It was important to her that Tulir understood her initial aversion had been based on shock. Their future had been dangled in front of all their faces. They couldn't have it now. Was it worth giving him the answer? Would that only make it worse?

Tulir looked at his hands. "My apologies for how that was handled."

"I don't like that you didn't tell me sooner. It happened behind my back, but I understand the risk you faced."

"It's not that I didn't trust you. Believe me, that wasn't it. It's that it wasn't just me at risk. And if it's any consolation, Harth felt terrible about me not telling you. It was my fault, not his. He respects you."

Lena pressed a finger to his lips lightly. "At first, I hated the idea of someone else, but thinking on it . . . I don't understand it, yet I do. You loving me doesn't stop you from loving him. I understand, because I can't stop myself from loving you. Does that make sense?"

"You're a good woman, Lena." He cupped her face with his hand.

"The kind you deserve," she answered. Leaning in, she whispered, "She better be good to you."

Tulir shook his head and licked his lips.

They kissed again. Lena lost track of herself and the time with it. Their hands wandered. Tulir made no protest. She could feel it in the heat of his touch—just this once. If fate never let them have it again, if she could never sink to being unfaithfully wed, they would let it be theirs just once.

A door opened. They broke apart. It wasn't the right direction to have been the bedroom door—sounded too close to have been the study door. There had been no knock.

Harth stood on the threshold of an interior passage. "I'm sorry, I shouldn't have—"

"I didn't think anyone—" Lena and he both attempted apologies simultaneously, and stopped short.

Tulir stood and rubbed a hand down his face. "I asked you to come. I wanted to talk because we haven't been . . ." He turned to Lena. "I'm sorry, the last—"

"I can go," offered Harth.

"I didn't mean to . . ." Tulir's statement ended in a grumble.

"Stay," Lena suggested before she could think on it. She stood and wiped a hand over her kiss-bitten lips. "We're all involved. We're all beholden to this horrendous timetable together."

Tulir wiped a hand over his mouth. He breathed heavily. There was more than lust behind his eyes. Lena thought she saw consideration.

"It's up to you," Harth said to Tulir.

There was so much to say. The conversations had been had individually; it was time they talked together, but she, too, deferred to Tulir.

He studied them both, then decided, "You should stay."

Chapter 17

THE LIGHT PEEKING IN from the windows woke Lena slowly. She had purposefully left the curtains open the night before to let the sun rouse her. It was earlier than when she normally started the day, but this time she needed a head start.

Tulir's head rested on her collarbone. She could tell from his breathing he wasn't awake yet. The presence of him felt like a comfort, and she soaked it in while she could. There was nothing short of love that she could use to describe what she felt. The high, the satisfaction, the warmth, and even the confusion. This felt right.

Light footsteps walked toward them from the direction of the study. Lena assured she was covered by the blankets instinctually. There was no true fear; a door hadn't opened. A glance across the bed to the other side of Tulir told her the footsteps belonged to the third person she knew was in the room.

Harth emerged from the study. The entrance put him on the empty side of the bed. He was dressed from the waist down, wiping his hands on a rag. He sat lightly in the place he had slept. Fingers reached out to ghost over Tulir's bare shoulder.

She could tell Tulir was waking the way his breath and grip changed. Delicately, she lifted his hand to her lips and kissed it.

He blinked awake slowly. A lazy smile warmed his face when he saw her. He used the hand by her mouth to trace the line of her cheek down to her neck. He smiled, purposeful this time, and pulled himself closer to kiss her on the shoulder.

Tulir shifted into a sitting position, then yawned and rubbed his eyes. A shiver ran through him as his bare chest was exposed to the chill of morning. He reached for Harth, who handed him a cup of water. He drank a few sips down, then passed it to Lena.

Careful to keep the blanket tucked under her armpits to avoid the same chill, she sat and accepted the water. With her eyes, she conveyed appreciation, not wanting to break the comfortable silence.

Harth took a deep breath. His hand was fastened to Tulir's bicep. The men leaned toward one another and kissed. They parted, but their foreheads stayed together. Harth raised his eyebrows in a silent question, and Tulir nodded.

The empty water cup was set on the bedside table. Lena saw them kiss and felt no strangeness witnessing it. She didn't gawk—it wasn't her place to stare—but she kept them within her periphery as she looked at the sunlight dancing through the pink-tinted windowpane.

Harth's hair was too short to look messy from sleep, recently cut since having gone to the Ovnite camp. He turned the way he was sitting for his back to face Lena. The new angle gave her a view of the scars that littered his back. For this, she averted her eyes.

"I wish you didn't have to go," said Tulir.

She could tell by the sound that the words were said in her direction. Smiling, she looked at Tulir. She couldn't say it was alright. She didn't want to say at least they'd had this. Too many finalities existed.

Harth slipped his shirt on as he got up from the bed, then walked to the chair at Tulir's desk where Lena's dress had been laid out. He picked it up carefully and walked it to her. In the last two steps, his eyes met hers and he handed it off.

"Thank you," she said.

He put his back to her and looked out the windows.

She sensed the degree of his unease. Lesser than it had been last night, and respectful enough to not consider rude. As she slipped the dress on, she recalled the layers of comfort she had needed to build the night before.

Talking first had been to their benefit. It eased the nervousness, as had the wine retrieved from Tulir's study shelf. The progression was simpler than she expected, as Tulir had a bridge to both their hearts. She and Harth hadn't touched more than the brushing of fingers. The night was centered around the person they were losing.

The trousers, she had left beside the bed. She slipped into them easily.

"Will you show Lena the way to her room through the back passages?" asked Tulir. He cleared his throat and ruffled a hand through his hair.

"The bed is in front of it. I don't think I could get it to move," said Lena. *How many mistresses have passed through those halls?*

Was that what she was now, a mistress? Did one instance constitute that? Or was the area grey because she had bargained herself one night in exchange for vowing not to sleep with a married man thereafter? She didn't think on it too hard.

"The door slides. You'll be able to get in," said Harth.

She supposed, "I may as well leave out the main door. They saw me come in last night, then not leave."

"The guards rotate every two hours to keep their eyes fresh. The man on the door will assume you left after he did," said Harth.

"What if he told the next guard?" Lena's clothes were situated as best she could get them without a mirror. "I'm decent."

"There's no reason for that information to be exchanged," said Harth. He was back to looking as if he had walked out of the barracks. The present shadow of stubble wasn't always on his face, but often enough to not raise questions.

"You won't have people suspecting you," said Tulir.

"I've got a good reputation that way." Lena flattened out her dress as it sat around her waist. She would have to change when she got to her room. Her hair felt messy and puffy. She combed through the strands with her fingers to help flatten it. Placing her hands on the bed, Lena leaned toward Tulir. He aided in closing the distance, but she stopped before their lips met. She whispered, "Know I'll want to kiss you later."

He breathed over her lips. His hand bracketed her face gently. "I'm not sorry."

"Nor am I." She kissed him deeply. "But I won't. Not once you're officially hers." She watched his eyes to assure he understood. The sorrow she saw reflected told her he did.

"I love you," he whispered.

The door to the interior passage opened.

"I love you, too." She pushed off the bed and walked away before the part of her screaming to stay won. She couldn't have him. They couldn't stay in bed all day and abandon their responsibilities.

Perhaps in another lifetime, thought Lena with an ache in her chest.

Harth closed the door to the interior passage with them inside. He mimed for Lena to keep quiet and pointed down a dark hallway. After a pause, he nodded and set off in that direction.

Lena stepped lightly. Just as she thought there was no way she was going to make it in the dark without slipping, a light appeared. Her head snapped up, afraid someone had opened a door. The light came from Harth's hand. She kept moving and tried to keep her footsteps as light as his.

They wound through several turns and went up a set of stairs. Somewhere that sounded far below, a door opened. Her breath caught and she looked back. They were alone. She knew others had knowledge of the passages. Their secrets were safe so long as they ran into no one.

How many times had Harth risked the trip? Did he always come to Tulir in secret, or did he knock on the door properly? He knew the guards' shifts; he knew the guards. The question was if he leveraged such knowledge. She doubted it.

Their journey ended at the bottom of a set of steps. He pushed in a stone on the wall, and there was a click. He used the hand emitting light to find a rope thatch and pull. The door shifted to the side.

Socks was on her bed. He crouched low, ears pointed back, and stared at them with wide eyes. A low grumbling meow welcomed them. She didn't know if he looked more ready to pounce or run.

"It's me," whispered Lena. She tapped her nails on the top of her headboard.

Moving slowly, Socks approached. His back was hunched, tail down. He sniffed. Front paws on the headboard, he got his face high enough to be close to her fingers. He sniffed again.

Lena scratched behind his ear.

Socks changed his stance to have his tail up. Head shoved against her hand, he immediately began purring. He had to gulp through the effort.

"He's not used to seeing you over here," said Harth.

Socks scampered away. When he got off the bed, he went to dive beneath, changed his mind, and ran behind her closet instead. It sounded like he knocked something over.

"You didn't pick the most graceful animal," he remarked.

Lena shrugged. She was looking at the rear of her headboard. It was flat, and the board extended from her calves to almost her shoulders. There were no footholds to use to maneuver over it. If Harth gave her a boost, perhaps she could clear it. Wouldn't be the most graceful entrance, Lena mused, but she could manage.

"Where'd you get him, anyway?" Harth also looked to have been evaluating how to get her on the other side. A tentative push against the headboard didn't move it in the slightest.

"He showed up," she answered. She bent to see how much clearance there was under the bed. That was Socks' route. She could probably fit.

"I'm not going to make you crawl under there," said Harth. He looked at the bed, then to her. "May I?"

"Yes," she agreed, not fully aware of what to.

Harth put one arm around her back and bent to get the other under her knees. He picked her up fluidly with a soft grunt. Hoisted over the headboard, Lena cleared it and was let to drop to the mattress.

"You alright?" he asked.

"Definitely beats crawling," she said with a laugh. She got to her knees to face him. "Thank you."

"Tell Scamper he doesn't have to break anything else. I'm leaving." He jutted his chin toward her closet.

"May I ask you something?" She gripped the headboard with her fingertips.

He hummed.

"We put it off because you were healing, then everything was changing, and we were so busy." She stopped her rattling and refocused. "I still want you to teach me how to fight."

Harth took a breath and looked down the lengths of the hallway.

"Is someone—?" She stopped her question when he put a finger to his lips. She listened. There was a sliding sound, very faint. Perhaps a few floors away.

Harth kept still for a few seconds after the noise stopped. The finger lowered. He nodded for her to continue.

"Someone will think we're having an affair," she joked.

He huffed a laugh and shook his head. "You want to learn to fight?"

"I do."

"Not to overstress the situation, but with our new neighbors, it wouldn't be a bad thing for you to learn," he agreed.

"I was thinking the same."

He shook his hand out where the light had been. Keeping his eyes on the dark hall, he said, "I'll be down in the courtyard in a few hours. We can get started then."

"Thank you."

He nodded, she returned the gesture, and he closed the passage door. It slid and clicked into place.

Lena listened for a few long minutes to try to hear him walk away. After time enough had passed, she shrugged and decided he must have left but made too little noise to detect. The ambient backdrop of the castle shielded light footsteps.

She sat on the edge of the bed and brought her knees up to her chest. She thought about Tulir. Everything had changed, yet it didn't feel like it had. There was an expectation she had carried that once she and Tulir had abandoned holding off on their lust, a veil would lift, and more things would make sense. She loved him, but then she had before. She craved his touch. If anything, that yearning had worsened now that it wasn't her imagination fueling it but her memory.

Socks poked his head around the side. He made eye contact with Lena. "Meow."

"He's gone. You're safe," said Lena. She patted the bed.

Trotting happily, he came to her. He jumped up and rubbed his face against her hands. The purring resumed.

"He's not that bad," Lena tried to convince him.

"Meow," said Socks. He pawed at her arm until she moved it, then tapped on her knee. When she extended her legs down flat, he plopped lazily onto them.

"He is curious," agreed Lena. She petted Socks while she thought. Thinking back to what Tulir had said, she had to agree with him on one front: There was a mystery to Harth that sparked intrigue. He surprised her to have been the man who had seen her nude, then handed her a dress, eyes averted, come morning. She and Harth had shared the night, shared the bed, but they had kept a respectable distance between them. He didn't reach for her, nor her him. Their touches had been tangles when they both couldn't stop touching Tulir, mostly when things had settled down and they were tucked under blankets.

Lena rubbed her hand up and down her bicep, then squeezed. Had Harth kept his distance exclusively for her benefit? In retrospect, the request to have him stay had been rash. Irresponsible. Had the potential to overwhelm her. But in the moment, it hadn't, and the memories didn't impose such feelings now.

There was so much their arrangement could have meant to all of them. Satisfaction for Tulir. Unraveling the mystery of Harth. Her general attitude toward Harth hadn't changed—she didn't want, or expect, to receive love from him—but she thought of the casual way he had lifted her over the headboard, and only after asking permission. There was a layer of comfort they could reach. To do what was best for Tulir in all circumstances, public and private.

Lena smiled and covered her mouth with her hand. She had expected more jealousy to rear once the light of morning uncovered what they had done. Perhaps guilt should have been there, too. It had all been rash and immodest. Society told her she should think of the men like that differently. They were deviants, weak . . . but Tulir hadn't felt weak when he had loved Lena and made her feel like a woman.

***

AROUND MIDDAY, LENA joined Harth in one of the courtyards. It was semiprivate, on a raised third floor, and adjacent to the Ovnite barracks' upper exit. She wasn't sure it had been a training courtyard before the castle's population had exponentially increased. The marks on the ground could have been from boots or weapons, or could have resulted from furniture they had dragged away to make room. There were raised flower beds along the edges. She supposed they were a benefit. If someone lost their balance, instead of falling over the wall, they would fall into dirt.

But she couldn't concentrate on any of that. There was a sword in her hands. It felt heavy, bulky. She knew what the swings felt like when done correctly, as she had managed it a few times, but the more she swung, the less correct it felt. She needed to improve her arm strength.

"Remember to keep your feet moving," reminded Harth. He had a short sword in one hand and moved slowly. His attacks gave her plentiful time to defend.

Lena swung her sword across her body at chest level. There was a ring when the metal clashed. She felt the reverberations up her arm as she stepped to the side and pushed his blade off.

Breaths came hard. She was sweaty. It had only been a half hour, an hour at most. Her arms felt like they were turning to jelly. *How do men fight for prolonged periods of time?*

"You want to take a break?" he offered.

"No," she refused and wiped her forehead. She adjusted her grip. "May I?"

"Please."

Lena stepped forward to attack. There wasn't a lot of energy in her reserves, but she pushed to perform. *Only a few more minutes.* She could muster the energy for a few minutes. Her swings were concise, but slow. She remembered to move her feet.

Harth backed out of a defensive stance and rotated the sword in his hand. "Not bad."

"I'm slow," she complained.

"I've trained a lot of men from the ground up. You want the correct form to start. Speed comes later. If you throw your weight around quickly but haphazardly, it gets you in trouble."

"It's good advice."

Lena turned and Harth looked up. Briet was at the edge of the courtyard with Tisa.

"Mind if we join you?" asked Tisa.

"Go ahead," Lena said, backing up. She switched to a one-handed grip and was made to pause by a yawn. "I'm done for now."

"You not sleep well last night?" asked Harth.

She grinned. His tone was that of casual friendly concern, as far as anyone else knew. He was too serious for anyone to assume there was a separate connotation. But Lena saw the glint of teasing in his eyes.

"Best sleep I've had." She passed by him, confident sway in her step. "What I got of it."

Her illusion of assumptions, of her exclusive reading of Harth's question, was fractured when she saw Tisa's quirked eyebrow. Lena felt herself turning red. She wiped her hand on her forehead and breathed deeply.

"There are targets we can shoot, yes?" asked Briet.

Lena reached the edge of the courtyard and sat on the stone flower bed wall. From what she could see, Tisa had brought neither a bow nor crossbow. Lena set her sword on the stone next to Harth's bow.

"There should be targets just around that corner," said Harth. He gestured to the supply cove behind the wall.

"Will you?" Briet asked of Tisa, who nodded and went to retrieve it. Briet continued, looking at Harth, "The king told me you're his best archer."

Tisa hauled out a large target and set it in front of a stone wall. Its legs were made of wood. The target face was wood a few inches thick, and the back plate was metal. The face was painted with rings, white along the edge and gradually growing darker to a black point in the center.

"Hopefully the king doesn't embellish the skills of his friends," said Briet.

Was it a test? A performance? Was Harth in a position to refuse? Lena thought of her new title. *Duchess.* How many hollow titles had been handed out? Had Tisa gotten one? Had Harth? Lena kept her hands folded neatly in her lap and watched.

Harth walked to where she sat. He deposited his sword next to hers, strapped the quiver to his back, and took up the bow. He looked back to Briet. "How far back?"

"How close do you need to be?" she returned.

"From here?" whispered Lena. The target was diagonal; there was no chance for a dead-on shot.

He notched an arrow and fired. It stuck out of the target's side, in the thin ring of wood.

"It's good," complimented Briet. She walked down the line of the target.

Harth approached the same sight line. "Anything in particular you want to see?"

"At the farthest point, it's what, two hundred feet, yes?" asked Briet, pointing to where she was headed.

Cicero joined Tisa along the sidelines. He coughed but straightened up quickly.

"Give or take," answered Harth.

Briet, at the far wall, turned to face the target. She stood sideways and raised her arm to point at it. Her finger pinched and moved in such a way it looked like she was notching an invisible bow. Her other arm dropped as she pulled the pinched fingers back. Blue threads of magic wound around her hand. By the time she had it pulled back fully, there was a thick haze of blue magic shaped like an arrow. She let go.

The magic arrow zinged silently and struck the target.

"Grey," called Tisa.

Lena blinked rapidly. The corner of her lip pulled up in a smile. Ther was so much magic could do. Whereas she had but seen the surface scratched, the Ovnite were learned in it.

The magic arrow dissolved, and the hole it left behind chipped at the paint. Tisa went to the target and removed Harth's arrow.

"Would you mind a quick competition?" asked Briet.

"Any rules I need to know?" replied Harth. He stood at the end of the range with her.

"Yes." She gestured at the target and smiled. "Hit it."

"We've each fired a tester shot. The Miss goes first." Harth backed away a few steps.

Briet nodded. She tucked loose blonde strands behind her ears. Shoulders squared, she took a deep breath. She repeated the process of conjuring the magic arrow and fired.

Tisa put up a hand and got closer to the target. "Nine rings, ring three. Grey."

"Your draw." Briet moved aside.

Harth pulled the arrow and notched it as he walked forward. Bringing the bow up on the last step, he fired. The sound the arrow made was a distinct whistle and crunch when it hit the target.

Lena made a mental note to listen for how Briet's sounded.

"Ring two, grey," called Tisa. She pulled the arrow from the target, and it broke.

"How quickly can you fire those in succession?" asked Harth. He took a step to the side but didn't clear the area.

Briet came up to stand beside him, preparing to shoot with her left hand so that they faced each other. She answered with two arrows fired in quick sequence. The arrows traveled silently but made a similar crunch upon hitting the target.

Two arrows pulled from the quiver, Harth echoed her tactic. The first arrow stuck into the target next to her magic. The second one seemed to strike the target but bounce back.

Briet shrugged.

Tisa came up to the target as the magic arrow dissolved. There was a curious look on her face when she pointed two fingers at Briet. "Did you know they could be dented?"

"What?" questioned Briet.

"He hit yours," answered Tisa. She kept pointing at Briet. "Ring two and three, grey." She pointed at Harth. "Ring one, black."

"And the other?" asked Briet.

Tisa shook her head. "I'm not going to call it a miss." She turned to Cicero and tapped him on the chest. "You're good to call, yes?"

Cicero nodded.

Tisa approached where Lena was sitting. "Afternoon, Duchess."

Lena rolled her eyes playfully and did a badly formed bow from where she sat.

"Your people eat all hours of the day," Tisa said with a laugh as she sat down on the stone near Lena.

"If that's the chief complaint, I believe we're alright," replied Lena. She nodded her head toward Cicero. "Is he alright?"

Tisa shrugged. "He's sick. It's not contagious, from what we can tell."

Lena thought to all the Ovnite coughing. "Do many of your people have it?"

"Many do, to degrees. Some have died," she said solemnly. She looked to the ongoing competition. Voice detached, she said, "I fear they're being exposed to something we were guarded from in our capture. There's no telling who will get it or how badly."

"The doctors have visited?" asked Lena.

"They've helped," confirmed Tisa. "They were the ones who assured us it isn't contagious."

"Ring two," Cicero called out, pointing at Briet.

Wishing to get the other woman's mind off it and satisfy her own curiosity, she asked, "The place you came from, did it look like this?"

"No." Tisa shook her head and patted her hands in her lap.

"Ring two." Cicero pointed at Harth. "Right on the cusp, though. There's black paint chipped away. It's hard to tell."

"Cicero?" yelled Briet.

"It's only a few inches wide." He stopped to cough, covering his mouth. Voice strained, he excused, "It's hard to tell."

"This place looks like Estnable. Not as large, but the stone. The regalness," said Tisa.

"What is Estnable?" asked Lena.

"The other place. The city that was within the wall. There was our Ovnite settlement and the Estnable fortress," explained Tisa.

"Ring one."

"What happened to them?" asked Lena.

Tisa rubbed her hands down the tops of her thighs. "For a long time, we were feuding neighbors. Now, what's left of the Est have assimilated into the Ovnite. Cicero, for instance."

Lena could tell it wasn't a topic the other woman wanted to elaborate on.

"Ring one, black," called Cicero. He pointed at Harth.

"I've learned I can take the king at his word," said Briet. She shot an arrow.

Cicero leaned forward and called, "Ring two, grey."

A tall figure leaned against a pillar near the storeroom. They were watching.

Harth nocked and quickly fired.

"Ring one, black," said Cicero.

"I concede I have some improvements to make, yes? Thank you for indulging me," said Briet.

Harth gestured with his bow at the target. "You're going to tell me how you do that?"

The figure in the shadows came forward and waltzed toward the target. *Kazio*. Talking at Cicero but loud enough for them all to hear, he said, "Didn't you tell him the bow was a coward's weapon?" He yanked the arrow from the target.

An arrow lodged into the target at Kazio's neck level, equal distance from it and the raised arm holding the arrow. His head whipped to the side, and he glared. Amusement coating his voice, he scowled, "A good trick." He broke the arrow away. "But is it your only trick?"

Harth stared back at Kazio. Facial expression unchanging, he went to where the swords lay on the stone barrier. Lena held out a hand, and he gave her the bow. He set the quiver beside it. He took both swords and moved into the middle of the courtyard.

"Short swords?" asked Kazio as he closed the distance.

"You're afraid to get too close?" Harth tossed a sword at Kazio.

He caught it by the hilt. It whistled through the air as he swung it a few times, and then he looked to Harth. "On your call."

CLEVEHOLD

Tisa got down from the stone perch. "I should retrieve Amundr for when one of them hurts themselves."

Lena nodded. There was a tightness in her chest. She didn't know what to expect from Kazio, and that scared her the most. Her gut said it would be a dirty fight. He was a young man putting on an act. He was a leader on Briet's council. A rational person had to exist in there, she reasoned. By the way he prowled with the sword, however, she couldn't see through to it.

Harth nodded, and the spar began. Swords clanked together melodically. Kazio was taller than Harth, but both men looked equally strong.

Tisa gave their spar a wide berth. Cicero walked toward her, and the two of them spoke quietly as they passed. Tisa nodded and kept walking. Cicero approached the stone barrier and took Tisa's spot on the wall.

Anxiety spurred in Lena as she watched the men fight. There was too much brutality in it for it to have been considered sparring. The clanks of metal were too rough.

The base of Kazio's sword glowed orange.

In the next swing, Kazio's entire sword illuminated. When it hit Harth's, there was no give or pushback on Kazio's.

The impact made Harth stagger back. He stayed on his feet. "No magic," said Harth. He pointed at Kazio with his sword and began walking a circle around him. "If you want to sword fight, sword fight. Let's not make this messy."

"He reminds me of Imogene," said Cicero.

Kazio and Harth resumed fighting. Lena had to look away. She asked Cicero, "Who is that, Imogene?"

"She was an Est soldier. Kazio's mentor," answered Cicero.

Lena took a deep breath, debated her question, and asked anyway. "What are the Est, and is that why his magic is different?"

Enthusiastic, Cicero explained, "The knights of the king were sent to squash a rebellion in the East. You know about the curse and the Binding. The knights were referred to 'of the night,' I think partly because of when they chose to attack. Over time, that was shortened from 'of the night' to 'Ovnite.' Blue magic. The rebellion, they were Nobles in the East with orange magic."

"Eastern Nobles." She proposed, "Estnable?"

Cicero nodded. "It's where Kazio and I came from. We're Est, originally."

"You're very knowledgeable for a fighter," she complimented. His conversation was a good distraction. The men were arguing about something.

"Wasn't always." He stopped to cough. "I was a scholar back home."

Lena's eyes lit up. *An avenue out.* "Would you like to see the Royal Library?"

THE FIRST FEW MOMENTS after Cicero entered the library, he only gawked. Selgen saw them come in, then disappeared around a shelf and walked off. Cicero didn't seem to notice.

"There's another library in Clevehold," said Lena. She ran a finger along a shelf. "Hopefully the occupying army doesn't damage it."

"Is it this size?" asked Cicero.

Lena shook her head. "Bigger. Three times the size, at least."

"How many books?" Cicero's eyes scanned up and down shelves.

She had never stopped to consider it. *Thousands. Tens of thousands. Maybe more.* "I'm not sure, but you're welcome to use the library while you're here."

He covered his mouth to cough, then cleared his throat. "I'm not sure I could read this much in a lifetime. In fact, I'm sure I couldn't."

"Perhaps you'll stay and try. Briet will need a council. So long as you don't think you'll miss your home too much," said Lena.

"I don't." He tapped on the spine of a book. "I don't think I'll go back there. To be honest, I don't know that anyone wants to return."

Was that why Briet had agreed so readily to stay? Was there no home to go back to? Lena guided them to sit on a bench by a window. "Will you tell me about it, your home?"

"I grew up in Estnable. The fortress they had was only a few stories high, but the layout was massive. I never really left it until I went to the Ovnite settlement." He stopped and looked down at his hands.

"How did an Estnable bookworm end up an Ovnite soldier?" asked Lena.

Socks trailed in. He meowed at Lena, took a long look at Cicero, and scurried back out.

"He's shy," she apologized.

"That's alright." He looked out the window. "Kazio and I, and a friend of ours, left Estnable and went to the Ovnite. We did it because the Est leaders wanted to break the Binding. We overheard it, but no one believed us. See . . ." He took a long breath. "Before the Stone King was killed *again*, if we had tried to break the Binding, it would have killed us all. We didn't have enough evidence to know for certain that the magic was broken. We worked with the Ovnite because we wanted to stop the Est from killing everyone. It was really with the best of intentions."

She put a hand to his shoulder. "I understand."

"Amundr and his wife, Ellisif, were the ones who helped us assimilate into the Ovnite. They trained us. Ellisif was a strong, courageous woman. Without her guidance, I don't know that I would have ever been a fighter." The smile he had grown speaking about her lessened. "The Est and the Ovnite were always feuding. The Est attacked. Ellisif was killed, shot in the back with an arrow. Amundr couldn't save her. The Ovnite numbers shrunk. We fought the Est again. We won, but we lost. The Binding was broken."

"I'm glad the remains of the Stone King's magic didn't kill you," said Lena. She tried to process his story, filling in the gaps with smaller details she had otherwise heard or inferred. A thought washed over her. Her eyes lost focus.

"What?" he asked.

Lena shook her head. "It's interesting. Our stories aren't the same, but they rhyme." He looked at her curiously, and she explained, "I had never left the city I grew up in. I was scared to think of the world beyond it. It didn't exist to me. Then, one day, it was all upended. I never would have gotten through what happened without Klaus and Avild."

"The historian?" questioned Cicero.

"Her and her husband. They had a cabin outside the city and kept us safe while we sorted things out. The people who were after Tulir, they came. It was just me and Klaus at the cabin at the time. He fought valiantly, three against one, and the only reason he lost was because someone outside shot him in the back with an arrow." Lena stopped and clasped her hands together. She heard Rether's laugh echoing in her ears, saw the way Klaus' eyes had bulged when he was gutted. The arrow would have done it. The blood loss just made it faster.

Klaus. Then Vilars. Effectively Selgen. Almost Tulir and Harth. Almost her. "We also lost, in a way."

"It's strange how this world can take someone like you and me and change them into . . ." He gestured between them, then continued hurriedly, "Not that I meant . . . because you had said—"

"No, you're right," she agreed. She took a deep breath and looked out the window. "We are at a strange intersection. The occupation beyond our walls. The wedding. Things I assume your people didn't consider when they crossed the sea."

"To be honest, and no unfairness to your people, I'm surprised by how different the world *isn't*." He coughed and cleared his throat. He looked pale.

"Would you like water?"

He waved a hand and insisted, "I'm fine."

"When the Stone King's magic turned on him, what had united the different regions fell apart. We're only just mending those discrepancies. Apparently, not well enough or fast enough."

"It put us in a better situation to compromise," he suggested.

She shrugged and clasped her hands together. "I hope that compromise endures. I'd love to learn to heal like your people do."

"I don't know it myself. It's Vitki magic. I can talk to Amundr about him teaching it to you."

"Maybe," she agreed. The thought of it made her uneasy.

"He isn't as scary as he looks." Cicero bumped shoulders with her. "He lost everything when Est attacked. It changed him."

"That's understandable."

"He has a big heart and bad eyesight but admits to neither. Once you get past the first layer, he's a good person, and a good magic teacher," said Cicero. "Plus, anyone with the patience to teach Kazio deserves mountainous credit."

She nodded and smiled. "I would appreciate it, then."

Chapter 18

THE DINING ROOM HAD been refashioned for the wedding. The hall of the Stone King was likely more appropriate for the occasion, but the connotations of the hall weren't easily overlooked. The dining hall may not have had the balconies for observers, but the room was large enough with the tables removed to house an absurd number of people. Where the tables were hidden, Lena didn't know.

Lena sat on a bench near the front of the room with the rest of Court. She had looked around to find her mother, Nela, or Selgen but couldn't locate them in the crowd. What she did observe was the lack of Ovnite. There were some, but not nearly as many as she had expected. Troubled, she thought about what Tisa had said the day before about sickness.

A blonde at the side of the crowd caught Lena's attention. She tried to wave for Avild to approach, but the other woman refused. They made eye contact. Avild didn't come any closer.

Lena debated getting up. No one would be so disrespectful as to steal her seat. There was still time before the ceremony. She left the bench and went toward the window Avild was standing by. "I'm surprised you came."

"I'm surprised you look so happy," said Avild.

Lena raised her eyebrows.

Avild shook her head and pinched the bridge of her nose. "I'm sorry. I don't like being here. Harth said it was the respectful thing for me to do."

"It is the respectful thing to do, which is why I'm happy to do it," said Lena.

"I am sorry to you personally that it came to this."

Lena took Avild gently by the wrist and moved them closer to the window, away from the crowd. There was an uptick in volume. More people were gathering in the middle of the hall.

"Tell me"—Lena looked around—"is this what all royal weddings are like? Historically speaking."

"This wasn't the traditional place. The concept and contract of marriage hasn't changed much over time," answered Avild.

A horn blew. Lena opened her mouth to say she should return to her seat and that Avild could join her. There was room, and she had aided the Council.

"It's nothing like my wedding," said Avild.

Lena smiled. "To Klaus? I expect not."

"Not him. The first one."

"The—?" Lena stopped her question at the crescendo of music.

"An arrangement brokered by my father when I was sixteen. He was an ugly man, over twice my age, and had land in the East," Avild explained casually as if she wasn't relaying a version of history not captured in the text.

"What happened to him?" asked Lena. The thoughts of returning to her seat were forgotten.

"One of Gudserk's men found him drowned in his own vomit the morning after the ceremony. He never so much as made it to bed."

Avild had killed him.

"No. I wasn't a fighter then," she had told Lena. *Then Avild had the man killed.* Stuttering to find the right way to start the question, Lena asked, "W-were there other suitors?"

"None that I responded favorably to." Avild's eyes were focused on the ceremony.

A man at the front began talking. Lena didn't know if it was the crowd, how far away she was, or the ringing in her ears, but she heard none of the words clearly. Tulir was at the front. She knew she should go.

Land in the East. Across the sea, east? There had been Nobles there once. They rebelled against the king. A king who had slighted them? A king who pitched a marriage of alliances only to betray his word? Lena wondered if she should bookmark the thought to ask Cicero about later. What did their history say of it?

Perhaps it was better to not know. Lena shifted her eyes from Avild to the ceremony, then to the tapestries that hung from the ceiling. Most were only colors and sigils. Tulir hadn't posed for any of himself; he thought it gratuitous. There was one of the Stone King's family at the back of the room.

The king, with his eldest daughter, only son, and young twin girls. The tapestry had been heavily damaged but, like most things, was restored with best efforts. When they had been remaking it, Lena had caught herself more than once. The masses thought it was the queen in the tapestry, not a third daughter. That was how history retained their memory.

The victors wrote history. The tellings and retellings of a lie made it true. That was history as all but four people in the room, in the *world*, knew. If that lie could have been sold completely enough, what other alterations to history existed based off a well-traveled rumor? If Avild didn't want the Stone King's eldest child to be remembered as his daughter, she wasn't. If Avild didn't want surviving records of her first husband, there weren't.

There was no telling how much centuries of history could change. How would people speak of current actions in a thousand years? Did Tulir have a nickname not yet realized that he would become known solely by, his real name long forgotten? Would people like Lena be remembered at all? The thought made her feel as the ceremony did—insignificant.

CLEVEHOLD

AT THE CONCLUSION OF the short ceremony, during which there was an exchange of rings and amulets, the room was flipped. Tables and benches were brought in from an adjoining room. Not as many as normal, but enough for food and drink. The head table was dressed per usual.

The fact they were amidst a siege wasn't forgotten, though Lena assumed the festivities intended to push aside that fact for at least a few hours. Food wasn't served in abundance, but alcohol was. The distilleries of Clevehold had moved their stock into the castle at the first whisper of trouble. It was a staple they had no shortage of. The main alcohol they served were beer and mead—heavy, hearty, filling.

Lena had considered getting drunk. The thought first crossed her mind when she had arrived at the head table. The structure had changed. She sat in the chair the servant pulled out for her. It was on the wrong side.

Seven chairs were on each side of the table. On the side Lena was sat on, from left to right were Charlot, Norman, her, Harth, Amundr, Kazio, and an empty seat with a place setting. She assumed it was for Cicero and proved his absence from the festivities. Across the table from Cicero's place was another empty seat, but this one wasn't dressed. Next to it was Tisa, Briet, Tulir—still putting him at the center—Rufino, Marisol, and an empty undressed setting.

The placement made sense. Lena smiled and nodded politely with the dinner conversation as she rationalized the groupings. The young king and queen sat across from more seasoned fighters, a physical obstacle between royalty and the rest of the room. To the immediate left and right of Tulir and Briet were their most trusted advisors. The next step in the logic made Lena realize she was balanced with Kazio—she decided not to think on that too hard—and at the ends were the other advisors. It meant Cicero was balanced with Norman, but if he had been here, Lena would have told him not to take it personally. Putting Norman there served the dual purpose of keeping him away from the Ovnite and keeping Charlot away from everyone.

"I hadn't heard anything. Had you?"

Lena looked up from her plate. Marisol was looking at her. "Sorry?"

"The postmaster's missing dog," said Marisol.

Lena wiped her mouth with a napkin. "I didn't know he had one."

Rufino looked down the Ovnite side of the table. "What do the necklaces represent?"

"The amulets on tether strings are our symbols of union. Akin to your wedding rings," answered Briet.

Harth blocked most of Lena's view of Amundr, but she looked that direction. He wore two. *One for himself and one for his lost wife?* Kazio and Tisa didn't have one.

"What are the small knives for?" asked Tisa. She put a hand over her bicep. "I've seen some of the Royal Guards carrying them. Harth has one, yes?"

"They're stitched into some of your shirts, as well," added Briet as she looked at Tulir.

What are knives usually for? She tucked away the urge to repeat the answer she had been given by drinking her beer. She should get drunk tonight, she decided. It was in her jealousy's best interest when, in a few hours, she would start overthinking how Briet knew the tailor work of Tulir's shirts already.

"When a guard makes a significant mistake, there's a punishment for it. The men have choices: the whip, shaving of one's head, or a stab to the upper arm with a small knife that sits over their bicep," answered Tulir.

"And they call us archaic," said Amundr.

"Why give the men choices?" asked Kazio. He drank his beer. "Why not pick hair? It grows back, yes?"

"They choose one punishment, and it's a career habit. It tells you a lot about the man. The one who chooses the knife is injured by his superior or the offended. Less public than the whip. The wound is small, but significant enough the man has to keep it clean for weeks to stop the festering. He'll feel the injury for months when he works the muscle," explained Harth.

"Those who pick to shave their heads can be suitable for mundane jobs, like the City Guard, but such vanity doesn't exist in the Royal Guard," added Tulir.

The music picked up before there was a retort. It was too loud to hear down the table. The sounds of people clapping and dancing added to the noise. Lena took the absence of conversation as her cue to advance her drinking.

"We should dance?"

Lena visibly winced hearing Charlot's whining statement-question. Tulir covered his mouth to hide his smile, and Harth nudged her with his shoulder. Lena raised her glass as if to cheers, then drank. Rufino did the same. Marisol wore a buttoned-up smile.

"Yes, dear." Norman and Charlot rose from the table and walked away. Their immediate absence was followed by silence from the Court.

Lena felt laughter bubbling up from her stomach and couldn't hold it back. It spread first to Marisol, whose smile grew as her eyes clenched. It worked its way down the table. Briet cracked into audible laughter before Tulir did. There was a strange laugh Lena assumed had to belong to Amundr. Harth had an elbow on the table and fist to a closed mouth, but the amusement was clear in his eyes. Tisa slouched low in her seat and alternated between normal laughs and high-pitched squeaks, which only made them all laugh more.

A cheer broke out in the crowd and Lena looked back to see what had caused it. On the musicians' temporary platform, a woman held up a violin. She showed it off to the crowd for a few seconds before wedging it under her neck. The crowd settled and held their breath.

The sweet melody of the violin carried through the hall, slow and sweet at first until the violinist stomped twice and switched to an upbeat sawing. Other instruments soon joined in, and people clapped along. Mugs of beer were raised.

"I love these things!" exclaimed Tisa. She looked down the line of men at the table and settled on Kazio. "You have to dance with me."

The remnants of laughter were still in his voice. "No, I don't."

"I outrank you," said Tisa. She stood.

Kazio made a so-so motion with his hand.

"I definitely do, yes?" said Briet. She pointed at the dance floor. "Go."

Kazio got up and bowed in bad form. "Yes, Your Grace."

Tisa didn't wait for him to stand upright before she dragged him away. There were a few shuffled steps before they righted and disappeared into the crowd.

"Drowned dog stack!" yelled a man. People cheered.

Lena took a deep breath and looked down at her glass. She should trade it in for a beer mug if she was going to drink like this. *Perhaps I should join the game.*

Across the table, Marisol whispered something in Rufino's ear. He turned red. Marisol stood gracefully, whereas Rufino bumped the table. He apologized, "Sorry, will you excuse us?"

"Enjoy the night," said Tulir, his glass raised.

Hand in hand, Rufino and Marisol made for the rear exit.

"Were they not enjoying the celebrations?" asked Briet.

"They'll be enjoying themselves privately," answered Lena. She hiccupped.

Briet smiled. "I see."

"Drowned dog?" asked Amundr. He said the first word with stranger enunciation than the typical Ovnite accent.

"A drinking game," answered Tulir.

"Ah." Amundr leaned forward, elbows on the table, and pointed at Tulir. "Is the king too noble to drink with his people?"

Tulir put down his glass. "Not if it's in good company."

Amundr laughed and stood. He pulled Harth's chair back. "You, too."

"If you insist," said Harth. He glanced down to Lena, then to the periphery of the crowd. Nodding to the side subtly, he then turned to join the men.

Lena didn't think much of the parting action until Avild approached the near empty table. It was just her and Briet left. *Where has everyone gone so quickly?* Did Harth think she needed reinforcements? Protection? A guardian?

Avild was on Tulir's side of the table. She gestured to his empty seat, still pulled out, and asked Briet, "Do you mind?"

Was your seat anyway, thought Lena. *Supposed to be. Wanted it to be. Never quite was.*

Lena drank. A servant refilled the glass.

"Please. I don't foresee them returning any time soon," said Briet.

Was she trying to talk like them? Was she a high society woman where she came from? *How fitting for a queen.* Lena decided to resume her polite, understanding nature in the morning. She was allowed rudeness tonight.

Avild sat. She had her own mug, mostly full, and raised it. "Congratulations."

"Appreciated," responded Briet. "Thank you for the part you played in getting us this far."

"To our alliance." Lena raised her glass and some sloshed over the side. "And to what's in the people's best interest."

The women clanked glasses. Briet took a gulp. Avild only sipped.

"Lena"—Briet paused to cover her mouth—"I know you were to be queen before everything changed. I agree that what's transpired is in all our people's best interests. I don't know who your other suitors are, but I make available my top men."

"That's very kind of you," said Lena. She was a duchess. The first bridge of the alliance had not seen the day's end and it was already her turn to get brokered.

"Nothing has to be decided immediately," said Briet.

"Of course." Lena waved her hand. "It will bridge ties. Avild, what do you think of them?"

"You are well-grounded. You should hope to pass the same on to your children," said Avild.

Fish. Lena felt her stomach churning. The day. The beer. The conversation. If she caught a whiff of fish, she would lose her stomach contents.

"Kazio, then. He leads the Vitki," said Briet.

Had Harth known Avild wanted to have this conversation? Was Lena meant to be sold like livestock? It was Briet's idea—today, it was—but Avild had known.

Lena drank.

"Not Amundr?" questioned Avild.

Cheers rang out in the direction of the drinking game. Lena looked that direction and sucked a breath in between her teeth. *The oddly balanced one with yellowed skin? No.*

"He's powerful, but a widower and not an available man," answered Briet.

Lena's shoulders dropped as she breathed out. A thought occurred to her—the tone. *Longing? No. Regret? Not quite.* Muted, whatever it was. She drank and let the thought go.

"Is he agreeable to you? Kazio?" asked Briet.

The smile Lena performed was supposed to have been polite and understanding. That was who she was. Based on their reactions, that was how it was received. It didn't stop the action from feeling sour. This was her future, decided by others. She just had to be present for it.

She should have been queen from the beginning.

"He is difficult. I won't pretend he can't be," said Briet. She sipped her glass.

Avild rested, her shoulders back and chest open with her forearms on the chair arms. "Not by way of being abusive."

"No, not at all. Such isn't tolerated within the Ovnite," said Briet.

"Such does occasionally happen here. Should it happen to a duchess, the man would go missing rather quickly," said Avild conversationally.

Lena felt a genuine smile pull up her face.

"I would expect nothing less. Only proof, if it were one of my men," said Briet.

Another violin song kicked up. The drinking game was in full swing. People were enjoying themselves all around. Lena angled her chair to face the festivities; it wasn't as if the women needed her input. The man Lena was going to spend her life with would be decided by a woman younger than her—granted, much more talented and worldly—and a near thousand-year-old princess in hiding.

Lena drank.

Had Klaus known about Avild's first husband? *Very likely.* How had that adjusted his view of the then-princess? Lena had envisioned the start of Klaus and Avild's love as stolen glances across Court. He was a Royal Guard, charming, deceptively strong for his size, and he stirred up daydreams of running away in the princess. Attempts to impress her with magic flares were thought to go unnoticed, but she was always watching him with a keen eye. They bonded over a mutual skill of archery. Avild offered to take him to the Royal Range, and he always managed to have been one of the guards with her when she left the castle to hunt. Cute. Subtle. Gradual.

Romantic.

Lena drank her beer to empty and, not seeing a servant around to refill it, borrowed a glass someone had left behind.

Love wasn't linear and gentle. Not really. Love overwhelmed you. Affection could begin as subtle. A natural comfort around someone. Once you realized love was taking hold, the floodgates were already open. Love made you rationalize the rash and not want to apologize for impropriety.

That had to have been the case with Klaus and Avild, too. They had known each other existed, but neither was an option for the other. Avild had her first husband killed—if Klaus wasn't already employed as a Royal Guard when it happened, she doubted the rumor wasn't relayed. Then, she let the whore's family conspire to kill her brother. Enough Royal Guards survived for Gudserk to send his men to chase a rumor.

Lena set her glass on her knee and drummed her nails against it. All the things Avild had told her, she took as fact. What if none of it were true? Or what if all of it, and all of their implications, were true?

What if Klaus had been here? If he had lived, would the Stone King still stand? Was it always about finding someone to pass the responsibility of power to? Lena was young. Impressionable. Malleable. She liked to think Klaus would have objected to her getting married off in the name of building bridges. Or perhaps he would have sided with Avild.

The most likely outcome, regardless of his personal feelings, was that he would have deferred to Avild. This was her world.

A smile bloomed on Lena's face. She was making the case to the wrong person. She wanted Avild to come to the library. She wanted Selgen to escape the city. Avild was the thinker, and Lena couldn't outsmart her. What Lena could do was make the appeal to Avild's heart.

The heart she had lost.

"Miss Lena?"

She picked up her head. There was a sway to her upper body. She blinked a few times. "Yes?"

"Pardon me, Duchess," corrected Harth. He looked pinkish high in his cheeks. There was a spill mark on the side of his trousers she assumed someone else had caused.

"Don't start with that," pleaded Lena lazily. She lifted her glass up, but before the liquid reached her mouth, the smell hit her nose. Her stomach protested. Maybe it was her mind. There was too much delay in her thoughts to decipher which. She lowered the glass.

"Would you like an escort back to your room?" he asked.

She shook her head and held the glass out to him, glad that he took it; the quick movement of her head made her dizzy. "I . . ." She wanted to protest, but the last bit of sensibility won out. "I think I might best do."

"Would you like assistance?" His right arm bent at the waist to offer an escort.

"Should I leave while they're deciding my future?" mumbled Lena. She turned enough to see across the table. Briet and Avild weren't there. "They decided, and they left."

"The bride went to find the groom for a dance," said Harth.

And Avild disappeared into the background and faded away. A spy. A thief. Lena braced her hands on the chair arms and stood. "Drowned dog. Did you win?"

He shook his head. "I've never had luck with chance games."

Lena swayed. She wanted to get back to her room. But she doubted her ability to do it on her own. She reached for the arm Harth kept prepared for her. His steps were steady, steadier than hers. She asked, "Did you not drink?"

"Just more practiced." He walked them to the rear door. They exited to the hall, but the noise carried with them.

Lena stumbled. She put her free hand to the wall to right herself. Laughing, she said, "I should have practiced."

"You alright to do the stairs?"

After a deep breath, she answered, "If you can."

He patted her on the arm and began their irregularly paced climb.

"I don't know whether to be proud or insulted you didn't overindulge tonight." Were those the right words? Lena wasn't sure. She was too busy being proud of herself for making it up the steps without tripping.

"I scheduled myself for the predawn shift on the wall. I figured too many men would object or show up sloppy. I only have a few hours before I have to be up there," explained Harth.

"Please don't fall off the wall," said Lena. She hiccupped.

Harth laughed. "I won't."

With no filter on her thoughts, she said, "You scheduled because you presumed you'd get no sleep tonight. I only hope I've indulged enough to sleep. I can go back to being rational and understanding tomorrow."

"If the worst of your indulgence is a slur in speech and step, then you're faring a lot better than most men down there," said Harth.

She pushed him off. He had meant it as a compliment, and that was the worst of it. The demure, accepting, well-mannered girl—that was all she was.

Lena gripped the material of her short skirt. Her back hit the wall. "Find the queen. I'll tell her what for."

"I didn't mean—"

"She shows up at our gates. Threatens us. Then she's planning *my* future."

Harth made a motion for her to lower her tone.

Lena hissed. "She wants me to marry that Vitki. He doesn't like me! Doesn't respect me!"

"I'm sure if you talked to Tulir, something else could be arranged."

"No." She let go of her skirt and wiped her mouth. "He'll talk to Briet, see the rationality in it, then he'll volunteer to be the one to talk to me about it."

"He wouldn't force you to do—"

"He'd be right." She slapped her hands on her thighs. There was a hollowness in her chest. "It would make sense! He wouldn't make me, but he would ask me. And there's nothing he could ask of me that I wouldn't do."

Harth opened his mouth, closed it again, then rubbed a hand down his face.

"I don't want to get sold off, even if it is the right thing," admitted Lena. Her voice cracked.

"I wish there was something I could do. About all of this."

The desperation in his voice didn't equal hers, but she saw it in his eyes. Where was the future they were supposed to have? Lived for one night only to have been danced away to the tune of clapping and violins.

Lena giggled. "You don't like Kazio."

"No." He shook his head and shared her smile. "No, I don't."

"We should get married," she considered.

He warned, "Lena."

"I'm going to get taken off the Council anyway. At least I wouldn't lose my connection to it completely," she justified.

"You aren't going to lose your place on the Council. And you're a duchess, beyond what I know you to be. Marrying a guard is below your station."

She scoffed. "A Royal Guard has been proven to be fit for a royal station. You're the Commander of the Royal Guard. And what is a Vitki leader, if not for a glorified magic guard?"

"Even if the stations were a fitting match, it ignores the purpose. Briet wants you to marry Kazio for the sake of . . ." He fumbled over the words, "Uniting. Mending."

Input logic to avoid making it personal. She had seen that before. She stepped forward and spoke kinder, softer, "We can make the appeal it's an arrangement made from emotion. I'm just a silly woman, aren't I? It would be an act of heart, the very thing that brought the Ovnite within the walls."

"Lena, I told you." He sighed and looked to the side. "I'm not . . ."

"You're a strong, rugged man who is good at hiding his feelings. You got an opportunity when my proposed station changed. I expect they'll be surprised, but not in denial of the story we tell." She took his hand in both of hers.

He let her.

"I remember all you told me. I don't expect you to change. I don't expect to get everything from you." She looked him in the eye when he turned. "But we could hide away together and share our heartbreak over the same thing."

Silence hung for a moment. Footsteps approached—two sets, and quickly. Tisa appeared around the corner with an Ovnite man in tow with her. They both looked giddy and drunk. Tisa stopped when she saw Lena and Harth, and her companion bumped into her.

"You took a right at the stairs, not a left," explained Harth.

"Right." Tisa backed up a step. "Sorry."

"This place is a maze," excused Lena.

Tisa nodded, then turned and pushed her companion back. They went back around the corner and their footsteps receded.

"Gives the story merit," supposed Harth.

Lena smiled and squeezed his hand.

He looked the other way down the hall. "I said I'd see you to your room, Miss Lena. I have."

"We're done talking about this?" she questioned. Her hands pulled back. "I suppose it was another fanciful idea to get me out of a mess I have no right being in."

Harth put a hand onto her shoulder, leaned down, and kissed her forehead.

"I'd be understanding," she said. *More understanding than a random woman, if the monarchy became so inclined to marry you off, too.*

"Can we talk about this in the daylight?" he requested.

"In the daylight," she agreed.

He smiled. "Good night, Miss Lena."

Chapter 19

THE SOUND OF ALARM bells made Lena jerk awake. Socks jumped from where he slept at her feet and dove under the bed. A headache pounded in Lena's ears. She zeroed in on the alarms. Something was wrong. What time was it?

Lena got out of bed and dressed quickly. There was a bad taste in her mouth. She guzzled a cup of water, grabbed a ribbon to stuff into her pocket, and fastened a knife to her belt. When she exited her room, someone ran past.

The rendezvous point. She was supposed to head there. As she walked toward the stairs, she tied up her hair. People were headed in all different directions. The light was all firelight. The sun hadn't come up yet.

Avild was coming up the steps as Lena descended. They met in the middle.

"Do you know what's happening?" asked Lena.

Avild shook her head. "I was in the barracks. It's not the Ovnite."

"I was asleep," said Lena.

"Missus Avild. Duchess." Salvatore met them on the stairs. "Are you alright?"

"We're fine," said Lena. *He doesn't have any idea either, does he?*

"Do you require an escort?" he asked.

"No. Go do whatever you need to," instructed Lena.

He nodded and left them.

"Where is the rendezvous point for the Court?" asked Avild.

Lena continued down the stairs, bringing the other woman with her. "The Stone King's Hall. We meet there. It isn't used otherwise."

"Interesting choice," commented Avild as they moved through the crowd.

"It's secluded, defendable, and a place we know no one else will be." Lena led them to the cell hall, sure to close the door behind them. They went down, crossed, and went up the second set of stairs. There, they ran into Harth, Rufino, and Marisol.

"Steepwharf?" proposed Avild.

"Their position hasn't changed, and they haven't abandoned," answered Harth. He was armed with his bow, looking to have come from watch.

"We don't know what's happening?" questioned Rufino. Marisol clung to him tightly.

"Let's all get to the hall. Perhaps someone there will have answers," said Lena.

The group of them entered, Rufino and Marisol at the front, Lena in the middle, the other two behind her. A shiver crawled up Lena's spine.

Kazio could be heard grumbling before she saw him.

"He did what he could, you know that. Now we have to wait," said Tisa. She was standing between Kazio and Amundr.

Norman, dressed in nightclothes, approached Lena's group. "What's going on?"

"Where's the king?" countered Harth. Three of the Ovnite and the Council, save Tulir, were present.

"We haven't seen him," answered Tisa.

"Briet isn't here, either," added Amundr. "We're missing them both."

"You up to going out there?" Harth proposed to Amundr.

"I'll go with you," offered Avild.

Harth advised, "Stay with the duchess."

"The historian is a personal bodyguard?" questioned Kazio sourly.

"You weren't sleeping on the job this time?" accused Norman as he glared at Harth. "Or just elsewhere?"

Amundr moved toward the exit door Harth held propped open.

Marisol whispered something to Rufino, and he held her closer.

Not the Ovnite, Lena repeated to herself. She swallowed heavily. The pounding in her head made her thoughts slow. Steepwharf hadn't changed positions. She didn't smell smoke. She thought of Nela, Selgen, and her mother. *Goodness, why did it take me so long to consider them? They must be terrified. Are they alright?*

Amundr backed away from the door while Harth kept it open but stood out of the way. More footsteps were approaching.

Briet walked in first. She had two swords, one in each hand, the blades resting on her shoulders. Tulir followed, dragging with him a beaten-up man who left a damp trail behind him on the stone floor. Three more guards followed, two of them dragging injured men. The last one spoke to Harth, then closed the door.

The swords were dropped off to the side. Tulir shoved the man he was hauling at everyone's feet. The man fell to his hands and knees. Blood dripped off his face.

"Look who we caught sneaking about," said Tulir. He was dressed in nightclothes, a billowing shirt and cotton trousers tucked into boots. There was blood on his knuckles.

The prisoners were Steepwharf men. Lena recognized their clothes. The material was lightweight and dried quickly. She surmised, "They came in through the tunnels?"

"They haven't been very forthcoming." Tulir kicked the prisoner in the side, causing the man to topple over.

In the distance, the bells stopped.

"Was anyone hurt?" asked Tisa.

"Nothing they won't recover from," answered Briet.

A prisoner groaned.

"No, she isn't talking about you," said Tulir. He looked to the guard who had arrived with them but didn't have a prisoner. "May I borrow that?"

The guard handed Tulir a knife off his belt.

"Anyone uncomfortable watching a man die should leave," warned Briet.

Kazio scoffed. "Their women fear blood?"

Lena looked to Norman, then flicked her eyes to the door. He was pale but crossed his arms and remained stationary. Lena shook her head.

"Sir, would you mind escorting my wife back to our room?" asked Rufino. He squeezed Marisol before letting her go. The man who had given Tulir his knife stepped forward.

"You"—Harth pointed at the one guard standing behind a prisoner—"exchange custody with Amundr."

The guard shoved the prisoner down, and Amundr stepped forward to stand over the man. The prisoner tried to hide his innate flinch at the giant man towering over him.

"I'm going to take my men to do a sweep of the grounds. I know where the tunnels let out. We'll block wherever it's been breached and track down any others who got in," said Harth.

"I'll send Drengr to help," offered Tisa.

"As Kazio will do with the Vitki," ordered Briet. She was also dressed in nightclothes more akin to Tulir's, not a nightgown.

"Understood." Kazio walked away with Tisa and Harth.

"Avild, you have this one?" Tulir asked as he gestured at the last prisoner.

She nodded.

Norman began, "I hardly see how that's—"

Tulir ordered the last guard, "Go see to the duchess' family—Selgen, Nela, and Christa. See they're aright and assure them Lena is."

"Yes, sir," he responded with a nod.

The prisoner in exchange stood quickly. A knife was pulled from his boot. With bloody teeth, he snarled and advanced toward Tulir.

An array of green claws intercepted him. A talon sliced his wrist, and he dropped the knife. A bear claw ripped at his thigh, and he fell to one knee. As he cried out, a second wave of green magic hit him, a gust of wind. The prisoner toppled backward and skidded across the floor.

Briet stared, open-mouthed, at Avild.

Lena clenched her arms around herself and steadied her breathing. Her heart was beating quickly. Despite her headache, she tried to focus.

"Do you want this one dead?" asked Avild. She stepped toward the groaning prisoner.

"Not yet," answered Tulir.

"We know these are Steepwharf men?" proposed Rufino. He stared intently at the one Amundr hovered over.

"Yes," answered Lena, "by their clothes."

"By their weapons, too. But they weren't guards. Not so far as I knew," said Tulir.

"I wonder." Amundr crouched next to his prisoner. "How many men died trying to find a way through those tunnels?"

"The ways are drowned. I suppose there could be pockets of air along the way, but it would be pitch-dark. They have no light that can survive down there," said Avild.

Tulir walked around the front of his prisoner. He used the knife to raise the man's chin. "How many of you tried to get in?"

Silence.

Tulir dug the knife in. Thin streams of blood trickled down the man's face.

"Was it just three you found?" asked Norman.

"Just these three wet rats," confirmed Briet. She walked to the window looking out over Clevehold and crossed her arms.

Lena picked up her head. "They came for you, or they came for her?"

"We were together when they found us," answered Tulir.

"Yes, but who were they after?" Lena's thoughts were murky, but she knew she was making sense.

"Whose room were you in when they came for you?" asked Rufino.

"Mine," answered Briet, facing the window.

"You came for her?" Tulir asked as he dragged the knife under the prisoner's chin.

Amundr kicked his prisoner over and rummaged through the man's pockets.

"They came to assassinate the queen on her wedding night?" questioned Norman.

"There's no way for them to have known of the ceremony. They came to kill the Ovnite leader," countered Lena.

Amundr held a vial from the prisoner's pocket up to the light. After squinting for a few seconds, he created light with his hand. The vial contained a murky yellow liquid.

"How did you know what she looks like?" asked Tulir. The prisoner he had made bleed kept his mouth shut.

"They know from the raid on Steepwharf," volunteered Rufino.

Amundr scoffed.

Lena looked at Briet's reflection in the window. The woman wiped away blood that had seeped out of her ear. Lena looked to see if anyone else noticed, but their eyes were on the vial.

"May I?" asked Avild. When Amundr tossed it to her, a green glow lit up her hand.

A cushion to catch? wondered Lena.

Tulir carved the knife up the side of the prisoner's face. The prisoner winced but kept his mouth closed. Blood stained his clothing. Tulir kicked him over. "We aren't going to get anything out of them tonight."

Avild uncorked the vial and sniffed. She dabbed her finger into it and rubbed the liquid between the pads of her fingers. "Whatever it is, it has to be injected or ingested."

"Poison or sedation?" asked Norman.

"They could be coerced into talking." Briet turned to face them. She was closest to Avild and her prisoner.

"I'm tempted to let them sleep on it. A few days without food, water, sunlight—it separates the boys from the men," said Tulir.

"Do you need all three of them?" Avild held up the vial.

Tulir looked to Briet. After she shook her head, he said, "I'd like to know what it does."

Lena looked at the knife by her feet. It was nondescript, but familiar. A standard knife from Steepwharf. A guard's knife. She picked it up and looked it over to confirm.

Avild gripped her prisoner by the throat. Lena kept her eyes on the knife. She heard the sounds of struggle and gargling as the man was forced to drink.

"Ten to one, that liquid won't kill him, only put him to sleep," said Lena.

"What makes you think so?" Norman asked critically at the same time Rufino asked, "Why?"

Lena walked to Tulir and handed the knife off to him. "Look familiar?"

He examined it. The prisoner at his feet squirmed, and Tulir stomped his foot. The prisoner stopped moving. Tulir shrugged. "Looks like a standard knife."

"A standard guard's knife from Steepwharf. They're fashioned a bit differently here, and you said these men weren't guards," said Lena.

"Harth and one of those Royal Guards were from Steepwharf, too. They didn't recognize these men," agreed Avild.

Briet looked at Tulir. "You have a knife like that, yes?"

Tulir sighed and clenched his jaw. "They wanted to make it look a certain way."

"Whether we blamed you directly or one in your employ, our leader killed by one of yours looks like a conspiracy, yes?" said Amundr.

"Despite us apprehending the men, it sounds like you're accusing us of something," said Norman.

Lena rolled her eyes at the use of "us."

"It's just the way in which he speaks," excused Briet.

The prisoner by Avild flopped forward heavily. His head smacked the stone and he groaned. His hand dragged forward, but he couldn't prop himself up.

"A sleeping aid or a paralyzer," surmised Avild. She kicked the man over for him to face the ceiling. His forehead was bleeding and blood seeped from his mouth. A loose tooth moved as he breathed heavily.

"Will their people bargain for them?" asked Amundr.

"The people of Steepwharf aren't inherently heartful people. I don't suppose they sent anyone they couldn't bear to part with," said Lena.

"A test of our defenses," said Briet.

"Something to toy with us," agreed Tulir.

Rufino sighed. "Something to keep us from sleeping at night."

"If you're going to keep them, where?" asked Amundr.

"There are cells. Down that hall at the bottom of the stairs. Magic protected, and away from traffic. We can keep them there," answered Tulir.

Avild hauled along the paralyzed prisoner. "We'll see if this one survives the night."

Chapter 20

LENA HAD TRIED TO DOZE off. She hadn't gotten back to her room until dawn. It had taken Socks a few minutes to emerge from under the bed, after which he sat with her on the couch and curled up in her lap.

A brighter light woke her as the sun bled through the stained-glass pieces. Socks was still in her lap. She petted him lightly to wake him. He started purring and rolled over, his short black and white fur shedding onto her clothes.

There was movement outside the window where there shouldn't have been, along the canal that ran through Clevehold. *A boat?*

Lena adjusted Socks against her chest as she stood. At the window, she looked out. A small boat was headed toward the castle. It flew a white flag.

She pressed a quick kiss to Socks' forehead and put him down. He meowed in protest, but she was already on her way to the door. The shoes she wore had stayed on since the pre-dawn threat. She kicked open Socks' door flap and left.

By the time Lena was at the outer gate, the message from the boat had passed inside. Tulir, Briet, and Kazio were there to retrieve it. Many people gathered around, but a group of guards created a protective circle around them.

Tulir unrolled the scroll and read the note.

Lena caught her breath and looked around eagerly. The bells hadn't sounded.

"They want to meet to discuss terms," said Tulir. He handed it to Briet.

Before she started reading it, Briet asked, "Do you think this is a trick?"

"They are bastards for betraying us." Tulir looked in the direction of Clevehold and combed a hand through his hair. "However, they are rule-abiding bastards."

"You can expect them to keep their word?" questioned Kazio.

Lena's heart sank. Tulir was considering it. She asked sternly, "You're not thinking of going out there? Terms, now, after what happened?"

Briet squinted at the scroll and read it again. Or was she just reading slowly? Did their letters differ, too?

"I couldn't live with myself if we went to war because I ignored our chance to broker peace," justified Tulir.

"They don't want true peace," spat Kazio.

Lena hated it, but she was inclined to agree with him.

"He's right." Briet rolled up the scroll and clutched it. "If it's a ploy for peace, it's for you, not my Ovnite, yes? My life was threatened this morning."

"I wouldn't ask you to risk your life for this," Tulir told Briet.

"You want to peace talk alone?" questioned Kazio. He pointed at Lena. "Or with her? No."

Amundr pushed through the ring of guards. "What's come over our neighbors?"

"They want to meet." Lena gestured at the scroll in Briet's hands. "It's likely a play to extract us from the castle and kill the king or Briet. Or turn us against one another."

"We've assumed their intentions. The question is, do we play into them at all?" proposed Briet.

Amundr narrowed his eyes at her. "You're not going out there."

"Your life was under fire. They're likely trying to find out if they succeeded and, if not, make another attempt. You should stay here," agreed Tulir.

"I'm not sending you out there alone. I have too many reasons, not all of them polite," refuted Briet.

Tulir smirked. "You're starting to sound like someone from the Western Continent."

The guards parted again. Rufino, huffing, joined them. He excused, breathless, "I got here as soon as I could."

Briet looked to Tulir and Lena. "Fill in your man."

"A boat with a white flag approached. They passed through the scroll Briet's holding. They want us to lower the drawbridge and meet them out there to discuss..."

Lena stopped listening to Tulir. A question Briet asked Kazio distracted her.

"How's he doing?" she asked.

"He did what he could." Kazio shrugged at Amundr. "Time will tell if he relapses."

"Cicero's strong," said Amundr.

Lena closed her eyes and cursed. *Of course it would be Cicero. The best of them.*

"Tisa and Gunna?" asked Briet.

"Tisa seems to have an overactive alcohol weariness. Gunna..." Amundr hummed.

Rufino said, loud enough to address all of them, "What they want is to corner you."

Kazio scratched the side of his face with a thumb and raised his eyebrows.

When everyone was looking at Rufino, he continued, "They've had time to think about their tactics. They want to meet today—purposefully minimizing the time you have to consider."

"There isn't much to consider, is there? Not if their thinking and attitudes haven't changed," surmised Lena.

"You intend to go?" Briet asked Tulir, and he nodded.

"If the king is intent to go, the question is, who do we send?" asked Amundr.

"I can't ask any of you to do that," said Briet.

Kazio offered nonchalantly, "I will go."

Lena furrowed her brow. "Your tune changed quickly."

"I'm not letting him barter my future, Duchess," he responded lowly.

"We can't risk the queen after last night—this morning. And you can't just send him," said Rufino.

"Amundr," nominated Tulir.

The Ovnite Elder nodded.

"Why should he go if I am to stay behind?" protested Briet.

"If this is the stupid decision my gut is telling me it could be, I need to know there will still be leadership left. You were the one who told me Amundr was too stubborn to be killed. You"—Tulir looked at Rufino—"your support can be counted on?"

"Yes, sir," replied Rufino.

"None of you heard me condoning pushing Norman out a window if it comes to it, understood?" Tulir looked to Briet. She nodded.

Lena stepped forward. If he was this insistent on doing something stupid, he wasn't going to do it alone. "I'm going with you."

Kazio snorted.

She ignored him. "I'm not a fighter, but I am a shield."

"It was enough to hold back my magic," considered Amundr. "And that place was your home, yes?"

"Which gives me all the more reason to want peace, if that miraculously is their true intention," said Lena.

Tulir looked as if he wanted to protest. His eyes lingered on Lena's. He wanted her to change her mind—she could see it. But deep down, he had to know she wouldn't.

"Rufino," Tulir got his attention, "get archers along the wall. We'll lower the drawbridge, but I want the gate sealed behind me. Bolted, not just closed."

He left them to begin preparations.

"I'll be up at post with the archers," said Briet. This was her conceit.

"No prisoners," said Kazio.

"May I speak with you a moment?" Briet asked him.

Lena rubbed her temples. There was still an ache pounding in her head, less so than the first time she woke. It had less to do with the beer and more with the empty stomach, she supposed, but she couldn't consider eating yet.

"Shouldn't you also take your queen's counsel?" asked Tulir.

Amundr made a clicking sound with his mouth, toying with his twin amulets absently. "I'm aware of what she wants."

"What did he mean by no prisoners?" Lena had an assumption as she felt a pit grow in her stomach, but she preferred to ask than assume.

"Should they capture us, death is preferable." Tulir fastened his hands behind his back. "That she should shoot him instead of let him be taken."

"Do you disagree?" questioned Amundr in such a way that it felt more like a statement.

The opposite of Charlot, considered Lena. *Where is Norman?* It was better the weasel wasn't here, but his absence troubled her.

"I hold up surprisingly well under torture," answered Tulir.

Briet returned to them, a hammer in one hand. She went to the wooden post near the gate's door, positioned a nail, and hammered it in. When she was done, the nail stuck out two inches.

"When you leave here, you hang your tether," instructed Briet.

"Why?" asked Tulir.

Briet pulled her own over her head. She hung it from the nail. "It's our custom. If you come back, I'll explain it to you."

"Alright," he agreed. He removed the amulet and hung it with hers. The two stones clanked against each other in the silent breeze.

THE DRAWBRIDGE WAS lowered. The full door to the gate didn't have to open; a normal-sized door was cut into the wood. Iron bars creaked as they were removed from the slats to open it.

Part of Lena was glad their meeting would be done on such short notice. This way, there wasn't time to properly stress over it. Her stomach was already uneasy. Her head hurt. The only added uncomfortableness was the saddlebag over her shoulder. A last-minute request.

She and Tulir were the first ones through the door. He put up his hand for her to take as she stepped over the threshold. He whispered, "You're certain?"

"I will not be excluded from your rash decisions," she answered.

Kazio and Amundr followed them out. The door closed behind them and they heard the clang of metal knocking together as the bars were put back. Across the drawbridge, near the exit to Clevehold, were three men seated at a table.

Kazio walked next to Lena on the other side from Tulir. He hooked a thumb into the strap of her bag and toyed with it. "What did you bring, Duchess?"

The way he said her title unnerved her. She kept her face forward and focused on identifying the men. Two were familiar. *Diederich. The Judge.* The third, in the middle, she didn't recognize. By way of answering Kazio, she pulled up the flap on the bag.

He tsked. "Women here are very different. Misplaced hospitality."

Lena ignored him. They walked the rest of the way in silence. Amundr said nothing but looked back pointedly at the row of archers on the wall. His steps were clunky and unbalanced. If Lena hadn't known it was how he always walked, she would fear he was going to fall off the edge. Was it from spending too much time at sea? Did it have to do with the yellowish tint of his skin?

The men stood. Diederich greeted lifelessly, "Tulir."

"Diederich. Alger. Judge," Tulir said and nodded.

"General," corrected Alger. He gestured to Diederich. "And Commander."

"We began without titles. I didn't want to show you up." Tulir pulled out a chair and sat down. His legs were apart, he didn't tuck in, and he rolled up his sleeves. The gouged scar on his arm was visible.

Lena hid her grin. She moved to the side of the table, close enough to keep Tulir safe. There were only three seats on their side. She hadn't planned to sit, regardless.

"Do you mind if we check the bag the Miss is carrying?" asked the Judge.

"Miss Lena," Diederich addressed her personally.

She reached into the bag and pulled out two glasses. Lena set both on the table, one in front of Tulir, the other in front of Alger. She then took out a bottle of wine and handed the empty bag to Diederich.

"Optimistic," he commended. His search of the bag turned up nothing. He set it down.

"Thank you for agreeing to meet with us," said Alger. He had shiny pins clipped onto his jacket. His jaw was flabby and his teeth yellow.

Kazio and Amundr both gestured at the chair on the open side of Tulir. They didn't speak but made noises as if they were. It sounded like gibberish. Kazio gave in with a shrug. He pulled back the chair, flipped the orientation, and straddled it. Amundr remained standing.

"I'm sure the short notice was purposeful," responded Tulir.

"These men in rags speak for you?" questioned the Judge.

"Foreigners, no doubt," grumbled Alger. He tapped his fingernails on the table.

Kazio looked back to Amundr and said something in gibberish. The Elder narrowed his eyes. Kazio spoke again, pointing at the man across from them. This, Amundr met with a scrunched nose and a nod.

"What language is that?" asked Diederich.

Lena wondered the same thing. It sounded nothing like their accent, nor the language Avild and Cicero had briefly spoken. Was it true gibberish? The corner of her lip upturned, which aided her pleasant expression.

"Foreign," responded Amundr.

"Don't pretend the answer would matter to men who never liked a thing they didn't fully understand," snarked Tulir.

Kazio made a menacing smile, similar to the one she had seen during their first meeting.

Lena glanced to Clevehold. There were people moving about. Curtains facing the castle weren't moving as much as they should have been with the wind. She made a point to stay close, but not impose. She clasped her hands at her stomach and toyed with the bottle lightly.

"Who are these two foreigners you brought?" demanded the Judge.

"The queen's men, her advisors," answered Tulir. He nodded at the two men with him.

"The queen?" questioned Diederich.

"I assumed you were familiar." Tulir's mouth opened in a smile. "You tried to have her killed early this morning."

"You made an alliance with these people," said Alger distastefully.

"And if one of my men hadn't warned me you were marching this way, would you have tried to kill me, too?" proposed Tulir.

Alger ignited, "You suppose to accuse—"

"It was rhetorical." Tulir put up a hand. "You couldn't kill me, so we're doing this."

Kazio spouted gibberish at Amundr and Tulir. It came across as angry, accusing.

"Later." Tulir said a second word in gibberish with the same inflection.

Amundr took a swaying step closer to Alger, who eyed him.

"The men," Tulir reminded. "At least three broke into the castle for an attempted assassination. Are you going to answer for that?"

"If a few rogues took it upon themselves to break into the castle, why should we answer for them?" asked Alger.

Tulir laughed and looked to Amundr. "Remember to tell them the rogue Ovnite who attacked Steepwharf don't have to answer for it, when we get to that."

Lena kept her mouth buttoned, but a puff of air escaped her nose. She gripped the bottle tighter. The situation had to be amusing. Otherwise, it would be terrifying.

"Do the foreigners understand why magic was outlawed?" asked the Judge.

"Why it still should be?" added Alger pointedly.

"We know why it was," answered Amundr.

"And they know how it came to be revived," said Tulir.

"After they attacked you and you showed your belly?" remarked Alger.

"Once we spoke of it like adults and found mutual common ground." Tulir directed across the table. "And came to know we had mutual enemies."

"You insulant—" began Alger.

The Judge put up his hand. "We came to speak. Common terms. Common accents. A deal easy enough for a novice to understand."

Tulir raised his eyebrows and waited. Kazio went to start his gibberish, but Tulir put up a hand. He turned the motion around to wave the Judge on.

"What we want is simple: disband the new heathenistic monarchy. Life will return to the way it was. The Stone King has no bearing on our future," proposed Diederich.

Slowly, as if talking to a child, Tulir replied, "You understand why I wouldn't want that? You don't have to like the legacy and lineage for it to be true."

"You think the station of your birth gives you any right?" proposed Diederich.

Alger picked at the table and muttered, "The indentured son of a whore."

Amundr raised his eyebrows.

"I've never had that impression. Not when I was born indentured, son of a courtesan with no father, and sold off. I don't hold it now," replied Tulir.

"But you've taken up as king as if a whore's lineage gives you any right," said Alger.

Tulir's nose twitched. "I've taken up as king to govern a city of refugees. The reign expands beyond Clevehold, but the people here are my main concern. The people of magic, shunned or escaped from their homes, by backward men like—"

The Judge tried to interrupt, "The law states—"

Voice serious and full, Tulir interjected, "It's *my* time to speak, and I'm far from satisfied. You remove me, you ransack the city, and you put to death all of those who have magic. Your selfish and archaic laws put at risk myself, my Court, and all those I never should have needed to harbor. My refuges here were your scared citizens in Steepwharf."

"People afflicted by magic will be given the chance to repent," said the Judge.

"Afflicted by magic," Amundr repeated mockingly.

"Repent." Tulir tapped a finger on the table. "Will those of us *afflicted* lose a hand or foot, or just our livelihoods?"

"Don't forget you left Steepwharf a criminal, boy," reprimanded Diederich.

The corner of Tulir's lip upturned.

Kazio turned to Tulir. He spoke in gibberish and ended with a question. "Criminal?"

Tulir nodded.

Kazio slapped Tulir on the chest and proudly smiled.

"What your people consider criminal doesn't hold much merit here," remarked Amundr.

"Would you like time to consider our terms?" asked the Judge.

Tulir scoffed. "You've given me nothing to consider."

"We have food to last the fall and winter. We have means to wait it out longer." Alger stabbed the table with a meaty finger. "We know of the Iste armies in the west and how they have not yet come to your aid. Disbanding the monarchy and magic is a question we're asking now. If you don't answer it correctly, it will become a demand."

"Your twin was the rash one, Tulir. Make your last act as king one that will let your people assimilate back into the world without death," bargained Diederich.

"Just because they came from that whore in quick succession doesn't make them twins," jeered Alger.

Tulir's jaw clenched.

"That's it, then," Lena sighed. She uncorked the bottle and stepped forward. "We may hate to admit it, but there's only one responsible course of action." She poured Tulir's glass full of wine. The glass in front of Alger, she made a show of turning upside down before she poured wine over the stem. The liquid cascaded down and seeped into the table.

"Miss Lena, we—"

"Duchess," she corrected. She tossed the bottle of wine off the drawbridge and into the river.

Tulir raised his glass and drank from it.

Kazio reached across the table and flicked the upturned glass at Alger. Wine from the stem notch splattered onto his shirt. Kazio smiled.

Diederich stood, his face much calmer than Alger's pulsating red. Diederich drew his sword.

Amundr took down his whip that had been tucked beneath the rags. As it unwound, teal magic made it glow. He pulled his lips back to snarl.

"I've got Steepwharf's best archer on the wall," warned Tulir.

Would the first blow come from a man at the table or a man hidden within Clevehold? Lena tensed and postured for a shield. She didn't want to give herself away yet.

"If it's come to a fight, boy . . ." growled Alger. He knocked his chair over as he stood and unsheathed his sword.

As Tulir slammed his hand down onto the table, green magic ate at the wood. It was dissolving around his palm. "Lest you all want to leave behind widows or discover reasonableness, we are at an impasse."

Fear glinted in their eyes. Lena saw varying degrees of it, and Alger's rage won out, but the fear couldn't be hidden. Fear at what the Stone King's heir could do. The man hadn't forgotten the volume of outlawed magic.

"We could burn this city," threatened the Judge. "Burn your castle with you all in it."

CLEVEHOLD

"Stone doesn't burn," said Lena. "What you do collapse, we will rebuild. Our defenses are greater than yours. We aren't the ones in danger here."

Silence stood for a moment. The table around Tulir's hand continued to flake away. Amundr's grip on the whip made the magic pulse. Alger and Diederich stood with swords drawn.

Kazio pulled a knife from his sleeve and stabbed the table.

The Steepwharf men flinched.

Lena felt her heart racing.

Amundr tsked.

Kazio shrugged, glaring. "They did not look properly intimidated," he said with almost a complete lack of his Ovnite accent.

"We part ways here." Tulir stood. There was a handprint left behind on the table. Light made clear how thin the wood was at the palm and fingertips. He stalled a moment before putting his back to the men.

Walking backward, Amundr eyed the men while reeling in his length of whip.

Kazio stood and let the chair fall forward. He motioned for Lena to go first. "Duchess."

"Sir." She nodded and walked. Her chin was kept level with the ground, but she looked up to see the guards along the wall. She watched them for any sign there was danger behind her.

"We needed to broker for peace, yes?" hissed Amundr distastefully. He walked alongside Tulir. "It was a waste of time."

"I realized that once I saw their faces. This worked out to everyone's benefit," replied Tulir. He shook out his hand.

Lena smiled.

They were nearly at the door. Metal protested and moaned as the slats were removed. Lena slowed her pace as to not reach it before it was open.

"Well handled," Kazio whispered over her shoulder.

Lena raised her eyebrows. The slow pace allowed him to catch up, and she looked at him. "I would return the compliment if it didn't stun me."

He tilted his head from side to side. "I was worried of my responsibility over you. But you are properly irresponsible yourself."

"Ah." She nodded and ran her tongue over her teeth. "Do I get to meet the man, now?" Lena reached for the heavy door.

Kazio held it open one-handed over her head. "Perhaps."

On the other side of the door, they were met with apprehensive murmurs. As the door closed behind them, Briet cut through the crowd. She ran up to Tulir and threw her arms around his neck. He embraced her back, and they met with a kiss.

The crowd erupted in cheers.

What would Diederich, the Judge, and Alger think of that, Lena wondered? Cheers at the return of the king. Clevehold wasn't defeated—she was invigorated. The sounds of the people proved it.

Briet and Tulir parted with smiles. She hooked the tether over his head, and he took hers as she handed it off and did the same for her. The crowd sustained their cheers.

"I'm not the only one playing the part," mumbled Kazio.

Lena looked away. She didn't want to see it, either.

"You can get a full report from your men, but as it is, the siege stands. We could not come to terms," Tulir told Briet.

"I expected nothing less." Briet held his hand.

The crowd pressed in around them. An eagerness poured out from them. They watched Tulir with strained patience for an explanation.

Tulir set up a box and stood on it. He put a hand to Briet, and she got up on the box with him. He addressed the crowd, "The men of Steepwharf and the coastal cities are out there, occupying your city—of that, I'm sure you're aware. We tried to meet with them and broker peace, as we were able to do with the Ovnite."

A different person cut through the crowd. *Tisa*. She looked pale. She grabbed Kazio and pulled him away urgently.

"Most of you know how magic is treated in those cities. It's why you had to leave. Nothing has changed. Should I open those doors, the men of the coastal armies would want you all to pay an immoral price," explained Tulir.

Lena felt fear creeping up her throat. She headed in the direction Kazio and Tisa had disappeared. What was wrong?

In the background, she could still hear Tulir. "They want to starve us out. They want to burn your city. They make threats, which only proves to me they don't care about your lives. Your safety. But I do." The crowd cheered.

At the outskirts of the crowd, Lena was able to see around people. Tisa was leading Kazio to the Ovnite barracks. She picked up speed as she followed and kept an eye on the door Tisa took them through.

Lena stopped on the threshold. It was their hut for the sick. Kazio was kneeling beside Cicero. Coughs erupted from the bed, interchanged with gasps. Cicero was turning blue. His hands clawed at his chest, and his eyes bulged.

"Help him!" Kazio barked. He looked afraid to touch his friend.

Tisa stood off to the side. She had a hand over her mouth, eyes blurry with tears. She shook her head.

Footsteps came up from the outside. Lena moved inside to get out of the way. Was there nothing that could be done? Where were the doctors?

Cicero's mouth moved as if he was gasping for air, but he made no sound. Blood vessels popped in his eyes.

"Get Amundr!" ordered Kazio.

Footsteps came up beside Lena. Amundr put a hand to her shoulder and moved around her. "I'm here."

"He can't breathe!" shouted Kazio.

Amundr went to the opposite side of the bed as Kazio. He knelt down and hovered his hand over Cicero's lurching body. He looked at Tisa.

"The doctor said"—her voice cracked—"they can't. They don't . . ." She covered her mouth.

"Save him!" shouted Kazio.

Amundr began steadily, "I already—"

"Fix him!"

Lena felt tears welling in her eyes. A shuddered breath left her as she came to understand. Amundr wanted to help Cicero. He had. Healing magic didn't work a second time once it was expended on an affliction. She moved to stand beside Kazio.

"You have to!" Kazio gripped the bedframe with white knuckles.

Cicero's arms tensed up. He jerked and twitched. Mouth open, they could see his throat was closed.

Teal threads of magic wound around Amundr's fingers. He placed one hand on Cicero's throat, the other hovering over his chest. Amundr closed his eyes. He, too, was holding his breath.

Cicero's arms fell limply to his sides.

Lena gripped Kazio's shoulder and squeezed.

A whined moan worked out of Amundr. The magic burned brighter. The body stopped moving. Amundr's grip released, and he sucked in a breath. Eyes open, he examined Cicero's unmoving form.

"That's not it," refuted Kazio.

"I'm sorry," said Amundr.

"No." Kazio wiped a hand under his nose. "Fix him."

Amundr began, "The sickness was too deeply—"

"Fix him!" Kazio shouted. His fist came down onto the bed. Lena felt the ire from the tension in his shoulder.

She didn't let go. "He did what he could."

Amundr sat back on his heels and looked at his hands before they dropped to his lap. "I can't fix death."

Tisa gasped out sobs behind them. People were gathered in the doorway. The speech was an ongoing murmur carrying in. People cheered in the distance.

"If you can't fix him"—Kazio wiped a hand over his face—"find someone who can."

Amundr stood slowly. He moved around to Tisa and whispered, "We can't leave the body here."

Lena looked back. She and Tisa both nodded.

Kazio sank forward, elbows on the bed. Lena felt the change in position as she hung onto his shoulder. He looked as though he was fighting to hold on to anger but losing to tears. He begged, "Amundr, please."

"I'm sorry," Lena whispered kindly and squeezed his shoulder. "You should get some air."

"Get off me!" Kazio shouted. He wrenched his shoulder forward out of her grip and repeated, voice cracking, "Get off me."

"They need to take his body away," said Lena.

"Get out, all of you!" Kazio spat as he waved to the door. Sobs bubbled up his throat and his shoulders jerked.

"Can we wait?" whispered Tisa.

Amundr tsked quietly. "It's not contagious amongst the living, but we don't want to keep the dead."

Kazio huffed deep breaths. He stood quickly and abruptly, enough to make Lena flinch. On the way out the door, he bumped shoulders with onlookers.

Lena followed out, head down and leaving space between her and the others. She couldn't stay with the crowd. There was an uptick in their mood. They were proud of Tulir. And why shouldn't they be? Whether Tulir's idea to risk meeting had been foolish or not, him going out there to broker and being refused was the most noble thing in the eyes of the people. He was the sensible one. He demonstrated understanding. Upon return, he had been swept up in a kiss with his new wife to reinforce the strength of their alliance. The speech, the crowd—at some point, they just fed off each other.

It was easy to forget going out there had been a risk. No doubt there were archers waiting in the buildings of Clevehold. Did the men of Steepwharf intend to be honorable and only take action if acted upon, or had the right target not walked out onto the drawbridge? Did it matter if no one had gotten hurt?

They'd had to return inside the walls to face death. *Why Cicero?* She hadn't known him well, but what she did know of him was curiosity and kindness. If any man deserved to choke on the muscles of his throat, it was not him. Given Kazio's reaction, the two must have been close. *The Est boys.*

She remained by the building until people came by to take Cicero's body away. After that, she felt compelled to leave. The barracks weren't hers. The sorrow wasn't hers to share. Cicero wasn't the first Ovnite they had lost to sickness. They were too practiced. But their mechanical reactions dragged under the emotional toll of losing a leader.

Lena found herself naturally headed to the Stone King's Hall. That was the rendezvous for emergencies, right? Didn't this constitute one? Or was it a waste to dedicate a room during a constant state of emergency?

Norman came to mind again, as did the prisoners. She would have to pass their cells. Men of Steepwharf wouldn't know the castle layout well. Even if plans had been drawn and known, knowing which room belonged to Briet was specific. *A rat within the walls?* But how could they traffic unnoticed?

CLEVEHOLD

As the likelihood of a traitor increased in her mind, the ability to prove such diminished. If there was a traitor within the walls, the prisoners would never give them up. Everything was conspiracy. That in itself would cause turmoil and internal strife. The Steepwharf men had gotten what they'd wanted, anyway.

The door to the stairs opened and an acrid stench wafted out. The stench of blood. The stench of the dead. Lena quickly moved inside and closed the door. Her footsteps were light going down, and she created a green shield around the final turn.

She sighed when she reached the bottom. "Avild?"

"You shouldn't be down here." The woman was cleaning blood off her hands. There were splatters on her shirt and trousers. Puddles were gumming up on the floor. By the confidence in her stance, none of it was hers.

Lena swallowed and let the shield dissipate. She didn't hear anyone else. The cell doors were open, no knife or sword in sight. "Did Tulir ask you to do this? Did Briet?"

"Officially"—Avild dropped the rag and examined her fingers—"no one did."

Despite her efforts to stay calm, Lena's heart sped up. She moved closer to the puddles of blood. In the cell, three bodies were piled up. Their faces were pale, vacant. There were ropes tied around their feet. Sticky blood was drying on their clothes and in their hair.

Lena set her jaw and looked away. This was what Tulir wanted? Or was it Briet's doing? Would those mouths have brought them to starvation that much quicker? Tulir had said something about waiting a few days to determine which of the prisoners were men. Lena wondered if Avild had another way of finding that out.

"Were they too risky to keep alive?" Lena's throat felt dry as she pushed the words out. If they had been conspiring with someone inside the castle, they couldn't any longer.

The smell of blood brought back the memory of Klaus being gutted. Then came Vilars, bleeding out from his thigh wound. Cicero's clawed hands and swollen throat joined them in the line of bodies. An echo of Rether's laugh made a shiver crawl up her spine.

"You don't need to be here." Avild walked toward Lena.

She reflexively backed up. The pile of bodies left her vision.

"You don't need to see this," continued Avild.

"I'm not Marisol. I can stomach blood," Lena snapped.

Had the men died proudly? Willingly? It didn't look like magic had been used. Would she recognize it if it had? If Avild had tried to trade lives, would it show? Lena swallowed hard. *No.* They were alone. Avild couldn't.

Why hasn't she tried? She couldn't ask that. Throat cleared and chin up, she asked, "This is how you serve the monarchy now?"

"When I last served the monarchy, I let people conspire," she admitted casually. "Now, these men can't."

"You said times hadn't changed that much."

Avild shrugged. "As you've grown to learn, at times, brash actions are better than no action. Risk exists either way."

Lena knew she should leave. She shouldn't have been party to any of this. Too much—all of it was too much. Lena turned in a circle. *No.* With reserve, she asked, "Can this castle endure attacks from the canal?"

"That's not the right question," responded Avild. "The hallmark of a siege isn't the attack. It's passive. It's waiting."

"The walls won't break, but that doesn't matter,'" inferred Lena.

Avild nodded. "Steepwharf's army will camp comfortably in Clevehold. They may poke from time to time, but they don't need to get in."

"Can we escape through the mountain?" Lena didn't know of a way, but that didn't mean it didn't exist.

"The advantage of building into a sturdy mountain is defensibility. The trade is the sturdiness. They never drilled into the mountain more than the vault. It was before my childhood, because I heard stories of it then—an evil was said to live under the mountain. Something that burns men alive."

"A magic within the rock?"

"Or a dormant volcano." Avild shrugged. "Regardless, the men could try to dig out, but the time it would take far exceeds how long the food will last."

"What would you do?" asked Lena.

"I'm not your queen," said Avild.

Impatiently, Lena asked, "What would your father do?"

Avild raised her eyebrows and crossed her arms. "My father cursed himself in his hubris. I'm not so inclined to revisit or head his ideas."

In a huff, Lena sat on the steps. Despite how long she had been exposed to the smell of blood, the copper tang still made her nauseous. Feeling like a distraught child and knowing she was going to sound like one, she asked, "How can all our plans change so quickly?"

"I'm sure you haven't forgotten your escape from Steepwharf," said Avild.

"It was your escape plan," reminded Lena. She had just been a pawn in it.

"It was your rashness."

Is that a compliment? Lena pulled her braided hair over her shoulder and circled back. "Steepwharf's escape is just what I mean. I had a boring life I was comfortable with. I could be picky about details, but overall, it was a good life." Lena extended her arm out. "Within a week, all of it upended."

"And it's happening again. Now, after you settled into another semi-boring role where you were almost content?" proposed Avild.

"Yes," agreed Lena. She let her arm drop. "Not boring, but consistent. Predictable. Almost two years of steady growth, progress, and building within the castle. In Clevehold. With Tulir. Now... now it's this."

"I'm sorry you loved him."

"I do love him," Lena corrected, "and I'm not."

"Worse, then, because it can't make this easier." Avild leaned on a stone wall that jutted out between cells. "It was supposed to have been yours. The power, the monarchy, in the way I thought the world could swallow it best—through the filter of a man."

"If I had tried to take up the crown to start, Steepwharf wouldn't have waited for the Ovnite to march," Lena mused. She shook her head. "It's not about the power. I don't need the title. Now, it's about doing what's best for the people. What Harth and I wanted to have with Tulir—it's background noise. Briet is what Tulir needed to stabilize this. That bridge ordeal could have gone very differently if it happened a week earlier."

Avild's eyes narrowed. "Harth?"

Lena's heart seized. *Wouldn't she know?* No, not based on that tone. How specific had Lena's ramblings been? Could she play it off as a slip or misunderstanding? The implication was too present. Floundering, she tried to speak and hoped the right words flowed, but she only got so far as "They are..."

Why hadn't Harth told her? It wasn't Lena's place. Was there an underlying reason? Was Avild not supposed to know? There were punishments for Harth's preferences. What did Avild believe?

Lena knew her face was red. She stood and thumbed over her shoulder. *Easiest to say nothing and run?* How guilty would that make her look?

Avild put up a calming hand. "I know of Harth and his... 'not the type for a wife,' as he puts it." She lowered her hand. There was no malice in her voice. "I've known for years. I have no less fondness for him, and it's a trust I would never betray."

"Right." Lena didn't quite feel relieved. That wasn't the end of it.

Avild pushed off the wall. "I didn't realize his fondness was for Tulir. I believed Tulir was too enthralled with you, and Harth has always kept himself well guarded. I didn't know you were Tulir's beard."

"I'm not. Wasn't." Lena shook her head and began again, "Tulir did love me. *Does* love me. There was no ploy. When I said Harth and I wanted to have something with Tulir, it was because we were . . . *us*. Brash and never too well defined. Tulir loves us both. There was going to be an arrangement."

"You were prepared to share Tulir then, but not now?" asked Avild.

Lena pulled up a sad smile. "The pretenses were different. Briet will never know about Harth. Tulir isn't married to me."

Avild closed her mouth and turned to the side. Her eyes were angled down, affixed at the bottom juncture. She pinched the bridge of her nose.

Lena assumed now wasn't the right time to tack on how, despite knowing Harth's preferences, given their mutual connection, she had asked him to marry her. When she felt enough silence had passed for Avild to think, Lena said, "Both of us want what's best for Tulir and the people."

"You aren't fools." Avild made eye contact with her. "So long as you don't let love make you fools, you can find benefit from being around people you trust."

Lena nodded. Trust was what Avild had lacked last time she served the monarchy. Lena didn't doubt a significant part of the woman before her was relieved to know they wouldn't make the same mistakes.

"The Council will want to meet to discuss what happened today." Avild gestured to the stairs. "You should go."

"Did you see it?" asked Lena.

"Enough of it. It was the right thing to meet, despite knowing nothing would change their stance."

"Not a waste of time?"

"Showmanship isn't always," answered Avild.

"Will you come to meet with the Council? They respect you."

Avild shook her head. "I have to do disposal."

"I can help," Lena offered automatically.

"I'll bear this one alone," responded Avild. "Better you keep your hands clean."

Chapter 21

THEIR SEATING ARRANGEMENT in the meeting room mimicked the wedding. Two days, it had been. Too much of the day had been lost in negotiations and fallout to allow them to meet the same day. It had also given everyone time to sort out their thoughts.

Kazio took his place next to Amundr, not letting Lena see much of his face before he sat. Norman was beside Lena and looked displeased at realizing he was technically the balance of Kazio if Harth's middle seat was unaccounted for. If it wasn't, as Lena had figured, that made Norman's counterpart open air.

Across the table sat Rufino, Tulir, Briet, and Tisa. A servant handed a large scroll to Tisa and said, "Sorry for the wait."

"It's alright," said Tisa as she set it down.

"Was there an issue in finding the maps?" questioned Norman.

"The librarian was missing. We had to find it ourselves," the servant apologized.

"Thank you," said Tulir to dismiss the servant.

Tisa and Kazio across from her worked to unroll the map. The other end reached down to Rufino and Lena, who secured it to the table. It left Norman on the periphery.

The map of the continent had been requested to give the Ovnite a better lay of the land. The map carved into the table was unpainted and served for those who knew what they were looking at; the map on the scroll added depth. The sea to the east showed the few islands dotted in the blue, the coastal communities were up-to-date, and the river winding up to Clevehold was more accurately represented. That side of the map was all cool colors, and the greens morphed into yellows and oranges as it shifted west. The plains were dotted with cities along bends of rivers.

Rufino resumed the question he had begun before the servant interrupted. "Why not send the Vitki healers with a band of fighters to keep them on their feet?"

"It doesn't work that way. Not all of our Vitki are healers, and the wounds are not always so quickly and easily dealt with," answered Briet.

Tisa pointed at the western side of the map. "How far away are the Iste?"

"They're here." Harth ran his finger along the mountain range Clevehold was nestled in. "But they've stalled."

"The bulk of their army hasn't crossed into the mountains," said Tulir.

"But we should assume they have sent scouts ahead to see what their friends on the coast are doing," said Amundr. He fidgeted in his seat, not looking at the map.

"Are we not going to consider the terms?" questioned Norman.

Of course he wants us to consider what cannot be.

"Consider the terms," Kazio enunciated slowly. His voice sounded hoarse.

When there wasn't an answer, Briet added, "Consider disbanding? Consider putting everyone in this room to death? Potentially everyone within the castle?"

"No one said death," said Norman.

Amundr laughed.

"The men of the coastal armies have a healthy distrust for magic," argued Norman.

Lena expected the scoff to come from Kazio, but Rufino was the one to speak up. "They would kill all of us. If they're generous, it ends at just us."

CLEVEHOLD

"Maybe not all of you," said Tulir. He spoke into his fist and looked at Norman.

"Are you considering it?" asked Harth.

No. That wasn't what this was. Lena waited. She moved her hand from where it was neatly folded in her lap to under the table, flat. She hoped Harth read her caution.

"I want to think like they're thinking. Norman, what are our main points to consider?" asked Tulir.

Norman straightened out his jacket. "They want the monarchy disbanded. Why shouldn't they? It's not our way. It was founded—respectfully, sir—by children who didn't know the first thing about governing."

"But you do," Tulir interjected on the other man's breath.

"Well, I . . ." Norman stuttered.

"You know what they want. You think how they think. You think what they think," continued Tulir casually. There was a mischievous grin hidden behind his hand. "You *are* them."

"Are you accusing me of something?" Norman laid his hands on the table.

"I have no evidence to accuse you of anything." Tulir switched his attention to Harth. "How many dogs and cats have the people of Clevehold reported missing since moving into the castle?"

"My men know of at least a dozen," answered Harth.

Tulir hummed. "And when you and Tisa searched the tunnels for possible access breaches, did that conclude the search for any animals?"

"We found . . ." Tisa stopped. Her expression narrowed. She leaned forward and put her elbows on the table. Curiously, she stared at Norman. "We found a few dogs and cats. Drowned."

"Animals who couldn't find the right path through?" supposed Tulir.

Lena's stomach dropped as her breath caught. Her eyes clenched shut. Socks was okay—she had seen him this morning. No one had gotten ahold of him and forced him to swim for his life.

"If you're quite done with your tangent," said Norman. "I only want what's best for the people. That's why we're here, isn't it?"

"Which people?" Briet questioned. "People like you, you're safe, yes? Magic is integrated into my Ovnite. Accepting your people's terms is a death sentence for mine."

"We would be massacred," said Kazio tiredly.

"The people of Clevehold and the Ovnite are the same people now, which is all the more reason we cannot revert and abandon," said Lena. "Look at what we've built here! As Tulir told those . . . those *imbeciles*, we have built a refuge in Clevehold."

"We are not one people." Norman punctuated each word with a poke to the table.

Amundr stood noisily, walked behind Norman's chair, and dragged it backward. He grabbed the smaller man and hauled him to his feet.

"What are you doing?" protested Norman. He squirmed but couldn't escape.

Amundr used one hand to drag Norman to the door and opened it with the other, then tossed the man out. Amundr snarled at the slammed door, then turned to the table. All stared at him. He gestured back. "Unless he speaks for you."

"The childishness in me approves of it," said Tulir.

"I'll have Norman followed, just in case he slips," said Harth.

"Why wasn't I informed?" asked Briet.

Amundr resumed his place at the table.

"Nothing could be proven, and the link only just dawned on me," answered Tulir. His hand moved away from his mouth. "We agree, submitting to them comes at too great a risk. We can't. The question then becomes, can we fight them without the Iste?"

"We don't have the numbers," said Briet.

"But we have magic," Rufino proposed.

"It will only get us so far. If we fight, and if we lose, we are back in here waiting, but worse off," said Amundr.

"We need the Iste." Harth tapped on the mountains to the west of Clevehold.

Tisa scratched at the edge of the scroll. "We suffer the siege."

"They don't have to kill us outright if they think they can outlast us," said Rufino.

"Do they know our people are dying?" asked Kazio.

Amundr wiped his hands on his trousers. "Who knows what the rat may have funneled out."

"What are the casualties up to?" asked Lena.

Briet sighed. "We are on the recovering end for those who will survive. But that leaves a third of my people dead or too sick to fight."

"Can the doctors not help?" asked Tulir.

"That is with the doctors," said Tisa. "The good news is, the doctors are hopeful those of us who never got sick, or didn't become very ill, will not get worse."

"Can we keep going like this? Food stores, supplies, morale," asked Harth.

Lena sat tall. "We keep doing what we've been doing. Tulir's speech yesterday brought up morale. The people were incentivized to hate, which will make them want to survive longer out of spite. We need to weed out any weak links and show unity." She didn't look down the table at Kazio, but she felt him there. "We have to avoid any sentiment that one party would have been better off without the other."

"Should another bid be sent to the Iste?" asked Rufino.

"Have it sent," instructed Tulir.

"If it must be said, that man is no longer invited to sit on the Council," said Amundr. He waved dismissively at the door.

"He's better off more permanently removed," grumbled Kazio. Lena was inclined to agree.

"I'm not going to have him killed. He may be of use," said Tulir. "He is absolved of his duties, though. That much is agreed."

Harth nodded. "A man like that—strip him of his power, his title, the finer things, and he won't be happy to have been kept alive."

APPROACHING RAIN MADE the air feel heavy and sweat stuck to her skin. Lena's arm ached. She admitted her second lesson with the sword was faring better than the first, but she still wasn't strong enough.

Avild and Kazio were off to the sides of the courtyard. Lena would have been lying if she couldn't admit their presence added a layer of stress. She also thought she saw Amundr out of the corner of her eye, though there was no time to dwell on it.

Sidestep. Block. Push. Lena panted and made a quick adjustment to her grip before she attempted to swing at Harth. His sword caught it, but he didn't push her off. Confused, she didn't move.

"What do you do?" asked Harth. He was fighting one-handed, bearing the weight of holding his sword against hers with just his right arm, as if it took no effort.

"Run away, wondering how I got into this mess," answered Lena between breaths.

He tapped his left hand to his chest. "I'm exposed."

Lena positioned her weight, shifted sideways, and shoved her shoulder into his chest. On impact, she felt how much resistance she was met with. He was prepared for her attack, but she still felt justified in saying, "I could never knock you over."

"Your sword is angled down. I could block you in." He paused a second to let her observe. "Before I do, you can—and please, don't—elbow me in the gut or groin and slip back out."

Lena tapped her elbow to his stomach, then pushed off.

"Never expose your back, if you can help it."

"No dramatic twirls?" She wiped her forehead with her sleeve.

"Only works if your opponent is very bad or very drunk," he answered.

Briet joined them in the courtyard. She gave Harth an upward nod. "Are you and the duchess about finished?"

"If you insist," said Lena in faux defeat. She rotated her shoulder and winced.

"You're doing well." Harth walked with her to deposit the swords on the stone outcropping.

"I feel like a little girl playing pretend," she admitted quietly. She didn't need Kazio or Briet to overhear.

"You look like a grown woman attempting to learn a new skill," he refuted. He donned his quiver and bow. "If I put a sword in Rufino's hands, he would do no better."

"I appreciate it," said Lena.

"Do you have time for target practice?" called Briet. "I can show you how to make arrows from air."

"Another time," he called back.

"Something to tend to?" Lena proposed quietly. She quirked an eyebrow and smirked. Underlying her insinuation was curiosity. She had promised herself she would not seek affection from Tulir after he was married, but Harth had made no such vow, not that she knew of. He was a good man. He knew the risk it would pose to Tulir to continue, but nothing was certain.

Quietly to Lena, he responded, "I'm appreciative of the results of the Stone King shenanigans most days, but it did get me promoted higher in the guard than I ever aspired."

Lena discerned the amusement in his tone and amplified it with her own. "Fair enough." She propped herself up to sit on the stone.

Harth left the courtyard. On his exit, he nodded at Avild, who returned the gesture. He then looked back to Lena once more before disappearing through a doorway.

"Arrows aren't my strongest suit, but I will spar," offered Avild.

Amundr and Kazio remained on the side of the courtyard. The former, she caught making a curious grin her way, and the latter scowled.

Is that what it looked like? Lena kept her head up, her expression on the cusp of amused. *Let them think. Let them wonder.*

Let it make Kazio uncomfortable.

"Throw them here?" Avild asked as she approached Lena. Both swords were tossed over. Avild caught one with each hand.

When Briet was handed her weapon, she asked, "Who taught you to fight?"

Avild rotated her wrist and swapped hands to the left. "My late husband."

"Was he good?" Briet started their rotation to circle each other.

"The best," said Avild. She stopped and nodded.

Briet returned it and made the first attack.

Lena didn't feel the same level of anxiety bubbling up over this fight. There wasn't any true danger to Avild. If her estimation was right, Avild was using her left hand to test the other woman.

The spar did, however, carry on longer than Lena had anticipated. Briet moved around more than Avild, but not enough to turn the tables. With Avild fighting left-handed, the match came across as decently even.

CLEVEHOLD

Avild stepped out of a block. "You don't often fight people your own size, do you?"

"The Ovnite men run tall, as do most women," responded Briet. She circled.

Avild smirked and remained stationary. "Moving bulk around and swinging strong will wear out a larger opponent." Her sword came up to point at Briet's throat as the woman neared. "But you won't outlast me."

Briet batted the sword away with her own. "Fight with your good hand and we'll see how long I last."

With a shrug and smirk, Avild switched hands in a toss. The women resumed sparring. Avild moved her feet, as did Briet, who looked like she was concentrating on moving less.

"Should we worry about the future prince or princess who could be at risk?" joked Kazio, a hand over his stomach.

Lena looked to the men. Their expressions had swapped. Kazio's face matched his tone, his posture was a relaxed lean. Amundr was tense, watching intently. His lip twitched and he squinted.

Briet grunted. Lena turned to the fight in time to see the queen land on her butt. The sword skidded away from her as she glared up at Avild. "Finish it."

Avild smiled and hooked the sword over her shoulder. She approached Briet with slow steps, her hand extending down. "You fight well."

Reluctantly, Briet took her hand. Briet was hoisted to her feet. The women spoke, but they were too far for Lena to overhear.

Kazio sighed dramatically. He picked up Briet's sword. "I'll fight the winner."

Amundr walked along the outskirts of the courtyard, closer to Lena. "This should be interesting."

"They both have an attitude problem," said Lena quietly.

"That's why it should be interesting," he agreed with a laugh. His brittle nails drummed along his chin.

Briet walked away and situated herself where Kazio had been standing.

"Lena," Avild called to her, "should I risk the future Duke?"

Kazio rolled his eyes.

"Titles are hollow if he can't fight," responded Lena. "I need someone who can protect me, don't I?"

Avild and Kazio nodded at each other. Their initial bout was surprisingly slow, but the tempo increased gradually. Avild moved around at the same rate she had with Briet. Kazio kept up diligently until she gave him the slip, dodged around, and tapped her sword to his back.

He grimaced and turned. "Is moving around too much the right thing, or not?"

"Harth told me you can use magic through your sword," said Avild.

The corner of his lip upturned. He looked down to where his hand was fastened to the hilt. After a few seconds, orange magic began to glow. He cut the sword through the air and the magic encased the entire blade.

"Where do you feel that?" asked Avild. When met with a confused look, she put a flat hand to her chest. "Where does it start from?"

"At the base of my neck until it burns down my arm," he answered.

She narrowed her eyes. "Burns?"

Lena looked down to her hands. *Is it supposed to burn?* The magic she used to create shields made her hands tingle, but there wasn't any discomfort in it. Did it matter what the magic was used for?

"A natural," commented Amundr. He was squinting at them.

She looked up. Avild had recreated Kazio's technique, except her blade had a green glow. With another set of nods, they resumed sparring.

Lena couldn't help but flinch at the first heavy impact. She recalled when Avild's sword had broken and shattered. To distract herself, she said to Amundr, "It's quite a trick."

"He's showing off," grumbled Amundr. He watched the spar with worried eyes, occasionally looking to Briet.

"It's probably for the best you're here, if it gets *too* interesting," said Lena.

"Or we could send you out there to break it up," he proposed, corner of his lip lifting. He swayed minutely as he stood with planted feet.

"Perhaps," she agreed. Her hands came together in her lap. "I don't know if Cicero spoke to you of it, but he said you were a good healer, if I wanted someone to learn from."

"He told me." Amundr flinched as a hard block from Avild sent both her and Kazio staggering back a few steps. They resumed sparring.

"Would you teach me?"

Amundr looked at Lena from the side and squinted. She felt to be under scrutiny, until she recalled what Cicero had said about the man's eyesight. Amundr asked, "How are your fighting skills?"

"Wanting"—she gestured to the courtyard where he had seen her spar—"but I don't plan to halt one training for another."

"Sword, shield, heal," Amundr counted off and shrugged. "We may make a Vitki of you, yes?"

Lena smiled. A better way to bridge the gap. A more trustworthy way. It would still have to involve Kazio, but if she could learn magic like they had, she wouldn't be a burden to anyone.

Amundr opened his mouth but stopped as his head snapped to the fight.

Lena's heart lurched as she did the same. Nothing looked wrong—Avild and Kazio stood apart, backing up from a block. Their swords still gleamed with magic. She studied Kazio. He looked pale, loose.

"Kazio," called Briet. She took a step forward.

Avild lowered her sword.

Kazio didn't react to any of them. His tone disjointed, he said, "Why Ulga thinks wrong—Dabria, shelf." He took a faltered step forward and dropped the sword. The orange magic zipped up his arm to his neck and made an aura around his head for a second before disappearing. He dropped to the ground.

Lena and Amundr ran to Kazio. Briet met them there, crowded around where he fell.

Kazio's eyes were open, but the pupils rolled back, his eyes black webbed. His body was twitching with tremors. Jaw clenched, a low moan worked out of his throat. Amundr knelt and held Kazio's head to stop the tremors from causing injury.

"This isn't the sickness," said Amundr. He moved Kazio's head into his lap and kept it stationary with one hand. The other, he used to search Kazio's body. There were no wounds. No blood. No bruises. "What did you do?"

"I didn't—" answered Avild at the same time Briet said, "It wasn't her."

Amundr squinted at Briet.

"Is this the first time it's happened?" asked Avild.

"Yes," answered Amundr. Teal threads wound around his hands.

"The second, maybe third. It stops on its own," answered Briet. She put a hand to Amundr's shoulder.

"Second?" he hissed.

Lena couldn't watch Kazio's body twitch. She covered her mouth and looked to Avild. *Has no one called for a doctor?*

"It was back East, before." Briet stopped her explanation.

Kazio stilled. His tense shaking body went lax. Eyes closed and mouth open, he was finally still.

"Kazio!" Amundr called, shaking him. He leaned down to hover an ear above Kazio's nose. "He's alive."

Lena let out a breath of relief.

"He'll be okay," said Briet.

Amundr made a clicking sound with his mouth. Delicately, he picked up Kazio and looked to Briet. "Why didn't you tell me?"

"The first time, Kasper healed him, or he snapped out of it. The second time he rode it out on his own."

Amundr stood with Kazio's limp body in his arms. Anger sharpening, he began, "Why—?"

"Because he asked for my discretion," answered Briet.

Amundr shook his head and walked away.

THE SUMMER NIGHTS MADE for longer days, but the nights still came too quickly. Lena found herself in her room after dinner, wondering how she was going to pass the night. The day had been filled with meetings and sparring, working her mind and body. She hadn't attended dinner in the hall because she was helping Marisol and Rufino do assessments of inventory. Word had been sent there was no change in Kazio's condition.

Now what?

A storm had rolled in. She didn't anticipate it was going to last long. She had tried to communicate this to Socks, but still he insisted on hiding under the bed. As long as the storm raged, he would hide. She put food down under there for him.

A knock on her door was almost muted by the rolling thunder. She didn't want to yell to ask who it was. The chance was taken as she opened it blindly.

"Duchess," greeted Tulir.

"Your Grace."

He smiled and shook his head. "May I come in?"

"Of course." Lena moved to the side and shut the door behind them. "I don't know what it says of my character, but I find myself hopeful the storm damages our neighbors."

"I don't care what it says of mine to say I was thinking the same." He looked out the window and rubbed his hands together. "It's what those bastards deserve, but I'm more worried what this will do to the Iste. They aren't accustomed to the wet."

"They'll be alright." She joined him at the window but kept a respectable distance.

"May the rain miss them," he proposed.

She nodded. "I would say we could drink to it, but I don't feel like indulging." All too well she remembered the pounding in her head, the dryness in her mouth, and the general sluggishness.

"For the best," he agreed. "I want to overindulge, but I fear where it would lead."

"I wouldn't let you make a fool of yourself," she promised. "In public."

He laughed, and the joy reached his eyes. The look endured until a flash of disappointment made him look away. He sighed. "I want to be faithful to Briet."

"You're honorable that way. I expect nothing else," responded Lena. She wanted to reach for him, physically comfort him. Was that still allowed? They were her own rules to set, she supposed. Yet breaking any physical bound felt like too much.

"At the same time, I don't want to be," he admitted in a rush, as if the words were chasing him.

"I need you to be, when it comes to me. I don't mean to sound like a hypocrite, but I can't be yours if she is. It's different," said Lena.

He nodded and combed a hand through his hair. "She's in a higher position of authority than you. There's additional risk and less protection for you." A short laugh made him smile as his hand dropped. "You're also honorable, in that way."

"This was what had to happen." Whether she truly believed that or liked it wasn't the question. She had to respect the logic as she understood it.

"Everything changed so quickly." He moved away from the window and rubbed a hand down his face. "Steepwharf is at our gates asking for our surrender. My own Council member was their advocate to revert."

"We know it wouldn't stop at reverting. Magic was illegal before, but it was gone, myths forgotten. Faced with this resurgence, people would be hunted," said Lena. She had grown to hate the little dots of light in the distance.

"Neighbors would turn on each other." He agonized a groan that developed into words. "But they'd be alive. They wouldn't starve."

Lena's eyes widened as she stared at him. "Are you considering surrender?"

"What are my choices?" he whispered. Tulir looked young, disheveled, lost. Stuttering, he gestured at the door, "The Ovnite are dying. The Iste have stalled."

Lena crossed the room for proximity. Risking it, she used her arms to bracket and ground him by lightly grabbing his elbows. "Surrender doesn't stop the Ovnite from dying. In fact, it would make it happen faster."

Tulir blinked away a tear. With strained resolve, he said, "The doctor said there's nothing that can be done. Their bodies don't know how to fight our diseases."

"Between the doctors and the Vitki healers, they can manage better here than if we opened those gates," assured Lena. She was about to tell him she intended to learn the art of healing from Amundr, but she paused.

Footsteps in the hall—too light to have been her normal guards on their route. Not quiet enough to have been sure it was someone trying to hide.

"Stay here," Tulir whispered before he moved away. He went to the door silently.

Goodness, how fearful are we of being in their own home? Lena wrapped her arms around her torso as she held her breath.

The person in the hall fell. Tulir opened the door quickly. His eyes widened, and he dashed out. Seeing his urgency, Lena followed in kind.

Briet had collapsed in the hall. Tulir reached her and turned her over with Lena there to help him. Briet's eyes were webbed black and bleeding. It looked like she was barely breathing.

"Get Amundr," whispered Tulir.

Lena took a step back, but she couldn't take her eyes off Briet. *What magic . . . ?*

"Lena!" yelled Tulir.

She sprinted to get help.

Chapter 22

LENA DIDN'T FIND SLEEP until the hour just before dawn. She had been with Amundr and Tulir, explaining what they could of what had happened to Briet. Their explanations weren't lengthy. Briet didn't wake up. Amundr had been able to stop the bleeding, and the webs had receded.

Breakfast had been missed, but Lena wasn't sure she could eat anyway. The demands of the day were ahead of her. She dressed and delayed, gave Socks a few extra minutes of attention, and then went about her duties.

A guard intercepted her. One of the men who had accompanied her to Clevehold, perhaps? It felt too long ago to tell. "Duchess Lena."

"Yes?"

"Your family requires your presence—sent me to find you urgently," he relayed.

Lena felt her chest constrict. *Nela? Selgen? Mother?* "Did they say why?"

"No. Just that you had to come right away," he answered.

"Who did you speak with?"

"Missus Christa."

Lena bunched up her short skirt with her hand. "I'll head there right away. Thank you."

She ran through the halls. The considerations of what could have happened tried to push into her mind, but she kept those thoughts at bay.

Internal debate would only slow her down. All active thought had to be focused on how to best navigate the crowd.

Out of breath, Lena didn't bother knocking when she reached the door. She opened the door and paused, waiting to take in whatever was urgent. She dropped the grip on her skirt.

"It's about time," said Mother. She stood.

Nela was sitting on the bed with a book. She looked up and then closed the book without marking it. "What's wrong?"

"What's . . . ?" Lena questioned. Nothing looked amiss. Her shoulders relaxed and her hand fell from the handle. Was it Father? Had they received word?

"Close the door," instructed Mother. She went about uncovering plates on their small table.

"A guard had me rush here." Lena said it as a fact, but her eye contact with Nela relayed all she needed to.

"You didn't have to run so fast your hair became indecent," said Mother.

What was the tone? Joking? Pandering? Something with a hint of condescension? Lena's heart was too loud in her ears to tell. She closed the door and smoothed a hand over her hair.

Nela stood from the bed. She asked quietly, "Are you alright?"

No. Lena was speechless. Taken aback. She didn't need one more headache with all else that was happening. But she couldn't say that, could she?

Mother pulled back chairs from the table. Casual, carefree, she said, "Why don't you join us now that you're here?"

Fish had been served on the plates.

Are you damaged? Lena didn't know if it was her lack of breath or her last remaining shred of patience that stopped the question from verbalizing. *How could she think . . . ?*

Nela also looked at a loss for what to say. Eye contact made with her sister again, she volunteered, "I had no part in it."

"What?" Mother straightened up. "No part in wanting to see your sister? Lena's ignored us since we arrived."

We're on the brink of war. If she had said it, it would have been through clenched teeth. She had to get out. The stench of fish crept up her nose. *Disgusting food, especially in the morning.*

"Part of Lena's duties is to keep all this running." Nela stood between Lena and Mother, the point of the triangle. "She isn't ignoring us, she's working."

"How does she know things are running smoothly with *us* unless she comes by?" questioned Mother, exasperated, as if it was the simplest thing.

"What ails you, Mother?"

Her mother had to pause a moment to consider. "Excuse me?"

Lena gestured around the room. "You have food—you're not starving. You have beds—you're not uncomfortable. You have clothes and blankets—you're not cold. The lock on your door works. You're in a private secure room. You aren't ill." She flattened her hands. "You look fine, so what am I missing?"

Mother scoffed and looked to Nela. When she was offered no help, she said, "Since when do you speak to your mother like that?"

"If that's all . . ." Lena nodded and clasped her hands together behind her back. That wasn't going to be it, but it would prompt whatever floodgate needed opening. She wouldn't have to wait long.

"Well, if it's all business," her mother spat the last word, "perhaps you can share with us the *business* of what's been happening. What's going on?"

"Mother, the guards tell us what they know daily," said Nela.

"Yes, but there's more to it than that." Mother sat down and opened her arms expectantly. "Well?"

A smile crossed Lena's face. If not that, the internal coil holding her upright would surely snap. "I cannot give you confidential information."

"Why not?" questioned Mother.

"Because anything not relayed by the guards is at the discretion of the Council. I cannot betray them."

"But I'm your mother," she insisted.

Surely, the rationalization wasn't that complex. Mother could have understood if indeed she wanted to. The insolence, the rudeness, the fish—all of it. She honestly acted in such a way because she was under the impression it was acceptable. She was permitted to treat Lena in such a way. *Why?*

The mockery of her tone reiterated in Lena's mind: *I'm your mother.*

"Goodbye," said Lena as she turned and opened the door.

"You're being unreasonable!" called Mother.

Lena kept her head high and walked away.

Mother screeched after her, "I didn't raise you to be rude and dress like a whore!"

A laugh simmered in Lena's throat. She kept walking. Her face bore what felt like a deranged smile all the way to the training courtyard.

Tisa was there, along with a handful of Ovnite. *Her Drengr?* Lena couldn't be sure, but they were tattooed. She ignored them and went for the supply cove.

More anger and anxiety bubbled up in her with each step she took. There had to be something here to help her get it out. Her fists clenched.

"Duchess," greeted Tisa as she came around the corner.

"You're looking well," Lena acknowledged, distracted.

Tisa walked forward slowly. "Are you alright?"

"I need to hit something." It would explode from her otherwise. She couldn't just bury it.

"Haybale," suggested Tisa. She tapped her hand on it. When Lena nodded, Tisa helped roll it out into the open.

CLEVEHOLD

"You know how to make a fist?" asked Tisa as she leaned against the side of the large bale. Tufts stuck out the side, and it smelled old.

Lena answered by punching the hay. It felt good. The material absorbed the impact, but not enough to douse the satisfaction. She left a dent. Lena repeated the punches.

At first, her mind ran through all the recent events that had spurred her anger, but soon her mind went blank. She wasn't thinking, only moving, feeling. Her fists tingled and she continued to punch, one blow after another. Power moved down her arms.

The next punch felt different. More precisely, she hadn't felt it at all. Her fist connected, and she saw it happen—there was a green flicker from her clenched fingers. She loosened her grip. The magic was gone.

"Duchess!" said Tisa, alarmed. She nudged the woman.

The hay had caught fire. The last place Lena had punched had a dent, and licks of blue and green flames ate at it. It didn't smell like burning hay. Lena looked at her hand again.

Tisa gripped the haybale by the edges and flipped it so that the flame faced the stone.

"I'm sorry," said Lena, not feeling it whatsoever.

"It'll smother." Tisa examined Lena. "You didn't know you could do that."

"Family brings out the best in us." Lena wondered if she should have been scared. Scared of the emergence of magic at unforeseen times. Scared of unintentionally lighting something ablaze. But she didn't. She felt good. She felt powerful.

"Would you like to train with the Drengr?" offered Tisa.

"No." Lena felt renewed, a better version of herself. Calm restored, she politely refused. "I have to go." She went to leave but looked back. "Thank you."

Tisa made a friendly salute. "Any time, Duchess."

LIZ BUNCHES

THE DAY PROGRESSED with far less theatrics than the morning. Lena was told ahead of time Marisol and Tulir would not attend dinner to monitor Briet. She hadn't woken up. It had almost been a full day.

Lena balanced a plate of food as she knocked on the door to Briet's room. She smiled when Marisol opened it for her. "Thank you."

"Is it that late?" asked Marisol. She yawned.

"It is." Lena moved inside and set the plate down on the desk. "Any change?"

"No," answered Tulir. He was in a chair next to the bed, elbows on his knees, watching Briet. The bags under his eyes were heavy.

"Amundr was in here not too long ago. She's not improving, but she's not deteriorating," explained Marisol.

It looked nothing like the sickness, nor what had ailed Kazio. Lena grinned pleasantly and put a light hand to Marisol's shoulder. "Go take dinner with your husband. I'll stay."

Marisol looked to Tulir. "See if you can get him to eat."

"I will," promised Lena.

"Thank you." Marisol left.

Lena went to the window and pulled back the curtains. There wasn't much light to let in, and the room was naturally dark. The bed was dressed in navy blue, the curtains the same. The furniture was a matching dark wood. There were paintings of the sea on the walls. The shards of glass in the window alternated between clear and seafoam.

How fitting, thought Lena. She cleared her throat. "Did you pick this?"

Tulir hummed. His eyes were affixed on Briet while his fingers absently toyed with the amulet hanging from his neck. Hers was on the nightstand.

"When's the last time you stood from that chair?" asked Lena. Before he could answer, she worked her way back toward him. "Up."

"I can't leave," he croaked from his dry throat.

"You can move so far as the sofa." Lena lifted him by his hand, and he was obliged to follow. She guided him to the sofa with an unobstructed view of the bed.

He sat back heavily and rubbed his hands over his eyes.

Lena sat down and crossed her ankles. The sofa wasn't very comfortable. The undertone color was purple against navy. Nothing about the room felt inviting.

Lena began, "I was summoned by my mother."

He looked at her with raised eyebrows. The worry on his face softened. "What did a duchess need to be summoned for?"

"She wanted to know what was going on. Apparently, what the guards are telling them isn't sufficient, and since I'm her daughter, I should tell her everything I know." Her hands dropped dramatically in her lap. She tilted her head to the side and squinted. "I don't think she's our informant, though. The patience the requestor would require is too great."

"It would rival yours"—he bumped shoulders with her—"and you don't often see that in military men."

"Poor Nela," said Lena.

"Your sister can be moved," he offered.

Lena debated it quickly. "No. They aren't the best companions to each other, but they should stay together. Once things calm down, we can figure something out."

"You miss Nela. I can hear it."

"I do," she admitted readily. "She was always around, then she just wasn't, and I've spent the last two years growing into a different person. I feel like I could reconnect with her without being in her shadow, but..."

"I understand." He patted her knee.

She took a deep breath. He did understand. Too well. She wasn't the only one forcibly separated from a sibling.

Lena smiled in such a way that didn't reach her eyes. "Nela won't be able to threaten or tease you anymore, Your Grace."

"I don't know that any title of mine can stop her from doing that. She's a fierce one, your sister," said Tulir. There was a longing in his eyes. Was he thinking about what it would have been like if he and Lena had gotten married, she wondered? Nela threatening him the morning of the ceremony. Dinners with Lena's family.

"I'll be interested to see if any of the Ovnite are as afraid of her as you are." She bumped him back.

"If Kazio has any sense, he will be." Tulir sniffled and stared at Briet on the bed. "Nela will have to wait until he's on his feet."

"I saw Amundr in passing getting food. He told me Kazio woke, and was grouchy and weak," she relayed. She hadn't gone to see Kazio. She would only prolong his sour mood.

"Good to know he's already himself again," replied Tulir. He leaned forward on his elbows. "I'm sorry the one who was chosen for you isn't what was expected. Briet told me about the conversation she and Avild had with you. I'm sorry."

"There's no hurry, and nothing is set in stone," said Lena. It was Briet's right to talk to her new husband about whatever she liked. But the rationality didn't mean Lena had to like it.

"Have you found yourself an alternative?" he asked and looked back.

Kindly, she asked, "Is this what you want to talk about?"

"There's something about Kazio I don't like. Not just the posing—I can't name it, and he's one of Briet's best men, so I can't justify it. If he's sickly, and you have a better prospect, I will help you get whatever you want."

"Harth," said Lena simply.

She was now in Tulir's shoes. She recalled that night at the private dinner when she had been trying to decipher what he was leading toward. Just as he had, she sat and waited for a reaction.

"What?" He stood and combed a hand through his hair. He whispered, "Harth?"

"Would it not be suitable?" she questioned, chin up.

"Lena, it was never my intention to bridge that gap between the two of you," he explained hastily.

She stood and spoke quietly, "I know I'm not what he wants. That wasn't what I was asking."

His eyes were wide, breaths quick. "Then what was?"

"Duchess and the Commander of the Royal Guard would make a good match. Especially since said duchess will likely be removed off the Council once this is all sorted," she justified.

"I won't have you removed."

"But it won't be only your choice, and as history has demonstrated, the choice isn't always yours to heartfully make." She felt herself becoming flustered at the need for defense. Didn't he understand? "I need to protect myself."

"I will protect you," he promised.

"You can't intercept everything," she countered. "Harth will never choose a wife. It's not in itself inherently devious, but I see now Norman was suspicious. You said yourself there's something about Kazio, and I now have a good reason to step away. This protects both Harth and I."

Tulir breathed heavily. He pressed his palm to his forehead and groaned. Bringing it down, he asked, "Why does it have to be this?"

Lena narrowed her eyes. "What is it you're feeling? It's not jealousy. That would have been better suited for Kazio. I don't desire Harth—I don't expect to receive it from him. For the purpose of children would be the only reason. In fact, it's adjacent to what you asked of me."

Tears had built up in Tulir's eyes. "What I wanted . . ." His voice cracked, and he stopped. He kicked the leg of the sofa. "I was trying to have the best of all worlds. Life is like magic . . . volatile when we overstep our reach."

"Tulir," she tried to get his attention.

"The trio of us, we were good together—you know it."

"We still are. The mold just changed," she reasoned.

"I should have done something differently."

"The fallout isn't your fault."

"I want you to be happy," he pleaded.

She stepped closer and whispered, "What made me happy was you. What I have now is my best chance."

"This is my fault," Tulir insisted. "The foreigners, the marriages, Steepwharf and the chip they have on their shoulder—I didn't foresee any of it. I failed."

"I still support you. The foreigners do, too. There is an abundance of men in this castle willing to fight for you." Lena reached for his shaking hands and held them in her own.

He hung his head. "I was a guard. Not a soldier, not a leader."

"The men out there are guards, too," she reminded. They had to be; Steepwharf didn't have an army. Their fighters were Tulir and Harth's contemporaries.

"What happens . . . ?" Tulir let out a long breath to steady himself. "What happens when Briet finds out how this all came to be?"

"Why does she have to?"

CLEVEHOLD

Tulir withdrew his hands and went to the window behind her. He looked out on the fading light. "It's all build on falsehoods."

"It was built the best way we could control it," reminded Lena.

He waved an arm. "Avild should have it."

Lena checked that Briet was still asleep and unmoving, then stood beside Tulir. She shook her head. "If you admit anything to Briet, our alliance will not survive. They already have reason to distrust us—Norman saw to that. We need the Ovnite, and they need us."

He repeated dryly, "Forged on a falsehood."

She put a hand on his arm. "But holding strong."

"I can't hold this together."

"I couldn't break my cousin out of jail on my own. I had help. Titles and standings be damned, you still have me."

He looked at her. His chin trembled, but his wet eyes shone with a hint of relief. "You're gracious."

"Be proud of what you've built. I am," said Lena.

"Would you have that same pride knowing how weak I am?" he asked.

"You aren't."

"But I want to be." He held her gaze.

Lena took a breath and looked down. When she came back up, it was with resolve. "We aren't fools. I won't let you be. You've helped me through my difficulties. I'm here for you. You'll eat, you'll sleep, and I will watch over your wife."

He kissed her on the cheek. "Yes, ma'am."

NOT MUCH CHANGED OVER the next two days. There were only five people at the table when they gathered for dinner in the Council meeting room. There wasn't a seat on Lena's left side any longer, Norman's and Charlot's placements having been removed.

Marisol was absent, at Briet's bedside. Tisa and Amundr were the only representatives of the Ovnite.

"Will Harth be joining us?" asked Tisa. She held her fork awkwardly and stabbed the meat.

"He scheduled himself a shift on the wall," answered Lena. There was less on her plate than usual—a result of their rationing. Though she didn't feel much like eating, she needed to. It couldn't go to waste.

Amundr refused the utensils and ate with his hands. He observed, at their table, "We grow thinner, and we've not yet been attacked."

"It's happening quicker than we expected," agreed Rufino.

"Has the sickness from the Ovnite spread to the others?" asked Tisa. The piece of meat she had tried to stab fell from the fork. She dropped the utensils and ate with her hands.

"Not as far as we can tell. There are other sicknesses going around, though. It's what happens when we keep everyone too close," said Tulir.

"We're well stocked in medicine," reminded Lena.

"If we keep the doctors spry and teach another hand or two to heal, we will endure," said Amundr. He looked to Lena.

She raised her glass to him. It was strange to see the empty seat next to her, but it allowed her to see Amundr up close. Slouch. Bad eyes. A grey-and-brown peppered beard he had let grow in. Still an imposing man, but just a man.

The rear door opened. Lena second-guessed what she saw, her chair clattering when she stood. Amundr did the same. Those on the other side of the table turned to look.

Briet and Kazio, leaning on each other, entered the meeting room. They were both pale, Briet more so, and it looked like Kazio was holding her up. She was changed out of her bedclothes and her blonde hair was tied back in a ribbon. Kazio was freshly shaven.

"Can't miss a Council meeting," said Briet. She grinned. Her steps were slow and shuffled.

Tisa pushed back from the table and went to them. "You're both impossible."

"I thought—" Tulir stammered and stood. "When did you wake?"

Briet hooked her arm over Tisa's shoulders. The woman took her weight, and she moved off Kazio. "An hour ago. They told me he was up, too."

Amundr tsked but grinned.

"Marisol?" questioned Rufino.

"Looked like she was more in need of the sleep, so I let her lie," answered Briet. Tulir moved her chair out and she sat.

Kazio made it most of the way around the table before his step faltered. Amundr was close enough to catch him and kept Kazio upright. The exchanged remarks were made in hushed tones. Their exact words couldn't be overheard, but it sounded like a scolding from Amundr and a rebuttal in jest from Kazio. Amundr halfheartedly pushed Kazio down into the empty seat between Lena's and his own.

Lena looked at Kazio and shook her head, but she couldn't help but smile. *Impossible, indeed.* She righted her chair and sat back down.

"Unless you're in the middle of something, I have an item of business you need to hear," said Briet as she settled in.

Kazio leaned in close to Lena, pointed at her plate, and whispered, "Is it not any good?"

She pushed her plate toward him.

"Are you ill?" Rufino asked Briet.

"I'll recover. Being invisible was taxing," answered Briet.

Amundr grumbled.

Lena repeated to ensure she heard correctly, "Invisible?"

"You managed it?" asked Tisa.

Briet nodded. "And I snuck into Clevehold."

"Without using the tunnels, yes?" presumed Amundr.

She shook her head. "I went over the wall, ran lines. Nothing anyone visible could get away with."

Kazio ate quickly. Whatever Briet was about to tell them, he either already knew or didn't care. Lena couldn't imagine scarfing down food right now. Her stomach was in knots.

"The Iste are out there, brokering. You're about to lose that army to Steepwharf," said Briet.

Tulir looked her in the eye. "You're certain?"

"Without a doubt. I left before they settled on final details, but that was more to pick over your corpse. They needed to decide who got which head."

"Aren't they your people in the west?" Amundr pointed at Rufino.

He swallowed and laid his hands on the table. There was a faraway look in his eyes. "They were."

"Do you know anyone personally enough you could make a counterbid to?" asked Tulir. There was panic blooming behind his eyes.

"Do they detest magic as the coastal cities do?" asked Kazio. Lena poured a cup of water and handed it to him, but Kazio wouldn't take it. He muttered, "I don't need to be mothered, Duchess."

"Just fucking drink," she whispered.

His lip pulled up in a half snarl. He took it and drank it down.

"They have a similar view on magic, not as extreme. I could send word to them to try, but if they've decided, despite my presence here, I don't know what my word will do," said Rufino. He pushed away his plate.

"Making that bid also gives away our insight. They don't know we know this, yes?" said Tisa.

"You're right," agreed Tulir. He rested his elbows on the table.

"We need to come up with an alternative," said Amundr.

Kazio leaned back, the plate cleared. "There's nothing to be done tonight."

Rufino mumbled to himself. Eyes unfocused. Pale. He blinked rapidly.

"We ignore this information?" questioned Lena.

"It will still be an issue tomorrow." Kazio gestured across the table. "The queen only just awoke."

"It will give us all time to think on it, sleep on it," agreed Briet. She looked at the plate someone had put before her. "How are the food stores?"

Lena paused to provide Rufino time to answer. It was technically more his area; Lena had only assisted with assessments. When it looked like he was too distracted to answer, she said, "Migrant birds are what we're eating now. Fish are still aplenty in the Royal Harbor. With the supplies from the Ovnite ships accounted for, we have stores that will last for a month more, we hope."

"I'm sorry." Rufino stood on shaky legs. "I have to go." He went to the door, fumbled with the handle, and left them.

"Treacherous," whispered Kazio. He held his empty cup to his mouth.

"He looks as though he's about to vomit." Lena leaned back and made eye contact with Kazio. She assured, "Trust me, Rufino isn't that good a liar."

Chapter 23

HARTH HAD MADE TIME to train with Lena in the afternoon. At the last minute, he changed the location from the front courtyard they had been using to the one in the rear, wedged between the castle and the mountain. Tulir was waiting for them there.

"I hope you don't mind," said Tulir. He handed a sword to Lena. "I informed Harth of what we were told last night. He said he had training with you and . . . honestly, I wanted to get away."

"He's angry Briet hid something from him," said Harth.

Lena nodded.

Tulir put a hand on his hip. "I don't need to know what she eats for breakfast or her bed count, but invisibility and going over the wall during a lockdown are 'share with the class' type actions."

"She did tell you when it worked," reminded Harth.

Tulir put up his hands.

Lena felt the weight of the sword in her hand. She didn't feel like sparring. The image of the fire she caused on the haybale revisited her. What if she lost control again? It hadn't scared her when she had done it, but it did now. It was one thing to ignite hay, another her men.

Handing the sword back to Tulir, she said, "You could do with some training."

"What are you trying to say?" he asked coyly.

"You spent two years not putting too much weight on that leg"—she tapped on his hip as she walked past—"and you need to unlearn that. You learned to fight left-handed—now you need to find balance." She turned and settled to lean against a wall.

CLEVEHOLD

"She's right," said Harth. He had done a walk of the perimeter. They were alone.

Tulir smirked at Lena. "I think I'm good with both my hands." She blushed and glared.

"Quit flirting and put your sword up," said Harth.

Tulir rolled his eyes.

And thus the dance began. Lena liked to watch them spar. They were both well trained, strong, and fought in a way she never could. Harth used more brute force tactics, whereas Tulir dipped into the grace of evasion while holding up a hearty defense. Slip past, pivot, strike. Every time Tulir tried it, Harth was prepared.

The sword in Tulir's hand was knocked away from him. He cursed.

"Trust your step," instructed Harth.

"I do!"

"Then don't flinch," said Harth. He pointed at Tulir's dropped sword.

Tulir removed his overshirt. The one beneath was sleeveless. Not in any way indecent, especially not for a man, but it exposed the gruesome scar on his right arm. Lena wondered, as she tried not to gawk, if there was a reason he didn't ask for the gouge to be healed. Was it that he had spent two years using his left hand to fight, and going back now wouldn't make sense? Or was it kept as a reminder?

The clanking of swords resumed. Tulir kept up, though at times it looked like a struggle or reach. Out of breath, they parted.

"You're doing well," said Harth.

"I wasn't sitting on my ass as king, was I?"

Lena wasn't in the way, but she kept herself mobile to avoid her placement becoming an issue.

Harth came after him with an overhead swing. Tulir defended. The strikes continued and Tulir was backed against the wall.

Swords locked, Harth leaned in.

Tulir was trapped. Teeth bared, he grunted, but he couldn't gain leverage. The swords moved up, closer to his neck. Tulir kicked Harth's knee.

The move disengaged the standoff and Harth stumbled back a foot, but Tulir grabbed him. Harth was turned and pushed to the wall. Swords to the side, Tulir pressed them chest to chest, their faces close to touching.

Harth punched Tulir under the ribs, and as he flinched, he pushed Tulir off. The swords came back up and Tulir swung.

"You have to be careful." Harth sidestepped and evaded.

Tulir chased. "Don't let me distract you."

Harth came after Tulir with renewed vigor. The spar was well formed, mostly tame, and it was clear Tulir was losing. They parted naturally after a few minutes.

Tulir switched the grip on his sword and shook out his hand. "Isn't your specialty archery?"

"Whatever comes over that wall," answered Harth. He nodded.

Tulir pushed back his shoulders and returned the nod. The sparring resumed. They slowed down, and Harth walked Tulir through a set of steps. He was trying to get Tulir to move without favoring one leg. Swords clanked in a steady rhythm and Tulir gave feedback as they moved. It looked like a dance.

Lena smiled. She thought of Klaus and Avild. The tackle in the grass. How Lena had interrupted them because a wooden spoon took down the bug net. With Tulir and Harth it felt better, warmer, just the three of them in their own world. This felt right.

"Run it at speed," instructed Harth.

Tulir did so. At the end of the string of movements, Tulir knocked Harth's sword to the side. Before the other man could get the sword back up, Tulir had a point at Harth's neck.

"Good," said Harth, pushing the blade away casually.

"A few more rounds of this and I'll be back to where I was," said Tulir.

"Which was?" asked Harth.

Tulir looked at him pointedly and shrugged.

"Better than me?" Harth scoffed.

"The standards were different for a public guard. It's not your fault," excused Tulir. He twirled the sword.

"That's what you think?" Harth pulled up the front of his shirt to wipe sweat from his brow.

Tulir eyed Harth's exposed skin and said mischievously, "You never took me up on sparring in Steepwharf. You can't tell me I'm wrong."

"I've been training since before you were born," reminded Harth.

Tulir turned to Lena. "Could you imagine it? An eleven-year-old kid running at you with a knife?"

"Will you pay attention?" she asked, suppressing a giggle.

"Lena should sub in. She listens better than you do," said Harth.

"You want to trade me out for something prettier." Tulir raised his eyebrows and theatrically raised his sword to point at Harth.

He knocked it away. Coated with reserved amusement, Harth said, "I want to trade you out for someone quieter."

"You never complained." Tulir shook his head, then backed up. "Alas, I would like to see the lady fight. Her with me—you trade out."

"Yes, Your Grace." Harth rolled his eyes.

Lena met Harth in the middle and took the sword. "We picked him."

"Didn't feel like a choice," responded Harth.

The sword felt heavy in her hand, but it no longer felt foreign. She decided there would be no wholehearted sparring. Not only was she unmatched to do so, but she wouldn't risk the fire. They could walk through drills.

Slowness was easier to convey if they spoke. "You told him everything about what Briet said?"

"All about how the Iste are quick to betray us," answered Tulir. He swung slowly, and she blocked. "Good."

"Are we taking her at her word?" asked Harth. He kept to the periphery of the spar, but not so far that he couldn't hear.

"She came to Tulir when she collapsed. The general area, at least." Lena paused to block and swing. "What reason does she have to lie?" Tulir took a step, and she remembered to keep her feet mobile.

"Can't expect a dynasty that was dormant for a thousand years to return without question," Tulir spoke through their slow-motion spar. He was observing Lena more than he was putting in effort. "Keep your elbow—yes, like that."

"Thank you," she said.

"Try one-handed."

Lena shook her head. "I'm not nearly that strong."

"One day you will be. You want the muscles to learn the right way," Tulir encouraged. "Believe me, I wanted to do a bastard hold when my right arm betrayed me, but your fighting is more about mobility and tactic than strength."

She held it in just her right. "Will I be learning with a shield next?" Her swings now required more effort, and she felt off-balance. They took it slow.

"Have you thought about what we do next? They're making deals with the Iste in secret, but they'll let us know soon," said Harth.

"I have." Tulir backed away and swiped his sword through the open air. "If she agrees, we should slip away with Briet, take the Court with us, and leave Clevehold."

Harth narrowed his eyes. "There are so many people that came here seeking refuge from people like Steepwharf's men."

"People who would be killed if we left them behind," agreed Lena. *This is his plan?*

"They'll be better off than if we made a stand. If the Council surrenders and disappears, they may show mercy," said Tulir.

"We abandon?" questioned Harth.

"It was forged under a falsehood. This is how we pay for it," hissed Tulir.

"You aren't paying a penance," said Harth.

Lena relaxed her arm. She looked at the sword in her hand. Was he right? *No.* Not as it stood, but he was almost there. She suggested, "We go to Estnable."

"Where?" asked Harth.

"It's in the East. It's where Kazio and Cicero come from," answered Tulir.

Harth looked at Lena incredulously. "You agree to abandon?"

"Not to abandon." She motioned for both men to move in closer. "Bring our ships, the ones we've been building. Bring our people. Move the dynasty."

"Bringing all those who took refuge won't be an easy feat," said Tulir.

"Will Briet bring or abandon us?" asked Harth.

Lena jumped in, fearful of Tulir's pessimism. "She has reason to agree. You met her for peace. You kept her people safe within the walls."

"Half of them are sick or dying under my protection," reminded Tulir.

"They would have gotten sick from coming to this continent regardless," said Lena.

Harth considered, "If the Ovnite had staged the siege, or had met Steepwharf outside the walls, their fighters and magic users wouldn't have been enough."

"What position are we in to ask them to take not just us, but our people? We would outnumber them," said Tulir.

"What position are they in?" returned Lena. "They are our allies, and I do not threaten, but what position would they be in to consider your request a question and not a polite formality?"

Tulir combed a hand through his hair. "We run?"

Harth blinked quickly. "It was your idea."

"You trying to talk me out of it, I expected," said Tulir.

Lena set the sword with the point on the ground and rested her hands atop. "It's not running, it's relocating. People came to the Stone King's city for refuge, but it isn't the city of Clevehold that gives it to them. It's how we protect them. We don't need this castle to do it."

"What makes us think Steepwharf won't follow us across the sea?" asked Tulir.

"They'll have enough to deal with here if they want to put themselves in power," answered Lena.

"Winter is approaching. Their ships are smaller, if they risk fights in open water. They won't directly chase us, and without that, they don't know where Estnable is on the other continent. It's not a guarantee, but the reasons to not follow are notable," said Harth.

"Thank you, both of you." Tulir looked as if he was going to say more, but his attention was directed behind them. Lena turned to see what he was looking at.

"The queen asked to see you, Your Grace," said a guard.

"If you'll excuse me." Tulir handed his sword to Harth. He wiped off his hands and approached the exit, turned, and walked the last few feet backward. Lightheartedly, he called, "To answer the Commander of the Royal Guard's question, you two bastards have my blessing! If you need it."

"There's a lady here," Lena faux ridiculed.

Harth rolled his eyes.

LENA WALKED INTO THE private room with her hands clasped in front of her. It was the place Tulir had brought her when he suggested their arrangement. She loved the view.

"Interesting place you picked," said Kazio.

"You said you wanted to meet with me somewhere private. This is more respectable than my quarters," she answered. The door behind her had been left ajar. She did not move to sit. There wasn't any innate distrust she had for him, but caution felt wise.

Kazio leaned back against the banister. He was tall, and more of the stone barrier was below his waist than above. He didn't appear to be the cautious type. "Is your king contemplating how to best our growing enemy?"

"Is your queen?"

He snorted and rolled his eyes. "What do you want?"

"*You* asked to speak with *me*," she reminded. She joined him at the balcony, a few feet away. She breathed deeply. "How are you feeling?"

"I'm fine," he said quickly.

"It's only been four days since you—"

"I said I'm fine, yes?"

Lena closed her eyes and smiled politely in a way that did not reach her eyes. She pushed off the banister. "You should enjoy the view." Turning, she walked toward the door. There was no time for her to waste. *Summoned to be insulted . . .* She could go to her mother for that.

"I'm sorry," he admitted as if it pained him.

She turned back toward him.

"Will you stay?" Kazio went to a small table by the wall and picked up a pitcher of wine. "Please."

"You confuse me," she confessed, but made the concession to stay by moving closer.

"My friend Cicero told me I don't respond well to people I don't know, and therefore don't trust." Kazio poured two glasses and held one out to Lena. "I'm not a diplomat by nature."

"I'm sorry about your friend. I didn't know him long, but he was kind."

Kazio raised his glass. "To Cicero."

She raised hers to cheers. She waited for him to take the first sip before she followed suit. It was bitter.

"Cicero was the better man," admitted Kazio. He observed his wine as he swirled the liquid around. "I expect my part in all this will change, yes?"

Lena took slow steps with her wine. "How so?"

"As Duke," he stressed the word strangely, then drank the rest of his wine.

She could go into her options, as she saw them. An opportunity was being presented to either refute or confirm his idea. But behind the snarl, she saw the man uprooted from his home, living a foreign life, carrying the baggage of deceased friends who had helped him get this far. "I don't like the idea of people deciding for me, either. I assumed you'd be relieved to be rid of me."

Kazio laughed. He approached but kept his distance.

Lena smiled back at him. This person she saw now seemed more genuine: a young man with a need to guard himself. Cicero had said their stories rhymed. How true was that? How similar was Lena to Kazio, and how much would it pain him to accept such?

She asked, "How old are you?"

He made a clicking sound with his mouth and scrunched his nose. "Not old enough, if what Tisa told me is true. About the real reason things are changing."

"Right." Lena sipped her wine. She took a deep breath and looked Kazio in the eye. "I want to be clear: I don't think I like you. I'm going to talk to you as if you're my equal. I'm going to ask you questions. The challenge you pose to me isn't something I have the capacity for right now. If all I'm going to get are smart remarks, I will decide I don't like you, and I will leave."

"You're free to leave whenever you like, Duchess."

She mimed his facial expression. Her heart began to beat harder. *What is this, a chase?* "You asked me here to have a discussion—one we've not fully had. You want to find out how much your aliment has changed your situation and if I have any influence over it. It also tells me you haven't had this discussion with Briet, but you assume I've had it with my men," she baited, sipped her wine, and waited.

His face went through several motions, and remarks danced behind the surface of his eyes. Remarks that likely would help him find out if Lena was willing to make good on her threat to leave. He reminded her of Tulir in that way. Ready with wit. Had Tulir had a harder life or Kazio an easier one, she may not have found Kazio as difficult to be around.

Did that mean she saw heart under Kazio's exterior? She supposed she had to, if she was comparing him to Tulir. Heart, loyalty, pride, and too smart for their own good. The kind of unseasoned smart that got them cornered into situations they didn't know how to handle. That was when the pride kicked in—better to not show it. At least Lena knew if Tulir got himself into that kind of trouble, his heart had made him do it for the right reasons.

"Twenty-six." Kazio made a so-so motion with his hand. "Or twenty-five. Somewhere in there."

"You don't know when you were born?" It didn't shock her to know he was a touch younger than her twenty-seven years. It led her to believe Briet was younger still. *Hard lives, indeed.*

"We celebrate milestones, not time."

"Surely your parents kept track of your age, as a child."

He shrugged. "Until I left them."

"Left them?"

"Our children don't stay with their parents. Our elders communally raise them, those with the best experience," he explained.

Lena hovered a hand over her stomach. "You don't raise your own children?"

"If you live long enough, you raise a future generation." Kazio scratched the side of his head. "Don't worry, men like me don't tend to live that long, yes?"

What would he pass on to his children? His ginger hair? His height? She had the latter running through her family. She had always imagined her sons would undoubtably grow taller than her, but with Kazio, her daughters could, too.

"That's not how we raise our children," she said, drinking the last of her wine. When she had envisioned her future, the children had dark hair and calm brown eyes—Tulir's eyes. Harth had brown eyes, too, though they were lighter with a green tint. Not the deep, dark eyes she got lost in.

"Your choices won't be as rushed as the king's," said Kazio.

Her choice. That's what he thought it was. The background truth existed: the decision didn't have to be rushed. The marriage of Briet and Tulir had been an act of unification as much as it was rash. If they had waited, much may have changed. *Briet may not have been looking at a future with brown-eyed children.*

Could have been for the better, or they could all have been dead.

"And what choices has the queen given you, her strongest man?" Lena set her glass on the banister.

He lightly sneered, "Don't mock me."

"I wouldn't," she defended. "Your affliction appears to be magic-use related. You're still a strong man without it."

"I am the Vitki leader. Magic is what makes me strong."

"Do you think the queen is weak?" she proposed.

He shook his head. "It's different." He looked out to the horizon. He went to set the glass on the banister, but by not looking, he placed it off-balance. The glass tipped backward and shattered on the ground. He cursed.

Lena put a hand to his chest to stop him from bending to chase it. "Why would you think it's different?"

Kazio stared at her for a moment. He seemed to notice the hand she pushed him with and straightened back from it. "What I have, this . . . it's with me. Magic brings it out, but I often feel it."

"When they said it had happened before . . . ?"

He shook his head. "Not to that extent. Sometimes when I wake, or I'll . . ." He bared his teeth and looked down at the glass pieces. "Sometimes, I'm confused. I don't know why or when. It makes me weak. Now, everyone knows."

If this ailment was within him, as he said, it stood to reason he could pass it on to a child, just as he could eye color. She folded her hands together.

"Nothing that helps my case, yes?" said Kazio.

"Honesty is always a positive attribute," replied Lena. When he looked at her, she continued, "As is courage."

"Our worlds aren't too different, but weakness that makes you unable to fight is cowardice, Duchess," he said definitively, leaning into her title.

She punched him in the arm.

He flinched and looked at her with a knit brow.

"You don't want to fight me?" she questioned. Her fists weren't up, but she kept her arms tensed.

"Fighting an unarmed duchess wouldn't prove courage."

"Is it because I'm a woman?" She stepped around the broken glass and kept her chin up.

Kazio shook his head, mouth open. He didn't know what to make of her, she supposed. She wasn't overtly assured of the point she was trying to make, only that she hated his self-pity. There wasn't time for it.

"My mentor, Imogene, she taught me to fight with respect," said Kazio.

"You're saying you don't respect me?" She used the flats of her hands to push him. There wasn't much resistance, and he stepped back.

"What is this?" He put his hands up and kept her at arm's length.

"I watched a good friend die. He died fighting. But what he didn't do was fight the whole way through. It was planned, strategized, and assessed. He fought when he had a plan. Waiting, not fighting, wasn't cowardice," she explained.

"I'm choosing not to fight a duchess," responded Kazio.

"Then you aren't senseless. You know when to delay and when to attack. If the overextension of magic is what makes you succumb, don't."

"It's that simple?"

"To find and know your limits?" she questioned.

"Why be so insistent to help me?"

"Why be so honest with me?" she countered. It was strange—she knew she was pushing him and that he was on the brink of anger, but she wasn't afraid. Sense told her she should be, recalling the image of Kazio as she first saw him, the fiery man leaning out of the Ovnite ship. Who she saw before her now was more him than that man was.

Kazio wiped a hand across his mouth. "To let you find the limits of my patience."

"Are we or are we not the same people?" she proposed to him. "It's us in here, and it's them out there. I need to know where our faults lie, for us to plan for them."

He shook his head. "Your fault is that you can't fight for yourself and need others to do it for you, Duchess."

The way he said her title crawled up her spine and forced a frown to her face. She dropped her glass in the pile with his and left him with the mess.

Chapter 24

"DUCHESS?"

Responding to the title had felt strange at first. After what had only been a couple weeks but felt eventful enough to have been a lifetime, she was growing accustomed to it. "Yes?"

"May I speak with you?" the guard asked. He was young, uneasy.

"If you treat an animal like it might bite, that's what it does." Salvatore moved around the young guard. "Don't give a woman a reason to be impatient."

Lena closed the book in her lap. She had thought to look in the library's medical books for anything related to the sickness the Ovnite were experiencing, but no new information had jumped out.

"Ma'am." Salvatore nodded. "Amundr has requested your presence down in the shipyard but hadn't specified his reasons."

Strange, Lena mused, but she expected such behavior from him at this point. She stood. "Will you accompany me down there, sir?"

"Yes, Duchess. We will take—?" Salvatore stopped abruptly when he ran into the young guard.

"Sorry, sir," the guard stammered, quickly moving out of the way.

Salvatore grumbled but kept his words clean. "Find an assignment."

"Sir?" the young guard questioned.

"The barracks," said Salvatore.

"Sir." The young guard nodded and fled.

"Do they fear me?" asked Lena once the young man was gone.

Salvatore led them through the castle as they spoke. "Many a young man signed up more recently. They come in two types when they start too old: no respect and no fear. Or interchanging those you should respect with those you should fear."

"I don't know that I've ever been feared before," considered Lena.

"Respectfully, ma'am, every man should have a healthy amount of fear toward his woman. We don't think like you do. Women with authority, especially—they know what they want. If us men don't keep up, women will leave us behind." Salvatore held the door open for her.

"Sounds like you have a good balance of fear and respect for the women in your life," she complimented.

"Married twenty-one years, two daughters, and a daughter-in-law. Wouldn't have survived otherwise."

Lena smiled.

"To be frank, Duchess, men of the guard can make for bad husbands. It can be dangerous, it can be exhausting, and dinner is often cold by the time we get home."

"I'm sure the respect your wife has for you permits for some allowances," said Lena.

He held another door for her. "There are many honorable men among the Royal Guard. So long as a woman can understand lack of presence does not mean a lack of love, the pair can endure."

"I believe I understand what you're saying, and I do."

They reached the shipyards. By the masts, she knew immediately more had been built. Not their size of ship, either, but the Ovnite's. Four had come, three had survived Steepwharf's attack, but there were five tall masts in the Royal Harbor.

"Took some smaller ones apart for material," said Salvatore as he led them through the yard. It smelled of fish and sweat. There were people on one of the ships, and threads of magic wound around their fingers as they worked in orange, green, and blue.

"We're lucky they can build so quickly," she commented. "But I guess the best luck would be not to need warships."

"Yes, ma'am," he agreed.

A cluster of men were off to the side by the lumber stacks. Lena looked to Salvatore curiously and he led her forward. She looked for Amundr; he should have been easy to spot over the crowd. The men noticed her and moved from her path. She and Salvatore traveled through the part they created.

Amundr was crouched on the ground next to a bleeding man. There were splinters of wood around. He waved them forward. "Come."

"He fell off a mound. Hasn't woken up," said a man as they passed.

A guard was in the clearing around the unconscious man and Amundr. The guard addressed Salvatore, "The doctor was here, but he was sent away."

Sent away? Lena stood on the other side of the unconscious man. "Is he alive?"

"For now," replied Amundr in that voice that made it difficult to tell if it was a joke or a threat.

"Doc said he's got broken bits," said a man in a heavy Ovnite accent.

"The leg, both arms." Amundr hovered his hand down the unconscious man's body. "And probably a broken foot."

Lena nodded. She understood. Rubbing her hands together, she knelt. "What do you want me to do?"

"Perhaps we should wait for the people to disperse," said Amundr.

He was right. If she was going to learn, better to do so without the pressure of a crowd. The last thing she wanted to do was not have sufficient focus and accidentally set a man on fire.

"Will you move the men away?" Lena asked Salvatore.

"You heard her. Clear out!" Salvatore and the other guard moved the bystanders away.

Lena's palms began to sweat. She rubbed them on her trousers. The man on the ground was breathing evenly, as if he was asleep. Had the doctor given him something, or was it the shock that knocked him out? Regardless, it was better he was unconscious. The odd bends of his leg and left arm made her stomach churn, but the bone sticking out of his right forearm was nightmarish.

She looked to Amundr instead. He had shaved, now back to his normal clean face. There were bags under his eyes. Did he always look that way, she wondered, or just in the time she had known him? As the men's feet were shuffling away, to avoid the silence, she asked, "Are you alright? You look exhausted."

"I've been tired all my life. I learn to live with it," he said candidly.

The immediate truth wasn't expected. She pursued the thread and asked, "Is that why you . . . ?" She made a slow ripple motion with her hand.

"Why I what?" He smirked and looked around at the thinning crowd. After licking his lips, he looked to Lena again. A hand went over his heart. "Some things, magic can't fix. When I pull the magic through to help others, it provides a personal reprieve, and some balance."

"Pull through?" she asked. Were they all afflicted with something or other? *A result of the limited diversity within the Binding?*

"You'll soon find out." Amundr looked over her shoulder to Salvatore as the man came back.

"Would you like me to stay?" offered Salvatore.

"That won't be necessary," answered Amundr. He waved dismissively.

"Duchess?" Salvatore looked at Lena.

Concentration. Privacy. She shook her head. "I'll shout if I need you."

"Yes, ma'am," he agreed, then left.

"Is it better to heal them when they aren't awake?" asked Lena. She wanted to distract herself from the blood and broken limbs, but with what? This was why she was here. Things needed to break to be fixed.

"For you, yes. His injuries are not grave. You may not be able to heal him completely," answered Amundr.

Lena pushed up the cuffs of her sleeves. "If I can't, then you'll fix it?" Before he could respond to her question, she remembered the answer. Once magic was used to heal it, it could not be compounded.

"It's not like mending a book," he answered.

"How did it happen?" Lena looked around at the splintered wood. Had something fallen on him? Had he fallen and something broke his landing?

"You're stalling." Amundr smirked. He pinched the fabric of the unconscious man's left sleeve and lifted it for a few seconds before letting it drop. "Start with his nondominant hand. Whatever state you heal it up to, the balance will have to heal naturally."

"Unless it's broken again?" proposed Lena. *Would redundancy solve it?*

Amundr tsked. "I'm not in the business of breaking ally bones."

"Right." Lena wiped the back of her hand along her mouth. "What about the volatility of magic? Can you fix it if, instead of healing, I harm him?"

CLEVEHOLD

"This magic only works if you are properly grounded. If you are not, the worst it can do is not work."

The unconscious man groaned. He would wake soon.

She had delayed long enough. It was time to find out if the Stone King's bequeathed magic was good enough to heal. Amundr had said she couldn't make it worse—there was no reason not to believe him.

"How do I do it?" asked Lena.

"Start with a feeling of tightness here." He pushed his fingers into the arch under his ribcage. "You will have to call it forward. Magic that originates from your spine will do damage. To heal, you must filter it through your heart, your lungs, the things used to keep you alive."

Lena nodded and straightened out her back. She didn't know if magic started in the same place for everyone, but when she concentrated and called it forth, the origin was the spot on her back where the magic had shot in. There was a pinch where it began. She breathed deeply and concentrated on pulling it forward.

She put a hand to her chest. "Since you're moving it through what makes you alive, can your emotional stability change the outcome?"

Amundr shook out his hands. He didn't look at her. "It might."

"I've done it, as you said," she told him.

"Feel your blood as it courses away from your heart. Feel it moving away, not just to your legs and arms, but to your head."

Lena felt a chill as she became aware of what he described. There was life flowing all around her. She looked down at her hands. A green hue glowed from them, not as fiercely as light. "I feel cold. Not from ice, but from within."

"Good," he encouraged. "Put your hands together and hover over the worst of the break. When you feel ready, apply pressure, and slide your hands apart."

Lena kept breathing deeply. The cold mist in her hands helped it feel less like panic. Her hands connected, her thumbs tucked between, and she hovered them over the broken limb. Feeling assured, she pressed her hands down. She didn't feel fabric or flesh, just the tingle and coldness of magic.

"Feel what's coursing through your connection to him," instructed Amundr.

The world around her was still. There were no birds chirping, no water slapping wood or stone. She wasn't sure if she or anyone else was breathing. The chill regressed the world into a slowness. She was steady.

As she pulled her hands apart, traveling up and down the man's arm, a band of green magic kept them connected. The film was opaque; there were lighter misaligned striations in the green. All at once, the lighter spots snapped to form parallel bands and there was a loud crack. The unconscious man flinched and gasped.

Lena yanked her hands away. The magic was gone. She blinked rabidly and felt her heart speed up. "What happened?"

"Typically, you hold on until it's done." Amundr ripped the unconscious man's sleeve open. The arm was red and purple with bruising. When Amundr poked at it, the unconscious man moaned but did not wake.

"Did I hurt him?" she worried. Her fingers ghosted along where Amundr had exposed the arm. The flesh was inflamed. She came too close to Amundr's fingers and when they brushed hers, he felt cold.

Amundr pulled his hands away and straightened his back. He looked at her curiously.

Too long, the silence hung. She pressed, "What did I do?"

"You healed the break. The lesser pains, the bruising, the muscle injuries—those will have to heal on their own," said Amundr.

Lena breathed easier. She shook her head. "Why look so disappointed, then?" She wiped sweat from her brow.

"Try the other arm."

The right arm was the one with the bone sticking out. Lena concentrated on the magic again. She filtered it forward, felt the chill, pressed her hands down, and set the magic to work. This time, as she pulled her hands apart, she resolved to keep herself attached until the healing was complete. The same failure didn't need repeating.

The striations snapped straight, and the bone pulled under the skin. Cracks aligned. The skin closed, and the bruising faded. It took an open second of clarity to realize the magic was opaque. She couldn't see the arm, but she knew the result, somehow.

Pressure built up behind her eyes. She had to breathe. Lena lifted her hands and welcomed air into her lungs. As she looked down, her eyes confirmed what her mind had told her: the arm was healed. Near pristine, save a scar.

Lena smiled.

Amundr spoke as he examined the arm, "My oldest friend was the shortest of my brotherhood. We often joked it was because he fell from a tree, broke both his ankles, and I had to heal him. It wasn't my best skill as a young man. We couldn't bring him to our Vitki mentors. We were too high up the mountain, and he insisted I could do it."

"But you could," assumed Lena when he stopped telling the story.

"Not well enough for him to walk. I had to carry him down. Good thing he was small. Near the bottom I was tired, off-balance, and I tripped." Amundr sat back onto his haunches and made a wave motion with his hands. "He created a shield. We skated it off the edge of a cliff, landed on the shield when it touched down, and skidded to a stop on the ice overtop the river. No one believed us. A young man like him, a shield that strong . . . it shouldn't have worked."

Lena rested her hands on her lap. The man hadn't woken up yet. She knew they should complete the healing of his leg while they had time, but she was more curious what Amundr was trying to tell her.

"From that day, I thought he would one day lead the Vitki. I was envious. I knew I was his competition. I never told him, though. Then, one day, we were adults"—he nodded toward Lena—"and I had learned something new. I was determined to make it work. I shot out magic from my hand like an arrow. Only, when I use the trick, it returns to me. I wasn't prepared for that the first time." Amundr showed her the underside of his forearm.

She squinted. "I don't see the scar."

"It went in here." He pointed to where the veins branched on his wrist. "And came out here." He poked at the soft junction before the elbow. "It bled horribly when the spike disappeared. It would have killed me."

"It was a good thing you were no longer novice healers," said Lena.

"My new wife surely would have been disappointed, had I died of hubris. No. Haldor took hold of my arm and healed it. *Too* well. There was no scar, no sign of my stupidity." Amundr lowered his arm. "I told the story. People didn't believe it, either. Both just stories with no evidence."

"Which meant he wasn't the chosen leader," said Lena.

"I spoke with him, the night after I was given charge of the Vitki, when our leader had died of a fever. I asked Haldor why it shouldn't be him. He made he realize something: I was the one

CLEVEHOLD

telling the stories of the sled shield. I was the one telling stories of the spike. He didn't deny them, but he didn't care if people believed it." Amundr rubbed his hands together and rocked subtly side to side. "He was very powerful, but he assumed he wasn't what the Vitki needed for a leader."

"He knew you were." Lena felt a crack in her smile but tried not to let it show on her face. The reason they hadn't put Lena on the throne and chose Tulir instead. Amundr couldn't possibly have known. There were too many variables in place for him to make a guess that good.

"As we became men, my skills of magic surpassed his. I never saw a hint of envy from him. Every time I tried to surpass my limits, he assured it did not leave me scarred." Amundr looked down at his brittle yellow nails. "Some people are fighters. Some are mediators. Others are those patient and powerful enough to heal their friends when they don't know their limits."

Lena breathed easier. Her smile returned. "We are prizes amongst brash friends."

"Most people here, of the West, have no idea what their capacity for magic is. Too long, you were muted. If the Stone King was truly as powerful as the legends tell us, King Tulir will make hefty strides these next few years, should he learn from the right people. But you, Duchess"—he gestured at the unconscious man between them—"you should tell your stories."

"What happened to your friend?" asked Lena.

"Memories and stories are all that's left of Haldor and his family."

Lena thought about what Cicero had once told her. The Ovnite didn't want to go back home. Every story of the past they told involved a high margin of death.

"You should finish the leg. It appears you don't need my help for it, Duchess."

LIZ BUNCHES

"Did they stick you with one of those titles, too?" asked Lena.

Amundr snorted and stood. "Fix the leg."

THERE WAS A TIREDNESS that had settled in Lena's bones, deeper than just normal exhaustion. It felt good, but also as if she needed to nap for hours. She couldn't justify it. After having healed the man at the dock, she was determined to return to the library.

The book on diseases was exactly where she had left it. She ghosted a hand over the cover. Her eyes closed, and she felt the tiredness behind them. *Perhaps a walk around the library before settling back in would be helpful.*

Lena walked through the aisles and made her way toward the back. If there were any others in the library, they were extremely quiet. There was a light breeze, which meant one of the windows was open. She hoped a bird wouldn't fly in.

Socks was sitting on the perch of the open window. Lena gasped and dashed forward. Her arms wrapped around the cat, and she backed away quickly. She exclaimed, "Are you crazy?!" as she snuggled Socks to her chest.

"Are you alright?"

Lena turned. It was Tulir. She gulped and kept a tight hold on Socks. "He was on the open ledge." She willed her racing heart to slow.

"That's a touch too high up to assume you'd land on your feet." Tulir scratched behind Socks' ears.

"Can you close the window?" asked Lena. She didn't want to let Socks go until she knew he was safe.

Tulir obliged and pulled it shut.

"Meow," protested Socks. He wiggled out of her arms, jumped down, and wound between Tulir's legs.

"You take it up with your mother," he responded.

Socks purred and rubbed his face against Tulir's calf.

Tulir looked to Lena. "He does make a strong argument."

"I didn't know he came in here on his own," said Lena.

Socks let Tulir pick him up so that he could climb onto his shoulders. Tulir bent forward to accommodate, and the white paws batted at Tulir's hair where the short strands stood upright.

"I'll make a royal rule: no unattended open windows," he offered in full seriousness. He reached up to pet Socks and earned more purrs.

"I can't have anything happen to him," said Lena.

"You hear that?" Tulir looked up at Socks. "Don't give your mother any more scares."

"Meow," said Socks. He jumped down onto a table.

"I keep telling him to watch his language," said Tulir.

Lena petted Socks until he rolled over to show his stomach. "He does his best to listen. He just has some bad influences," she excused, looking at Tulir through her eyelashes.

"You would think kings would be expected to swear! This shit is stressful."

She laughed and shook her head. "*That's* what you're going to teach him?"

"You've earned a few to say yourself." He turned to the side and motioned toward a sitting area. "Now that you look like your heart won't beat out of your chest, would you like to sit?"

The excitement had woken her up, but she still felt the pull of exhaustion. "Yes, let's sit."

Tulir led them to a nook off to the side and pulled out a chair for her. It felt strange. The options were a sofa, large enough for two, or a pair of stand-alone chairs. Not long ago, the closeness would have been favored without question. Now, she was sitting across from him.

"I didn't mean to derail you, if you were looking for Selgen," Tulir apologized when he sat.

Lena sank back into the chair. "I wasn't looking for anyone."

"Are you alright?" His eyes narrowed, focused on her knees.

She picked her leg up and yawned. When she was finished, she explained, "It's not my blood. There was an accident at the docks. Everyone is fine now."

"What were you doing at the docks?" he asked. He looked tired. Not work worn, but from a lack of sleep. His short hair was sticking up because he had been running fingers through it. She knew his stress symptoms well.

"I was there for the accident." She yawned, covered her mouth, then clarified, "After it. Amundr is teaching me how to heal."

"If everyone's okay, I presume that means it went well?" he asked, and she nodded. "I guess it takes a lot out of you."

"It's good. Not only does it feel good, but he told me a story of sentiment." She smiled and shrugged. "I hope that means it went well. Bridges, and whatnot."

"I don't doubt that's something you're good at."

She nudged his knee with her foot. "Enough."

"It's natural." He leaned his elbow onto the chair arm and placed his head in his hand. He looked relaxed.

A thought occurred to her. "I should tell Salvatore everything is fine."

"I'm sure whoever was with you will tell him," said Tulir.

She cringed and laughed. "No one will, because no one was."

"Lena," he led, exasperated.

"I know, all these men I'm seen with! I'm such a whore."

"Your reputation isn't what I'm worried about. Your safety is," he pressed. He rubbed a hand down his face.

"I won't tell you that Amundr is harmless. He's probably the most dangerous of the Ovnite, actually. But it was public. I was safe. I'm learning," she justified. She heard the small thumps of soft feet and looked over in time to see Socks scampering toward the hall.

"What makes you say the *most* dangerous?" Tulir leaned back into his comfortable position. "I'm not disagreeing, just wondering why you think so."

She took a long breath through her nose. The thoughts were tired and slow as she considered them. She thought on the answer a moment before she explained, "Avild. If people look at the Ovnite council and they look at your Council, they'll probably think Amundr's counterpart is Harth, but it's not." Lena looked around.

"We're alone." Tulir looked sheepish when he continued, "I had the staff who followed me in here leave."

"From the bits I've put together, Amundr was the leader of the Vitki, which was, and sort of still is, secondary to the Drengr. He stepped down, and I think it had to do with his wife dying. Amundr trained Briet and Kazio, and he's comfortable enough with what he gave them to step back, but not step away completely." She sat forward. "Amundr and Avild are grounded, confident, and knowledgeable in a way that means they don't have to show off. Usually."

"That makes sense. The one who looms." Tulir rubbed a finger over his upper lip. "Who has the misfortune of being Norman, in this exchange?"

Lena waved a dismissive hand. "Norman's permanently thrown out. Replace him with Avild."

"Briet." Tulir pointed at himself.

"Naturally, though, I think you're better looking," agreed Lena.

"Tisa?" he asked, pointing at her.

"Maybe?" Lena considered it. To do so, she had to ignore the considerable strength and fighting skills of the other woman. "Tisa and Briet do seem to have more roots."

"The Est boys came in later," said Tulir.

"I will take Tisa, only because Rufino for Cicero makes the most sense. Innately kindhearted. Helpful. Supportive. Not gunning for a title."

Tulir pulled back the side of his mouth. "What we're left with doesn't match up."

She covered up another yawn. She whispered, "Perfect sense, if you notice how Kazio looks at Briet."

He raised his eyebrows.

"I don't see it as reciprocated. Granted, she is reserved," said Lena. She elected not to share the inkling she had that Briet was interested in Amundr, the widower. Lena smiled into her fist. Was the Ovnite's internal dynamic as complex as theirs?

"I suppose I'll keep an eye out for ginger children."

She wished there was something she could do to make him feel better. Reassurance. Encouragement. She wanted to kiss him. She shook the tired thoughts from her head. "Regardless of that, Kazio would die for her in the way I have no doubt Harth would for you. Not that others wouldn't. There's those willing for duty, those who would admittedly"—she put a hand to her chest—"be afraid. Or there's men like that . . . they would do it as if it were second nature for the person they deem worth it."

"This is the ginger one we're talking about? The second strangest?" Tulir poked at the chair arm.

"Harth's reserved and stone-faced, whereas Kazio's *showy*. I don't know. There's a wall you have to be let through, and then another one thereafter you didn't expect to be there. That's when you notice which are their natural traits and which are for show. Who they are versus what they want you to see." She felt she had rambled long enough. There was justification to ask if her words made sense, but she avoided doing so.

"Harth's a better man than Kazio, walls or not," said Tulir.

Lena hummed. When she saw how fast Tulir's eyes narrowed, she explained, "When Avild, Harth, and I were at the Ovnite camp, Avild broke her arm. It was my fault as much as it was Amundr's. Harth came around the corner with a man he had been friendly toward. He saw the broken arm and the webs in her eyes, and he read from Avild what they were going to do about it. If she had said, 'Clear it out and burn it down,' he'd have started by putting an arrow through his new friend's throat."

Tulir shrugged. "Avild's practically his mother."

"If you needed to be completely rid of Briet—no body, no evidence, no questions asked—who would you go to first?"

Tulir considered it for a second. He didn't have to verbalize the answer. He conceded.

"It doesn't make Harth *not* a good man. It's the other side of self-sacrificing. He would do whatever it took—die for you, kill for you. Remove himself from your life if it made you happier," explained Lena. She took a deep breath to fend off a yawn.

"I'd do brash things for you. Like break a man out of prison, no questions asked," said Tulir.

"You had to follow me through the Rose District first to see what I was doing," she reminded.

He waved a hand.

Lena leaned forward. "But would you have killed that guard?"

"I didn't have to for the escape to work."

She shrugged. "What if I had asked you to?" She waited. "That's my point. It doesn't make anyone the lesser man."

"I don't know that I agree he would have just . . ." Tulir made a slicing motion across his throat.

Lena leaned back. "I maintain that he would kill for the same people he would die for."

"An attribute for a good husband," he agreed. He scratched the side of his head. "But I guess that means we're talking about both of them, if you think they're so similar."

She had almost forgotten they were talking about Kazio. "I still have reservations about Kazio. He's a good man for us because we're on the same side. In the instant Briet and I want different things, though, he would turn on me."

"But what if I maintain your marriage to him strengthens the bridge between cultures?"

"I would combat it to say Kazio isn't a completely healthy man. I want healthy children." Lena knew his hypothetical was only intended to toy with her personality assessments, but it also forced her to self-reflect. Not long ago, she had thought she would do anything Tulir asked of her. Did that still stand?

"And if I said risk it, I don't care?" he said with a shrug.

Lena smiled lightly. She folded her hands together. "Avild told me of her first marriage on the day you were married. Her father had arranged an awful husband. She was sixteen. The middle-aged groom never made it to their wedding bed."

"Point taken," he agreed. "Not that I would make the mistake of thinking I could force you to do anything."

"I suppose that's where my loyalties differ," she considered. "I compromised a lot earlier in my life. It came naturally. It was expected. I love you. I would do so much for you, but I'm going to examine my options first."

"And you're afraid you'll be taken off the Council." He nudged her knee with his foot. "Natural."

"And what kind of woman is Briet?"

He drummed his hands on the chair arm. "A good one. One good enough where I want to give her the benefit of my behavior. I very much get the sense she didn't ask for her station—she earned it."

CLEVEHOLD

"You're allowed to fall in love with your wife."

He was about to make a retort, but he stopped. Lena heard it, too—a set of footsteps. They both sat up straighter.

"Norman," said Tulir as the man came into view. He didn't get up.

"I came to speak with you," said Norman.

"You are," Tulir said simply.

Lena didn't get up or look back. She heard other people. Guards in the hall, she presumed.

"About the Iste and Steepwharf," Norman continued impatiently.

"Why?" asked Tulir.

Norman cleared his throat. "I had assumed, following my wrongful separation from the Council meeting—"

Tulir cut in, "Why?"

Norman having knowledge of Istedinium's and Steepwharf's alliance was news, but Lena wasn't surprised he had either found out or simply assumed it would happen. *No doubt he paid off the guards standing by in the hall.*

"There's no legitimate reason to keep me removed. The only reason you could remove me was because I disagreed with you. It's daft and arrogant," argued Norman.

"I thought my issue was too much heart?" questioned Tulir.

Lena snickered.

"And gall, it seems," returned Norman.

"There's nothing for us to discuss."

"Because you're too daft to accept their offer?" proposed Norman.

Tulir's jaw clenched.

"The offer that would have us all killed," reminded Lena.

"I wasn't speaking to you, I was speaking—"

"To the king," she interjected. "I am on his Council, whereas you are not. He's been kind thus far, but you are testing his patience."

"The Ovnites are weak and dying! If they don't all succumb, they will flee, and what will become of the king's Council then?" snarled Norman.

"You use that backbone with me more than you use it on your wife," said Tulir.

Lena covered her mouth to stifle a laugh.

"You're an insulant child who's going to get all your people killed," said Norman. "A king needs to be willing to compromise. You *will* be broken."

"Can you be a touch clearer if that was a threat? I want to know what I'm reporting to the guards." Lena calmly folded her hands.

Norman scoffed.

Tulir stood. "You're excused, sir, before this escalates."

"On your hollow authority," grumbled Norman.

"Not so hollow that I can't invoke discipline," replied Tulir. "If the formalities are needed, you may have it. You are no longer on the Council. You have no authority over our decision-making. You are not being arrested because I have no concrete evidence. Your innocence could be refuted by trial and testimonies, but I have neither the manpower nor the patience to watch you try to weasel your way out of it. You're a free man, Norman, because you are not a threat."

Norman's mouth hung open. He breathed loudly. "You think I have nothing? Do you think nothing will come of it when I go to the queen and tell her that her new husband is a deviant? A man who lets his Commander use him, as if he were a woman?"

Lena's heart sank. It was one thing to assume his presumptions and another to hear it confirmed.

Eyes narrowed, Tulir leaned closer to Norman and whispered, "Why threaten this to me instead of going to Briet first? Lest you're a liar."

"A king knows when to compromise." Norman backed up and straightened out his dress shirt.

Lena heard another voice in the hall. *Salvatore?* Had he come back to check on her? It sounded like men talking. She hoped for them to stay in the hall, out of earshot.

"Apparently, I've been compromised." Tulir stepped forward.

"I could walk out and tell her, right now." Norman fumbled another step back. He kept his chin up but couldn't hide the waver in his voice.

"Did you witness it yourself?" Tulir rolled up his sleeves, revealing the scar and the knife he had strapped to his forearm.

"S-sir," Norman stammered. He backed into a table.

"I can't be checked for virginity like a woman can be. Beyond that, I'm now married to a woman. One I have very much been able to please. She's not one to lie for my ego. Where does that put your accusation of deviance?" He unsheathed the knife and twirled it casually. "Without evidence or testimony, you want to threaten a king and the Commander of the Royal Guard—the two people who arguably have the most loyalties within the castle."

"I'm not a sole witness," hissed Norman.

"So go tell her." Tulir pointed at the door with the knife. "Go tell her the Commander, who plans to marry the Duchess, and the king who she just . . ." Tulir trailed off, scratching the side of his head with the knife. He looked back to Lena. "What if she does believe him?"

Her heart was pounding, but her breath was forcibly steady. She smoothed out her skirt and replied, "What if that was an insult she couldn't bear her people to find out, and she had to silence the rat?"

"The queen is always armed," supposed Tulir.

"You seem to forget the punishment for such—"

"Those were Steepwharf's rules." Tulir tapped the knife against his palm. "You would have to get people to believe you. The people *I'm* protecting. The hypothetical punishment would be carried out by men whom *I* pay to employ."

Norman reached under his shirt and pulled out a knife. The handle was ornate, his family crest. He wielded it weakly. "Queen's pleasure he damned. Perhaps she also is a deviant! Gets me rid of the whole lot of you."

Lena kept her eye on Norman's knife. Tulir could kill Norman easily, but that wouldn't be enough, would it? Not if there were other witnesses. No—they needed a way to negate Norman's story. Tulir's pride had already leaned too much into confirming what could have only been an off-base assumption.

The guards in the hall. Not just Norman's men—Salvatore had returned for her.

"Guards, help!" cried Lena, lacing her voice with panic. She rushed forward, took advantage of Norman's confused state, and grabbed his knife. One hand, she clawed beneath his to get to the handle; the other, she grabbed firmly around the blade. Pain ran through her palm. "Guards, please!"

"What are you—?" Norman grunted as he struggled, but lost the knife to her.

Footsteps rushed into the library. She had a few more seconds.

Lena elbowed Tulir back, then sliced the knife across her dress collar down to her bicep. The cry she let out was genuine. The knife clattered to the floor and skidded to a stop by a bookshelf.

One of Norman's men came around the corner first, but Salvatore followed.

"He attacked me," whimpered Lena. The blood from her hand was dripping. Tears of pain stung her eyes.

"I didn't do—"

Tulir roared, "I'll kill you for that!" He raised his knife at Norman and stalked forward.

Salvatore got between Tulir and Norman. He had one arm up at Tulir, the other on his sword. "What is all this?"

"She's mad! She took my knife," answered Norman at the same time Tulir yelled, "He came in here trying to kill Duchess Lena."

Lena put her hands over her ears. She felt the blood of her palm soaking into her hair. The cut across her shoulder stung as she moved. She hadn't meant to cut deeply, but it had to bleed. She sobbed and closed her eyes.

More guards ran in, based on the heavy steps. She heard Salvatore order, "Detain this man!"

"This is madness. I haven't done—it's a trick! It was her!" shouted Norman.

"Duchess," said Salvatore.

"Are you alright?" asked Tulir.

Lena opened her eyes and slowly brought down her hands. Her chin was trembling. Tears blurred her vision, and she blinked them away. Norman was gone.

"Your Grace, do you mind?" Salvatore gestured at the clean knife in Tulir's hand.

"Sorry." Tulir handed it over. "I couldn't get there fast enough."

Lena stammered, "W-why would he?"

"Norman attacked you? Both of you?" asked Salvatore.

"We were in the library and—" Tulir stopped when Salvatore put a calm hand up.

"Respectfully, sir, if you don't mind, I'd like to hear it from the Miss first."

"Of course," agreed Tulir.

Lena took a wet breath. "We were talking in the nook. I heard someone coming. I came out. He had that." She pointed at the ornate bloody knife on the ground. "He cut me before I could yell." She stopped to cover a sob, careful not to do it with the bloody hand.

Salvatore assured, "It's alright, you're safe now."

"I'm so sorry," apologized Tulir.

"I yelled. Tulir came. I tried to . . ." She looked at her bloody palm and cursed. "I should have used my shield. I'm so stupid."

"It's not your fault," said Tulir.

Salvatore picked up the bloody knife. He examined it carefully.

It was a Northerner's knife. Norman was bound to have more like it. The knife was part of a set, a proud set. Knives so ornate, he would never loan them out. No one could deny blood on a knife.

"I should h-have," stammered Lena. She looked at Tulir. "If he was coming for you . . . the shield—I should have . . ."

"Why don't you take Duchess Lena somewhere more private?" suggested Salvatore. He handed Tulir his knife back.

"I'll see her to her chambers to be cleaned up. On your way to the hold, can you have Amundr sent for?" asked Tulir.

"I'll see it done."

Tulir went to Lena and rested his hand on her uninjured shoulder. "And Norman will be handled?"

"I could call for a judge, but . . ." Salvatore deferred to the ornate knife.

"I would have him hanged in an instant, but hold off on justice. When she is ready, we will have Lena decide if there should be a trial," said Tulir.

Salvatore nodded and let them leave.

Tulir led Lena to her room slowly, one hand on her arm, the other resting lightly on her spine. She imagined she looked a sight, with the torn dress and blood in her hair. They were just about to enter her room when her name was called, and they turned.

CLEVEHOLD

Harth. Worry was etched into his face. "They said Norman attacked you."

Lena broke from Tulir's hold and ran to Harth. She was brought in for a tight hug and let herself weep. Blood was getting on his clothes. People were watching. His hold on her was secure.

"When are we displaying justice?" The words rumbled out of Harth's chest.

"We'll speak on it privately," said Tulir.

"His casual contempt for her stood, but this won't," responded Harth sternly.

How well he plays the part he wasn't cast for, thought Lena. It was shaped perfectly: Norman hated Lena, there was a background, and a reminder. Tulir was attempting levelheadedness about Norman's situation, not accusatory. Norman would say anything to get his head off the chopping block. In the end, it was his knife and her blood.

Norman could spout everything he knew about Tulir and Harth's affair, down to Tulir's prideful confirmation. An affair that involved King Tulir, a man who could have insisted Salvatore kill Norman on sight, and the Commander of the Royal Guard—hardworking, well respected, and consoling his future wife after an attack. The accusation, when told in its entirety, would sound like madness. Desperation. Any of his men who had supposedly borne witness would be sensible to keep their mouths shut or otherwise be accused of conspiracy.

Lena looked up at Harth through wet eyes. "Can we go?"

He ghosted his hand along the side of her face, where the blood was drying in her hair, then rested it on her neck, his thumb on her cheek. There was regret in his eyes. A failing. Beneath the layers of worry, an ire brewed.

"Someone is retrieving Amundr to heal her," said Tulir.

Harth's eyes met hers and his jaw set. In that instant, Lena knew he would kill Norman. It would wrap all of this up.

No. He deserved to know the truth first. With her gaze, she pleaded for patience.

He offered a small nod. She imagined, if he spoke, it would be an apology. For not being there. For letting it happen. To assure her the anger was not directed at her, but would be unveiled on the man who did this.

She threaded her uninjured hand in his. "Let me get the blood off me first."

Tulir held the door open for them to enter her room. She guided Harth to follow, and they stepped in. Tulir closed the door behind them.

Before she could begin the explanation to Harth, Tulir pulled her by the wrist and backed her against the wall. His face pressed to hers in a wild kiss. They both breathed heavily, and a low moan pushed up her throat. She tasted her tears and copper as their lips moved together.

They parted, their foreheads touching. He looked at her, bewildered and in love, and whispered, "An absolute natural."

She wiped her mouth and looked to Harth. He looked lost, but only half as angry. She didn't have words to begin the explanation—Tulir had stolen them off her tongue—but her eyes said enough for him to take a deep breath and a step back.

"I can't stay." Tulir pulled away from her completely. He said to Harth, "You have her?"

Harth demanded with barely contained fury, "Are you going to give me a good reason I shouldn't go down there and kill that rat?"

"Would you stay here just because I asked you to?" whispered Tulir.

"*Just?*" Harth questioned.

CLEVEHOLD

Tulir opened the door. "Stay with her. That's what I need you to do."

There were watchful eyes on them. The scene was perfect. An angry soon-to-be husband, his distraught woman, and the king trying to calm them both down from acting rashly. Lena could almost hate herself for how well the scheme had worked.

Lena put a hand to Harth's chest and felt the rapid heartbeat beneath. "Please stay. Let's have the king handle it."

"Has Norman ever personally threatened you?" Tulir asked Harth, his tone indicating privacy, but people were close enough in the hall to hear.

"No," replied Harth. His jaw was set.

"Then I need you to stay away from the cells until you've cooled off. Be with Lena. She's yours," urged Tulir.

In it was a silent *now*— *"She's yours now."* How many people had seen Tulir in Lena's chambers, or the inverse, prior to the Ovnite arrival? They had been set to marry. Their affections hadn't been secret. Lena almost grinned, but she put a hand to her mouth. She was property, high-value property, passed from one man to another. On any other day the thought would have made her angry. Today, it loaned less credibility to Norman's ramblings. A woman two men had affection for—surely possible. Their true intended arrangement? No one would believe such a thing.

Tulir walked away and let the door shut.

Harth turned away. He took off his bow and quiver, vacillated on where to set it down, and settled for the floor by the window. He put a hand to his hip, the other covering half of his face.

This was his first time in her chambers, she realized. The closest he had gotten was the threshold of the secret corridor. She offered, "You can sit."

With strained patience, he requested, "Please, tell me what's going on."

She looked to the closed door. "Will you put water in the basin, please?"

"Where are you hurt?"

"I have a cut on my hand, and one from my collarbone down. I'm going to change out of my dress, but I have a wrap beneath to keep me decent." She retrieved rags from the dresser.

Harth poured the water and set the basin on her desk. He dipped a rag as she handed one to him. Delicately, he wiped it across her injured palm. It wasn't deep, but it stung.

"Your head?" he asked as he concentrated on cleaning the cut.

"Blood from my hand." She did her best not to wince as he wrapped the hand. His eyes kept flicking to hers, and she wanted to be resilient. Wanted to assure him the flinches weren't for him, the same way he had silently communicated his anger wasn't for her. She pulled at the torn collar of her dress. "Will you help me?"

He did so silently. He was careful to pull it over her head in a way that made her minimally bend the injured arm. Dress in his hands, he asked, "Salvageable or floor?"

"I'd like to burn it after today," she answered. "Floor."

He dropped it off to the side.

She adjusted the top of her wrap. The sleeveless undershirt had been sliced through by the knife and the torso no longer connected to the shoulder. Luckily, it was tight enough that it didn't flap down. She tucked her arm across her chest to secure it in place.

A wet rag dabbed against the blood dried in her hair. They were far from the door, but Lena still tried to be as quiet as possible when she said, "Norman knows about you and Tulir. All of it."

Harth paused. Then he dipped the cloth and continued to dab at her hair. Red flakes broke off, and the water turned pink.

"He threatened to tell people—Briet, primarily, but it wouldn't stop there. Tulir tried to talk him out of it by reminding Norman who he was threatening."

CLEVEHOLD

"Norman tried to attack Tulir, and you got in the way?" Harth hovered the rag over her shoulder. "May I?"

She nodded. The cloth stung. "Norman is going to say—after he threatened Tulir and Tulir confirmed his suspicions—that Tulir pulled a knife, Norman took out his own, and I took the knife from Norman and inflicted my own wounds."

"Did you?" He held the rag to her bicep, where the blood was still flowing.

"If Tulir killed him, and other people knew what Norman did, it would look like Tulir was trying to cover it up. This way, when Norman tells the story, the *whole* story, how unbelievable does it all sound?"

He sighed and deposited the rag in the water. "That should be good enough until the healer comes."

"I won't let that happen to him, or you," said Lena. "Norman has to die. I don't like it, but he must. Doing it this way was the only way to protect us all. If we fall apart, it all falls apart."

Harth rubbed a hand over his mouth. His eyes were guarded, expression neutral. "He's a risk. It's smart."

"You don't approve?" she asked, trying to look him in the eye.

"It never should have come to that." Harth balled up his fists and walked to the window. "You didn't need to get hurt for this."

"No one should be threatened for this, but that's the world we live in. It's the game we play." She wrapped a robe around her shoulders. "And, hell, if this is how we get rid of Norman, I wish we had done it before he started drowning animals to smuggle people in."

He looked at her curiously.

"What?" It was her turn to grow impatient.

"You used me," he said simply.

She licked her lips. "I used your reaction. I used your presumed standing with me, my previous standing with Tulir, Norman's disdain for me, and my tears. The blood is new. I used that, too."

"You could have had me turn around and kill Norman."

She shook her head. "I've never killed someone, but I assume it sits better in your soul if you know the real reason why."

There was a knock at the door. Harth's posture changed to defensive, then he released the new tension. He went to the door and let Amundr in.

"I was sent for."

"Yes." Harth led Amundr to where Lena was sitting. Harth got to her first and kissed her on the cheek. "You surprise me."

Lena smiled and angled her head down. Harth moved to the side, not far, and allowed Amundr to approach.

"I didn't expect to see you again so soon." Amundr had changed into different clothes. It surprised her to not see him in rags, though she assumed the blood from earlier was being washed out. Now, he wore the clothes of Clevehold. The sleeves and trouser legs were not quite long enough.

"I assumed I couldn't fix myself," she answered. She took the robe down off her shoulder, keeping as much as she could covered.

"In that, you were right," said Amundr.

"Do I need to go?" asked Harth.

"That is up to her," Amundr answered, looking to Lena.

Lena was able to meet Harth's eyes, relieved to see there was no resentment. "I would prefer you stay. You can go, but only if you agree not to go down to the cells."

Amundr knelt in front of her. He poked lightly at the shoulder wound. His hands were cold. "That won't be necessary."

"What do you mean?" She tried to avoid flinching as he touched it.

CLEVEHOLD

"Norman isn't in a cell. Or, rather, only his body is," said Amundr. His hand glowed teal and he ran it down Lena's shoulder. "Luckily, it wasn't deep."

"They hung him already?" questioned Harth.

"Didn't have to." Amundr held out his hand. "The other one."

Lena was too stunned to speak. She laid her injured hand in Amundr's. With the other, she grabbed Harth's hand. There was a heavy contrast between the warmth of Harth's hand compared to the chill of Amundr's.

"When Salvatore came down with the bloody knife and the story, it was quickly considered settled," explained Amundr as he healed her hand.

His heartbeat pulsed with hers as the magic worked on the wound. The beats felt irregular, not in intensity but in occurrence. He removed his hand before she could think too much on it.

"Was that it?" Amundr looked at the side of her head.

Lena nodded. She felt as if she had no voice. *What has Tulir done?*

"To whom do I owe a barrel of beer, besides you?" asked Harth.

"I don't think the barrels necessary." Amundr rose. "The king has repaid Kazio by keeping him out of his own cell."

Chapter 25

"WE SHOULD WAIT FOR Harth, yes?" asked Briet.

Lena shook her head. "He's dealing with the guards. They're attempting to find out if it runs any deeper than Norman."

"Does he think there's a chance Norman wasn't working alone?" asked Tisa.

"No one else has come forward," said Tulir. He was staring at the map spread out on the Council's table. The firelight burned low. They didn't need to see the etchings of mountains and rivers; they knew the terrain well. Even the Ovnite did, Lena supposed, for how long they were all staring at it.

The sun wasn't yet fully up. Lena didn't know who had called the meeting in the early morning hours. Perhaps no one formally had. Yet they were all awake, and it didn't feel like there was time to delay.

"Do we know if the plot was only against you?" asked Rufino. He had only just been informed of Norman's attempt and death. It appeared he was still processing, but there wasn't a hint of grief in his face.

"Aside from his ramblings, we may never know the true intentions," said Amundr. He leaned back in his chair, elbow on the armrest. He fiddled with his two amulets mindlessly.

Kazio snorted. He had also changed into Clevehold clothing. His seemed to fit better than Amundr's. He caught Lena looking and narrowed his eyes.

She looked down at her hands. The cut was completely gone, not even a scar left. She rubbed at the spot, expecting it to hurt. *This did better than Avild's serum.* The pain and mark were both gone. Lena took a deep breath and set her hands down on her lap.

"In the future, even if the outcome is clear, do not act so hastily," said Briet. She stood behind her chair and leaned onto the back. Full color had returned to her face.

"Time is not a thing we have an abundance of, yes?" replied Kazio.

"There is a process in place for a reason," said Tulir.

Kazio shrugged. "The process would have made the same conclusion I did."

"You are no judge," said Briet.

"The outcome was mine to decide," said Lena. She got up from her chair and circled to the window, too antsy to stay seated.

"Would you have made a different decision, Duchess?" Kazio leaned back and looked her up and down. "Or did you need to defer to your soon-to-be husband first?"

"I'd have had him publicly executed *after* we got answers."

Kazio licked his lips. "I don't think you want to hear the things he was spouting in his desperation for freedom."

"Unless the man can be revived from death or you're going to lock him up"—Tisa pointed lazily at Kazio—"I believe this matter is closed."

"So long as he understands the conditions of his leniency," said Tulir.

Briet stared at Kazio threateningly. "He understands, yes?"

Kazio inclined his head.

"I hate to be the one to ask, but does anyone here have any suspects of treachery?" Rufino looked around the room.

A Council of five, sprouted to ten, down to eight. Seven, in present company. Lena could marvel at the pace things had changed were she not exhausted. Part of her wanted to see Norman's body and the damage Kazio had inflicted. It would have been within her right. Tisa was correct, though, as was Kazio.

Time was scarce, justice had been delivered, and the discussion was closed.

"I have no suspects," said Lena.

"I don't know much of your politics." Tisa leaned forward onto the table to look at Rufino. "But aren't those *your* people about to betray us?"

Rufino was about to stammer a response, but Tulir spoke first. "All correspondence since the first landing of your ships in Steepwharf has been copied by the two postmasters. Anything carried by ship, mule, man, or bird was duplicated before it was sent."

Lena's arms dropped.

"That is more than healthy paranoia," remarked Kazio.

"No one was told, other than the postmasters. Not even the guards. The order came directly from me, and I shared it only with Briet up to this point," said Tulir.

"What about everything that came in?" asked Tisa.

"That was harder to manage and was only implemented more recently. It's technically possible for any of us to have received treacherous correspondence, but I don't believe we have. And I know for a fact no one has sent any," explained Tulir.

"Not even the weasel?" questioned Amundr.

"He may have been receiving orders from outside. My fear is the plot was outlined before that. Steepwharf was ready to march west before your arrival. Norman's ploy was in place before we knew you existed—this just spurred him into action," said Tulir.

Well played, with enough of the truth. Was it possible to copy everything outgoing? Surely it was now, but there had been fluid travel from the time Steepwharf was attacked to when the Ovnite arrived. Had Tulir been that prepared, or was he willing to stake his reputation on Rufino's loyalty? He said Briet had known. Did that mean it was true or did she trust Tulir enough?

Either way, Lena was on the outside of it.

"I've sent nothing to my people since receiving Briet's information. We agreed it was better to keep it secret, and I have," said Rufino.

"The resentment isn't deep-seated from the Iste?" asked Amundr.

"Do I understand why they're doing it? Yes. Trade. Numbers. Seasoned fighters. But that doesn't mean I agree," pleaded Rufino.

"I don't see his loyalty being in question," said Briet.

Kazio took a deep breath and put up his hands.

How much had Briet seen? Invisibility was a wonderful trick. It would have been stupid to assume she let on all she knew, at all times.

Lena looked at the ground. Their privacy was under threat at the discretion of the king and queen. Was this what wartime pressure looked like? Did these kinds of acts sprout the type of fear that had molded Steepwharf into what it was?

"What kind of numbers do they bring?" asked Tisa.

"Too many for us to contend with," answered Tulir.

"Too many for you?" questioned Kazio.

"For our forces combined," clarified Briet. She tucked loose hair behind her ears. "This alliance between the coastal armies and the plains armies means we're in no position to fight them outright."

"We can't outlast them in a siege, not with their combined resources," said Rufino.

"Is it too much to hope they'll turn on each other?" proposed Tisa. "The right push?"

Lena shook her head. "Eventually, but not quickly enough. They have a common goal."

"A common enemy can be the best tether, no matter how temporary, yes?" considered Amundr.

Briet stood tall. "Which means we should put our effort into loading people onto our ships and leaving this place."

"We have five functional ships of Ovnite caliber. It will be tight, but we can get everyone onboard," added Tulir.

Tisa straightened up. "That's it, then?"

"You want to stay and fight for this place?" asked Kazio incredulously.

It wasn't about that. Lena stepped toward the table. "They've already made up their minds. They're just letting us know."

Tulir met her eyes. The look he gave her was sterner than she expected. She kept her chin up but pulled her lip up in a small smirk.

"Where will we go?" asked Amundr. His frail yellow nails poked lazily at the edge of the map.

"Home. Across the sea," answered Briet.

"We all came to the same conclusion, but the Council exists for a reason," said Kazio. He gestured around the table. "That's what I was told, yes?"

"This is everyone's opportunity to make objections or suggestions," said Tulir.

Lena pressed her shoulders back and clasped her hands behind her back. She stayed on the side of the table with Kazio and Amundr, where the most resistance was felt. If she assisted Tulir's perspective, the Ovnite men would have more reason to oppose.

"Why would we go back there?" asked Amundr.

"Their ships are smaller than ours. They won't want to fight at sea. They won't follow us. They'll know where we are in the East, but if we stay there, they'll have no reason to pursue," explained Briet.

"Except that they want you dead," refuted Tisa. She pointed at Lena. "They already tried to kill both of you once."

CLEVEHOLD

"If we're out of sight and out of mind, the alliance between the Iste and Steepwharf will fray. They want different things. If both were hell-bent on war, with their combined strength, they'd have attacked by now," said Tulir.

Amundr said to Briet, "We said we wouldn't go back there."

"We had a lot of ideas before we crossed the sea. If we're being completely honest, after we sacked the King's City, there was no plan. The Est land was fertile, livable, and anyone in the region who may try to take it, we can easily overcome," Briet responded to him directly, maintaining eye contact.

"We go back to that place where half our people died, let someone else sack the city we came for, return home with even lesser numbers, *and* with the person we crossed the sea to kill. Let's not forget that," said Amundr.

"What reason is there for the reminder?" asked Lena, wondering if she should infer it as a threat.

"We're allies of a common enemy. We've just agreed those alliances fall apart once that enemy is no longer present, yes?" pointed out Tisa.

"Especially since we are moving the dynasty back to the land *we* already had ownership over," added Kazio.

"The Ovnite survived because the gates were opened," said Tulir.

"And more of our friends are dead now," rebutted Kazio.

"I understand our tethers may not mean anything to the Est, but they mean something to me," said Briet as she pulled on her amulet string.

Kazio waved his hand. "Tethered as a business transaction."

"Tethered all the same. If it means so little to you, remember this got you shelter, food, doctors—"

"And Cicero is—"

"Wouldn't have sat in to second-guess me!" yelled Briet.

Lena was surprised Kazio stayed quiet for that one. It felt like the first instance where she truly saw it. They had referred to Kazio and Cicero as the Est boys; their magic was orange, where all others' was teal or blue. Lena had seen it, but in the silence, she felt it. Kazio wasn't one of them. Not through and through. She stood by her assessment: Kazio was loyal to Briet and would die for her, for the Ovnite people, but certain stitches of his assimilation weren't pulled taunt.

"We have decided to abandon the castle. For that, we need a plan," said Amundr with strained patience. He didn't like the idea of returning—it was clear on his face—but he replaced his criticisms with loyalty.

"I think the first question is if we broker our way out of here, or escape," said Rufino. He looked to Tulir, Amundr, and Lena, ignoring the tension between the others.

"They want us to leave, but they'll want their hands around our throats when we do," said Lena. She pulled her chair out to sit. To Tulir, she said, "You had an idea we could make a deal before."

Kazio rolled his eyes and scoffed.

Lena slammed her hand down onto the table.

"I wouldn't trust them to keep their word, even if they gave it," replied Tulir as if the outburst hadn't happened.

"The only difference it would make is if we gave them warning," said Briet. She drummed her fingers on the wood. "We escape, we run."

"Like cowards," muttered Kazio.

"You're not special for wanting to give them a kick in the face for what they've done. We all do," spat Lena. She felt heat rising in her spine.

"I want to *kill* them, not kick them, Duchess."

"This isn't helping," said Tisa.

"You want to run, like cowards." Kazio stood and gestured broadly to the windows, then to Amundr. "Except for you, who would rather die than go back, yes?"

Amundr tsked.

"You—you, who agreed there was no sense in dying for this place?" Tisa questioned Kazio.

Lena looked to Tulir and hoped he would read her worry. The Ovnite were fracturing. This couldn't persist.

"Everyone, rise," said Briet amidst the renewed argument. Tisa was about to counter, but Briet yelled, "Everyone to their feet!"

They all abided.

Briet began to pace around them. "We will be standing when we face our enemies. Like it or not, that day will come soon. Is this what we want them to see us as? Disjointed? If we cannot band together here, we cannot do it out there." She pointed harshly at the window, then let her arm come down slowly. "Certain things are decided. Our people are one. We will pack up and, on those five ships, sail east back to Ovnite and Estnable. We will not attempt to broker, because it would not be honored.

"You may sit when you have a legitimate concern we need to discuss, assuming the acceptance of those points, or a proposed solution, assuming the same. If the next words out of your mouth are arguments, or petty hang-ups, or grievances, you will use your standing position to remove yourself. Yes?"

Lena breathed through her nose and kept the airflow restricted. She needed to yawn, but it wasn't time to break the silence. Briet had the room.

Amundr pulled his chair forward and sat. He ran his finger along the smaller river that ran out of Clevehold. "Is there any viability in an alternate water route? We cannot go by land."

"Between the waterfalls and rapids, it wouldn't make for a good escape route," answered Tulir. He leaned forward, hands splayed out. "We only have one way out, and they know it, but there's nothing we can do for it."

"We can manipulate the riverbed, yes?" suggested Tisa.

"The waterfall will pose too much of an issue. Water displacement will make it too shallow in other places," said Briet.

"We add it to the knowns: our route out is how you sailed in," said Lena. She looked to Kazio who stood close to her, wanting an indication he had cooled down.

"The Elder needed to be closer to see the map," he whispered.

Lena was sure only she heard him. She hated her reaction of laughter, stifling it with a closed mouth and a hand to hide the grin. It morphed into the yawn she had been suppressing.

"The next question is when. What time of day gives us the most advantage?" said Rufino. He took his chair back in hand, then looked to Briet. She nodded and he sat.

"Leaving in the night poses challenges. We could run ashore or miss a trap," said Tisa.

Briet nodded. "We don't know the terrain well enough, and there's too many places they could be hiding. We need light to guide the way."

Tisa sat and pointed along the river as it bent out of Clevehold. "We can anticipate where they will assemble. It's where we were. By the time we make it that far, they'll know we're coming. Darkness won't make a difference."

"We shouldn't be the first to strike," said Lena. If not for Briet's threat to walk, she was sure Kazio would have said something. "We should let them be the first to draw. Like Tisa said, they'll know we're there. There won't be an element of surprise."

"It still gives them an opening," said Amundr.

Lena sat, elbows on the arm rests. "There's a small chance—I stress, a hopeful and minute chance—that they see we're fleeing and let us go."

"Beyond that, it also allows us to conserve our resources," agreed Briet.

"Not in the night, and not the first to strike," summarized Tulir.

"Our boats are larger than theirs. We have the high ground advantage," said Kazio. He grabbed his chair.

"Were your legs getting so tired that you had to state the obvious?" asked Tulir.

Briet snickered.

Kazio gripped the chair and pulled it away. It was deposited behind him. He rejoined the table where it had been, standing. Finger on the dot of Steepwharf, he said, "We also have that magic they so dutifully fear. We use that, make a show of it."

"Can we dam the river, flood them out?" asked Lena.

"Once we're past them," answered Briet.

Amundr amended, "Possibly, but not at the risk of slowing us down when we're downstream of them."

"Undue violence could encourage them to follow us. We are willing to fight, but only so much as we need to in order to get past," reasoned Tulir.

"Fear or not, we do not have the numbers," said Tisa.

"We should escape in the early morning hours. With any luck, their men will be asleep, just waking, possibly hungover, or still drunk," suggested Rufino.

"How soon can we be ready to leave?" asked Lena.

"We'll need to load the ships, organize storage for goods and people. We don't want to move so fast as to incite panic, but we shouldn't delay," said Tulir.

"We'll need enough supplies to survive not just the journey but also the initial settle, yet not so much that it weighs us down," said Briet.

"Two days." Rufino drummed his fingers on the table. "We have a headcount of people and numbers from rationing.

Calculating, organizing, loading—I think we could get it done well in two days, if we work through the night."

"We only have half-moons. Tell the workers to be careful. I don't want any extra light to give us away," advised Tulir.

"We'll keep our healers on standby," offered Briet.

"I'll go to the vault. People work better when they're getting paid," said Lena.

Tisa sighed. "I'll do a headcount of fighters, see who we'll have up top."

"I want a report by nightfall tonight if this two-day timeline is doable. Our aim is to leave the morning after next." Tulir stood up straight.

The meeting ended shortly thereafter, each with an idea of their assignment. Amundr left with Tisa, discussing the Drengr; Tulir and Rufino left, talking about grain stocks and how to make them most portable; and Briet left on her own, but only after grumbling something at Kazio.

Lena took a deep breath and licked her lips. *Don't think of it as a deadline. Just think of it as tackling one thing at a time.* "Kazio?"

He raised his eyebrows at her.

"Would you like to see the vault?"

"Depends." He scratched the side of his face with his thumb. "Do you plan to lock me inside it?"

She laughed and shook her head. Not waiting for him, Lena began to walk away. Soon, she heard him following.

Lena had so many questions. She yearned to know more about Estnable. Ignorantly, she had hoped the unknowns had all been dealt with prior to the Ovnite's arrival. Now, they were open to entirely new ones.

Norman was another thing she wanted to ask about—what had he said? What did Kazio know? Why had Kazio killed Norman for her? *Is it too obvious if I thank him?*

CLEVEHOLD

But she noticed as they walked that Kazio was decompressing. Little bits of tension started chipping away as they got deeper into the castle. She let him be, telling herself there would be time later.

The vault had three guards posted to it. Lena nodded at them, and they gave her space.

Kazio tilted his head back. "Is there a ceiling hatch?"

Lena smiled and placed her hand onto the wall, revealing the door to the vault. This time, she didn't watch the wall dissolve. She watched Kazio instead and felt a twinge of pride at the amazement on his face. "Clever, isn't it?"

He reached forward to touch the magic. Lena quickly grabbed his wrist to stop him.

"Afraid I'm going to steal?"

"I must walk you through it. Otherwise, it could think you have malicious intentions." She hadn't considered this part; this was the first time she was bringing someone else into the vault. Did she have to hold his hand?

"Do you think I have malicious intentions, Duchess?"

The vault will let us know, she considered. Instead of prolonging her worry and allowing her thoughts to become more cluttered, she stepped through and pulled Kazio by the grip she had on his wrist. He followed and was able to step through, unharmed. The green haze of light coming off the ceiling and walls was solid, with a flicker matching his heartbeat under her fingertips.

"An obnoxious amount of unused metal, just sitting here." Kazio scrutinized the piles of gold.

"Gold is too soft to be good for much," said Lena. "Also, I'm going to invoke chivalry and make you ferry it for me."

"*That's* why I'm here."

Lena shrugged. She became aware of his warmth, not just under her hand but from how close he had to stand due to her grip.

She went to let go, but as she did, he grabbed her wrist instead. Stunned, she looked up at him with a furrowed brow.

"I'll still be safe when you let go, yes?"

Her expression relaxed. "Do you suspect *me* of malicious intentions?"

Kazio let go, hand hovering near her, before he purposefully distracted his fingers by picking up a piece of gold off a nearby pile. "How many of these things do we need?"

"We'll bring Rufino thirty. He can let us know when more are needed." *Do we need to pack gold?*

"And the, uh . . ." Kazio pointed at the haze where they had entered the vault.

Please don't ask me too much, willed Lena.

He smirked at her. "What happens if you close it, and I have a toe over the line?"

Lena shrugged, a closed-mouthed smile creeping up on her. "Probably best if you don't."

Chapter 26

"SELGEN IS DEAD."

She didn't know the name of the guard who told her. Too many she knew by name were busy, she supposed. It was the type of news that had to be relayed quickly. The guard looked scared to tell her and hurried to leave.

He's dead?

Lena put down what was in her hand. It was heavy—too heavy. She didn't remember what she had been doing with it. She focused on breathing.

"I'm so sorry." Marisol was at her side, a solid comfort. Alive.

"He's dead," repeated Lena. It sounded hollow. Felt hollow. Did they have it right?

"Do you want me to go with you?" asked Marisol.

Go where? She couldn't leave. There was too much to do. A report was needed by sundown—they only had a few hours. What could Selgen have wanted that could take her away from their preparations?

He died.

Lena shuddered. Breaths she had to consciously take flooded her lungs too quickly. Her legs felt weak. *No.* It wasn't right.

"No, I'll, uh . . ." Lena looked at her friend. "No, thank you."

"Do you need anything?" asked Marisol.

Lena shook her head. She didn't want to speak. Her words would have been too steady and felt like a betrayal, or they would waver too much to have been coherent. Right now, she couldn't take the sound of either.

The walk to the lower levels was done by a known route, though there may have been a faster way down. Luckily, Lena's feet knew where she was headed. She didn't have to think about it. Long way or not, she arrived at the morgue.

No, that can't be right, she thought. *That's where the dead are kept.*

That's why I'm here.

Should she knock? She debated, hand resting on the wood. They would know she was coming. No one should believe death without a body to see.

Lena opened the door.

"Duchess," she was greeted.

Formal titles. Made up. None of it was real. She gulped. "I was told my cousin was here."

"Yes, Duchess Lena," he agreed. He reminded her of the shopkeeper in Steepwharf who bought the sapphire. A tall burly man, naturally intimidating, with a soft look. He was wiping his hands on a cloth. His hands were all black.

"I would like to see him," she said evenly. She decided against emotion until she knew for sure. It wasn't him. Couldn't be. They were so close.

"I also sent for his other kin. You can wait for them, or we can send for someone else," the man offered. He tucked the cloth into his back pocket.

"I'm fit to see him alone."

Words rattled in her mind. A past life. *Are you here to be courted, Miss Lena?* It wasn't fitting for her to be alone with a bachelor. She needed a chaperone.

"It is your right, but I must warn you, it isn't fresh," he said.

She nodded. There was no consideration for what his words implied. "Take me to him."

The room he led her to was at the rear of the small building. There were overpowering scents of salt and mint to combat the decay and rot. She was reminded of the library: a pleasant smell that mixed with a thick scent that could strangle you. Death was affixed, opaque. If you shined enough light on it, there was the appearance of something bleeding through, but it was a lie. The light didn't come from the other side; it was a reflection. You could see and smell the dead, but they got nothing of you.

The man stopped at a table. A heavy burlap blanket was draped over a body. He waited for a final nod of confirmation before he pulled the blanket back.

The smell permeated her nose before her eyes accepted what she was seeing. She clenched her eyes shut and shook her head. The image of his distorted blue face followed behind her closed eyelids. After she heard the fabric replaced, she opened her eyes and looked at her hands. "How did he die?"

"He bled himself," he answered solemnly.

Pale. Vacant eyes. Hollowed out. She couldn't see him anymore, but she felt him staring at her. "Who found him?"

"A servant. They were cleaning and noticed a smell. He had told them not to enter his room."

Selgen had always been peculiar. Secluded. Exhausted. "You, uh . . ." She rubbed a hand over her forehead. "You said it wasn't new. How long do you think?"

"A few days, ma'am."

"No one else has to see him." She straightened her back and looked at the burlap. He was staring at her from under it. Mocking her. "I'll let them know I confirmed it was him."

"Yes, ma'am," he agreed.

"He'll have to be burned, right?"

"We have been burning all the persons and clothes with blood on it. That's how we think the sicknesses have been spreading to the Ovnite, but he can be buried, if you prefer."

Why would they do that?

Because he's dead. She forced a deep breath and regretted it. Death was in her lungs.

He can't be here. He can't be dead. Why would they find him like this? Who did it?

He did.

"You can speak to your family about arrangements," he offered kindly.

"Thank you," she whispered. She walked out. She had to leave. Had to get the smell out of her nose. She was only there for him. If she wasn't there, he wouldn't be.

Lena didn't stop moving until she hit the open air. Then her feet felt too heavy. Her balance wavered. She put a hand up to steady herself. *Stone. Breathe.*

"Lena?"

She looked up and saw her sister. "Nela?"

Nela wrapped her in a tight hug. The pressure of tears and struggled breaths mounted. She tried to say, "He's dead," but it was too muffled.

"Are you alright?" Nela asked into Lena's hair.

Was she alright? *He's dead!* She wanted to say it aloud, but it caught in her throat. *He's dead.* She couldn't push it out.

"It's him?" Nela pulled back far enough to look Lena in the eye. She nodded.

Nela stuttered the beginning of a question that changed into "Did they say how?"

Lena felt her chin trembling. All she could say was "Himself."

"He—?" Nela stopped and hugged Lena again. "Let's get away from here, alright?"

Lena nodded. They walked to a bench carved into the inner wall. Nela held her hand when they sat. There were tears in their eyes.

"When was the last time you saw him?" asked Nela.

Lena looked down. Her stomach convulsed as if she was going to vomit. Her nose ran, and she wiped it with her sleeve. "I don't know."

Nela was talking. It sounded muffled. Her words were probably an explanation. A comfort. Nela squeezed her hand like when they were children. It was all going to be alright, the gesture said.

When?

The wedding. No, he hadn't been there. *The market? A dinner?* Lena clenched her eyes shut. Rocking slightly, she thought harder. She only came back with an ache. She didn't know.

Himself.

A life traded for a willing life.

Lena opened her eyes and gasped. *Where is she?* Tears were wiped away. The press of fabric against her eyes was harsh. She could see now. Where was Avild?

Her stomach lurched again. *How stupid. Pay attention. You never pay enough attention.* Bile crept up her throat.

"Lena." Nela was kneeling in front of her, hands on Lena's shoulders. "Talk to me, honey. You're white as a sheet."

She shook her head. How could she explain? She hadn't been paying attention.

"I'm so sorry. I know you two were close," sympathized Nela.

Close. He had come to her. She was heartful enough to help. Lena had tried. She took the sapphire to try. Lena blinked and she could see the high ceiling of the mine. Selgen, bound by ropes. Blindfolded. Exhausted. Dead.

Lena gasped. "There's too much."

"Tell me what I can do," pleaded Nela.

No. Couldn't be. Nela didn't get scared. She held it together. She held the family together by grit and spite.

"We lied, Nela." The words slipped out before she could think about them. Lena wiped her mouth and whispered, "Avild helped me. The sapphire. The knives. We lied."

"You aren't making any sense, honey." Nela brushed her hair back from her face.

Lena took an uneasy breath. "I took the sapphire. Tulir helped me break out Selgen. Tulir went north. I brought Selgen to Avild and Klaus. The man killing people, taking hands, he came for us." A voice in Lena's head begged her to stop, but she couldn't. "That's how Klaus died. Avild came to the castle. The Stone King, all this, was secondary. Built on revenge."

"That doesn't make it a lie," Nela said softly.

What didn't she understand? Lena gripped her sister's hands tightly. "Last time, everything was about keeping Selgen alive. I got him out. He was going to live. Then we got to the castle, Tulir was hurt, and we left Selgen in a cell. We left him there with his memories. We *left* him there." She had to stop when the sobs morphed her words into something indiscernible.

"It's not your fault," murmured Nela.

Lena put her hand to her heart. It was going to beat out of her chest. "I left him, and I never went back. All of this. I left him!"

"No, Lena, listen to me," Nela began.

"I don't know. I didn't know. He was dead for days. Where was I?" sobbed Lena.

Nela shook her. "You had bigger things to attend to."

The scoff came out wet. She wiped her mouth. *Bigger things.* "More than family?"

"Do you know how easily this place could have switched into chaos? I can't say I know all that's going on, but I see how big of a part you play in it."

"What good is all this if the people I love die?"

"I'm still here." Nela held her tightly. "Your friends. Everything you've built. Secondary or not, it means something to a lot of people. It's still here."

"I never thought..." Lena trailed off. He was supposed to have been there. All they'd had to do was get past the hurdles. Why couldn't he have waited? Why couldn't he have held on a little bit longer?

Unless he had been persuaded. She felt nauseous again.

"You won't do any good hurting yourself with it," reasoned Nela.

"If I could have—"

"I've got what ifs of my own, alright? What if I went with you that night? What if I followed my gut and got off that boat instead of finishing the ticket? I should have been there for you. I should have been there for him. I don't have a castle to run," said Nela.

"It isn't your fault."

"Then it isn't yours." Nela brought her sister in for a hug, then wiped tears away with her sleeve. "I want to understand. I want to help you, if you'll let me."

"I've burdened you with too much already," whispered Lena.

"You're my sister. It's not a burden."

Lena tried to take more steady breaths. There was a hole in her chest, but she no longer felt as if she was going to throw up. "I'm sorry for everything I must have put you through."

"Promise me something." Nela held one of Lena's hands in both of her own. "If the rumors are true and you plan to leave, please say goodbye."

There was so much to tell. Too much she had said already. Nela was trustworthy; it didn't have to include everything. She couldn't imagine getting married without her big sister there, even if it was a façade.

"Duchess," someone called.

"You'd better go," said Nela.

"You could come," said Lena as she stood. She saw her sister's face preparing for a refusal and continued, "You talked about getting away."

"Duchess," they called again.

"You don't need to worry about that right now," said Nela.

Lena squeezed her hands once more. "Promise me you'll think about it?"

What had Nela threatened? *"If I go in, you're going in with me."*

LENA REPORTED WHAT she could for Tulir's assessment. They would meet or beat the target of two days. It wasn't a formal meeting, and she left once their talk was through. He didn't give any indication he knew Selgen was dead, and she didn't offer it. Her mission for the day was done.

She searched the upper floors, the courtyard, the library—all the civilized places someone could blend in. Then the Stone King's Hall. The cells. When all the good prospects came up dry, she resorted to the guard's barracks. If she couldn't find Avild herself, she could find the person most likely to know where she could.

"Are you looking for someone, Duchess?" a guard on the door asked.

"Yes, Harth. Is he here?"

Did he bunk in the barracks, or did his station warrant alternate quarters? It should, she thought. But he still could have been here.

What else didn't she know about him?

"He isn't, ma'am," the guard answered.

"Do you know where I can find him?"

"On the wall, I suppose. Or in the armory."

CLEVEHOLD

"What about Missus Avild? Have you seen her around?" Lena clasped her hands behind her.

A second guard came to the threshold and leaned on the open doorframe. "Who?"

"The historian. Short, blonde."

The new man smiled and hooked his thumbs in his belt. "Not many beautiful women come down to the bunkhouse."

"Not unless we got means," said the guard. He mimed flipping a coin.

She was aware of how they were looking at her, how late it was, and how alone she was all at once. Clearing her throat, she stepped back. "Thank you for your time."

She took hasty steps to get away from them. The fear, she tried to stomp out in heavy steps. Lena walked along the interior wall until she reached the Ovnite barracks. If she couldn't find Avild, she would find the person who had helped her.

Some Ovnite, like Tisa, had taken up residence in the castle. Lena couldn't see Amundr doing that. No, he would have elected to stay down here.

It had to have been him. Magic was plentiful among the Ovnite, but Avild would have needed someone grounded, someone with skills and recklessness comparable to her own, and possibly most important—someone who understood the pain of losing a spouse.

There were murmurs and nods as she walked through. Amundr would have been easy to spot, had he been there. She was about to enter one of the buildings.

"Duchess."

Lena cringed. Somehow, it sounded unpleasant coming out of Kazio's mouth, like a mockery. She wanted to make him appreciate it or choke on it. Turning to him, she smiled tenaciously.

Kazio jogged the last leg to reach her. "I turned in my report to the king, don't worry."

"I'm looking for Amundr. Is he here?"

"He's asleep, likely," he answered. "What can I do for you?"

"Will you wake him?" The patience in her voice was strained.

"Did something happen?"

"Kazio—"

"Why?"

"Would you just . . ." She trailed off into a grumble. He was intent on making things impossible.

He shrugged. "Give me a reason. I'll be helpful again."

"The reason is, my cousin's dead," she snapped.

"The mopey librarian?"

Her fists clenched at her sides. "This isn't a joke."

"It must be, if you're coming here accusing Amundr of killing him." Kazio crossed his arms and got around her to lean on the doorframe.

"I'm not." When he raised his eyebrows, she repeated slower, with conviction, "I'm not. I do want to ask him something related to it, though."

"Ask me."

Lena's jaw clenched and she breathed through her nose. "Has Avild been here, or with him, that you've seen?"

"The little fighter who tried to kill me?" He held a hand up to his mid chest.

"Yes." She rolled her eyes. "And hardly."

"She comes and goes as she pleases," he supposed.

"Has she asked Amundr for his help, or you for yours?"

"No. Why?"

She watched his eyes intently. He wasn't lying. Satisfied enough, she said, "I should go."

"What are you afraid of?"

The question caught her off guard. She stammered and closed her mouth. After a shrug, she deflected, "Unlike some, I'll admit, a lot of things scare me."

"You told me honesty was a positive attribute. I saw you come out of the guard barracks looking disappointed. Now you're here, asking about the Ovnite Elder and your historian, as it has to do with your librarian cousin's death, yes?" He leaned in. "Why?"

She wasn't like Tulir. She couldn't be truthful for the sake of pride. Also, she supposed, there was nothing she could insinuate to make him uncomfortable.

"I have secrets. As do you. Everyone does, given the mess we're in. I mean it, I'm not accusing Amundr of murder. I am, however, looking for Avild to get answers, because the circumstance of my cousin's death made me suspicious of something specific."

"I'm sure the circumstances, as you see them, could link Amundr to Avild. Believe me, he had no part of it," said Kazio. He straightened up. For a few seconds, his face was soft. There was a kind of curiosity in his eyes. Then he looked away.

"Avild saved his life out there," she informed him.

"Which made them even for the threat and the attack, yes?"

"That wasn't how it happened."

Kazio smirked. "Then I guess they don't see eye to eye."

She wanted him to have been right. More than that, she wanted to stop chasing down a bad feeling. *Stay.* She wanted to stay. "How are you?"

"I'm fine," he brushed off.

She nodded. An acknowledgment not to push. "How are the others? Gunna?"

His arms came down to his sides. "She died. Not too long after Cicero."

Lena mumbled curses. The anger built up all too easily. Where had she been? Why wasn't she ever there when it mattered? Why couldn't she pay attention?

She punched a wall. The sting and shock rocketed up her arm. A fire burned in her spine. She wanted to do it again. Her fist collided with the wall, and she felt a drip of blood rolling off her knuckle.

Kazio wrapped around her from behind. He gripped her forearms and held on as she struggled, his arms too strong for her to pull away.

"Let go!"

"You cannot heal your own wounds."

He let go. Out of his grip, she stumbled a step. His hands were out to catch her, and she smacked them away. "What's it to you? I'm of no use. I'm not there when it counts. I'm not a fighter."

"You're no Drengr, but you're not useless, Duchess."

She combed her hands through her hair. She wanted to scream. To punch another wall. For him to hold her back again. Something. Anything.

"When I was a younger man—"

"Younger than the novice you are now?"

"You set such a high bar, Duchess."

"Very few of us do." She looked around. People were staring. At them. At her. She was supposed to have the answers. "What are we doing?"

Kazio looked her over. "We're calling it a night." He moved into the building.

"That's it?" She followed.

He opened his arms and tilted his head to the side. "I thought you didn't like fighting with me, Duchess?"

"Stop calling me that!" she shouted.

"What do you want me to call you?" He walked to her, looming over with his height advantage, and forced her to back up. "What do you want me to say to you?"

Lena's back hit the wall. Her breath caught. She looked him in the eye and waited.

His hands came up to the wall, bracketing her in. She didn't know if it was just the two of them. It felt like they were alone. Fear was absent, replaced by intrigue.

Throat dry, unable to stand the silence anymore, she lied. "I guess I came looking for a fight."

He laughed low in his throat. "You'll get your fight soon enough." He leaned in close, face a few inches from hers. He whispered, "Duchess."

Lena tightened her fists at her sides and parted her lips.

Kazio pushed off the wall and turned away. "You should go, before you burn down the barracks."

She shook her head and clenched her teeth. Her footsteps were heavy on the way out. She almost missed the small fist-sized singe mark on the stone.

THE FUNERAL WAS AT dawn. Mother wore a black dress and a veil to keep herself covered. Nela wore her typical blue clothes with a dark cloak overtop. Lena stood in line with them as they lowered Selgen into the ground. They buried him in the garden, typically not a fitting place for a body. Lena had no doubt the only reason he was getting a funeral was her station.

Tulir, Briet, Harth, Rufino, and Marisol were in attendance. People who she supposed were colleagues of Selgen's watched from the sides. Few words were said over the body.

Numbness and fire were opposites, but Lena felt both. She had cried all her tears. Onto Nela, onto her pillow. Her eyes were puffy and dry.

Did Briet know the man they were burying had been Tulir's former employer? She was there to hold his hand. How much had she been told? The tethers meant much to her; she had made that clear. They were sharing a life as if they had fallen in love. How much of Selgen did she know?

Lena wanted to avoid the bitterness, but there was no will to fight it. She wanted to be the better person. To them, the way she spoke and behaved, she was. But damn if, in moments like this, she wasn't bitter. Her heartbeat was steady, heavy. She had to bear it, because what other choice did she have?

The funeral must have ended. The crowd dispersed. Had either of them shed a tear, she wondered? Did Tulir feel any guilt over not knowing Selgen's last whereabouts, or was that just her, too?

Mother sobbed loudly. Lena looked at her. Nela gave Lena a sympathetic look as she guided their mother away. It was time to go. No one else was stuck.

"Would you like to go, Miss Lena?" Harth asked from behind her.

They were supposed to leave. This was the part when people shoveled dirt onto the box. The wood could splinter. She wasn't supposed to stand by to see the pale flesh and smell the rot. He was being polite about the direction she was supposed to take.

Lena nodded. She let herself be led away as the shoveling started behind them. She was tempted to look back, to watch. Shouldn't she stay there until the end? What constituted the end? Or had that deadline been long since missed?

The wood splintered. She flinched at the sound but kept walking. They made it inside, and the noises faded. The fire of anger was growing. Her jaw clenched.

CLEVEHOLD

They came to the post room. There was no mail to traffic in a siege. Lena reached back and threaded her fingers with Harth's. She pulled him inside and closed the door behind them. Alone.

"Where is he?"

Harth furrowed his brow. "Who?"

Hand taken back, she rubbed her palms together and paced the empty room. "Is he hidden within the castle somewhere?"

"Lena, who are we talking about?"

She smiled. His tone was kind and patient. She had expected an undertone of happiness. He hid it well. She looked him in the eye. "Klaus."

He flinched back. "He's here?"

"That's why she did it, right?" Lena gestured to the door, through which Selgen's rotting corpse was being pelted by dirt.

His expression fell. He followed the line of her hand, then shook his head. "No."

"It had to be someone willing to die. She knew how to push him."

"Lena," he cautioned.

"She has access to people powerful enough. One of the Ovnite—Amundr is a prime candidate."

He narrowed his eyes. "Do you hear yourself?"

"Tell me it doesn't look that way," she argued. "He's dead! She's gone."

"I'm sorry your cousin committed suicide."

"No." She shook her head. Loose hairs fell from her quickly done braid. "He wouldn't."

"He was troubled and plagued by his memories," he said cautiously.

"No."

"With the hopelessness, the—"

"No!" she yelled. A sob tried to pull up her throat. She covered her mouth. *No more crying.* She needed answers.

Harth approached slowly and put hands lightly over her arms. "I'm sorry."

"He was doing better." She hated the conviction lost from her voice.

"Not everyone gets a linear recovery."

"A life for a life. Someone willing . . . that's what you said." She looked up at him. "Isn't it? You were the one who told us what she was capable of."

"She didn't do this," he soothed.

"I know what she is to you, but you know she could. It's why she left before." Her voice wavered, and she took in wet breaths.

"It's why she left again."

Lena sniffled and shook her head.

He used his thumb to wipe away her first tear. "I know she didn't do it, because she wasn't here."

She blinked. Avild had been missing for days. Had she left right after? Did Harth really not know? They were his parents. Did Avild think his loyalties had shifted too much to tell him?

"The day she was training with Kazio, and Amundr healed him. Do you remember?" he asked, and she nodded. "The next day, she left."

Lena shook her head. *How?* was the first question, but she supposed that didn't matter, did it? Invisibility, scaling the mountain, walking through walls—Avild was capable of anything. "She told you she was leaving?"

He gave a light squeeze on her arm and broke eye contact. "She talked to me about Klaus. About the way things used to be. She isn't the type to say goodbye, but I know what it looks like."

"That doesn't mean she left," said Lena.

"Things are churning up. There's well-grounded magic here. The throne. Amundr's power. She walked away."

She could see he was convinced. She wanted to believe him. If she did, Selgen's death had truly been of his own doing.

"Do you trust me?" His eyes were clear of deceit. There was something akin to love in them. Not romantic. Not familial. Something enduring.

"I do. I believe you." She felt it as she said it. A shuddered breath ran through her. She thought of Selgen alone in his quarters. *He was always alone.*

"Is there anything I can do for you?"

She shook her head. "I'm sorry."

"For?"

"I don't know." Her hands came up, and she licked her lips. "For any position I've put you in. Anything I've accused you of. For any malicious ways I've thought of you." When he raised his eyebrows, she elaborated, "I don't recall all my thoughts from Steepwharf, but they weren't all kind, I'm sure."

He squeezed her hand once more before he pulled it back and rubbed a hand down his face. "I apologized to Selgen about a year ago for all of it."

"You were doing your job when you arrested him. Besides, the damage was done at that point."

"You know now that I recognized what was in his eyes. He had to be locked up. Selgen wasn't the villain, but he was the vessel." Harth put a hand to his hip and looked down. "I didn't know then, but I think the knives were a plant. Easy wrap-up."

"Did Tulir ever talk to you about it?"

"After he did, I'm almost certain. The testifying man turned up rich and dead." Harth looked to Lena. "I'm glad you broke him out."

"I wish it had been more."

"I wish I had gotten to the cabin sooner. I wish Klaus had stalled for longer," he said as he walked toward the bare counter.

She looked down at her hands. "I suppose saying it wasn't your fault doesn't help."

"You saw it—when you said Klaus was alive—before I questioned it, I wanted it. To say one more thing. To get that pat on the back and proud look one more time. No, it doesn't make it easier, and I've replayed in my head who knows how many times what could have been different. Knowing now what we know of the Ovnite and their healing." He flattened his hands on the counter and tapped his fingers rhythmically. "You can't avoid the guilt. But you can do your best to take it in doses."

She nodded. A thought occurred to her. "I know what I'm apologizing for. I made a proposal to you. You said you would think about it, then it ran away from us."

"Those conversations are better had sober."

Shrugging, she replied, "I've never felt more so."

He nodded.

"What was it like, for you?"

Harth raised his eyebrows.

"I didn't know about your and Tulir's..." She sighed. "But you knew about him and I. Sharing him—what was that idea like for you?"

"You have my apologies, for what transpired behind your back."

Lena shook her head. She supposed in a different version of their lives, where her and Tulir's marriage was underway, more discussions around secrecy and rebuilding trust would have been had. With the Ovnite arrival, they had skirted around it. Gotten past it.

She had never been more certain she could trust Tulir, and Harth, and understood their secrecy enough to feel justified in saying, "I don't want you to feel guilty over it. I understand why. Now, I hate the thoughts that creep in. The queen may have him, and I may not, but it's clearer to me from that hatred that it wasn't sole ownership I needed. I loved—*love*—him. But I know I'm not the only one."

"I was of a similar mind. You made him happy. More than securing a future, more than a union to hide behind, he loves you. I couldn't give him everything."

"Neither could I." Her steps around the empty counter were slow, measured, and she watched her shoes on the stone before she could summon the courage to look him in the eye. "What do you think of my proposal, Harth?"

His hand hovered over a shirt pocket, then came down. "We need to get through our escape before I make you a promise I possibly can't keep."

"You won't die there," she instructed.

"Lena—"

"You won't," she interrupted. Her chin was up. "If you do, I'll be sold off to the Vitki, scoundrel or otherwise. I understand and play my part in this game too well to refuse. Don't let them do that to me."

"If something were to happen, I don't suppose you couldn't fight or figure your way out of an uncomfortable situation."

"I'm tired," she admitted. "I'm asking to not have to. If people like you and I have to compromise, better to do it with a friend."

"I understand." He took her hand and kissed it. "I don't want the king and queen selling me at market, either."

She laughed, and he smiled.

Chapter 27

"COME IN," SHE ANSWERED absently. Lena was on the brink of pulling her hair out. He had to be somewhere.

The door creaked open.

"Duchess," said Kazio. He was dressed in Clevehold clothes and a leather vest that reached down to his thigh. Was that their armor, she wondered? Unlike their clothes, it hadn't been burned.

"Why did you wear the rags?" asked Lena. She bent down and looked under the bed as if he was going to materialize there between now and the last time she looked.

"The clothes were symbolic." He kept the door propped open. He moved into the room but kept away from her furniture. Hands clasped behind his back, he continued, "The humble origins of the Vitki and the magic that binds us."

She looked behind her dresser again. "But your magic isn't blue."

"I didn't request special ones, but if we make new . . ." He narrowed his eyes. "What are you looking for?"

"Socks."

Where else could he be?

"Your socks?" he questioned, looking down at her feet.

"He's my cat. He's black with white on his paws. He hangs around, and I've been trying to find him, but I haven't seen him since . . ." She wracked her brain. *Norman?* Had she seen him after that? His dinner had been eaten.

"I'm sure he'll turn up, yes?" assured Kazio.

Lena stood straight and took a breath. This wasn't what she was supposed to have been doing. They couldn't leave without him.

CLEVEHOLD

Kazio. He was there, standing over her, staring at her. Hand on her hip, she asked impatiently, "Did you need something?"

"I was coming to ask if you were alright, after the funeral this morning." He shifted his weight as he looked around her room.

"I am, thank you." She studied him. "You look like you have something on your mind."

"Not your burden."

Her hands flared out. "Distract me."

He raised his eyebrows and smirked. Looking away, he said, "I spoke with our superiors. I'm going to be on the lead ship to carve the way."

What she wouldn't give to face Steepwharf head-on and spit in their faces. Could she have justified being there, too? Her sword skills were wanting, but she was a good shield and a quick-learning healer.

"Did Briet ask you to lead?" She leaned on her desk.

"I offered."

Lena smiled and crossed her legs at the ankles. "You care for her."

"As you care for your king, yes?" he returned.

Maybe, in some ways, it was that simple. "You may sit."

"I don't intend to stay."

He had come all this way to ask if she was alright? It was possible, she supposed. She leaned back onto her hands and lifted herself to sit on the desk. "Be honest with me. You want to be on the lead ship because you want to be in the fight."

"I'm not afraid of it."

"But you fight best with magic. Magic is a risk to your health."

"Your legs were so tired to stand that you had to state the obvious?" He walked slowly toward the window, kept away from the bed.

She opened her arms, palms up. "Why do it?"

"It's my duty."

"It's undue risk if you go down. You know that. She knows that." Lena clasped her hands together and kept her eye on him. "She must have a reason for allowing you this indulgence. What is it?"

"Is that what you want?" He looked over his shoulder. "Indulgence?"

"Humor me," she snarked.

Kazio scrunched his nose and looked back to the windows. Shoulders squared, he spoke quickly, "When the Binding around my land was broken, many people died."

"I know. So, is it survivor's guilt?"

His head tilted from side to side. "I betrayed the people who raised me. The Est. They had a plan to break the Binding. I thought it was suicide. I went to the Ovnite. Convinced them to fight. We lost. The Binding broke. The Est were right."

"Them being right was a combination of chance and withheld information. You had no way of knowing. You thought it would kill everyone," recalled Lena from the stories Avild and Cicero had told her.

"Rationality and hindsight do not help the dead," he countered.

"You were made the leader of the Vitki for a reason."

He rubbed a hand over his mouth. "The Est and the Ovnite were feuding. Maybe if I hadn't defected, the Est would have skipped massacring more than half the Ovnite. Or maybe if I hadn't overheard the intention, I would have been an Est soldier killing the last of the Ovnite."

"Hindsight doesn't help the living, either. You knew what you knew." She got down from the desk. "You want to give them something else to remember you for."

CLEVEHOLD

A smirk pulled up the side of his face. "You asked about Gunna. The two of you met?"

"At the Ovnite camp. She was kind. Avild and I stopped her from going into a fire when she couldn't save Kasper," she explained. Was that right? Had Avild been there? The night was a blur.

"She was a good woman. They would have made strong children." Kazio sighed and looked at his shoes. "After the fight with the Est, I found Gunna. She had been missing but washed up on shore. I'm no healer, but I got her to cough. I got to reunite her with her husband, Kasper. He was so grateful and insisted he owed me a great debt. Now, they are both gone."

"It wasn't your sole idea to cross the sea. Even if it had been, it was action borne of what you knew. None of this is your fault," reassured Lena. She reached out slowly and put a hand on his shoulder. Would he make a mockery of her for offering comfort, she wondered?

He picked his head up and looked at where her hand rested. "I would lay down my life to keep what's left of my friends alive." His eyes met hers. "My pride isn't the reason I was the one to meet you first on your ship. It's not the reason I will be at the lead again."

Breathing in dramatically, she paused to consider. On the exhale, she joked, "It at least has to be *part* pride." She was happy to see him smile at her remark.

"Yes, Duchess," he agreed with a toothy smile. "I will never fully be without it."

THE VAULT CLOSED FOR what Lena knew would be the last time. Men carried away trunks and baskets of jewels and gold. It wasn't all of it—not nearly. Rufino had rationed a specific amount of weight allowed for each ship. In the case of needing to shed weight, this would be the first to go.

She glanced back at the wall as it reformed. The vault posed so many issues. Initially, she had worried Briet would catch on to why only Lena could access it. Tulir's secret could have been unraveled. That issue, they would now leave behind.

The future issues regarding the vault were for Steepwharf to discover. None of them would be able to enter it. Anyone would rightly assume the castle had a vault. Would they dig for years to find it? Magic wasn't on their side—one last stand for the Stone King was to stop them from ever getting it. Lena grinned at the idea of the three men they had met on the drawbridge walking about with axes and crowbars, taking down walls.

With her last task done, she headed up to the private room with her favorite view. She wanted to see it one last time. With the sun going down, now was the perfect time.

She opened the door and was compelled to immediately apologize. Someone else was already there.

"No, please." Tulir crossed the room. "Stay."

"I just wanted to see it one more time," said Lena.

"I did, too," he agreed. Met at the door, he opened it the rest of the way for her. "I'm going to miss this view."

Lena smiled and walked toward the balcony. "Too bad we can't take this with us."

"Would you like the door closed?"

"I don't mean to make you leave," she said hurriedly.

"I don't mean to."

She paused. She wanted to look at him, take him in. Her eyes were given one guilty trip up and down, then changed directions to look at the sunset. "Whatever you're comfortable with."

The door creaked and clicked closed. What did she expect from him? What did she want? A fully rested version of her had answers to those questions—what she should and shouldn't do. Was part of maturing realizing how muddled that became?

"I apologize for when I kissed you," he said.

Lena nodded. His statement made her point. She wasn't sorry it happened, but it shouldn't have. "It was a trying moment."

"To say the least," he agreed. He leaned his elbows onto the banister and looked out. His hair caught flecks of sunlight, making him look warm.

"I—" She stopped when he also started to speak. She allowed, "No, please."

"I don't want you to think it's only you who doesn't want to continue what we have." He sighed. "I'm a bastard. I don't want my children to be."

Lena breathed deeply. She wanted to imagine a time when there had been no conflict. No trouble at the gates.

She couldn't. Even the smell had changed. Things were too different now, too crowded.

"You and Briet will be good together. I don't know what to make of her, but she is strong-willed. A well respected and skilled woman. For a rush match, it was a good one."

Tulir smiled and looked down. "She and I . . ." He stopped and put a finger lightly to his mouth.

"Tell me," requested Lena. She turned and leaned sideways on the banister. Friendly and open, she said, "Talk to me about her like we're good friends, because we still are."

He looked up and checked her eyes. Whatever he was looking for, he must have found. "When she and I caught the intruders from Steepwharf, it was a whirlwind. We had retired to her room. No sooner than we were redressing, they came. We both took up swords. Like the bedding, it was awkward, clunky at first. We didn't know how to read each other, but there was something. A baseline. Something to build on."

"I hope she makes you happy enough."

Tulir scratched his hands through his hair. He straightened up, took a deep breath, and shook his head while looking at her.

"What?"

"I should have anticipated you being too understanding," he commented.

She couldn't tell if it was pride or disdain he spoke with. She chose not to read into the emotion. "There's scorn beneath my understanding, believe me."

"My remark was in no way foul." He relaxed his hands and put his back to the banister. "It's only human to have emotions. Negative ones against a situation you would reject, if you could, is to be expected. I had hoped you would never have to use your agreeable, understanding temperament on me."

"Did you think we'd never fight?" she jested.

"The last conversation we had in this room, I asked something completely outlandish of you. A selfish want of mine, but if I . . . I wanted you to know up front, before the marriage, not to find out the hard way. To say you took it in stride was an understatement."

"I'm pretty sure I slammed the door," she reminded him.

He laughed and nodded. "You did scare me with that. Then you showed up after, and Harth was there, and I hadn't told him . . ."

"Invisibility would have been useful there."

"Or the ability to"—he snapped his fingers—"make it all stop."

"What was Harth's position on it, when you declared dual monogamous loyalties?" she wondered. A breeze blew in, the smell of the mountain air whisking away the smell of the crowd below. She breathed it in.

"He assumed I would marry. He's fond of you." He pulled at the amulet around his neck. "He didn't expect I would tell you, after I backed away from it so many times. I think the last thing he expected was that night."

"Too brash?" she proposed. Nothing he could say could taint her memories.

"Adventurous was more the term I would use."

"I'm not worldly. The other side of that coin is not having stringent views of the world. Granted, if it hadn't been for the impending situation, something like that wouldn't have happened as soon. But . . ." *I wanted you to have it. I love you. I wanted a window to what could have been our lives.* She didn't have to finish it aloud for him to hear it.

She licked her lips and drummed her fingers on the stone banister. "What do you intend to do, now that it's Briet as queen?"

The breath he let out made his shoulders sag. "The future has been made more complicated. I want to be fair to you. To me, 'fair' would mean not sleeping with your husband."

"Given my options between him, Kazio, or an unknown—adventurous or not, I want the safest option. It helps and protects us all." She wanted them to share the heartbreak and the secrets, leaving less room to be compromised.

"Not that missing you won't hurt me, but . . ." he began cautiously.

"I can't change what he wants any more than I can what I want. I still can't say I fully understand how you love us both, so I can't speak to if those loves are different." She checked that the door was closed. "I'm not going to hold him hostage. You're all he has, and I don't see him risking being with someone else."

"I don't want you to hate me. Or him."

"It won't be akin to your and Briet's 'enough,' but I believe Harth and I can have our version of enough. What I need from you both is the promise you'll be careful. What happened with Norman cannot happen again," she stressed.

"It's done. He acted alone," dismissed Tulir.

"You stood there boasting to him. That wasn't responsible."

"What good is the power of the king if I don't use it? What good is the ability to make men like that feel small if I don't?"

Lena put her hand up for caution. They could discuss his proud mindset once the war had been won. "What I'm advising is secrecy. Absolute."

"I understand," he agreed.

She lowered her hand.

He toyed with the ring on his left hand. "I expect nothing will be formalized until we cross the sea?"

"A wedding is a good thing to keep pocketed for when you need to lift spirits."

"Are you prepared to leave?"

"Mostly. All but one item. Have you seen Socks?" She was afraid of the answer.

"I haven't," he apologized.

She cursed. There was too much noise. He was scared. She feared the poor thing wouldn't know she was leaving until new people came.

"I can have people look," he offered.

Lena didn't realize how much it had affected her mood until she blinked and a tear fell. She wiped it away. "No use. He hates most people."

"I'm sorry."

"Him and this view are the only things I'm really going to miss about this place," she admitted. "There's a whole new beginning waiting."

"Briet and I discussed who should succeed us." He pulled his hands off the banister. "Should we not make it—?"

"Don't talk like that," she cut in.

"She thinks it should be you," he finished.

"She thinks?" Lena questioned.

"Amundr and Tisa wouldn't take it up. Kazio is a bad choice. You're a duchess." Tulir pushed away and took slow steps. He stepped purposefully hard on his left leg. "As impressive as the Ovnite have been, if I don't make it and Briet does, it may be safer if you leave."

"Leave?"

Apologetically, he explained, "If I could be selfish, I would have you run away. Leave all this. It's not what we left Steepwharf for."

"I won't abandon these people," she said definitively.

"I know," he agreed, bittersweet. "I doubted it highly. Avild was the one who put the notion in my head."

"I understand why."

"Still, I spoke to Harth—not behind your back, as things have progressed—but if it gets too treacherous or you change your mind, he'll have a contingency ready."

"Which is?" she asked.

"I've told him to omit me from the plans in the case of my capture."

Lena rubbed her hands together. It wasn't up for consideration. "We're all going to make it. We have a good plan and enough people."

"I hope in a few days, you can complain I worried too much," he said lightheartedly.

"I wish we had more . . . both time and people."

"Avild?"

"Harth told you she left?" she asked.

"I asked after what happened to Selgen. My condolences."

"Your inquiry was politer than mine, I imagine."

"We had a good enough reason to ask. Her disappearance was suspicious. Yet, I don't think she's abandoned him."

"Klaus?"

"Harth," he clarified. "Avild admitted to him that when she and Klaus left Steepwharf, they were going to do so with finality, and without him. He was angry at the idea of them leaving without so much as a goodbye."

"She has," she reminded.

He shrugged. "Perhaps she just had to step away."

"Time will tell," Lena agreed noncommittally.

"As long as Harth may be in danger, I wouldn't count her out."

A KNOCK MADE HER WAKE. She blinked and rubbed her eyes. *Still dark.* She felt around for Socks. The room was empty. She cleared her throat and responded to the knock, "Thank you."

She swung her feet over the side of her bed and increased the brightness on the lamp. Her sight confirmed what she felt—empty. The food she had left out hadn't been touched. As she dressed, she tried to ignore it, but she willed herself to see the straggly tail come around the corner. To hear the clicking of nails he never fully retracted. The different caliber of meows that made her sure he understood.

He hadn't come back.

Lena made the bed calmly. She wouldn't sleep in it again. All she needed for clothes and personal items had been consolidated into one sack she could throw over her shoulder. A knife was strapped to her belt. She would never explore the interior passages again. She would never eat in the dining hall again. There were so many lasts she hadn't known.

The people were what mattered, not the grounds, yet it angered her to think that tomorrow, someone else could sleep here. The castle could be occupied or torn down. Everything inside was forfeit.

She put down the sack and picked up a candelabra. There was an ornate design near the bottom that gave her a good grip. She brought it to the window, the custom orange and yellow stained glass. She swung the candelabra through it. Bits shattered and fell.

The destruction felt good. She swung again. Shards of glass landed at her feet or blew away in the wind. They couldn't have this.

The door opened as Marisol rushed in. "Is everything alright?"

Lena dropped the candelabra onto a pile of glass. "I wanted to leave them with a little less."

"You didn't hurt yourself, did you?" Marisol took her hands and looked them over.

"No, thankfully." Lena felt awake. "Are you and Rufino ready?"

"As much as we can be," Marisol agreed. She was dressed in layers, trousers peeking out beneath her calf-length skirt. She looked pale.

"Are you alright? Ill?" asked Lena. She moved them away from the mess and breeze.

"Morning sickness, I think."

Lena smiled and looked to the woman's stomach. "Finally?"

Marisol grinned and nodded.

Lena brought her in for a hug. "That's wonderful."

"Could have come at a better time," said Marisol.

"By the time this baby is born, it will be better," assured Lena.

Marisol smiled and looked back to the door. "I should keep doing my sweep."

"And I have to meet with the Council. Is Rufino already there?" Lena picked up the sack.

Marisol took it from her. "I'll add it to what needs to be brought down. And yes."

"Thank you," Lena said in parting. They exited her room to go their separate ways. Before Marisol got far, Lena called back, "You haven't happened to have seen Socks?"

"No, I'm sorry," called Marisol.

Lena nodded. "Thanks again."

THERE WERE FIVE BASKETS placed in a row on the floor. The eight members of the Council were gathered. The last of the plans were in place. The baskets were pointed at as they spoke, stand-ins for ships.

"The river is wide enough we can pass two abreast," said Harth.

"One ship can provide cover for another, which means we need heaviest support on our lead and tail ships," said Amundr, pointing with his boot.

"The lead ship is the most likely to be boarded. What the middle three need to worry about most is their exposed side when they pass," said Tulir.

"Archers on those ships," suggested Briet. "Shields on the lead ship."

"Yes, but also an archer on the rear." Tisa tapped Briet on the shoulder, then pointed at the fifth basket. "That's where you should be. The rear needs to be defended, and we want to give them something to be afraid of following."

Briet nodded.

"If you're on the rear, we need to pick a middle ship for Tulir," said Harth.

"I'm not going to hide," protested Tulir.

"The two of us shouldn't be in the same place, yes?" said Briet.

"I'll be on the lead ship," volunteered Lena. Tulir looked at her warily and she added, "We need shields there."

"I will be up there as well," said Amundr.

"Cicero and I . . ." Tisa stopped, closed her eyes, and shook her head. "*I* will stay with Briet at the rear."

CLEVEHOLD

"We'll put Rufino and Marisol on one of the central ships. They'll be below with the rest of the nonfighters. Not with any of us," said Lena.

"If we were on horseback, I would be of more use," said Rufino.

Tulir patted him on the back. He poked the second basket with his foot. "I'll be here, close enough to provide support, if need be."

"You and your wife on three, yes?" Tisa asked Rufino, and he nodded.

"Everything is going to be ready in time?" asked Kazio. He circled around to the other side of the baskets.

"All our provisions are loaded, or being loaded, as we speak," answered Rufino.

"Those who will be rowing know their assignments," added Tisa.

"I'll make the last-minute moves to the men up top, but our fighters know what to do," said Harth.

Briet crossed her arms and stood at the head of the baskets. She wore leather armor, like Kazio. Assessing, she said, "The ships are going to be crammed and heavy. They won't be as nimble as on our way here."

"There was a learning curve on the way over. We'll do just as well, yes?" said Kazio.

Rufino narrowed his eyes. "You aren't sea people?"

Amundr laughed. He had his whip but wore no armor. The clothes he wore didn't fit him any better than before.

"We'll have time to talk about the kind of people we are once we get out of here," responded Kazio.

"Harth is a seasoned sailor. Smaller vessels, granted, but perhaps you should be with the lead," said Lena. She liked the idea of having him there to watch her back.

"I'll be on the second ship with the king," said Harth.

"He will be kept safe," reminded Briet.

"I trust the companies we have assigned to each ship, but I don't trust anyone more than myself to defend him." He jutted his chin out to Tisa. "You understand."

"We'll sail well enough, Duchess," said Kazio.

She had half a mind to scold him but settled for a sour look. He smiled.

Tisa crouched next to the baskets. "What needs to be done in the last few hours?"

LENA FELT STIFF IN the armor they had given her. Most plate was already accounted for, and chainmail was too heavy, which left her with leather armor loaned from the Ovnite. She adjusted it as they made final arrangements.

There were nets at her feet that she and deckhands were sorting through. Pointing at a pile on the left, she instructed, "Leave them. They won't last. We won't bring anything we can't use or repair."

"Good scrap," the man argued.

"We have better scrap," refuted Lena. "Leave it."

"Scrap is only good if you can find someone to tie the right knots."

Lena moved out of the pile to reach her sister. "I was coming to say goodbye once I was done, I swear."

"You may not want to see Mother. It's your right, but it won't end well," said Nela.

Lena sighed. "I suppose she has her own idea of what's going on here and out there."

This was it. She was leaving her family, again. At least this time, she could say goodbye to someone.

A coin purse was unbuckled from Nela's belt—the one Lena had used for her savings and left behind on their kitchen table. Nela held it up. "I'd like to buy passage."

CLEVEHOLD

Lena dove for a hug. She felt like laughing even as tears pricked her eyes.

"I'm not too late, am I?"

Smiling, Lena pulled away to ask, "Mother won't come?"

"There's a whole group of them that won't."

Father is on the other side of the line. Mother will be safe. They couldn't make everyone go, and there was no risk of leaving the ones who wanted to stay.

"This could be dangerous," warned Lena.

"Are you trying to talk me out of it?" asked Nela. She returned the coin purse to her belt.

"I want you to come. I hated leaving you." Lena squeezed her fist. "But it's not your magic. This isn't your fight."

"I believe in what you're doing. I believe less in the people of Steepwharf for what they've done."

Lena didn't want to talk her out of it, instead thinking about the ship at the least risk. "You should go on the fourth boat."

Nela did as instructed. Everyone was getting loaded on, and everything with them. There was a crowd gathered of those who would stay behind. Lena didn't look for her mother among the faces.

Nets, cargo, people—the last block of time passed quickly. She and Amundr loaded the last items onto the ship. Dawn was about to rise. That was their cue.

Men on the doors of the Royal Dock would get onto the fourth and fifth ship. The formation had to be tight, and they all had to move in tandem to protect one another. Their window was on the brink of opening.

Amundr mumbled something. A curse, gibberish—both were equally likely with him. He was glaring at the bare shipyard.

"He's late," said Lena. The planks on the other ships were being taken up. They couldn't wait.

Ginger hair cut through the crowd, jogging to the ship just as they were about to take the plank up. There was a basket he held securely under his arm as he leapt up.

"Last on board," grumbled Amundr. He turned away from Kazio to shout orders to get them underway.

"What held you up?" Lena asked.

There was blood on his face from a thin slash. As she looked him over, she saw more on his hands and forearms. Basket under one arm, he poked a finger under the lid to lift it slightly.

A white paw clawed his finger. He flinched and pulled away, and the lid closed.

Lena's heart flipped.

"He wasn't the easiest to catch," complained Kazio.

"Meow," said Socks from within the basket.

"Let's bring him below!" said Lena excitedly. She could hardly believe it. The hatch at the back of the ship led to the captain's quarters. There were no people in the room, as it was being used for storage. Lena went down the ladder first and took the basket. Kazio followed her down.

Lena opened the lid.

Socks backed into the corner of the basket, ears back. He hissed.

"It's me," soothed Lena. She moved her fingers toward him slowly.

He sniffed. His ears came up. Jumping out from the basket, Socks went immediately to her lap. He shoved his face against hers and began to purr.

"I missed you, too," she cooed.

"Meow," he agreed.

"He wasn't so friendly before," muttered Kazio.

Lena looked up to him, her smile bright. She held on to Socks tightly, feeling the vibrations of his purrs against her heart. "I appreciate this. More than you know."

"Then you wouldn't mind fixing up his damage?"

"Meow," said Socks.

"You don't mean that," she replied. She nuzzled her face against his fur. "I never thought I'd see you again."

Socks wiggled out from her grip. He sniffed the basket, looked around, and meowed. He turned back to Lena. Head shoved against her leg, he purred.

"Let me feed him first," said Lena. She felt the ship start to move and heard the gates opening. They had to get back up top soon.

Kazio's arms flopped at his sides. "Of course."

There were rations and bedrolls in the captain's quarters. She got a ration out and picked off bits of meat, then set the bedroll and the food down for him. Socks went to it immediately. She stood back and smiled, watching him eat.

"You think he'll be safe down here?" she wondered aloud.

"He'll be fine," said Kazio. He added, quieter, "Captain Guard Cat will claw the shit out of whoever tries to get down here."

The ship picked up speed. She turned to Kazio. "We should go."

"Sure we don't want to bring your warrior up top?" He held up his hands, lined with blood-dotted claw marks.

"Right," she remembered. "He's fine, once he gets used to you." The elation she felt made it easier to concentrate. The technique of bringing her magic forward and feeling the blood flow through her made healing his hands and arms simple.

Unsure how to heal the one long scratch on his face, she rested her hand on his cheek over it. He closed his eyes. She couldn't feel the heat of his skin under the magic, but she felt the pressure as he leaned in.

It was healed. She pulled her hand away to see if her assumption was correct. "Not even a scar."

"I can't believe you like that thing," he commented.

She looked back and smiled. Socks was chasing his tail. They both laughed as he rolled off the bedroll trying. Lena shook her head, returning her gaze to Kazio. "You get used to the little idiot after a while."

Chapter 28

THERE WAS A LOW MURMUR of voices, but the loudest sound was the natural creaking of the ship. Water sloshed up the sides and licked the canal walls. Full sails weren't down; traveling through Clevehold was too risky at speed. The rowers weren't engaged yet. The wind carried them smoothly. The gates had been left open behind them.

Empty.

Quiet.

If not for the fixed-up buildings and clothes left behind on the lines, Lena could have mistaken this for the Stone King's city as it stood when they first arrived. A pit grew in her stomach. Somehow, seeing it in this state was worse.

When she had first arrived here, the canals were littered with fallen stones and sunken ships. Buildings were half collapsed. The place had become truly desolate after having been abandoned for a span of time longer than Lena could conceive. The city itself had felt like a myth materialized.

The Stone King's city had become Clevehold. They had built it—people, hope, dreams—they had built it all. Refurbished. Reinvigorated. Revived. Children had run in the streets. Couples had been married in the gardens. People had come not only to settle but to visit—the true hallmark of a civilization. Clevehold had become a spot on the map.

Now, clothes on the lines flapped in the wind, left behind. Rats scurried along the streets, foraging for forgotten food. The city could easily have been moved back into—that was the heartbreak. They'd had it. They'd lost it.

They could only hope to remake it.

The lead ship passed by the library, another place she had visited for the last time without knowing it. The place she had wanted to take Cicero. Both aspects of that dream had died.

That was where it had all started. Where time and consideration had caught up with her, another half-formed plan fueled by anger and will. They had done what seemed impossible then. Why not one more time?

She didn't look back as the library passed out of view. Not at it. Not at the castle. The spirit of Clevehold wouldn't be lost if they could get the people out.

A fog appeared in front of them. At first, Lena thought it was a trick of the light, but it soon thickened. Sunlight tried to pass through, but the mass seemed to reject the rays. The haze then became brown. It was large and appeared to stick out of the river. More details materialized.

A ship.

"Is this you?" Lena looked to Amundr.

"Not mine." He shook his head, eyes trained on the ship. Down to the sail position, it looked like a duplicate of theirs.

Lena went to the bow and watched closely where it met the water. The false ship hovered, not quite reaching the canal. As the real ship pushed through and created commotion in the water, the haze at the bottom of the false ship was almost indiscernible. The false ship rocked; the sail billowed.

"Avild didn't leave after all," whispered Lena.

"The historian?" questioned Kazio.

Lena smiled and pushed off the rail. "Has to be."

Kazio turned to Amundr. "So, she *is* powerful enough to knock you on your ass, yes?"

The men began to jest and bicker. For some reason, Lena thought of Charlot. *Dreadful woman.* Perhaps it was the way Kazio had upturned his statement into a question. No one would miss her. Still, there was an echo of pity. She had lost her husband abruptly after losing their station. Lena was almost certain Norman and Charlot had adult children. Traitorous man or not, they were all suffering right now. *In the castle already picking at the scraps, no doubt.*

Lena hated the idea the coastal armies would take the castle. *Damn them all for what they've done.* Wicked woman or not, she couldn't help but hope whoever took the castle took pity on Norman's family.

"We're coming up on the threshold, Duchess," warned Kazio. He motioned for her to come closer to the mast.

"Their ships are farther down than I'd expect them to be," said Amundr. He was staring ahead, squinting. Beyond the last of the buildings and the trees, there were masts poking up. Grey and blue.

"Tisa was right, at the bend," said Lena.

"They should have started their attack in the city," a man in partial plate commented.

"Maybe that's why we didn't give them a warning, yes?" proposed Kazio. He reached up a hand to hook over a crossbeam of the mast as the ship rocked.

"They're all running into formation now, no doubt," said Amundr.

"What, we aren't hoping for a civilized wave as they let us by?" asked Kazio.

"Hoping, not expecting," said Lena. She tensed her arm, ready for a shield.

"Are you worried, Duchess?" He rested a hand onto the hilt of his sword.

"Close your mouth and open your ears." Amundr unhooked the whip from his belt.

The false ship passed through the stone pillars that marked the edge of the city. Beyond the threshold were trees, tall and lush green, reaching up to the dawn sky. Men moved around the Steepwharf ships, but they were miles downriver. Between them and the Ovnite ships, the land looked trampled. The banks were slick with mud. The longer Lena looked, the more evidence she saw that men had been camped out.

A horn sounded, followed by men yelling. Groups rushed out from the cover of trees, most on foot but some on horseback. *Iste riders.* They converged from both sides, heading toward the ship leading their convoy. Grappling hooks were swung at the false ship.

The metal fell through. A few more men attempted the maneuver, and the grappling hooks sunk into the water. The men looked to each other with confusion. Arrows fired out from the trees and left holes where the magic faltered. Lines from the hooks and ropes opened up lines in the illusion, and the image of the ship blurred. The details became muted.

The illusory ship devolved into a wave of fog washing up both banks. Men yelled and coughed. The horses reared.

On their ship, men were yelling out orders. Arrows were being fired back into the fog and trees. They were clear of the stone arches now, out in the open.

Lena created her shield and stood by Kazio. She kept an eye out as arrows began to fly at their ship. The fog must have disoriented them, she realized. Though threatened, the attack was lackluster, but they would soon sail beyond the fog.

Out in the open on the starboard side, Amundr was firing his stinger. It wasn't quite like the arrows Briet created; they didn't appear to pierce, but rather agitate. He was aiming at the horses. He made one rear and buck its rider.

Kazio snarled a smile, focused on the left bank. He clenched his hand. Orange threads swirled around it.

Men screamed, and Lena followed the sound. Men and horses tripped and fell in the mud into newly formed sinkholes. Some were deep enough for the person to disappear within.

Far beyond the fog, Lena looked back. The third ship was beyond the stone pillars, the fourth soon to follow. They were taking fire and returning it, but not nearly as heavily as the first ship. On both banks, men yelled in a strange language and pointed at the lead ship.

This was what they wanted, wasn't it? Lena fought her fear. She had to be ready.

Arrows struck Lena's shield, a cluster of three. Two were at her chest height, the third at her neck. They didn't pierce. The tips melted away and the sticks fell.

Kazio's hand brushed her arm and she looked back to inquire. He was pale, eyes unfocused. Lena backed up, keeping her shield to cover them both. "You're alright," she instructed. He had to fight.

"Get down!" someone shouted.

Lena caught a quick glimpse of a contraption on the right bank. Large flaming arrows. Diederich aiming at the ship.

She elbowed Kazio, and it was enough to make him fall. She crouched down at the same time she heard loud clanking.

Fired at them were metal rods shaped like arrows, doused in some sort of oil and set aflame. Lena knew, because one came over the bow and lodged into a portside banister. Another struck behind them.

Hooks came over the port and starboard sides.

Lena relinquished her shield and used both hands to shake Kazio. He was dazed but awake. His hands moved slowly, and he blinked heavily. "You have to get up!"

There was commotion as men and women came up to the portside to cut away the hooks and remove the rod.

Diederich yelled from the bank for his soldiers to board.

Kazio mumbled gibberish.

The magic was already pulsing in her spine. She moved it forward, felt it move through her. She put a hand onto Kazio's chest. It was either there or his head. She could try that next.

The green glow lit up his chest.

No. She panicked and pulled back. *One attempt at this.*

His hand came up swiftly to grasp hers. Alertness in his eyes. He breathed heavily.

"Get up," she instructed. Her hand was offered to him.

He denied it and got up on his own. His steps were slow. His sword was down.

Iste men had made it onto the ship from the portside hooks. Kazio roared as he moved to face them. His sword glowed orange as he cut through them before some even had the chance to pull weapons.

"On the banks!" an Ovnite yelled.

The flaming arrow machine was being reloaded. Diederich bared his teeth as he cranked the handle to aim. Lena ran to a cluster of people working the sail, attempting to gain speed. The shield reemerged to protect them.

At the bow was Amundr. He stared at the machine as they lit the arrows. He stood tall, a wavering giant posed at the tip of the ship.

Diederich yelled, "Fire!"

The flaming metal arrows shot out.

Amundr's shield caught them all. The teal barrier extended from him halfway down the starboard length of the ship. With an animalistic grunt, he pushed the shield away. The flaming arrows were returned with speed. One fell into the water while one pierced the ground near the machine, setting a man on fire. Two were directed at the Steepwharf ships.

CLEVEHOLD

They were getting closer. Men on the ships were readied. The glint of their swords in the growing dawn light made her scowl.

"Without!" Kazio shouted, followed by gibberish. There were bodies at his feet. He cut through the air with his sword, the orange glow fading. Staggered steps made him collide with the banister. He went to his knees and a tremor started in his arm.

Lena ran to him. *Why doesn't he know where his limits are? Briet never should have agreed to let him onto the lead ship.* What was Lena going to do, drag him below? She grabbed Kazio by the leather armor at his shoulders and heaved. Too heavy. She pulled again.

Amundr stumbled back from the bow. A trickle of red ran down his neck. He did a quick shake of his head and rubbed a hand over his face.

No. Everyone had to stay alert. They were almost at the Steepwharf ships—Diederich was reloading the machine. *Not now. Not yet.*

She groaned as she pulled Kazio, making no progress. The leather armor she was wearing made her clothes feel more constricted. Sweat and fabric stuck to her. "Come on," she grunted.

Threads of orange magic zipped up Kazio's arms, into his chest, and lit up his eyes before they screwed shut. Kazio collapsed and convulsed.

What was the worst that could happen—it doesn't work? She knelt beside him and pressed a hand to his chest. She felt the coolness flowing out of her and into him. When at first it didn't work, she fought harder to compel her magic. "Get up," she pleaded through clenched teeth. "C'mon."

"Come where, Duchess?" he mumbled. He blinked hard. Propped up onto his elbows, he looked around. A hardness coated his expression, and his upper lip twitched.

"I need you to do something." She pulled at him until he was on his knees, then put her shoulder in his armpit to help him stand. He was unbalanced and had to lean on her. She directed him to look at the mechanism and Diederich. "Remember him?"

Kazio weakly snarled.

They were nearly alongside it. "Open the ground."

"Duchess," he slurred.

"No excuses. Do it," she commanded. Her hand was flat to his chest. Hers glowed green as his created orange threads, feeding him coolness as she felt him burning beneath her hand. There was feedback other than pressure. She felt him.

The ground opened and devoured the machine, and Diederich with it. The man with the torch tried to run away but slipped into the sinkhole. The arrows caught fire. Screams were silenced as the ground swallowed them up.

"Appreciated."

Kazio relaxed and let his hand down. He was out of breath, but there was color in his face. Moving off of Lena, he bent down to pick up his sword.

"More men incoming!" shouted a guard.

Amundr turned fluidly toward the shouting but stumbled. His lips pulled back over his teeth. The whip was gripped tightly in his hand.

Time. They needed more time. Lena cursed. She didn't know magic for that.

The ship. The duplicates. The banks littered with dead and injured. She closed her eyes and concentrated. *More of it. Make the men see more of it. More carnage.*

More helplessness.

Horses galloped. Men shouted. The shouts turned fearful.

Lena opened her eyes. The land was filled with bodies—triple, quadruple what she had just seen. It didn't look like a few fallen horses and a company of fallen men. Dozens of corpses lined the banks. Men who charged were faced with blood and chaos. Some chose to turn around and run.

She looked down at the line of ships. They were clustered together, and arrows fired to and fro. A company of horses harassed the rear ship. They were answered by blue arrows. No other ship had been boarded.

The wind picked up hard enough to make Lena flinch as it whistled roughly in her ears. Her hands came up, and she retreated to the mast. *What is this?*

The gust howled and churned the river before them. The sails of the Steepwharf ships caught the breeze, and green-tinted pockets of wind hauled the ships up the left bank. It was hard to tell how many Steepwharf ships there were based on their positioning, and how the wind stung her eyes to stop her from looking. The first Steepwharf ship tilted until it crashed sideways. By the sound of it, more than one ship succumbed.

Men on the right bank yelled and pointed up at a tree. Lena didn't need to understand the words to catch the intention. The origin of the gust: a woman in the trees.

If she's here in the trees, who has been . . . ?

Arrows were fired into the tree. The wind dissipated. Men continued to yell orders, some going up the trunk, others circling below.

"They're beached!" shouted an Ovnite.

Lena looked forward. They would have been coming up on the first of the Steepwharf ships, were they not destroyed. The Steepwharf vessels outnumbered theirs easily, but most were smaller, fishing boats refurbished for war. They couldn't stand up against the wind. Clumps of wood and sails covered the bank, and the men who escaped the ships threw whatever was within their reach. Better prepared men shot arrows.

Their resistance was not crushed yet. Larger ships had survived. Wedged on the left side, the men on deck were shouting angrily. From the ground, men were funneled onto two ships that sat one behind the other. The mast of one was bent in half, but the men aboard paid it no mind. Ropes and planks in hand, they were waiting. The other ship was heavy with men, ready to make sail. Men on the shore worked to push the hull back into the water.

"The men are going to be ready when we pass," warned Amundr.

"Make the berth wide!" yelled an Ovnite.

"No! The river is wide enough. We use our shields, run up alongside, bottleneck who tries to board, and let the others pass us," said Lena.

"We can run!" shouted a guard.

The men on the ground were busy pushing their sailable ship off the bank. Amundr pointed at them. "If we don't fight them, they'll be in the water to fight those behind us."

"They'll be vulnerable from the right bank." An Ovnite pointed to the group harassing the tree. They hadn't caught her yet; otherwise, they would have refocused on the approaching ships.

"They have enough defense to skirt by, so long as they can avoid being boarded," said Lena.

"We have the wind on our side," added Amundr.

Their ship was angled to run up alongside Steepwharf's. Amundr put up a hand to stop arrows from the bank. Men and women readied their weapons, but there was an air of uncertainty.

"We should—" began a protest.

"This is what we're here for!" yelled Kazio with his full chest. "*These* people." He pointed with his sword and taunted, "And their silly little boats."

The fighters cheered.

"Signal the second ship to go around," instructed Lena.

"Yes, ma'am." A guard ran aft.

The Steepwharf ships were smaller—that much was clear up close. The Steepwharf men would inherently have an issue boarding, but not for a lack of effort. They were prepared with ropes, planks, ladders, and long spears. Men from the shore were funneling in, waiting eagerly for their chance. Alger stood on the ship, armed and ready.

Just long enough for the others to get by, she reminded herself. Fear was brewing. She couldn't let it. There was no room for it.

She ran to the starboard side. They were alongside where the men were fighting the tree. Claws were ripping into the men on the ground. A man fell from midway up the tall tree, screamed as he flailed, and hit the ground with a thud.

The second Clevehold ship was coming up to pass them. There were a few feet of room between ships.

There was a groan and a wet sliding sound. The ship jerked, and Lena clutched the banister. Steepwharf's ship was back in the water.

There was movement high up in the tree. A person launched out of it. Lena's breath caught. *Did they—?*

She couldn't finish the thought. Avild collided with the second ship's sail and disappeared as the fabric swallowed her up.

Lena smiled. There was clattering behind her. As she turned, she reached for the knife on her belt, but it was gone. When had she lost it?

Steepwharf boarded. She looked around frantically, picking up an unclaimed sword. A bastard hold would have to do. She didn't have to be great, only good enough.

A Steepwharf man charged at her and Lena swung. The man seemed surprised. Using this to her advantage, she attacked. Her strike was blocked, but she recovered quickly. Teeth bared, she tried to remember everything she had been taught. *Move your feet. Read the body language. Know when to lean.*

On a block, she lost the left-hand grip. The sword flung right but she kept hold of it. Left hand up, she reflexively closed her eyes and made a shield.

She heard the body drop.

Eyes open, she saw the man was in two pieces. There were two parts that had clearly been severed, angled up at the ribcage. Torso here. Legs there.

Did I . . . ?

The shield?

She didn't take time to consider it.

Clevehold's second ship had cleared them. Gusts of green-tinted wind filled their sail, and their third ship was coming up fast. Lena looked up. Avild was in the crow's nest of Clevehold's lead ship, pushing them along.

There was movement close, on the right. A hand on her shoulder. Lena grunted and turned with a swing of her sword.

Tulir deflected it with the vambrace on his forearm.

Right over the scar, she thought as her breath caught. She blinked rapidly. Out of breath, she scolded, "No way to defend."

"Any stronger or quicker, I wouldn't have." He pointed at the sword. "May I borrow that?"

She handed it off. "Never come with your own?"

"The man I had hold mine went overboard." He mimed a stab.

"Why did—?" Lena couldn't finish her question. A Steepwharf soldier ran at them, sword raised overhead. She prepared a shield.

An arrow struck the man in the throat, and he fell backward.

"What happened to your new trick?" Tulir called back in the direction the arrow had been fired from.

"What happened to staying on our ship?" returned Harth. He fired into the crowd of Steepwharf men. They were only able to board at one chokepoint. With Vitki on one side, Amundr on the other, shields held the rest back. Alger waited on the enemy's side, shouting orders at the men.

"You got off as well," said Tulir.

Harth smirked and fired. "Always you first."

Lena stepped over the dead man at her feet. Where was she needed? Tulir moved in to fight the soldiers as Harth picked off stragglers trying to board outside the chokepoint.

A yell made her turn.

Kazio.

He dropped again. She would have rolled her eyes if her heart hadn't plummeted.

By the time she reached him, tucked between a large wooden crate and the portside aft banister, her magic was ready. She pressed her hand to his convulsing chest. She had never taken the time to properly parse her appreciation for the Stone King's volume of magic and groundedness, but when Kazio's tremors stopped and his eyes opened, she recognized the uniqueness of a third revival. Relieved, keeping her ears open for those around, she said, "You know, there are other people I should be helping."

Kazio put a hand to his throat and gasped. He breathed quickly, and a moan exited as he sat up. His eyes found Lena and he reached for her.

There was a skirmish farther down deck. She crowded Kazio's space and he backed up, wedged between the crate and banister.

"No more magic," she told him. This recovery had been slower. He didn't look hurt elsewhere. Lena tapped on his chin and looked over where he'd grabbed at his neck. It looked fine. She was about to ask what his detriment was, but she saw it in his eyes. *Fear.* He hadn't been able to breathe.

She looked around for his sword. Beneath the feet of men a few feet away, she saw broken shards. That was what was left of it.

"Can you get back up?" she asked, but was unsure he heard her.

Lena saw Amundr struggling to keep his shield steady. The man groaned, stepped back, and let it drop. Men came forward, climbing over the railing. As Amundr yelled and reinforced his shield, it sliced through the men. Blood sprayed as bits of bodies collapsed. Amundr pushed forward, forcing the board back.

Alger had gotten through the hole unscathed. He snarled, red in the face, jowls quaking, and raised his sword. He was met with an arrow to the eye.

She looked starboard. Clevehold's fourth ship was pushing past, gusts in their sails. "Just a few more minutes," she thought aloud.

"Where did this come from?" asked Kazio, voice hoarse. He poked her arm.

She winced and looked. There was blood on her sleeve. A quick examination told her it was a shallow wound. She hadn't noticed. "I got in a fight."

"You were fighting?" He huffed a breath and looked around.

"Because we have to," she urged. She couldn't leave him here—he was bait, yet she didn't have the strength to move him.

"Yes?" he questioned with a clenched jaw.

Hand on his chest, she pushed the magic forward. *Cool him down, get him up.* She felt him again, magic pushing back against hers. His hand came up to wrap around her wrist. Open-mouthed, he gaped at her.

She pulled back and let the glow dissipate. "I'd've kept fighting, but the king took my sword."

Kazio nodded and sniffed. "Well, if the king is here . . ." He put his hand out.

Lena took it and helped him up. He wasn't armed. That was all she was able to think as she saw him move toward a Steepwharf soldier. Kazio was going to help a fellow Ovnite in trouble. Did he realize his sword was in pieces?

The soldier was grabbed by Kazio and yanked back. Kazio let out an animalistic yell, then punched the soldier on the chest twice in quick succession. The soldier's sword was raised, but his arm appeared stuck. He looked down to where Kazio had punched him. There was a hole burning away his flesh. The soldier staggered and dropped.

Kazio looked at his fist, then to Lena, his eyes wide. His expression solidified into determination. His fist had threads of orange and green magic snaking between his fingers. He was steady.

There wasn't time to think. She jutted her chin to the shield line. The Vitki had been thinned. Amundr was being attacked from the other side.

The shield line broke.

A wave of soldiers pushed onto the ship.

Lena looked around frantically and climbed up onto the crate. With a bird's eye view, she watched the two sides clash. More men were climbing up ladders and planks to board. On her ship was chaos. There were people to heal, but there was no chance of getting through the crowd unharmed. She couldn't become the liability.

Amundr used his whip and wound it around a soldier's throat. When pulled taunt, the teal glow intensified and sliced through. Blood spurted as the head rolled away.

Men were burning. Kazio was using his newfound magic to set the blaze. *New skill? Loaned?* It didn't matter, she realized; he was upright.

Tulir kicked a man in the chest, sending him hurtling back over the banister. Before the splash, Tulir was already swinging at the next opponent.

Harth fought with his broadsword. There was a gash on his arm, but the fierceness with which he moved made her doubt he felt it. The bow was gone and the quiver on his back was out of arrows.

Arrows. Lena took a deep breath. She couldn't just stand there. Standing tall on the crate, she did her best to mimic Briet. The action felt funny. Lena had never fired an arrow.

Her pinched fingers released. Magic shot forward. It wasn't as fast as an arrow, nor did it travel as straight. It bent through the air quickly and changed directions enough times to hit a different target than intended, luckily still a Steepwharf soldier. The man jumped back and snarled at Lena. An Ovnite took advantage of the distraction and sliced across the soldier's back.

"Claws!" a familiar voice yelled—Avild from the crow's nest. She was pushing Clevehold's fifth ship up alongside them. "Be ready to make sail!"

Lena shook out her hands. The sea of soldiers. A broad target. She took a deep breath. *Claws.* She knew what those looked like. They smelled like the library. Felt like a broken nose and glass shards.

Palm toward the group of soldiers pushing in, she clenched her fist slowly. The feeling originated in her spine and traveled down to her palm, extending into talons and nails. Green haze flowed from her. This wasn't a tingle or a coolness—this felt like power.

Men yelped as the claws ripped into them. Water splashed as they flailed and fell into the river. Monstrous green claws gouged their chests, opened their necks. Lena gritted her teeth and clenched her palm more. The claws moved from man to man, thinning their ranks. Too much chaos on one ladder caused the entirety of it to fall into the water.

A gap. Ready to sail. Lena looked forward. All other Clevehold ships were ahead of them.

CLEVEHOLD

"Get down before you fall down!"

The words broke her concentration, and the flow of magic stopped. She gasped a breath. Had she been breathing? It felt like she hadn't remembered to.

Lena looked for Kazio. The crowd was smaller, the fighting lessened. Her focus dialed in and she found him on the deck, next to the crate she stood on.

Tall enough to grab her by the waist and strong enough to bring her down, he set Lena on the deck. No sooner had her feet touched down, he took one hand off her waist and moved it to her face. He leaned down and brought her in for a kiss.

She tightly gripped the fabric of his shirt. Breathless, he kept her upright. A jolt beneath their feet made them part. The kiss had only lasted a second.

Eyes filled with wonderment and locked on hers, he whispered, "Duchess."

Shouting faded behind them as they left the Steepwharf ship behind. Scared the enemy would ready their sails, Lena parted from Kazio to look over the side and see the state of Steepwharf's ship. She had to laugh—there was a wedge of land that kept the ship in place. They could not pursue.

Lena looked up to the crow's nest. Avild was getting down.

"It wasn't her." Kazio pointed at the blonde standing at the rear of Clevehold's fifth ship, then looked back to the wedged ship. "Should we have . . . ?"

"Retrospect doesn't help anything," she responded. The aftershocks of power resonated through her. She felt heavy and light at the same time. Hearty, untouchable. Was this what being grounded felt like?

In the same way she knew a wound was healed before seeing it with her own eyes, she knew not only had they won, but those important to her had survived. She could feel it. So, she looked for it.

As she moved from aft to middle, she took note of what they had.

An Ovnite was hauling the last living Steepwharf soldier overboard. Others, Ovnite and guards, were working together to haul away the dead. Under a corpse, Lena saw a broken bow. She recognized it as Harth's. It was split in half below the hand hold. She picked it up.

Avild reached the deck. She nodded at Lena, who returned it.

"On a ship?" asked Lena.

Avild raised her eyebrows. "Pardon?"

He has to be. She couldn't have run from the city to the woods and get up the tree that fast. Couldn't have left him behind in Clevehold.

Later.

Amundr and the other Vitki were busy healing. Amongst the dead, there weren't too many of their own. The people chosen had been the right ones. The plan had been carried out well.

Tulir was portside bow, wiping blood off his sword.

She knew eyes were focused on her as she approached the bow of the ship. In one hand was a broken bow; the other glowed green. She was messy with blood not her own, save the arm wound. Her hand had crunched out a dozen or more men. She was walking with her chin high, past the corpses of her enemies.

They had won, but they were silent. Waiting.

Harth's eyes were on her as she approached. He was who she headed toward. Before him, she held up the bow.

"You can mend this. And I"—she pressed a hand to the wound on his arm—"can mend this."

"You put your skills to good use," he complimented. He didn't take the bow.

CLEVEHOLD

All eyes were on them.

Waiting.

Healed completely, Lena moved her hand up to the side of his face and made her request without words.

Harth took the bow only to drop it. He wrapped one hand behind her neck, the other on her waist, and dipped her backward as he leaned forward. Hesitating only half a second, he kissed her.

Hoots erupted across the ship.

Lena's eyes clenched as she smiled through the kiss. It was tender, sweet and slightly coppery. She held a tight grip, but not because she feared he could let her fall. Her other hand carded through his short hair.

After almost a minute, he brought her up. She made a show of delaying wanting to leave the kiss. The hoots and commotion continued. Harth beamed back at her.

Tulir leaned back against the port railing. He clapped, smiled, and shook his head.

Celebrate, as you should, she thought as she looked down the length of her ship. Clevehold was behind them. Only the peaks of the castle were visible behind the forest. Bends in the river took them out of sight of enemy ships. At their current speed, it wouldn't be long before they reached open water.

She held Harth's hand. He squeezed it.

Kazio sauntered to the bow of the ship. He jutted his chin out, looking beyond them. "Your Grace, I think you're in trouble."

Lena turned into Harth to look ahead. His arm came up to bracket her shoulders. They were looking at Briet at the stern of the ship ahead of them.

Briet shouted, "You're on the wrong boat!"

Laughter was added to the general upbeat commotion of their ship.

LIZ BUNCHES

Tulir pushed off the railing and put his hands up in surrender. "Sorry, love!" He gestured east. "We're all heading the same direction."

Don't miss out!

Visit the website below and you can sign up to receive emails whenever Liz Bunches publishes a new book. There's no charge and no obligation.

https://books2read.com/r/B-A-OUKBB-TDLGF

BOOKS 2 READ

Connecting independent readers to independent writers.